*There was once a girl
who dreamed of romance, and love,
and forever. . . .*

Somewhere Rachel had forgotten all about the magic.

"You've gotten awfully quiet," Miriam said.

"I was just thinking . . . about Christmas."

"About your grandfather."

"Yes. I used to think this was a magic place. That anything could happen here. Even miracles," Rachel said solemnly. "Do you still believe in miracles?"

"Of course," Miriam said.

"I think I gave up on them."

"I think you've given up on everything, dear. And you just can't do that. You've got to believe, Rachel."

"Believe in what?"

"You'll see. . . ."

Twelve Days

———✦———

Teresa Hill

A SIGNET BOOK

SIGNET
Published by New American Library, a division of
Penguin Putnam Inc., 375 Hudson Street,
New York, New York 10014, U.S.A.
Penguin Books Ltd, 27 Wrights Lane,
London W8 5TZ, England
Penguin Books Australia Ltd, Ringwood,
Victoria, Australia
Penguin Books Canada Ltd, 10 Alcorn Avenue,
Toronto, Ontario, Canada M4V 3B2
Penguin Books (N.Z.) Ltd, 182–190 Wairau Road,
Auckland 10, New Zealand

Penguin Books Ltd, Registered Offices:
Harmondsworth, Middlesex, England

First published by Signet, an imprint of New American Library,
a division of Penguin Putnam Inc.

First Printing, October 2000
10 9 8 7 6 5 4 3 2 1

One year at Christmas, a couple I know received a call from a social worker desperate to find a temporary home for a little girl.

My friends, it seems, were still on the county's approved list of foster parents, although they'd already decided not to take any more foster children into their home. They'd gotten their hearts broken once before by the system.

But the social worker begged. It was Christmas, and the child had nowhere to go. In the end, my friends took the little girl into their home and their hearts. She came to them on Christmas Day, and I'm happy to say, she's been there ever since.

It takes a special kind of courage to love a child who's not your own, at least not in any legally recognized terms. I admire people willing to take the risk. And of course, the writer in me couldn't help but think—a child in desperate need of a home at Christmas. . . . There must be a story of my own there. And here it is.

What follows is fiction, but this book is dedicated with love to my friends Scott and Jan and to their daughter Krysta.

Chapter 1

On the first day of Christmas, eleven-year-old Emma sat in the backseat of the social worker's car, her little brother Zach on one side of her, baby Grace sleeping in a car seat on the other side.

The light was fading fast, streetlights coming on, and the entire neighborhood glowed with the light of thousands of tiny Christmas bulbs strung on just about everything she could see. Snow was falling, big, fat flakes, and everything was so pretty.

For a moment, Emma thought she might have stepped inside the pages of one of the Christmas books she read to Zach or that maybe she'd shrunk until she was an inch high and was living inside one of her most prized possessions—a snow globe.

It was so beautiful there, inside the big, old, magical-looking house, so warm, so welcoming. Emma could make it snow anytime she wanted with just a turn of her wrist, a bit of magic that never failed to delight Zach and the baby. She thought nothing bad could happen in a place like that and often wished she could find a way to live inside the little ball of glass.

Blinking through the fading light and the gently falling snow, she thought for a moment the neighborhood they were driving through looked oddly familiar, though she was sure she'd never been here before. She would have remembered the big, old houses reaching toward the sky, with all those odd angles and shapes, the fancy trim and silly frills that seemed to belong to another place and time.

Rich people's houses, she thought, the knot in her stomach growing a bit tighter. What would anybody with a house like that want with her and Zach and the baby?

Zach leaned closer to the window, his nose pressed flat against it, fogging a little circle of glass. "It's almos' Chris'mas. Ever'body has their tree and stuff up."

"I know, Zach." There were wreaths on doors and on the old-fashioned black lampposts topped with fancy metal curls, the lights perched delicately on top. There were stars made of bright Christmas lights, even Christmas trees in people's yards.

Emma had never seen people go to so much trouble for Christmas. They must have spent hours. And the money . . . It must take a lot of money to decorate a house like this just for Christmas. She couldn't imagine what the insides of those houses must be like. She and Zach and the baby didn't need anything fancy. Just a place where they could stay together. She couldn't bear it if they were separated. Emma had to make sure that didn't happen.

The social worker pulled the car into a long driveway and at first Emma thought they were going to the house on the right, all castlelike and fairy-talish.

Aunt Miriam—that's what she'd told them to call her—turned off the car and pocketed the keys. She twisted around in her seat and said, "Let me make sure someone's here before we take the baby out in the cold, okay?"

Emma nodded, knowing they were running out of chances.

"Zach," Aunt Miriam said. "You stay in your seat belt and in that backseat. Emma, don't let him near the steering wheel or the gearshift. Cars aren't playthings. I'll be right there on the porch. You yell if you need me."

"Yes, ma'am." Emma put her arm around Zach. She could take care of him and the baby. If someone would just give them a place to stay and something to eat, she could take care of everything else.

Aunt Miriam got out of the car. A blast of cold air came in before she got the door shut again. Emma shivered a bit. This had to work, she thought, closing her eyes and wishing, praying. This might be their last chance.

Zach brushed past her to get to the window on the other side of the car.

"Zach!" she scolded.

"I gotta see! I gotta see the house," he said, then wailed, "Oh, no!"

"What?" Emma leaned over the sleeping baby to look herself. It was like all the other houses, big and expensive, certainly like no place they'd ever lived.

"Chris'mas!" Zach cried.

"What?"

"It isn't comin' here," he cried. "No Chris'mas."

"Oh," Emma said, realizing now what was different about this house.

She should have known they didn't belong in a place like this. From the moment they pulled into the neighborhood, it had all seemed too good to be true.

The nice lady from social services had brought them to the only house on the street with no Christmas lights, no tree, no ribbons, no bows, no fake reindeer statues decked out in lights on the lawn.

Christmas wasn't coming here.

Emma didn't believe it was coming for her and Zach and the baby, either.

The doorbell rang, disturbing all the silence in Rachel McRae's house, and she honestly thought about ignoring it, as she often did these days.

She was sitting in her great-grandmother's rocking chair deep in the corner of the living room, in what she now realized was near darkness. When had it gotten so dark? Surprised, she looked at the clock on the wall. Five-thirty? She frowned. Where had the day gone?

Sam would be home soon. Maybe. She hadn't even started dinner, hadn't done much of anything. She'd slowly retreated from everyone and everything over the past few weeks. Once again, she found herself at the end of a long day in which she'd done nothing. It all seemed to be too much for her lately. She had the odd feeling that the world was moving too fast all around her and she couldn't quite keep up.

The doorbell rang again, and Rachel decided it would be easier just to open the door and deal with whoever was there this time.

Moving slowly and quietly through the house, she flicked on the overhead light and blinked as her eyes adjusted to the brightness. At the front door she flipped on the porch light and pulled open the door, finding her aunt, a kind-hearted, sixty-something-year-old woman with more energy than most half her age, standing on the porch.

"Aunt Miriam? Hi."

"Hello, dear." Her aunt smiled. "How are you?"

"Fine," Rachel said.

"You threw a lovely party for your father and all of us over the weekend."

"Thank you." It had been her father's sixtieth birthday, which had turned into a family reunion somehow. Her family welcomed any excuse to get together. "Do you want to come inside?"

"Not just yet. I just wanted to make sure you were home. I brought you something," Miriam said, turning and heading for her car.

"Oh, okay. Do you need help?" She crossed her arms in front of her, shivering a bit in the cold.

"No, we can get ourselves inside, Rachel."

Ourselves?

Rachel frowned. She wondered who Miriam could have brought to visit. It couldn't be family, because they'd all been here over the weekend, all forty-six of them for brunch on Sunday. She'd spent Monday putting the house back together after everyone left. It wouldn't get messed up again until the family came for Christmas. Rachel and her husband, Sam, weren't messy at all, and it was just the two of them, probably it always would be.

Neat, clean, and quiet, that was Rachel's life. Her sister Gail, who had four children, the oldest of whom was twelve, actually said she envied Rachel at one point over the weekend when the chaos level hit its peak.

Envied?

Rachel had nearly broken down. She'd hidden in the laundry room, wiping away her tears. Sam had caught her coming out. As he always did lately when he saw that she'd been crying, he stiffened. His whole body went on alert, sending out all those signals that said, "Don't start, Rachel. Not now."

Not ever, she supposed. They weren't going to talk about it. It didn't matter if they did. Nothing would change. So many bad things had happened, and there were no children in this house. Probably, there never would be. How in the world was she supposed to accept that? How was she supposed to go on?

Rachel crossed her arms in front of her, shivering a bit from the cold, and walked to the edge of the porch. That's when she saw the little face inside the car pressed against the window. A nose smashed flat against the glass. A mouth. A child-size hand.

For a second, Rachel thought it was Will, that Miriam had brought Will back to them, when Rachel had given up on that ever happening. But the door opened, and a boy much smaller than Will hopped out. He was four or five, Rachel guessed. She had lots of nephews and cousins. She knew about little boys.

Will was eleven, so tall and lanky, with arms and legs too big for the rest of him. He'd been too skinny and wary at first, but then he'd crawled inside of Rachel and taken root there, growing and changing and blossoming, right there in Rachel's lonely heart. She'd forgotten how much she'd always wanted a baby, and remembered that she simply wanted children.

And then Miriam had taken him away. Rachel and Sam knew they'd likely never see him again.

This wasn't Will. Looking up again, Rachel saw a second child climb out of the car, a girl in a thin sweater, an ill-fitting dress that was too short and showed her thin legs and bony knees. *She must be freezing,* Rachel thought.

The girl took the little boy's hand, and they stood staring at Rachel and the house. She couldn't help but wonder if they were scared. They had to be cold, and she'd bet they hadn't had enough to eat lately, maybe not for a long, long time. It hurt to think about that, hurt in places Rachel hadn't hurt for a long, long time, places in her heart she thought had died. It would be better if all those sad, lonely corners of her heart just shriveled up and died. Miriam knew that. She had to understand. So Rachel couldn't understand why her aunt was doing this to her.

Then, in the worst betrayal of all, her aunt leaned into the car and came out with a baby in her arms.

"Oh." Rachel closed her eyes. *A baby*.

Miriam walked right up to Rachel and put the child into her arms, giving Rachel no choice but to take it.

The other two children gazed up at Rachel waiting for her reaction, their own expressions hard to read. Sadness, uncertainty, fear? Little children shouldn't ever be afraid.

So although Rachel wanted to shove the baby back into her aunt's arms and run inside, locking the door behind her, she didn't. Not at first. She didn't want the children to think she was rejecting them. She wasn't. She was rejecting pain and her own memories and the most dangerous thing of all. *Hope*.

For years, Rachel had had a dream. An utterly illusive fantasy that one day she'd open her front door and someone would put a baby in her arms. It was her own personal version of the Publishers Clearing House Sweepstakes. They could put her on national television if they wanted, broadcast live from her front porch, if she ever won the baby sweepstakes.

A little shiver ran down Rachel's spine. She'd had the baby dream just a few days ago. It had snowed in her dream, she remembered, and it was snowing today. She'd missed that, too; there was a soft, pristine white blanket of snow covering the ground, and it was cold. Just like in her dream.

The dream, too, always started with the doorbell ringing. Sometimes Rachel opened the door and saw no one. Then she looked down and found a basket at her feet, an oval-shaped basket filled with something that might have been mistaken for laundry. But the linens would wiggle, and she'd pull them aside and find the baby waiting for her. In a basket at her front door, like a present.

Sometimes—the last time she had the dream in fact—she opened the door and found a person standing there. She didn't know who, didn't see anything except the baby in that person's arms. She held out her arms and found them filled with a warm, soft, sweet-smelling baby. Right there, on an otherwise absolutely ordinary day.

Just like today.

"Miriam?" Rachel protested as her aunt herded the children inside, as if she still lived here.

"Inside, Rachel. These children are cold and tired. They're probably hungry by now, too."

"I hungry," the little boy piped up.

"See," Miriam said, as if that excused everything.

"You didn't stop by for me to feed them," Rachel pointed out.

"No, but I know you would never turn away a hungry child. Your mother raised you better than that."

"And surely your mother raised you better than this," Rachel said, about to be seduced by the warm weight of the baby in her arms.

They all traipsed down the front hall and to the right, to the big kitchen. Miriam walked right to the refrigerator and opened it.

"Oh, Rachel. You've been baking already." Miriam turned to the boy and the girl. "You have never had anything as delicious as pumpkin bread made with my mother's recipe. She used to live in this house. I did, too. I used to sit in this kitchen, right where you are, Emma, and watch her bake. We'd have a fire, and the whole house would smell so good, and then when it was finally done, we'd put real whipped cream over it. The bread would be hot enough to melt the cream, and it would run down the sides, like ice cream. It's delicious."

"Bread?" the boy said, obviously not impressed.

"More like cake," Miriam explained. She'd already gotten the bread out of the refrigerator and was headed to the cabinet for plates. "You do like cake, don't you, Zach?"

"Uh-huh." He nodded vigorously.

Oh, God, Rachel thought. He was hungry. And he was so thin. He didn't have a warm coat, either. He just had a thin jacket, like the girl. Emma and Zach, she thought. Hungry and cold. In her house.

"You can't do this, Miriam," Rachel complained.

"In a minute, dear." She put slices of bread in the microwave to warm, and found the whipped cream. And then when the bread was ready, put a generous dollop on each slice. She got out the milk, asked Rachel for glasses, and when Rachel provided them, she poured milk for the children and settled them on stools at the breakfast bar. "We'll just be in the other room, all right?"

Zach obviously had no problem with that. He was digging into the pumpkin bread, the whipped cream drizzling down the sides, just as Miriam promised. Emma looked more cautious, more aware of what was going on.

"We'll be right back," Miriam assured her.

Rachel followed her to the living room. She shoved the baby at Miriam and was so mad she was shaking. "What do you think you're doing?"

"I know you and Sam are still smarting over losing Will. I know you're still worried about him, Rachel, and I'm sorry, dear. I am so sorry."

"Sorry? We loved him, Miriam. I can't sleep at night for wondering what's happening to him now. What his so-called mother's doing to him."

"She hasn't missed a beat so far. I checked this morning with Will's teacher, with his mother's counselor, her employer. So far, she's doing great."

"So far? What does that mean?" Rachel was relieved, but still so angry, so worried. "It means nothing, Miriam. Nothing except that the pressure hasn't gotten to her yet, or she hasn't let some awful man move in with them yet. Or that she's still worried enough that someday she might actually lose Will for good that she hasn't let herself mess up yet, but she will. You know she will, and she'll hurt him. I'm so scared that she's going to hurt him."

"I'm sorry. Rachel, if it were up to me, Will would be with you and Sam. You know that. But so far, no one's appointed me God of Baxter County. Judge Forrester's that, and he thinks Will's mother deserves another chance."

"I hate this," Rachel said. "I hate it, and I can't do it again. You know that. Sam told you that."

"I know. Believe me, if there was anything else I could do, I would. But I don't have anyplace else to take these kids."

"Oh, come on, Miriam. Don't try that with me."

"I don't. They're siblings, we think. All three of them. A nearly teenage girl—no one wants teenage girls from troubled homes. A preschooler and a baby. The baby's about a year old. She's crawling, and she's into everything. Before long, she'll be walking. Zach is an absolute joy, but he's a boy and he's five. He's a barrel of energy. He needs so much time and affection and reassurance."

"Well he's not going to get it from me," Rachel said.

"I don't have a home that can take all three of them. I'd be pushed, as is, to find three different foster homes to take one each," Miriam said. "It's the middle of December, Rachel. Everyone's swamped in December. With the Christmas festival starting, and people who've made plans to get away for the holiday, people who are sick. You know that awful flu's going around. We were stretched to the limits before, and now we have all this to contend with."

"I can't help you."

"I'll have to split them up. Can you imagine what that's going to do to them? We've been looking for a place for them since late last night. They slept on the couch and in the chair in my office while I phoned everybody I know trying to find a place for them. They're tired, and all they have left is each other. The only time I've seen them really panic is when I admitted that I might not be able to place them in the same home."

"Miriam, I can't do this," Rachel said more firmly.

As if Rachel hadn't said a word, Miriam went right on. "We found them at a motel on the edge of town. The Drifter. Who knows how long they'd been there. Three days or so, we think. Their mother abandoned them."

"Abandoned?" Rachel asked, her sense of outrage rising above her sense of self-protection.

"Yes. The kids wouldn't say anything, but finally we found the man who checked them in. He remembers a woman he assumed was their mother, but he hasn't seen her since she paid for the room three days before."

"How could anyone leave a five-year-old and a baby in a motel room for three days with a little girl?"

"Emma," Miriam said. "She's eleven. Almost twelve. The boy's Zach, and the baby's name is Grace."

Rachel's face began to crumble. "How could you bring me a baby?"

"You and Sam are still on the list of approved foster homes, from when you took Will. I know you said you didn't want to do this anymore, but I'm desperate, Rachel. You know how strained the whole system gets this time of year. People just fall apart over the holidays. If you could just help me out until after Christmas . . ."

"No," Rachel said.

"I can't bear to separate them. If it weren't for that, I would never ask this of you. But I don't think I can look Zach and Emma in the eye and tell them they have to say good-bye to each other. I don't think I could tear them away from each other, and that's what

I'd have to do. I'd have to physically tear them from each other's arms."

"Don't do that," Rachel said. "Don't put that on me."

"It's been hard for you. I understand. Life has been unfair to you and Sam. But you can't give up. You can't shut yourself up in this house and hide any longer either. It isn't healthy."

"Don't tell me what I can and can't do, Miriam."

"Now you listen to me. I didn't want to do it this way, but if that's what it takes, I will," Miriam said. "If you don't take these children, I will call your father and all three of your sisters and your brother, and I will tell them that I'm worried about you. That I think you might be seriously depressed and that you've been sitting here in this house all alone every day for the past few weeks. I will make sure they don't give you a minute's peace trying to save you from yourself."

"You wouldn't."

"Try me," Miriam dared.

Rachel paused, considering the seriousness of the threat. Her family, hell-bent on saving anyone, was something to behold. They could make her life utterly miserable. Even worse were the other things Miriam had said.

"You don't really think I'm depressed, do you?"

"Not yet," Miriam said. "But I think it wouldn't take much. Sit here worrying and feeling sorry for yourself for a few more weeks, and you will be."

Rachel stood there, scared and feeling trapped.

"It's Christmas," Miriam said. "Give them a decent Christmas. Give me some time to find someone to take them all or to find their mother."

"I can't."

"It won't be like it was with Will. Don't let it be. Don't even think that someday these children might be free for you and Sam to adopt. Just take them into your home, take care of them for a few weeks."

"I can't do that."

"What if it was Will, Rachel? What if we need to place him in foster care again? If it weren't for people like you, I'd have no place to put him."

"Will should be here already," she said. "He would have been safe here. We loved him, and we would have taken good care of him."

"Then take care of these children instead. Do for them what you can't do for him anymore. Give them everything you wanted to give him."

"It's not the same thing," Rachel argued.

"It's exactly the same thing. They're every bit as lost as he was."

"It's too hard, Miriam. It hurts too much to lose someone I love."

"Then don't love them. Like these children a lot. Give them the best you can, temporarily."

How could anyone take a lost child into her home and not love that child? Especially children who needed so desperately to be loved?

"This is what they need, Rachel. This is what foster care is. It isn't perfect. I know that. But it's all these kids have right now. It's what's going to keep them safe and warm and well fed and not quite so lonely. You can do all that for them. Staying together means everything to them. Emma begged me to take them back to the hotel and leave them there. She's sure she can take care of them herself, as long as they can stay together."

"I just can't."

"No, you won't. Because you're scared and you're thinking of nobody but yourself."

Rachel gasped, hurt. "Miriam?"

"Life hasn't been fair to you, Rachel, and I'm sorry, but life isn't fair to anyone. Everyone gets hurt along the way—some more than others—but don't you dare think you're the only one." Miriam shook her finger under Rachel's nose. "Let me tell you something, you always had a safe, warm place to sleep at night and food in your belly and someone to take care of you when you were little. You had a whole lot of some-bodies. Two parents and me and Aunt Jo and your grandparents and a whole host of other people. You still do. You've never been where these kids are now."

Rachel was shocked and a bit ashamed.

"I can't think of you right now," Miriam said. "I have to think about these kids. I'm all they have, and I'm going to make sure they're taken care of. That means their needs outweigh the fact that I know you and love you and hurt for you, for all the bad things that have happened to you. I know this will be difficult for you, but you have the time to take care of these kids, and I know you have the love."

"But—"

"I'll find out where they belong or I'll find someone else to take them. Right after Christmas. I promise."

Rachel sat there, stunned. Miriam took advantage of that, too. She put the baby back in Rachel's arms. Baby Grace snuggled, all warm and soft, against her neck. She made a little rumbling sound as she breathed, and she was surprisingly sturdy, the way one-year-olds were. Rachel hadn't even looked at her face, but she knew it would be perfect. Absolutely perfect.

"Sam will never agree to this," she said, a weak protest at best.

"Don't ask him. Tell him. Or better yet, I'll tell him."

Rachel laughed, giving in. Oh, God, she was giving in, because she had a baby in her arms and she couldn't stand to think of these poor children scattered from one end of town to another. "I've never seen this side of you before," she told her aunt. "I never knew you could be so fierce."

"Tough love." Miriam grinned. "We had a seminar at work last month. I've been nice too long."

Rachel laughed a bit, looking out her window and thinking. It was almost Christmas. Somehow, she'd missed that, too. When Will left it had been hot—Indian summer—and now it was almost Christmas.

She used to think Christmas was pure magic, especially in this town, in this neighborhood, in her grandfather's house. She and Sam had lived with him the first two years of their marriage, working on the house when they could, with Rachel taking care of her grandfather until he died and left the house to them. Rachel had always loved it here. She'd always seen this as a special place. At one time, she would have said a magical place.

Her grandfather, Richard Landon, was an oddball in a little town like Baxter, Ohio, never quite able to keep a job, his family always on the brink of financial ruin. His heart had always been in his art, and Rachel thought it was the height of irony that the town had come to revere him after his death in a way no one had when he was alive.

He loved Christmas and this town almost as much as his work, and the result became pure Christmas magic. He made snow globes, big, heavy balls of glass on intricate bases of swirled pewter, and inside were exquisite scenes of Christmas in Baxter. His sense of light and warmth and wonder radiated from his work. Somehow he had managed to take the magic of Christmas and capture it in a sphere of glass, where it snowed at will and Christmas music played and even grown-ups, just by watching, felt like kids again.

Collectors now paid huge sums of money for original pieces, and his designs were mass-produced in the only factory in town. People had jobs here because of him. He'd immortalized the town in his work. All four churches, city hall, the town square, all the major historic buildings, and most of the Victorian houses in the historic district. Even this house where Rachel lived. *His house.* The first Christmas house in his first famous Christmas scene. Rachel lived here now, in the midst of all that Christmas magic.

Somehow she'd forgotten all about the magic.

"You've gotten awfully quiet," Miriam said.

"I was just thinking . . . about Christmas. And Granddad."

She reached out and ran her fingers along the glass in the fancy window by the door. It was diamond-shaped, and filled with hundreds of tiny diamonds of beveled glass. It sat in just the right spot that the light hit it in the afternoon and seemed to dance its way across the hardwood floors in the front room. He'd always loved playing with glass and light, and had tried to teach her.

"We did this together," Rachel said, "when he was too weak to do much more than tell me how to fit it all together. Sam installed it the week after he died, but I remember him making me take him outside on the porch and making me hold this up to the sunshine so we could both watch what it did to the light. He said it would be our way of letting the magic inside."

Rachel hadn't watched the play of light across the floor in a long time.

"I used to think this was a magic place. That anything could happen here. Even miracles," she said solemnly. "Do you still believe in miracles?"

"Of course," Miriam said.

"I think I gave up on them."

"I think you've given up on everything, dear. And you just can't do that. You've got to believe, Rachel."

"Believe in what?"

"That things can change. That they can get better. You'll see."

"I told myself that for so long," Rachel said.

"Well maybe you'll just have to tell yourself a little longer." Miriam gave her a gentle smile. "Without hope, you have nothing, Rachel, nothing but the life you have right now, and I don't think that's enough for you."

"No. It isn't." But she'd hoped for so long. She'd prayed, and it didn't seem as if anyone were listening. "I've been patient. I've waited so long."

"The good Lord doesn't work on your timetable. He has one that's all His own. You shouldn't forget that. Shouldn't try to rush Him, either."

"I want to believe. It's just so hard," she complained. "I feel like one of those little blow-up punch-toys we had when we were kids, with the clown faces. You hit it, and it bounces right back up. I feel like I've been bouncing back forever, and there's just no more bounce left in me."

"Then you know what?" Miriam asked. "You get to

lay there on the floor, Rachel. Are you ready to just lay there on the floor forever?"

Rachel smiled a bit. "Tough love, huh?"

Miriam nodded. "I think I like it. People aren't going to mess with me anymore."

Chapter 2

Sam would not be happy. Rachel left her aunt in the house with the children and with great trepidation made her way through the backyard to his office, in what was originally the carriage house.

Long ago, Sam had wanted to be an architect, but instead he'd spent the last twelve years doing construction work in Baxter, Ohio, a little town of eight thousand people on the banks of the Ohio River, west of Cincinnati. A place he had never wanted to stay. He had worked with a local construction company and later started his own business. People were restoring the old places in record numbers in Baxter these days and willing to pay top dollar for quality work. The business had thrived in the past few years, when everything else had seemed to go so wrong, and Rachel was proud of what he'd accomplished.

She opened the door, smelling sawdust and wood, missing the old days when he worked in the basement, when he was closer, and she saw more of him. He wasn't in the shop, but he had a small office in the back.

As she got closer she heard him talking. Peeking in, she saw that he was on the phone and decided to wait until he was done to give herself time to think of what to say.

She hadn't taken the kids upstairs to get them settled because she didn't want them or Miriam to see, but some of Sam's things were in the front bedroom.

Because he wasn't sleeping in her bed anymore.

Rachel wasn't even sure why. She just knew she hurt, that everything hurt. She didn't know if Sam did or not, because they didn't talk about it.

But they had to talk today. She had to find a way to talk him into this. Sam hadn't wanted to take Will at first. He'd been willing to adopt, although that had never worked out for them. But he'd been strangely reluctant to even consider foster care. He said they could never know for sure what they were getting into with a foster child, what kind of environment the kids came from, how much damage had been done. He'd argued that some children were just too far gone to ever be saved.

Unsalvageable children, written off completely. Rachel hated that idea.

But after twelve years, she and Sam had tried everything else. She didn't see how they'd ever have children any other way, and now she feared they never would. When Will left, Sam said that was it. They were done trying. They weren't going to get their hearts broken like that ever again.

Which meant she'd just have to talk him into this, just until after Christmas. She'd promised Miriam.

Rachel forced a smile across her face and had to brace herself, just for the sight of her husband, the man she loved and had wanted from way back before all the bad times. But just before she opened the door, she heard something odd.

"So the place'll be ready by Christmas?" Sam asked.

That was odd. She didn't know of any job he was finishing by Christmas. In fact, he'd been at loose ends since he finished the Randall house five days ago, a full week earlier than he was scheduled to, and his next clients weren't about to let him start renovating their house until after the holidays. Sam did not like to be at loose ends. He didn't know what to do with himself.

"Okay," she heard him say. "A few days later? Hell, Rick, you know I'm not picky. If anything's really wrong, I can fix it. Christmas is on a Monday this year, right? How about the Tuesday after Christmas?"

What in the world? Rachel wondered.

"I'll take it. A bed, a bathroom, and a kitchenette is fine. I don't need anything else."

A bed? Why did Sam need a bed?

"Yeah, I'm sure," Sam said. "This is what I have to do."

Oh, no, Rachel thought, sinking down to the floor, her back against the wall. *Oh, no.*

"No, I haven't told her," Sam said. "Her whole family was just here for her father's sixtieth birthday, and now it's almost Christmas. If I move out now, nobody'll talk about anything but that. It'll ruin the holiday, and there's just no point, especially if I can't get into the apartment until after Christmas. I'll wait to tell her. We'll do it nice and quick. That'll be the best thing for everybody."

She couldn't hear what Rick said, but Rachel thought, *Please. Please let him try to talk Sam out of it.*

"No. I'm sure. It's over," Sam said. "Look, I've got to go. Thanks."

And then there was nothing but silence. Rachel shoved her hand against her mouth. She was breathing too hard, and her chest hurt, but she managed to muffle the sounds and somehow she wasn't crying. She was too stunned to cry.

Sam was leaving her.

The Tuesday after Christmas, he'd be gone.

And he wasn't even going to tell her.

Sam. Leaving.

They'd been married for twelve years. He'd seen her through the most awkward years of her life and, later, the hardest ones. She'd believed he would always be by her side, no matter what.

Apparently, he had other ideas.

Rachel stood up to go. She didn't want to know his secret. Maybe if he could live with the pretense, so could she.

She'd taken three steps toward the door when she bumped into a stack of wood on the floor, making an awful racket.

Sam called out, "I'm in the office. Come on back."

She closed her eyes and swore softly. She just wanted to hide somewhere, until she wasn't so shaken, so stunned. Until it didn't hurt to breathe.

But he knew she was here, and she had to talk to him about the children. She'd promised to take care of them. They were only staying until after Christmas, too. Sam and the children might well leave her on the same day.

Rachel closed her eyes and pulled open the door at the same time he came out. They nearly ran into each other. He caught her, his hands on her arms; it was the first time he'd touched her in days, maybe weeks, and they stood there awkwardly staring at each other, too close and way too full of hurt for two people who were supposed to love each other forever.

Sam let go almost immediately and backed away.

He looked guilty, and she wondered if she looked guilty herself.

"Hi." She forced the word out, looking down at his cluttered desk, at his phone, at his window, anything but him. Then lied without one twinge of guilt. "I didn't think you were here."

He looked as shook up as she was. She thought he was going to call her on that but all he said was, "I was taking care of some things in the office. Did you . . . need something?"

"Yes." She needed so very much. She couldn't begin to tell him now, so she concentrated on the children. "Miriam's here—"

"Is it Will? Did she bring Will back?" he asked urgently, and for a second the old Sam was back. The one who cared. The one who didn't live behind all the walls they'd erected.

She missed him, she realized. She missed her husband a great deal.

And he was leaving her.

Right after Christmas.

"No," she said. "Not Will. He's fine, she said. So far, so good."

Sam made an exasperated sound. So he was still angry, she thought. He still hurt, too. She hadn't known that, and he probably didn't know how angry she still was, either. They didn't share much of anything anymore.

"Rachel? Are you all right?"

"Yes. I just have to tell you something, and you're not going to like it."

He paused, his gaze narrowing on her face. He didn't even seem to breathe. She wondered if he thought she was leaving him, or asking him to leave. Truth was, it had never even occurred to her. She felt so foolish now, but the thought had never crossed her mind.

"Miriam found some children in trouble," she blurted out. "Two girls and a boy, all from the same family. They don't have anyplace to go."

"What does that have to do with us?" he asked carefully.

"We're still on the list. Of approved foster homes—"

"No," he said right away.

"We are. They never took us off—"

"I don't give a damn about any list."

"She needs us," Rachel argued. "These kids need us."

"We agreed."

"No, we didn't," she realized. "You decided. You just told me that we wouldn't do this anymore."

"We can't," he said. "It nearly tore us apart the first time. You know that. You know how hard it was."

"My whole adult life has been hard," she said. "Every bit of it, and when I think about it, I honestly can't see it getting much worse than it is right now."

After all, Will was gone, back to his pathetic excuse for a mother. Rachel's husband of a dozen years was leaving her, and she spent her days in a rocking chair in a dark corner of her house not seeing anyone or doing anything.

Sam stiffened, looked harder and sadder than ever. "You'll get yourself hurt again, Rachel."

"Maybe," she said. "Maybe I'm just doomed to live my life with one hurt after another. I don't know. But these kids don't have anybody right now, and I'm going to help them."

"What?"

"I am. I'm doing it," she insisted, standing up to him as she seldom had in their entire marriage.

He was a good man, good down to the core, both protective and considerate of her. Normally, she would have talked this over with him and likely gone along with what he decided, but not anymore. He was leaving her. She'd have to think for herself, and she might as well start now.

"It's just for a little while, Sam. For Christmas. Miriam says all her foster homes are full. She doesn't have any other place to put these kids," Rachel said. "They need someone, and I can help them. I'm not doing this for me. I'm doing it for the kids."

"I won't do it," he insisted.

"Fine. Don't. It's not like you're at the house that often anyway, anymore. Show up for breakfast and supper, if you want, and I'll feed you. Dump your clothes in the laundry room and I'll make sure they get cleaned. But that's it. I doubt you'll even have to see the children."

"Rachel!"

"I mean it," she said, a little breathless at standing up to him. "I'm going to see that they have a safe place to stay and a nice Christmas."

"No matter what I say?"

"I know what you have to say about this." And he was leaving anyway.

Rachel didn't want him to go yet. For once, she wanted her house full of children, wanted to know how that felt. Maybe she'd pretend that these were her children, that this unreal time was her life, the way she'd always believed it would be. Maybe she would find she couldn't do without that. That no matter what the risks involved, she had to reach out and take that chance, one more time, to find the life she'd always imagined for herself.

These children she would borrow for a time, weave her fantasies around them, her life with children at Christmas, the way she always thought it would be. For that, she supposed she needed Sam's support.

"I haven't asked you for anything in the longest time," she said softly. "And I promise, I will never ask you for anything ever again. But these children need us, and I need to help them. Give me this, Sam. This one thing."

"It's a mistake," he insisted.

"Well, it's not like we've never made a mistake before," she said, then broke off at the look on his face. The hard, harsh, painful look.

What did he think she meant? That it was all a mistake? Surely he didn't think that. She'd never wanted anyone but him, but she'd always worried that given a choice, he never would have married her. Like a coward, she'd never found the courage to ask. She didn't have it even now after twelve years.

"It's not like we've never been hurt before," she said, not even looking at him now.

"That's no reason to get hurt again, Rachel."

He waited there a long time, looking at her and then looking away. She saw him work for every breath he took, saw him shake his head back and forth, as if he were about to refuse.

"Just until after Christmas," she said.

"All right," he said finally. "If that's what you want."

And it wasn't until later, when she was alone and headed back to the house, that she realized what she'd done, what she'd promised him. If she couldn't ask him for anything else, that meant when the Tuesday after Christmas came and he was ready to go, she couldn't ask him to stay.

Sam stood just outside the back door and stared at the back of the house.

There were children inside. It literally took his breath away, the thought of children inside his house.

And they were staying. His wife had decided. She'd feed Sam and do his laundry, and other than that he could just stay out of her way.

Sam was still smarting from that, still in shock, honestly. She had never made such a monumental decision on her own, never suggested that she'd be just fine without him. He'd spent weeks worrying about that—about whether Rachel would be okay without him.

But he wasn't gone yet, and it was still up to him to protect her as best he could. Determined to do just that, Sam stalked into the house. The back door opened into the laundry room, a catchall area for winter coats and boots and shoes. He kicked his off, hung up his coat, and stepped into the kitchen, warily looking around for the children or his wife or her busybody aunt, Miriam.

He found a little boy shoveling pumpkin bread into his mouth and gulping down a glass of milk that looked two times too big for the boy's hands. The boy was four or five, and he had dark hair that hung down into his eyes. He needed a haircut in the worst way, had on jeans that were frayed nearly all the way through at the knees, and worn sneakers that had to leave his feet wet and freezing in the snow. The boy had big, dark eyes and a mischievous grin. His mouth was sticky with cream and cake crumbs, and he was going at it as if he hadn't eaten in days.

Sam had taken a two-by-four to the chest one time when somebody swung a board around unexpectedly and caught him unaware, and the sight of the hungry, ill-cared-for boy felt much like that. A two-by-four to the chest.

The boy reached for another swig of milk and discovered Sam at the same time. Startled, he set the milk down, missing the counter. It hit the floor, milk and bits of glass going everywhere. The boy gave a startled cry, then looked at Sam as if he were some kind of monster that might attack at any second.

"I'm sorry," he gulped.

Sam frowned at the boy and then back at the mess. The boy went to scramble down off the stool, and Sam barely caught him in time and put him back up there. Sam let go of him as quickly as possible, refusing to think about what it felt like to have a little boy in his arms.

"Sit there," he said. "There's glass, and you don't need to be down there in it."

"I'm sorry," the boy said again, almost crying now.

Rachel, Miriam, and a girl with a baby in her arms rushed into the kitchen. "What happened?" Rachel asked.

"I broke it!" the boy wailed. "An' I made a mess."

"It's all right, sweetheart." Miriam stroked the boy's hair.

The girl gave the baby to Rachel. Sam looked away, not wanting to see Rachel with a baby in her arms. It had been hard enough to watch her with her nieces and nephews this weekend. Then the girl grabbed some paper towels and reached for the mess.

"I'll get it," she said.

"No," Sam said, maybe more sharply than he should have. "There's glass. I'll get it."

"I can take care of him," the girl said, a little breathless and maybe scared herself.

"You're just a child," he pointed out.

"I'm almost twelve."

"Which most people consider a child," he said, too harshly yet again. She looked as if she was about to cry, too.

Rachel stepped in and said, "You know, this is my fault. I should have given him a plastic cup. Then we wouldn't have anything but milk to clean up."

"I'm sorry," the boy said again.

"It's okay," Rachel insisted. "Zach, this is my husband, Sam, and he's not mad at you. He's just worried you were going to get hurt. You, too, Emma."

"Hi," Zach said tentatively, all big dark eyes and too much hair.

"Hi," Sam said, doing his best to wipe the scowl off his face.

"Emma, say hello to Sam," Rachel instructed.

"Hi," she said, obviously hurt by the fact that he'd called her a child.

"And this"—Rachel turned so the baby curled up against her shoulder was more or less facing him—"is Grace. Isn't she just an angel?"

Sam turned away. He and Rachel had a baby girl once. She hadn't lived a day. They were cursed when it came to children. He'd accepted the fact that they weren't ever going to have any, and he didn't want to see this angel of a baby girl in his wife's arms.

"Why don't you all clear out. I'll clean up the mess," Sam said, then turned to the boy. "Come here, Zach."

He lifted the boy off the stool, carried him to the edge of the kitchen, and set him on his feet.

"I'm really, really sorry," Zach said solemnly.

"No big deal. We have more glasses than we need in this house. More milk, too."

The boy turned and left. Rachel and the baby and Miriam left. The girl, Emma, lingered behind.

"You don't want us here, do you?" she asked.

Sam scowled at her. He couldn't quite help it.

"You don't like kids?" she suggested.

"I wouldn't know. I've never had kids."

"Why not?"

"It's a long story," he said. "One I'd appreciate you wouldn't discuss with my wife. She tends to get a little upset when she talks about it, and she's been upset enough already."

"I won't upset her," the girl claimed.

"Oh, yes, you will." He was certain of it.

Looking scared, the girl asked, "Are you gonna send us away?"

"Rachel said you're staying, so that's it. You're staying," he said, then decided as reassurances went, it sounded fairly weak. "And I'll be in a better mood tomorrow."

"Okay," she said tentatively.

"It's not that I dislike kids," he explained. "And I'm not usually like this. I'm not usually so loud or so . . ."

"Grumpy?" she suggested.

Sam winced. "Yes," he said grumpily. "It's just . . . It's been a bad day."

It was the day he had finally said it out loud. He was leaving his wife.

That made it real, didn't it? He hated it, and saying it out loud made it real. It seemed he could hear the clock ticking in his head, counting down his last days with Rachel. He'd set into motion a horrible thing, and he worried that he could never take it back, now that he'd started it.

Sam looked up and saw the girl regarding him warily. *Damn.* "Don't worry," he said. "Rachel's . . . well, she's the best. She'll take good care of you."

"I can watch Zach and the baby. I'm good at it. If you'll just let us stay, I can keep them out of your way. We won't be much trouble." Seeing Sam throwing paper towels over pieces of glass and puddles of milk at the moment, Emma reconsidered. "Well, not much trouble."

"I meant it, Emma. You can stay," he said, not looking at her, concentrating on the mess. Working with wood was messy. Messes didn't bother him. Rachel getting hurt would. "Until after Christmas, anyway. That's what Rachel's aunt said. She'll find someone else to take you by then."

"Okay."

"And you don't have to take care of anybody," he felt compelled to add. She was just a girl. "Rachel's always wanted kids. She'll enjoy having you here."

"She seems nice. Just . . . sad."

Sam dumped the worst of the mess in the garbage can in the corner and frowned. "She is sad. Maybe you and Zach and the baby can cheer her up."

Sam wanted that. He wanted all the old hurts to go away, and he didn't see how that was going to happen if they were still together. So he was letting her go, hoping she'd find someone else who could make her happy. He sure as hell hadn't, not for a long time.

And maybe somewhere along the way, he'd learn to be happy, too.

Happy without Rachel? He shook his head. He'd never imagined that, and he thought it was the ultimate in irony, now when he'd given up and decided to go, that someone had brought three children into their lives, however temporary that might be. He'd always thought she could have been happy with him if they'd had children.

"We could help," Emma said quite seriously, but hopefully. "Zack is kind of silly, and everybody likes Grace. Everybody smiles at her."

The look on her little face was so earnest Sam could hardly look at her. He felt like the big bad wolf, snarling and showing his teeth, terrifying already traumatized children. God, he hated himself today. He leaned against the doorjamb, suddenly so tired he could hardly stand up, feeling so old, so worn down. Hell, he was only thirty-two years old. How could he be this tired?

"We'll have a better day tomorrow," he said. Surely he could do better tomorrow.

Emma bid him a wary good-bye. Sam finished cleaning up the mess, then went to find Miriam. She owed him some answers. They faced off on the front porch, so the kids and Rachel wouldn't hear.

"What do you think you're doing, Miriam?"

"Trying to help those children."

"Bull."

"It is not. And watch your mouth. I'm a lady."

"Miriam—"

"Sam, don't hate me anymore for what happened with Will, okay? I love you and Rachel, and I tried my best to help you and that boy. Taking him away from here was one of the hardest things I've ever had to do."

"I don't want to talk about Will," he said. "I want to

talk about these kids. What do you know about these kids?"

"Not much. They're all siblings, we think. We think they gave us their real first names, but they won't tell us their last name or where they're from or what their mother's or father's name is. A clerk at the Drifter said they checked in four days ago with a woman he assumed was their mother. She paid cash for two nights, gave him a false address in Pennsylvania and a fake name, and he never saw her again. He opened the room on the third day, when she hadn't checked out or paid for another night, and found the kids inside, waiting for their mother to come back."

"Shit!" Sam said. "She just left them? Left a baby that age and a boy and a girl who's all of eleven and didn't come back?"

"Near as we can tell."

"And that woman could show up tomorrow, and you'd give those kids back to her, wouldn't you? If she came up with the right story, and you believed her and the judge believed her, you'd give her her kids back?"

"I don't know, Sam. I don't make the rules. I just have to follow them."

"Well let me tell you something, the rules suck!"

"Sometimes, they do."

"Oh, hell, Miriam." He got all choked up, worried he would embarrass himself, like he had when she'd come to take Will away. "Rachel can't have these kids here and not fall for them, and I don't know if she can take getting hurt again. I don't think she can take losing one more person she loves."

Sam winced at his own choice of words. Maybe he was thinking selfishly here. Maybe he was hoping she could take losing one more thing. *Him.* But that was it. Nothing else.

When he'd come out of the office and she'd looked so uneasy, Sam had thought for a moment that she'd heard him on the phone, that she knew. He had no idea what she'd say to him. Maybe she'd ask him to stay. Maybe she'd say she still needed him or that she just didn't want to be without him. But he wasn't holding out much hope of that, either.

"I don't want her hurt, Miriam." That was his bottom line.

"Neither do I, but I don't think she can hide inside this house much longer and never come out, either. I know sitting in that rocking chair of my grandmother's isn't doing her any good."

"What are you talking about?"

"Rachel," she said. "God, are you in as bad a shape as she is?"

"What's wrong with Rachel?" he growled.

"She doesn't do anything anymore. She hardly ever comes out of this house. She just sits here. Sam, where have you been?"

"Right here," he argued. But hell, he hadn't. He'd been working and sleeping in his office or in the front bedroom upstairs.

He'd been avoiding her and their problems, thinking they might get better on their own somehow, but it wasn't going to happen. Then Rick had mentioned that his friend Stu was moving out of the spare room above Rick's shop and did Sam know anybody who might want it. The more Sam had thought about it, the more he had known it was time. There was no point in going on any longer the way things were between them.

Rick's place was cheap and it was close to Sam's

shop and office. He wouldn't move his office right away. He couldn't take being so far away from Rachel, at least not at first. He'd still keep an eye on her and help with the house. As much as they'd done to the old place, it always needed more.

He'd decided. All he had to do now was hold out until after Christmas, tell Rachel and go.

Then all he had to do was learn to live without her.

Now it seemed he'd been so caught up in his own problems that he hadn't been paying enough attention to her.

"What's going on between the two of you?" Miriam asked.

"Nothing," he lied. The family gossip system was more highly developed than any communications satellite in the world. He wasn't interested in being fodder for the family roundtable. This was between him and Rachel.

"Sam—"

"We haven't gotten over Will, okay?" That shut Miriam up. She still felt guilty, and Sam was mad enough to use that against her right now. "So, Rachel doesn't go anywhere?"

"Not for weeks," Miriam said.

How could that be? She'd always been busy, taking care of her sick grandfather, helping Sam get the business off the ground, and later with her stained glass. She did amazing things with the glass, first on jobs Sam had taken on and then on jobs of her own. She helped her sisters with their kids, helped take care of her father now that her mother was gone. She volunteered at the church and for Meals on Wheels and all sorts of organizations around town. He'd always been proud of all she did, all she gave to everyone around her.

"I know she cleared her schedule a lot while she was working on the Parker mansion the past year, but . . ." She'd finished that weeks ago, hadn't she?

Sam had trouble remembering what day it was lately. Until he'd given himself a deadline to move out, he simply hadn't cared.

"All her volunteer stuff?" he began, shaken and trying not to show it.

"She's turned it all over to other people. No one's seen her outside the house in weeks—before the birthday get-together, at least. Everyone who's knocked on your front door has found her here, full of excuses as to why she can't do things, and yet she never actually seems to do anything," Miriam said. "Looks like you've got some things to take care of."

"Yeah. You, too. Find out who these kids belong to, Miriam. Quickly."

"I will," she promised. "Take good care of Rachel."

Sam held his tongue. He'd never been able to take proper care of Rachel. Still, the thought of her sitting here all day in that damned rocking chair in the corner . . . He had come home one evening around dusk and found her sitting in the dark, asleep in the rocker.

It had seemed odd, but she said she hadn't been sleeping well. He wouldn't know about that because he hadn't been sleeping in their bed. So he had let it go. He'd turned and walked away, as he so often did these days. He wondered what else he'd missed.

Chapter 3

The afternoon was chaotic between getting the children settled and Rachel holding her breath while Sam was outside arguing with Miriam on the porch. But he gave in, because when he came inside he had some plastic shopping bags from Wal-Mart. At first, all she could think was that was so odd. Sam didn't shop, except for building supplies. And then she realized he'd given in—that the children were staying and these were their things.

Rachel saw Emma staring at the bags. Her cheeks turned ruddy and she hid her face against the top of the baby's head. They had so little.

"We'll go shopping tomorrow," Rachel said, thinking to reassure her.

"We don't need much," Emma insisted.

"Then we'll just get what you need," Rachel said. But they wouldn't. They'd get a lot. "It'll be fun. Especially picking out things for Grace. They have the cutest clothes for babies. I have nearly a dozen nieces and nephews; I shop for them all the time."

Usually, it hurt, shopping for children she'd never have. But this time, she'd enjoy it. She'd dress Emma in something brand new, too. Something stylish, if she could figure out what stylish was to an eleven-year-old girl. It would be a good day. She'd make it one.

A moment later, Zach came whizzing around the corner. He'd found a set of Matchbox cars her nephew left behind and was on his hands and knees racing in a circle through the house—the hall, the living room, the dining room, the kitchen, and back to the hall. Every thirty seconds or so, he came through like a whirlwind, and this time, he zoomed into Sam. Still on his hands and knees, he looked way up at Sam and said, "Sorry."

Sam took a breath and let it out slow. "It's okay, kid."

"Can I ask you somethin'?"

With a pained expression on his face, Sam said, "Sure."

"Have you been bad?" Zach asked quite seriously. "Is San'a mad at you?"

Rachel started to laugh. She couldn't help it. Sam stared at her, a dazed expression on his face. She couldn't tell if he was really mad or if it was something else. But she stopped laughing.

"Not that I know of," Sam said finally.

"Has he told you something he hasn't told us, Zach?" Rachel asked.

"Uh-uh. I haven't talked to him yet, but I wanna. Can we do that? Do y'know where he's at?"

"I do," Rachel offered. "Santa's coming on Saturday. There's going to be a parade and everything. It goes right down this street. We can't miss that."

"I gotta tell him some stuff," Zach said seriously.

"We'll make sure you get to talk to him," she said. "Why do you think Santa's mad at Sam, Zach?"

"'Cause Chris'mas isn't comin' here."

"What?"

"We saw all the lights and the trees 'n' stuff on all the other houses. They're all ready for him. But I guess he's not comin' here. No Chris'mas."

"Oh." Rachel laughed again, realizing the problem. "It's the first day of Christmas, isn't it?"

Zach looked puzzled. "I thought it wasn't comin' for another couple o' weeks."

"I mean today's the first day of the town's Christmas festival. It's something special we do here," Rachel said. "Come and see, and I'll explain."

They went to the window. The children crowded in around her, and she found she liked the press of little bodies all around her, the sounds of awe in their voices, and the way Zach had his nose flat against the cool pane of glass and laughed as it fogged up. Then he touched the little triangles of blue trim around the edges.

"Somebody colored 'em?" he asked.

"Something like that," Rachel said.

She painted glass herself at times, but this she'd ordered special from a company in Wisconsin to match what had already been here when she restored these windows as best she could. At one time, she'd loved the way the pretty panels seemed to frame the world outside.

She looked carefully and really saw, for the first time maybe in a long time, that world outside the walls of her house. Thousands of twinkling lights gleamed back at her. Every house on the street was all decked out for Christmas but hers. It was the first day of Christmas, and she and Sam had ignored it.

"Baxter has a Christmas festival," she explained. "The Twelve Days of Christmas."

"Who's Baxter?" Sam asked.

"The town, Zach." Rachel laughed a bit. "It's famous for its old-fashioned Christmas festival, our own version of the Twelve Days of Christmas, except ours lead up to Christmas instead of starting on Christmas Day. We take the holiday very seriously around here. Especially in this neighborhood."

Sam and Rachel lived in a five-square-block area known as "the district," a place full of old Victorian houses, most of which had been lovingly restored. Many of them had been used as models in her grandfather's work, as well.

People came from all over to see the Christmas of Richard Landon's creation, and now Rachel had unwittingly violated a tradition that was practically sacred. She and her neighbors took pride in putting up an elaborate display of lights and seasonal colors for their own enjoyment and the town's visitors. Many of them would be strolling and riding through "the district" to look at all the lights over the next twelve days. Everyone was ready, except her and Sam.

"We just forgot, Zach. That's all," Rachel said. "Santa's not mad at us. Not that we know of, anyway."

"So, he comes here?"

"Of course. He'll find you here. We'll tell him all about it when we go see him. And we'll get the Christmas decorations up tomorrow. You can help."

"You got some'a those?" he asked, obviously unconvinced.

"Yes." Rachel looked to Sam, who'd remained silent through the whole exchange. "I think Zach needs to see the decorations. I can check the lights after the children are in bed, and we can decorate tomorrow."

"And a tree?" Zach added. "We'll have a tree?"

"Of course. We'll cut it down ourselves." Rachel re-

alized she was actually excited. "My aunt Jo lives on a
Christmas tree farm, and she has a sleigh. If we ask
nicely, and we catch her when she's not too busy, she'll
let us take the sleigh into the back fields and find a tree
to cut down. It'll be fun."

She and Sam used to do that every Christmas. Just
the two of them cuddled up beneath the blankets, riding through the snow. It was magical in a sleigh in the
snow at Christmas.

It had been so long ago. She couldn't remember
why they ever stopped. And that made her think, *Sam.*
Christmas. What would it be like without him? She
couldn't imagine that or a thousand other little every-
day things without Sam. She wondered briefly if he'd
found someone else. Wasn't that why men left their
wives? Because they'd found someone else? Rachel
couldn't imagine Sam with another woman, couldn't
imagine him hurting her that way. Of course, she never
imagined he'd leave her, either.

"Are you okay?" Emma said. "You looked all sad."

"Just for a minute," she said. "I was thinking about
the sleigh. It's been a long time since I did that. But
we'll do it this year. Promise."

She didn't dare look over at her husband, couldn't
find the courage to ask if he'd come with them. She'd
implied that she didn't need anything from him anymore, but it wasn't true. She needed so much from
him.

She wondered if he'd simply be here on the fringes,
going through the motions of Christmas until time ran
out and he walked away from her for good.

Zach and Sam found the decorations, twelve boxes
full. The number alone impressed and reassured Zach.

They opened three boxes, so Zach could rest easily knowing Christmas was indeed coming to this house.

He giggled and tugged at things that Rachel had packed in precise order, messing things up, but she didn't care. She sat on the floor with the boxes all around her, Grace patting the sides of the boxes and pulling herself up to stand while hanging on to them. She giggled and slapped her palms against the top of the boxes, obviously quite pleased with herself, either because of the noise or the fact that she was standing.

Rachel gazed at her in awe, as if she were a magical creature come to life, right here in Rachel's living room. "She's beautiful," Rachel told Emma, the little mother who was hovering next to Grace's side.

"And clumsy. She's always falling down and hurting herself."

"I'll be careful with her." Rachel would treat her like spun glass.

"Look!" Zach exclaimed, pulling out a long length of glittery gold garland she usually draped around the tree.

"You like that?"

He giggled. She didn't even scold him for ignoring her request to leave everything in the boxes for now. He came up to her and draped the garland around her neck and shoulders, like a scarf.

"You can wear it," he said.

Touched, Rachel said, "Thank you, Zach."

"It's for the tree, Zach," Emma said.

"She can wear it!" he insisted.

"I will. I love it."

She'd wear sackcloth and ashes for this little boy if it would make him smile. And then Rachel thought of another thing that might make him smile. Nearly an hour later, Rachel sat with Zach practically in her lap, Emma on her other side holding Grace. She pulled out an oversize book, the cover of which was graced with a painting of a Victorian house all decorated for Christmas.

"Do you recognize this?" Rachel pointed to the house.

"Uh-uh," Zach said.

"It's this house," she said, delighted to be living in her grandfather's old house on this cold winter night, so close to Christmas, with children gathered around her. She felt as if she were sharing a bit of true magic with them.

"Uh-uh," Zach said.

"It is. You'll see tomorrow, when we get all the decorations up."

"Your house is in a book?" Zach asked, leaning closer.

"Well, it actually belonged to my grandfather. This is a painting he did of the house at Christmas a long time ago."

"An it's in a book?" Zach was amazed.

"Yes. He's a bit famous. A few years ago, a publisher was interested in illustrations for a Christmas story, and he came and got a bunch of my grandfather's paintings, and now they're in this Christmas book. Isn't it nice?"

"Uh-huh," Zach said.

Zach settled in a bit closer to hear the story. Emma didn't seem as interested, but she sat there quietly, holding the baby. Rachel read, telling them about all the different things in the pictures that she could show them when they went into town the next day. She wasn't sure Zach actually believed her, had to admit it was probably hard for a little boy to understand. But he would see for himself soon. It would add to the magic even more.

Later, she tucked Zach into bed, let Emma put Grace down, then walked an unusually quiet Emma to the room down the hall where she'd be sleeping.

"You'll be all right here? By yourself?" Rachel asked gently.

"I will. But Zach's used to sleeping with me. Grace, too. We all sleep in the same room."

"Oh." Aunt Miriam said the children should have their own beds, preferably their own rooms. But she didn't say they had to actually sleep in them. Obviously, they were used to being together, and Rachel didn't want to make this any harder.

"Why don't we try it like this, Emma. And if Zach or Grace get lonely, they know where you are."

"Okay," Emma said.

"Is there anything else?"

Emma looked troubled. "This is really the house in the book?"

"Yes. It looks a little different now, because it was about thirty years ago when my grandfather painted the picture." Her grandfather wasn't a brilliant painter; he'd done the paintings as a first step toward making the models of the buildings he used in the snow globe scenes. But he had a gift in the way he used color and light and in selecting such beautiful scenes. Once the snow globes became popular, so did his paintings.

Emma frowned again, her brow wrinkling in concentration, and asked, "Is this a magic house?"

"I used to think so when I was your age. It's always been a happy house," she said, refusing to think about the last few years when it had been just her and Sam.

"And I want you and Zach and Grace to have a good Christmas here with me and Sam. Do you think we could do that? Make it a good one?"

Emma nodded.

"Then we will. And I don't want you to worry, Emma. We'll take good care of you here. All right?"

"Okay."

Rachel gave her a kiss on the forehead and a gentle hug. "Call me if you need anything."

Sam lingered on the fringes of the nighttime rituals. He watched as Rachel supervised—teeth brushed, hands washed, faces washed. The baby tried to eat the washcloth. She truly did try to eat everything.

He made sure he got upstairs ahead of the rest of them to set up the portable crib Miriam had brought in the middle bedroom. Then as Rachel came upstairs with Zach and the baby, he slipped into the front bedroom and cleaned his things out of there. Miriam said the children needed their own beds, which meant Rachel would need that room for one of the children.

He was still trying to decide where to put his things when Rachel came into the hall and caught him standing there with a handful of clothes. Her cheeks flushed, whether with anger or embarrassment, he couldn't tell, and the look she gave him made him feel like a thief, like he'd stolen something from her, something personal and very important, by walking away without a word from the bed they'd always shared. This after nights of making sure he was gone from the house before she woke up in the mornings and didn't go to bed at night until she was already asleep. So they didn't have to say anything about the fact that he slept somewhere else.

"I'll, uhh . . . I can sleep on the sofa in the family room," he said.

She nodded, keeping her head down, not letting him see anything else that might be in her eyes right now. He understood. He didn't want to have to look Rachel in the eye and talk to her about where he'd be sleeping now or maybe about why he'd started sleeping somewhere else in the first place.

He didn't even want to think about it now. It made him remember how alone he was, even in the same house with his wife. Right now, he felt more alone than ever. Watching her with the children tonight, he couldn't help but think that this was the way things should have been, the way things would never be for him and Rachel.

"Do you need anything?" he asked. "For the kids?"

"No," she said, still not looking at him. "We're fine."

Which he took as a dismissal, which still stung. Suddenly, he felt like a stranger here, as if he were on the fringes of something he wanted desperately, staring at it from the outside looking in, knowing he'd never have it, the way he'd felt most of his life. But never with Rachel. It was only with her that he'd ever imagined he might belong anywhere.

But not anymore, Sam reminded himself. Then, like the coward he'd become, without another word to her, he slipped downstairs and went back outside to his workshop. To his space, where nothing had changed.

Sam made himself wait until after ten o'clock to go back inside. He found a plate of food Rachel had left for him and heated it in the microwave. Then he took it into the living room, thinking he'd watch the early news before going to bed. But there was Rachel sitting in the rocker, the garland that had been around her neck now draped across the back of the chair, the baby in her arms.

He felt hot color rising in his cheeks, embarrassed that he'd walked away earlier without even showing her the courtesy of telling her where he was going and when he'd be back.

"Is the baby okay?" he asked, sitting down on the sofa across the room from her.

"Probably just unsettled by being in a new place," Rachel said, not looking at him, either, her attention focused fully on the baby. "She fussed a bit after Emma put her down, so I brought her down here and rocked her. She went right to sleep, and then . . . Well, it's not exactly a hardship to hold her."

"I heard you talking to Emma about shopping."

Rachel nodded. "Miriam gave me some money but it won't go far. They have so little. She suggested I try the church thrift shop—"

"Buy whatever they need," he said. "New. Heavy coats, gloves, hats, boots. Whatever they need."

"Sam—"

"We can afford to buy the kids coats. And get the girls some nice things. The boy, too. Not hand-me-downs." He knew all about hand-me-downs.

"Okay," she said. "Thank you. I know you don't want to do this. I know you think it's a bad idea, but . . ."

"It's what you want. We'll do it."

She sighed and looked back at the baby. Grace had caught the tip of Rachel's finger in one tiny fist, holding on tightly, and Rachel was running her thumb over the baby's tiny hand, mesmerized, lost. Sam looked at the garland Zach had given her earlier. He remembered the way she looked, all sparkly and glittery, her hair glowing golden as well. She'd laughed, and he'd been startled by the sound. He didn't remember the last time he heard Rachel laugh, and he missed it. He missed so many things about her.

Sam couldn't help but think of how perfect she looked sitting in her great-grandmother's rocking chair with a baby in her arms.

"I know it's silly," she said, "but today, when Miriam came . . . It was just like in my dream. The baby dream. I was sitting here all alone, and the doorbell rang, and she walked up to me and handed me Grace. I'd given up on anything like that ever happening."

Because of Sam. He knew it.

They couldn't have any more children. They'd tried adoption twice, only to get their hopes dashed both times, and then they'd gotten Will, which had also turned out bad. Now they had more children, who weren't staying, either.

"Rachel, she's not yours to keep."

"I know." She nuzzled her face against the baby's cheek. "I was just saying . . . it was so like my dream. I'd given up, totally. I couldn't even hope anymore, because it was too hard. It hurt too much. But I think I was wrong, Sam. How can I just stop hoping?"

He wondered what his wife hoped for these days, but he didn't ask. All he said was, "Just don't forget this baby isn't yours."

"I won't. I promise. But I'm going to enjoy the time I have with her. I'm going to try my best to enjoy this Christmas with these children."

"We can do that, I guess." He didn't like it, but he'd do it for her. Because she'd asked this of him and it was one thing within his power to give. And then, with his throat thick and tight with regrets stored up over the years, he said, "I never meant for it to turn out this way, Rachel."

"Me, either," she said.

They weren't talking about kids anymore. They were talking about their marriage, about the mess they'd made of it. She'd given up on him, he feared, just as he'd given up on the two of them.

Still, Sam wondered if she missed him, at nights like this when it was just the two of them talking and in their bed. She'd never said a word about him sleeping somewhere else, never asked him to come back, and suddenly it seemed as if it had been forever since he'd touched her.

He didn't want to think that he might never do that again, might never have the right. What would she do if he turned to her now? he wondered. If he took her in his arms and buried himself in the familiar comfort of her warm, soft body?

Sam groaned. He still wanted her, and it had been so long.

All those nights, he thought, he could have been with her.

Emma lay all alone in the bed they'd given her in the front room. She never slept alone. The baby fussed, and she got up to see to her, but Rachel got there first, and Emma decided that was okay. You could tell when people honestly liked babies, and Rachel did. Emma trusted her, even with the baby.

Things were much better tonight. They were together and warm and their stomachs were full, and Sam, although he seemed mad at the world, said they could stay. Emma was a bit scared of him. Some men didn't like kids and some men were just plain bad. Emma couldn't tell for now about Sam.

But he'd promised they could stay until Christmas, and Emma believed him about that much, at least. That should give her and Zach and Grace plenty of time. They could stay here with Rachel, who was so nice, and Sam, who they'd just stay away from, and everything would be fine.

Emma heard footsteps coming down the hall and a moment later Zach climbed into the bed with her. She'd been waiting for that, too.

"You think it's okay?" Zach said, snuggling into the warm spot she'd made in the covers. "Miss Rachel didn't say I had to stay in that other room."

"I know. She won't mind."

"Do you think Mommy's coming soon?"

"Uh-hmm," Emma said.

"But we didn't stay at the motel like she told us. What if she can't find us?"

"She will. She promised."

Truth was, Emma was worried. She had been uneasy when their mother said she had to go away and that Emma had to take care of Zach and baby Grace for a whole day. It was just supposed to be for a day. Emma hadn't gotten really scared again until it had gotten dark and their mother still wasn't back. The second day, she had to work hard not to let Zach and the baby see how scared she was. Still, Emma knew what to do. She took care of them. She had even remembered what to do when the police and the social worker came. She hadn't told them her last name or where they were from or what their mother's name was. But they had taken her and Zach and Grace away.

"We had to go, Zach. The policeman said he couldn't leave us there by ourselves, remember?" She'd tried to make them leave the kids with her, tried to make them understand that she could take care of Zach and Grace, but she hadn't been able to do that.

"I didn't tell 'em nothin'," Zach said proudly. "Just my name and Grace's name and yours. And that I'm five."

"You did great," Emma said.

"Do you like it here?"

"I think it's a great place to wait until Mom comes back."

"They sure have good food here," he said.

"I know." He'd eaten enough for three boys. Rachel had warmed up lasagna for dinner and let them have all they wanted. Emma's stomach had hurt when she was done, and as she had been helping put things away after dinner, she had noticed that the refrigerator was full. Sam and Rachel must never run out of food.

"I still miss Mommy," Zach said.

"I know. But we're together, so we'll be fine. All we have to do is wait."

Emma believed it. She believed everything her mother said.

She waited until Zach was all warm and boneless with sleep, then got up and dug through the Wal-Mart bags for her snow globe. She polished the glass where it had gotten smudged with fingerprints and stared inside it, as she never had before. Honestly, she didn't think she was imagining things, but she had to be sure. It had been a long time since she believed in magic, after all.

Emma grabbed her coat and shoved her arms through the sleeves, but she couldn't find her shoes. So she just put her socks on and padded downstairs. She didn't hear anything, but the light was still on in the family room. Someone might still be awake. She was extra careful to be quiet when she slid back the lock and opened the front door.

It was cold, and her feet sank into the snow with every step she took, getting wetter and colder by the minute.

She went clear across the street, and when she turned around, there was the house, in the midst of the glistening snow, moonlight and streetlights and the lights from inside setting it aglow. It had beautiful windows, like the kind you saw in church, with all sorts of pretty colors in the glass. Little rectangles of blues, reds, and yellows framed each window in the front of the house.

It was the windows that cinched it for her when she held her snow globe up in front of her, looking from it to the house, then back again.

She didn't notice the cold at all anymore, and she wasn't even scared of being out here in the dark by herself in this new place. She wasn't scared of anything.

Because they were just the same.

The house in her snow globe and the house where she and Zach and Grace were staying were just the same.

It had to be a sign, Emma decided. She'd always looked at the house inside the little glass ball and thought nothing bad could ever happen there, and now she was living in that house. Which meant everything was going to be okay. Emma was sure of it.

Chapter 4

On the second day of Christmas, in those odd moments between sleeping and waking, Rachel rolled over in her bed, instinctively reaching for Sam, but he wasn't there. She forgot sometimes before she truly woke up, and this morning she remembered something else, something even worse.

Sam was leaving her.

The memory stopped her cold. It hit with enough force to take her breath away even now, and she felt every bit as lost and as scared as she had yesterday when she'd heard him on the phone.

Rachel lay there, almost paralyzed. She'd thought it couldn't possibly be as overwhelming the second day, but it was.

Sam was leaving.

The words seemed to echo around inside her head, drowning out everything else for a long, frightening moment. Her eyes flooded with tears for a moment, and then the moisture overflowed. She just let those tears fall.

Oh, Sam.

She wondered, not for the first time, if he'd ever really loved her, something that hurt just about as much as anything that had happened to her in the last twelve years.

Maybe Sam never really loved her at all.

She might have stayed right there worrying, but she heard the baby fussing and before she could get up, Sam appeared in the doorway with a sniffling baby Grace in his arms.

"I heard her crying," he said. "I assume she's hungry."

Rachel glanced at the clock. It was six-ten. She had no idea when the baby normally woke up and ate, but it seemed reasonable that this was the time.

"I made a couple of bottles last night and put them in the refrigerator." Rachel started to get up. "I just need to warm one up."

"I'll get it. You stay here." Sam put the baby in the bed beside her. "It's still early. She might go back to sleep, once she's fed."

"Thanks," she said.

Grace settled in beside her, tucked into her side, and hiccuped and fussed a bit more and then just stared up at Rachel. It was nice, she decided, having a warm, soft baby in bed with her early in the morning.

"You must have been so scared," Rachel crooned to her, the baby's eyes focusing in on her face, as if taking in everything Rachel had to say. "To wake up in a strange place, in that odd little crib. Not knowing where you are or where your mommy is.

"But we're going to take good care of you. I promise. Sam's bringing your bottle, and then we'll give you a bath, and we'll find you something warm to wear. Today we're going shopping. We'll find you such gorgeous things. Something pink, I was thinking.

Do you like pink, Grace? It'll be perfect against your little pink cheeks and your mouth."

Grace purred up at her, still fascinated, blinking sleepily and stretching some more. This was the way Rachel had dreamed she'd spend her mornings, curled up in her bed in the first flush of dawn with a drowsy, hungry baby beside her, here in her house with her husband.

But they'd never had that. Rachel still felt guilty about the baby she'd lost not long after she and Sam got married. There'd been complications and she'd hemorrhaged badly. In the heat of the moment, the doctors felt they had no alternative but a hysterectomy, which meant there would be no more children. Not from her body. She felt as if her body had betrayed her, as if she'd let Sam down and her life had taken a wrong turn way back then, and she'd never been able to get it back on track.

Grace cooed up at her. The baby batted her hand against Rachel's, and Rachel fought back tears as she tried once again to soothe her.

"You're so adorable. I just don't know how anybody could walk away from someone like you," she said.

Rachel hadn't been able to walk away, not from the memory of her daughter or from Sam. Her father had wanted her to go to college in the fall, as she would have the year before if not for Sam and the baby. But Rachel couldn't. Her grandfather was getting weaker by then, and he needed Rachel. So did Sam. He worked like a demon at his job and on the house. Rachel helped him, took care of her grandfather, and told herself that someday there would be children. Except it had never worked out, and here she was thirty years old and childless, about to be husbandless. It seemed she would be starting all over again, just as her father had urged her to do, except she'd do it at thirty instead of eighteen.

Rachel had no idea how to even begin.

"I guess you're starting over, too," she told the baby, brushing her cheek against Grace's. "And we have things to do, you know. We have to decorate the house for Christmas, because Zach's worried that Santa isn't coming, although I'm sure he is. It's no telling what he'll bring you. I'm sure you've been such a good girl."

Grace shoved the side of her fist into her mouth and started sucking furiously, but stayed quiet except for the noises she made trying to satisfy her hunger.

"I know," Rachel sympathized. "I'm sure you're just about to starve. But Sam's coming. We'll get your tummy all nice and full and everything will look better then, I promise, sweetie."

She crooned to the baby a bit more until Sam was back with the bottle. Grace reached for it the minute she saw it, and soon she was sucking away, quite happily tucked into her spot at Rachel's side.

"She's really adorable, isn't she?"

Sam stood there awkwardly and said, "Yes."

"Emma told me Grace is almost one, so she must have been born around Christmas."

"She's not a present, Rachel."

"I'm sure she was to somebody."

"Somebody who abandoned her at a cheap motel on the edge of town."

"We don't know what happened." Rachel was torn. She wanted these children to have someone to love, but worried they'd be left again someday in another motel, in another town. Who would take care of them then?

"If you and I had children, you would never leave them anywhere, no matter what happened to you. You'd defend them to your last breath."

Yes, she would have. She would have done anything for them, just like she would do anything for these children.

"I know it's an awful thing," she said, "to have left them there. I'm not going to defend their mother for that. But they seem to be such good kids. Kind and gentle and loving. I think someone must have taken good care of them along the way. That was all I was thinking in saying we shouldn't judge this woman without knowing anything about her. I want to believe there's someone who cares about them, someone who wants them."

"If there is, Miriam will find her."

Rachel nodded. He didn't want her to get too attached to the kids. She knew that. She was telling herself that about once every minute. And that she could do as Miriam said—give the kids what they needed now.

Which made her think about Sam and what he needed. It had been a long time since she thought of what Sam might need or want from her, but he was here now. Suddenly she didn't want to let him go this morning. Time was ticking away. She didn't know how many more times they'd have to talk. Suddenly there were so many things she wanted to know.

"Why did you start sleeping somewhere else?" she blurted out.

He paled, his jaw clenched tight all of a sudden. He

glanced in her direction and quickly looked away again. "It seemed like the thing to do."

"What does that mean? You didn't want to be with me anymore?"

He didn't answer for the longest time, finally saying, "Sometimes it's easier. To keep some distance between us. You told me that. You felt it, too."

He was right. Sometimes everything hurt. Seeing his face when he saw her too caught up in her own pain to do anything for anyone. Seeing that same kind of pain in him and not knowing how to fix it. Did he think he was fixing it? By walking away? Did he think it too late to do anything else?

He must. He was going.

Rachel started shaking. *Come here, Sam,* she thought. *Just come to me.*

"I miss you," she said truthfully, painfully.

He flinched, his jaw going even harder than before. "Well I thought if it bothered you—having me sleep somewhere else—you would have said something about it. Honestly, it seemed like you didn't even notice at first."

She stared back at him.

"Do you even know, Rachel?" he said bitterly. "Do you know when it started? Or how long it's been going on?"

Rachel started to cry, thinking with something akin to panic, *How long had it been?* She dipped her head down low, over the baby's, trying to hide from him, because he hated it when she cried.

"Too long?" she asked. Too late to change things?

"Three weeks and five days," he said.

Rachel closed her eyes, thinking, *That long?* It seemed like a lifetime. Her marriage had all but died, nearly a month ago, and she hadn't even noticed. How could a woman miss something like that?

"I'm sorry," she said. "But I do miss you."

Sam stood there and stared at her. She could feel anger radiating from him and a strong sense of self-control. Even now, he wasn't going to tell her. He was going to bury it. Ever since the baby, they'd buried so many things.

"I'm sorry," she said again. Sometimes it seemed they did nothing but apologize to each other.

"It's hard to sleep in the same bed with you and not touch you," he said, still angry. "And it's really hard to touch you and see you cry."

"Oh." It came out as the breath rushed from her body. She remembered now. For the first time, she knew why he was sleeping somewhere else.

And it was her fault, too. There had been times when she went for days with no one breaking through the barriers she'd erected, but before Sam still tried. One night in particular, the last time, she remembered, it coming to her in a rush—Sam, the richness of his touch, the terrible need she had for him, and then it was like all the sadness she had inside her just burst through. He froze, and she'd told him not to stop, because she was so very lonely and she still needed him, even if it hurt. He'd held her in his arms while she cried, but he'd hardly touched her since that night.

"I remember," she admitted. "It's just . . . It's easier in a way, when you're hurting that much, to not feel anything at all. It hurts sometimes just to touch you. To be close to you."

Sam said nothing, just stood there.

"I'm sorry," she said again.

"Me, too."

And that appeared to be that. "Thank you for letting the children stay," she said.

"Sure."

"We can try to have a nice Christmas, can't we? We can . . ." Pretend, she thought. They'd gotten so good at pretending.

"We'll see that they have a nice Christmas. And then they're going. Don't forget that, Rachel."

"I won't."

He was going, too. If she thought her house had been lonely before, she couldn't imagine what it would be like then. No children. No Sam. No nothing.

Sam left, and Grace finished her bottle. Rachel burped the baby, then they just lay there in the warm, soft bed and dozed for a while longer, and Rachel had another dream. She dreamed her baby hadn't died. That it was nearly twelve years ago. She was eighteen again, and they were in Rachel's bedroom on a cold winter's morning close to Christmas, Rachel and her baby, with their whole lives ahead of them. Sam still loved her, and life still held all the promise she'd ever imagined. She was still so young, so hopeful, so sure that everything would work out just as it was supposed to.

Then she woke up and remembered it all once more. She lay there for a moment, almost feeling justified in feeling so bad. She remembered telling Miriam she felt like one of those punch-toys, with no bounce left in her, and Miriam saying, *"Then you can lay there, Rachel. Are you ready to just lay there on the floor forever?"*

Rachel sensed that she was at a crossroads—her last chance to decide what she was going to do with the rest of her life. At the moment, it seemed certain that

things were about to get worse, and there didn't seem
to be anyone ready to pick her back up again. It was all
up to her.

Surely she wasn't so weak that she couldn't save
herself. Surely she wasn't ready to just lay here and
wallow in her misery for the rest of her life.

Grace stretched and cooed and started to fuss once
more.

"You're not going to let me fall apart, are you,
sweetheart?"

Grace seemed to agree. She burst into a grin and
tried to grab on to Rachel's cheek with one pudgy baby
hand.

"Then I guess it's a good thing you're here," Rachel
said.

After all, she didn't have time to fall apart. There'd
be time enough to dwell on all the bad things later, if
she simply couldn't help but do that. For now, she had
things to do.

Get up, Rachel, she admonished herself. *Move.*

Rachel got up. She got Zach bathed and dressed,
and Emma took care of herself. Then Rachel and
Emma bathed Grace.

At Emma's suggestion, they put her in the deep sink
in the kitchen. Rachel just about worried herself to
death over something as simple as giving the baby a
bath. There was the water temperature to consider—
baby skin was so sensitive. The temperature in the
room; she didn't want Grace to get cold. It was nearly
impossible to hang on to a soapy, squirming baby, she
discovered. Grace loved the water and patted her
hands on the surface, dousing the front of Rachel's
clean shirt, but the baby giggled and looked so pleased

with herself, Rachel just smiled and decided to live in the moment.

She worried over getting soap in Grace's sensitive eyes and worried over how to get her hair wet and rinsed and about Grace trying to eat the washcloth again. Emma hovered right behind Rachel, and Rachel thought Emma's devotion to the baby was adorable.

"I have three sisters," Rachel told the girl. "All older than I am. My oldest sister, Ellen, claims she spent all her time taking care of me when she was a teenager."

"I don't mind taking care of Grace," Emma volunteered.

Rachel smiled. "I didn't think you did, and you're very good with her, Emma. She's lucky to have you."

They got Grace out of the tub and wrapped in a big blanket, then took her into the living room and laid her on the sofa while Rachel wrestled with her over the business of getting her dry and dressed. Grace cooed and swung her arms and legs and kept rolling over and trying to crawl away.

"Is she always like this?" Rachel asked.

"She's always busy, and she doesn't like to be still anymore," Emma said, staring at the pictures on the mantel. "Is this you and Sam?"

Rachel picked up the wriggling baby and glanced over her shoulder to the photograph. *Oh, God,* she thought, feeling another big tug on her heart. *Sam.*

"That's from the summer we first met," Rachel said.

"He's kind of cute," Emma offered.

Rachel laughed. "You're going to be twelve soon, right? I was about your age when I saw Sam for the first time."

Emma said nothing, just blushed, and Rachel sensed

that she was shy at the idea of boys as Rachel had been when she was almost twelve. Seeing Emma now and that old picture, Rachel remembered so clearly being thirteen and absolutely breathless at the sight of Sam McRae.

"He was the first boy I ever really noticed. The only one, really. You know what I mean? When I was just discovering boys and deciding there was something wonderful and interesting about them."

"Yes," Emma whispered, wide-eyed.

"Do you have your eye on a certain boy?" Rachel asked.

"No," she said, too quickly. "Well, maybe, but I don't think he even knows I exist."

Rachel nodded. She knew how that was, and she would bet Emma didn't have a lot of time to waste admiring boys. Poor Emma probably spent her time taking care of her brother and sister. She wouldn't have lazy afternoons to spend wandering through the mall with her friends, giggling and whispering over every boy they passed, or going to parties or anything like that.

"When you first met Sam," Emma asked, "what was it you liked about him?"

"Everything," Rachel said. "Absolutely everything. He was only a year ahead of me in school, although he's two years older than I am. He's from Chicago, but after his parents died, he missed a lot of school. By the time he settled in here in Baxter with his grandfather, he was a year behind. He seemed so much older than the other boys, so much taller and broader and more solid.

"He was quiet, kept to himself, and all the girls made fools of themselves over him. He had those

black eyes and black hair, and he was so intense, so serious. I don't think he was very happy here. You know
how some people, particularly when they get old, seem
to have permanent scowls on their faces, and they're
always mad about something?"

"Yes," Emma said.

"Sam's grandfather was like that. He was rude and
unhappy and kept to himself. I can't imagine he was
thrilled to have Sam with him, and Sam must have felt
the same way, because he never seemed to be there. I'd
walk into town with my mother or my sisters, and I'd
see Sam standing on the corner of some street, just
watching everyone. Or he'd be in the park, planted
against the trunk of a tree as if he were the only thing
holding it up. He made people nervous, I think, because he was so big and had a way of watching everyone, hardly saying a word or ever smiling. My mother
called him 'that wild boy.' "

Emma laughed.

Rachel laughed, too, then shook her head. "Nobody
here really knew him or what he was like then. They
just knew his grandfather and didn't like him. Small
towns can be like that. People watch everybody else,
and they always have an opinion. I don't think they
were fair to Sam back then."

"But you liked him?" Emma said.

"Yes. I couldn't stop thinking about him. I had long,
imaginary conversations with him in my head, because
I was too shy to talk to him in person, and I just stared
at him, the way he stared at everyone else."

"Did he like you?" Emma asked.

"Mostly, he ignored me. He called me a little girl
one day and told me to run along home to my mother.
He didn't even know my name, and I was absolutely

crushed. I was sure he was a much better person than anyone realized. He got into some trouble as he got older. Mostly just fighting with the boys his age, but he was so much bigger than the other kids, and people were ready to blame him for everything. It wasn't fair at all."

"So how did you get him to notice you?" Emma asked.

"I didn't really. Jimmy Richardson did. Jimmy was an obnoxious boy, but his father owned the Ford dealership in town and unlike Sam's grandfather, everybody liked Jimmy's dad. I was fifteen and Jimmy was pestering me, grabbing me and pinching me and trying to kiss me. I think it was his way of flirting, but I didn't appreciate it. One day after school, Sam grabbed Jimmy and told him that when a girl said to take his hands off her, Jimmy had better do it. Or else. Jimmy didn't appreciate that at all and they got into a fight. Sam got into trouble. Jimmy didn't.

"I tried to tell everyone what happened, but no one really listened. They all said Sam overreacted, that everything would have been fine if he hadn't grabbed Jimmy like that. But I was there. I know what happened. I didn't want Jimmy's hands on me at all, and Sam was just trying to help."

"So you were friends then?"

"More or less. I spent a lot of time defending him to anyone who'd listen, and Sam spent some more time ignoring me and telling me I was wasting my breath trying to change anybody's mind about him. But in the end, we did get to be friends. He's the best friend I ever had."

Rachel's voice broke. She had to work hard to clear her throat.

He'd been so big and tall and handsome, quiet when she got him alone, intense, sexy in a way she was just beginning to understand at the time. But kind to her, protective of her, gentle with her. Sometimes she thought her heart would burst from happiness, just to think that someday she might be his.

Her parents had been horrified—their daughter was smitten with that wild boy who had to be up to no good. But nothing they said could convince Rachel to forget about him.

She and Sam hadn't dated much. She hadn't been allowed to date until her sixteenth birthday. But she saw him at school. They'd arrange to meet at the edge of town and go for long walks along the river, and they'd talk about everything. He loved listening to stories about her family, and he told her how much he wanted out of Baxter. He was actually very smart, though he didn't often let it show. People had wrongly judged him, and he took stubborn pride in showing them exactly what they expected to see in him.

People also blamed him for her pregnancy, as if she hadn't gone eagerly into his arms, as if everything everyone had always said about him was coming true. But she'd been happy then, despite how scared she was. Because she knew he was a good man. A very good man.

And now he was leaving her.

"Are you okay?" Emma asked quietly.

"I'll be fine," Rachel claimed, looking over at the rocking chair. This could have been like any other day in her life recently. She could just let life knock her flat on her back and not get back up. Instead, she had children to take care of. She was going to give them a good

Christmas and have a few more days with Sam. She wasn't going to let herself think beyond that.

"Let's go find Zach," she said.

The boy followed Sam around like a lost puppy desperate for attention. He didn't even look where he was going, sometimes stepping all over Sam's heels, and he was way too eager to please. He'd smile up at Sam with those puppy-dog eyes and that quirky little grin, and sometimes he still looked afraid. That part got to Sam every time. Zach was still afraid but not enough to leave Sam alone.

"I thought Rachel was taking you to buy clothes this morning," Sam said.

"I got clothes on." Zach shrugged, as if he didn't care in the least. "She made me wash behind my ears and brush my teeth and ever'thing."

Sam stared back at him, seeing himself at Zach's age and someone else entirely. Someone else Sam had loved and lost. Any instinct he'd ever had about how to deal with kids seemed to have deserted him in this moment. He didn't like feeling so inept.

"So . . . where's your mother, Zach?" he tried. If he couldn't deal with them, maybe he could find out where they belonged.

"I'm not s'posed to tell," the boy whispered.

"Why not?"

"She told me not to."

"Who told you not to tell?"

"My mom."

"Before she left you at the motel she told you not to tell anyone where she was going?"

Zach nodded solemnly, looking a bit upset. Damn. Sam truly didn't want to upset him. But it was for the kids' own good and Rachel's. Rachel who looked so perfect, so content with a baby in her bed in the morning. Rachel who'd finally noticed he was sleeping somewhere else and said something about it. He almost thought it would have been easier if she'd never noticed.

Sam looked back at the boy, thinking the kid just had to go. All of them had to go before Rachel started thinking that maybe these children would stay and that everything would be better. Neither one of them could afford to think like that, and he could question a lost little boy if he had to, to protect Rachel.

"So, your mother . . . What else did she say, Zach?"

"That she's comin' back. We were s'posed to wait for her. Right there. Because she's comin' back."

Sam doubted that. "Has she ever left you before?"

"With Emma, y'mean?"

Sam suspected Zach got left with Emma a lot, and Emma was great with him. But she was just a little girl herself. "I mean has your mother ever left you anywhere and not come back? Not for a long time. Like days?"

"When she went to get Grace out," Zach said.

"Out?" Sam grinned in spite of himself.

"Of her tummy. Grace grew in her tummy. From an egg," Zach whispered. "You know, kinda like a chicken. I don't understand it all. But they had to go to the hospital to get 'er out."

Like a chicken? Grace would love hearing that someday. Zach laughed a bit. He was a cute kid when he laughed.

"So, that's the only time your mother ever left you? Overnight?"

Zach nodded. "She's a good mommy. She's comin'

back. Maybe we should be there. Don'cha think? How's she gonna find us if we're not there?"

"I bet Miriam left a note or something, Zach. If she comes back, Miriam will tell her where you and Emma and the baby are."

"I love 'er a lot," Zach said solemnly.

Sam nodded, his throat going tight again. He hadn't been much older than Zach when his own mother died. He remembered being bewildered and so eager to please, to find a place to belong again, and worrying that he never would. Damned if that fear wasn't coming true now. Soon he'd have a room over a garage and not much else.

Sam started to wonder where the children would go, too, after Christmas. Miriam couldn't have been serious about splitting them up.

"What's your mother's name, Zach?" he said with new urgency.

"Mommy," he said.

Sam sighed. "What's her last name? You know, when people say Mrs. So-and-so, what do they call her?"

He refused to say a word.

"It'll help us find her, Zach. You want us to find her, don't you? Then you should tell me everything. Where did you live? Before you came here?"

"Lotsa places," he said.

"In Ohio?"

"I think so."

"What town?"

"I dunno."

"Did you ever memorize your address? For school? Have you ever been to school, Zach?"

Zach shook his head. "Is that bad? Am I gonna get in trouble?"

"No."

"'Cause Emma has to go to school. We get in trouble when she doesn't."

Sam nodded. He wasn't surprised she had missed a lot of school. And he wondered what he could get Emma to tell him. She'd know so much more.

"Zach," he tried one more time. "If you'd just tell us what you know, I promise we'll do our best to find her."

"She's gonna come back," Zach said stubbornly.

"I know she said that, but . . ."

Tears welled up in the little boy's eyes. "She's comin' back!"

"What are you doing to him?" Emma yelled and ran to Zach's side. She put herself between Zach and Sam, like a mother defending her child—she probably thought Zach *was* hers—and attacked. "You made him cry!" Emma put her arm around the little boy. "What did he do, Zach?"

Zach sobbed. "He made me talk about Mommy."

Emma glared at Sam. "He's just a little boy."

"Emma, if you know where your mother is, you should tell us so we can find her."

Unmoved, Emma didn't say a word, just stood there holding Zach against her side. Sam looked up and in the open doorway saw Rachel with the baby in her arms, looking as angry as Emma. He turned back to the children.

"She told you not to tell, right?" Sam said. "Before she left you at the motel. She told you she'd be back, too, but she didn't come back, and now we need to find her. Do you understand that? You need to help us find her."

"Sam! That's enough!" Now Rachel planted herself between him and the children, telling Emma, "Take Zach to the house, okay? I'll be right there."

The girl nodded, in tears herself now.

"Everything will be fine," Rachel reassured the girl. "You'll see."

"She's coming back," Emma said, her lip quivering, her expression forlorn.

"Emma," Rachel said, trying to undo the damage he'd done, "we're going to take care of you. You'll be fine here. I promise. Now I need to talk to Sam. Please take Zach into the house and let him eat his breakfast. I'll be right there." Emma nodded. Rachel turned to the boy. "Zach, Emma and I were worried about you. We didn't know where you were."

"I was with him," Zach said, pointing to Sam.

"Well we didn't know that. You shouldn't come out here without telling us. You shouldn't leave the house at all without me or Sam or Emma, okay?"

"'Kay," he said solemnly.

"Go inside with Emma and eat." The two of them left, and Rachel, looking like a warrior woman, wheeled around to Sam and said, "What did you think you were doing?"

"Trying to find out where they belong," he said. "If they have a home, that's where they should be."

"So you're going to interrogate them until they crack? You had them in tears, Sam. Do you want them gone so badly?"

"No. I said they can stay, and I meant it. But there might be someone out there looking for them. Did you ever think of that? Someone might be worried half to death over them by now."

"I'm sure Miriam is checking. She doesn't need you to give them the third degree. They're little kids, Sam. They have to be so scared."

"Which is why they should be with people they know, people who love them—"

"If such a person exists," she said.

"Yes, if there is such a person, that's where they should be."

"Why don't we let Miriam worry about that."

"Miriam's not here. We are."

"And we're taking care of them. That's all she asked us to do. We need to give them a place where they feel safe," Rachel said. "You make it sound like you can't wait to get rid of them."

"That's not it," he insisted.

"Did you ever really want children?" she said.

"What?" Sam stared at her.

"Children. Did you ever really want them?"

"I wanted our baby," he said.

"Did you?"

"Of course I did, Rachel."

But Rachel didn't look convinced. She stood there holding Grace tighter, Grace who snuggled against her so trustingly, so innocently, just as the baby had entrusted herself to Sam that morning when he'd found her awake and crying in her crib.

She'd had big, bewildered tears rolling down her cheeks, and her arms were thrust out rigidly at her sides, her hands balled into fists. She was kicking her feet and working herself into a frenzy, no doubt because no one had come to tend to her.

He'd stood there practically choking on his own

breath and thinking that surely if he waited long enough someone would hear her and come get her. So that he wouldn't have to touch her and wouldn't have to think of the other baby girl who'd come into his life so briefly and torn his heart apart.

But no one had come, and she'd gone right on crying and kicking her little feet until he picked her up, with great trepidation and very little skill, not that she seemed to mind. She settled against him with the kind of trust that tore at his heart once again. She was still taking big, gulping breaths that shook her entire body at first, but she snuggled against him like a cat and then started making breathy mewing sounds.

The slightness of her body had scared him. Her scent had been somehow familiar, and he couldn't put her down fast enough, but the impression of her there lingered long after she was gone from his arms. She'd made him think of his precious daughter, whom his wife didn't even realize he'd wanted desperately and still missed?

"She was our baby," Sam said.

"You wouldn't still be in this town if it hadn't been for her. Or for me."

"Maybe. Maybe not."

"You always wanted out of here, Sam. You couldn't wait. You told me so all the time."

"Maybe when I was teenager," he said, not understanding what this had to do with anything at the moment. "This wasn't the nicest place for me to be then."

"And you couldn't wait to get away."

"I guess I couldn't," he admitted.

"You must regret that you never did."

"I really hadn't thought about it," he said, honestly perplexed. Did she regret everything that ever happened between them? "Rachel, everything was different then."

Even now, when he was leaving Rachel, he wasn't planning to leave town. He'd spent years building his business and his reputation. And even if he and Rachel weren't together, he couldn't imagine not seeing her every now and then. He wondered if it wouldn't hurt as much to see her once he was gone.

"I thought you must have so many regrets," Rachel said.

"About what?"

"Being stuck here all this time."

Was that how she felt? Stuck? "This is where our lives were."

"I know, but . . ."

"What?" She thought he really cared where they lived? Not as long as he'd been able to be with her.

"If it hadn't been for the baby . . . we wouldn't have gotten married—"

"Wouldn't we?" he asked, an old, familiar ache of insecurity gnawing at him again. He doubted he'd ever have presumed to ask if she hadn't been pregnant with his child. He wouldn't ask now if she'd agreed only because of the baby. It didn't matter anymore. Soon they wouldn't be married at all.

"You would have left here, if we hadn't gotten married," she said. "You would have gone to college and been an architect. That's what you wanted."

"It's what a teenage boy wanted, Rachel," he said softly, thinking about that long-ago dream. "I'm not that boy anymore."

"Still, I . . . I wasn't sure you ever wanted the baby. Not like I did."

He gaped at her, putting the whole issue of their

marriage aside and thinking—as he never let himself
do—of their daughter. Their precious baby girl.

He still hurt. His heart hurt. He still had an image of
her in his mind, one that came to him at the oddest of
times, a memory so fleeting and yet so clear. Once
upon a time, they had a daughter. His and Rachel's.
She'd been tiny, born two months too early and under
the worst of circumstances, and through the tears in his
own eyes, he'd seen her, lying so helpless and so very
still in an incubator at the hospital in town. He'd
known from that first look that there was no hope,
none at all, and he could only imagine what she might
have looked like one day, had she been born under different circumstances and lived.

He remembered, and he still hurt. He could hardly
look at the baby Rachel now held in her arms, as he
had trouble watching her with any child she'd held
over the years.

"I wanted our baby," he said roughly.

"Sam? When I told you . . . that day . . ."

Sam frowned. He remembered stone-cold panic,
one night, maybe two, when they hadn't been as careful as they should have, a foolish thing for which he'd
blamed himself. She never had. He'd waited for her to
shout at him, to be angry, but all she'd done was tell
him so softly that they were going to have a baby and
fought the urge to cry.

She had seemed to brace herself for him to say
something back— something ugly and irresponsible
and maybe to walk away from her. As if he could
have ever walked away from her back then. He still
wasn't sure how he was going to do it now, in less
than two weeks.

"Rachel, I don't remember exactly what I said then,

but . . . Oh, hell, I was eighteen and just graduating from high school. You still had a year of school to go, and your parents were having a fit. The timing sucked. We knew that."

"You looked so scared," she said.

"I was. I didn't know anything about being a father or a husband. I was afraid your father was going to kill me or try to separate us again, and if he did that, I didn't know who would take care of you and the baby."

"Oh."

She looked up at him, and he tried to read the emotions flickering across her face, found that he couldn't.

"Why are we doing this, Rachel? It doesn't change anything," he said wearily. It just hurt. It made everything hurt even more than before.

"I always thought I wanted her so much more than you did," she said, and she believed it even now.

He stared at her. He'd told her in no uncertain terms already, but she obviously still needed more. He said it once again. "You were wrong. I always wanted our baby."

Sam was afraid he still hadn't gotten through to her, but he had no idea what else he could say.

She sniffled, rubbed her cheek against the top of Grace's head, and said, "All of it would have been different, don't you think? If we had our baby."

"Yeah," he said. "I think it would have."

If he'd been more careful. If it had been years later when he married her and had children with her, when he had so much more to offer her. If they'd never gotten into that accident. If the baby had survived, and Rachel hadn't been hurt so badly. If there had been other babies, maybe she could have been happy and forgiven him. Maybe it wouldn't all be ending this way.

Even these children . . . Maybe if they'd come sooner and gotten to stay, it would have been enough. And a part of him was already thinking that even now maybe it wasn't too late for him and Rachel. Sam really didn't want to leave her. It just hurt too much to stay.

But these children wouldn't stay, either. Children never did in this house.

"I'm sorry," he said.

"Me, too."

She took the baby and left, leaving Sam feeling more alone than he ever had in his life.

Chapter 5

Rachel was shaking when she walked out of Sam's workshop and she might have fallen apart, if not for the stern talking-to she'd given herself earlier. Whatever happened, she was going to deal with it.

She found Zach inside looking none the worse for his little interrogation from Sam. He was quite happily eating leftover lasagna, Emma hovering by his side.

"I warmed up the food in the microwave for Zach," she said. "Is that all right?"

"You do that at home?" Rachel asked. "Cook in the microwave?"

"Yes. It's okay?"

"Of course," Rachel said, then thinking to add, "we always have plenty to eat here, Emma. You and Zach can have whatever you want."

Emma's gaze fell to the floor, and Rachel saw a flush of embarrassment in the girl's cheeks. She went to Emma and put an arm around the girl's shoulders, felt terrible just thinking of the burden Emma was carrying. To be so young, she was doing amazingly well under these circumstances.

"You always take care of Zach and Grace, don't you?"

"I try," Emma said, her head down, refusing to look at Rachel.

"I think you're doing a great job," Rachel said.

Certainly much better than Rachel would have herself. Even with all Rachel had lost, she suspected Emma's life had been infinitely more difficult than her own. Emma could get knocked down one day and bounce back the next. Not only that, she still managed to take care of everyone around her. She doubted Emma gave much time or effort at all to feeling sorry for herself. Miriam said Emma was a little rock the whole time they'd been at Miriam's office, not knowing where they'd end up or if they would all be together.

Rachel hugged the girl more tightly, awed by the courage she'd shown.

"What's wrong?" Emma said, finally looking up at Rachel.

Rachel shook her head, unable to speak for the moment. She'd been so caught up in her own problems, she'd lost track of everyone and everything else—including her husband.

Sam was so strong. He was the man she'd leaned on for fully half her life. He didn't run when things got tough. Look how long he'd fought to make things work between them. So for him to be leaving her, he must have been unhappy for a long time. Which meant Rachel must have missed so much. She was ashamed all over again.

"Rachel?" Emma tugged on her sleeve.

"It's nothing," Rachel said, automatically denying, as she so often did. Emma didn't buy it. "I was thinking of something else, something to do with me. And I shouldn't be doing that now, because you and I have lots to do today."

"We do?" Emma said, still looking worried.

"Yes." She was ready to outline her plans when the phone rang.

"I forgot," Emma said. "Mrs. Kramer called. I wrote it down here. And somebody else. One of your neighbors."

Rachel thanked her and picked up the phone, wondering what was going on. "Hello."

"Rachel, dear. It's Margaret Doyle. How are you this morning?"

"Fine, thank you." A third neighbor? Rachel was stumped. "How are you, Mrs. Doyle?"

"Just fine, dear, but I was a bit worried about you. Are you and Sam all right?"

"Yes," she said, probably hesitating a bit too long. Why would Mrs. Doyle be worried about her and Sam?

"I was just wondering because . . . Well, it's the second day of the Christmas festival and . . ."

"Oh," Rachel got it. The festival. The Christmas decorations.

They couldn't forget, not when the whole festival had been Sam's idea. He'd been one of the first to see what the restored Victorian district and the growing popularity of her grandfather's work might do for the whole town. Downtown had been dying, stores moving out, heading for the outskirts of town and the big shopping malls. They'd worked hard over the years, restoring not just the district, but downtown as well, bringing back all that old-fashioned feel to it. The charm and the uniqueness, which had at one time merely seemed old and out-of-date, were being celebrated now, along with Richard Landon's work. The combination brought thousands of people to Baxter, Ohio, for Christmas. And they expected it to be all decked out for Christmas.

"I'm so sorry," Rachel told her neighbor. "We didn't get the house decorated yesterday because . . . Well, we had some unexpected guests come to stay with us."

Rachel suspected Mrs. Doyle, Mrs. Kramer, and whoever else had called this morning had to be the only people in town who didn't know three children had been found abandoned at the Drifter motel and that Sam and Rachel had taken them in. Otherwise, she'd have heard from two dozen people by now. She explained as quickly as she could and let that be her excuse for having put up no Christmas decorations.

"Oh, my," Mrs. Doyle said. "How terrible for those poor children."

"Yes, I know. But we're going to take good care of them, and we'll get the decorations up today. I promise."

With Mrs. Doyle satisfied, Rachel turned back to Emma and Zach. "We have to decorate the house."

"I like dec'rations," said Zach, who was stuffing himself quite happily.

"Good. You can help."

"You put up all those fancy things, like at all the other houses?" Zach asked.

"Yes, we do. We're just a day late this year." And had left this little boy thinking Christmas wasn't coming here. She could just imagine what he'd thought when Miriam had brought them to what had to be the only house on the street with no Christmas decorations yesterday.

"Don't worry, Zach. We're going to fix everything."

Before they could think of decorations of their own, the children had to have clothes, coats, boots, the works. Rachel and the children piled out of the car and began their shopping excursion at Mary Jane Walter's shoe store, where Mary Jane fussed over the kids, especially Grace, and turned the cash register over to a college girl home already on break so she could wait on them herself.

"What do we need here?" she asked Zach, who'd turned shy all of a sudden and hid against Emma's side.

"Snow boots," he suggested hopefully.

"Definitely. Boots, dress shoes, and sneakers, too," Rachel said. All Zach had were sneakers and they had holes in them. "And for Grace . . . I don't know. She's not walking yet."

"But she will. And when she does, she'll need shoes." Mary Jane held up some little white baby shoes, tiny and perfect.

"She'll eat 'em," Zach claimed.

"She wouldn't be the first," Mary Jane said.

They got Zach outfitted with boots he adored and chose to wear out of the store, sneakers that he found acceptable, and dress shoes that left him grumbling.

"Dress up?" he asked. "Why?"

"In case we go anywhere . . . nice," Rachel said. "Where people dress up."

He frowned down at the still shiny shoes on his feet, clearly not seeing the appeal.

"Don't worry about it, Zach," Mary Jane said, ruffling his hair. "You can wear the boots today."

Which was enough for him. He set off to the corner of the store where Mary Jane had a collection of toys for kids to play with while their parents shopped. Grace was easy. They just measured and put the shoes on her. She had no opinion whatsoever about them. But Emma seemed uneasy about the whole process. She seemed ready to accept the snow boots but didn't want to try on anything else.

"Emma, you've got to have more than boots," Rachel insisted.

"You've outgrown what you're wearing. I know they have to be uncomfortable," Mary Jane added.

"They're fine," Emma insisted.

"Just try these." Mary Jane held a pair of shiny brown leather shoes.

Emma glanced at them and shook her head. Rachel had never seen her so stubborn. "One pair is plenty," she said. "The boots are fine."

"They're fine for the snow and the rain, but your feet will roast in them once spring comes," Rachel said, and she might not have anyone to buy them for her then. "You'll need sneakers when the snow melts, and if we go somewhere nice and you dress up, you'll need dress shoes."

"We don't have any money," Emma whispered urgently, her eyes big and sad and pleading with Rachel.

"That's all right. I do. I want to do this." In truth, Rachel had been shocked by how little the children had and the shape their things were in. It was amazing to think of having so little, of being so alone. And this was one thing she could fix easily. "And don't worry.

Miriam said the state will provide some money to buy some basic things for each of you, so . . .''

"Oh." Emma's cheeks got red again.

Rachel realized she'd made it worse. Eleven-year-old girls cared a great deal about their appearance, she remembered. But it would still be hard to think of the child welfare system buying your clothes, especially if you were proud and strong and brave and just eleven years old.

She gave the girl a quick hug and said, "Let me do this, okay? I insist."

And Emma gave in. She took the first things Mary Jane suggested and wore her new boots out of the store, too, carefully insisting that her old shoes go into the box and go home with them, as well.

Rachel winced when Mary Jane rang up the total. She hadn't wanted to let Rachel pay at all, but Rachel insisted. And she'd spent a small fortune just on shoes. She wondered if Sam had any idea what kids' shoes cost.

But truly, it would be no hardship to her and Sam. She and Sam would never be considered wealthy. Their early years together had been rough financially. There had been years when they'd plowed nearly everything they had either into the house or the business. But the business had taken off in the last few years, and neither one of them had ever been big spenders. These days, if they ever truly needed anything, the money was there. She'd never imagined needing a warm coat for a child and not having the money. True poverty had always been an abstract concept to her until she'd met Emma, Zach, and Grace.

"You know, those kids deserve to have the best Christmas ever," Mary Jane said.

"I know. I bet most Christmases, they get so little. It won't make up for not having their mother, but I want to spoil them this year." If it brought them some temporary pleasure in this big bad world, it would be well worth it.

She thanked Mary Jane and off they went through what seemed like the entire downtown. They were on their last stop, a store specializing in things for babies, when she ran into her sister Ellen, who was forty-two and just going gray, looking more like their mother every day. Ellen had teenagers and a husband, Bill, of twenty years who seemed to adore her and now a thriving second career selling real estate. A seemingly perfect life.

Rachel introduced the older children to her sister, and then when Emma took Zach off to play in the corner of the shop where there were some toys set up for children, let Ellen fuss over the baby.

"What an absolute doll!"

"Isn't she?" Rachel relinquished the baby, as her sister demanded without a word merely by reaching for her.

"Oh!" Ellen held Grace close and smelled her hair. Even though Rachel hadn't had any baby shampoo or lotion to use, Grace still smelled wonderful. Whatever the baby smell was, it didn't come from a bottle. "She's so beautiful. How could anyone leave her like that?"

"I don't know," Rachel said. Miriam still hadn't found out anything about the children's mother when Rachel had talked to her a few hours ago.

"It's so awful."

Rachel nodded. People did awful things to children in this world. It was one of the things that had fueled

Rachel's anger over the years, wanting children so badly, thinking she had so much to give, when there were so many people who had them and didn't give a damn about them. Or worse, hurt them.

"Maybe if their mother doesn't come back," Ellen suggested. "I was telling Bill last night that maybe you and Sam—"

"No." Rachel stopped her right there. "I've been hearing that all day, and with most people, I just let it go because . . . Well, because." People didn't need to know everything about her life. But with her sister, she was more forthcoming. "I can't think that way. I promised myself and Sam that I wouldn't. Not after what happened with Will."

"But, Rachel—"

"This is just until after Christmas, and it's . . ." Rachel started to say it was okay, but of course it wasn't. If things had been different, she'd love to keep these children, to make them her own. But Sam was leaving, too. Rachel had her goals firmly in place. They were simple and very straightforward. "We're just going to give them a good Christmas. That's all."

And then she could start trying to fix everything else, starting with what was inside of her.

"Ellen, do you think I'm selfish?" she blurted out to her sister in a moment of pure panic and fear.

"No."

"Do you see me as someone who thinks of no one but myself?"

"No, you're just . . . You're the baby of the family. I guess we've all always tried to take care of you, to make things as easy for you as we could."

It was true. They had. There'd always been somebody to pick her up and dust her off and help her out.

"You do." Rachel took a breath, scared. "You think I'm selfish."

"That's not what I said. I just know that it's hard for a mother to let her baby grow up. My Steffie's in middle school now, and I still find myself wanting to take care of her. We all did that to you. Not just Mom. All of us."

"That's how you see me? Like a woman who still needs someone to take care of her. Poor little Rachel."

"That's not what I said, either."

"Do you think I'm a nice person?" Rachel asked.

"Of course I do."

"I'm just not strong enough—is that it? I just haven't handled things as well as I should have."

"I think you're someone who's had her share of problems—"

"My share?" As if we were all allotted a certain amount and maybe someone was weighing them all, to see if they were evenly distributed?

"More than most people," Ellen said.

"Have I really?" She'd always thought so, but . . .

"Rachel, you lost a child. I can't imagine anything harder than that."

She nodded. It was *that* hard. And yet, other people had lost children and found a way to go on. She'd tried grief groups before. She'd seen people who seemed to be able to resolve it somehow, and she'd resented them for it. She hadn't wanted to come to terms with any of it. She'd hung on to the hurt, to the anger. She'd been waiting for someone to come along and say they'd made a mistake, that this was not her life and that she was going to get everything back. She'd been waiting for God to bring her baby back.

Those other people who'd dealt with their losses

had just made her mad. She wanted them ranting at the injustice of it all, the way she had been for a dozen years. She wondered if they'd hurt as much as she had, if they'd actually loved their children as much as she had, and yet how could they not have loved their children and suffered the same way she had? She knew they had.

But they hadn't sunk into a dark hole and not come out for twelve years.

"Hey?" Ellen asked. "What's happened?"

"I don't know," Rachel said shakily. "I've just been thinking that I haven't handled anything well, not for a long time."

"We do the best we can, Rach. That's all anyone can expect from us. Have you done the best you could?"

Rachel hesitated, panic creeping in once again. Had she? At the time, it felt as if it was all she could do to simply get through each day. And after that phase had passed, she'd been so angry. At everyone. She'd never really moved on from there, and it had been twelve years. She felt every one of them now, every day, now that it seemed she and Sam were about to lose everything.

"I don't think I have done the best I could." It wasn't easy for her to admit that, but surely at some point, she could have been stronger, done more. "I look at Emma and I feel ashamed. She's been abandoned by her mother, maybe by the only person in the world who cares about her. And instead of falling apart, she's taking care of her little brother and sister. I haven't even seen her cry about it. She just goes right on. . . ."

"Rachel—"

"She's only eleven, and here she is, so much stronger than I am."

"Did something else happen?" Ellen asked.

"No," she lied. She wasn't ready to let the family in on this. Not yet. It was too new, too raw. Besides, this wasn't about Sam. This part was about her. She was ashamed of what she'd done. "I've just been thinking . . . about me and my life. I think I've messed it all up, Elle."

"It's been hard," her sister began.

"I know, but it doesn't really matter, does it? It's my life. It's what I've got, what I have to deal with. I have to do better than this."

Ellen hugged her and then stood there looking at her with a worried expression on her face. "We've all wanted to help," she said. "We just didn't know what to do anymore."

Rachel felt tears filling her eyes, knowing it was true. All she'd ever had to do was reach out her hand and someone would help her. She was truly blessed in that.

"Thanks. It's just hard sometimes." To let anyone into her world, so filled with pain and maybe with self-pity. She was shamed to let her sister know how bad it had been, how badly she'd dealt with it. "And I'm going to do better."

"Good," Ellen said, then started looking around the store. "Now, what does this beautiful baby need?"

"Everything."

When they got back home, the car loaded down with packages, Sam was outside on a ladder hanging Christmas decorations.

Rachel sat there and stared up at the house. It was always colorful, with its dove gray paint with bright white and blue accents and multiple stained-glass windows she'd painstakingly restored over the years. It had porches upstairs and down and an octagon-shaped turret room in the corner, which she absolutely loved. There were arched doorways and three fireplaces, hardwood floors and wide wood trim, even the original, old-fashioned cut glass doorknobs. She absolutely loved it, especially at Christmas.

She put butter-colored candles in every window that could be seen from the street. Not real ones. The fire risk was too great. But very nice electric ones, to set the windows aglow with warmth and light. They used only soft white lights on the house, along all the rooflines, windows, and porches, wreaths strung with the same white lights in the biggest windows and on the doors, even on the white picket fence out front. And there was a giant fir tree in the front yard they decorated in the same white lights and big, red velvet ribbons.

It was a sight to behold when it was all done. It was also a big job and, at one time, one of her favorite days of the year.

"Miss Rachel?" Zach asked, pulling her back to the present. "Are we goin' somewhere else or can we get out now?"

She realized she'd pulled into the driveway and neglected to turn off the car, and Zach had obviously been taught not to climb out of a car still running.

"We're staying, Zach," she said, cutting the engine and setting the emergency brake. She'd lock the car, too, and hide the keys, just in case. She couldn't stand it if anything happened to these children while they were here.

Zach scrambled out of the car and gazed up at the house in awe, babbling about all that Sam had done, which was to finish stringing the lights along all three stories. Emma got Grace, and Rachel got out and stood there, staring at the house.

She remembered one Christmas so long ago when, as they were nearly finished decorating, Sam had made *her* his present, wrapping her in a long strand of red ribbon and carrying her inside. He lay her down on the rug beneath the tree. They'd already turned off all the lights in the house except for the candles and the lights on the tree.

There in the Christmas glow of it all, he'd slowly unwrapped her, kissing every inch of her as he went and telling her that she was the best present he'd ever received. All he'd ever wanted, all he'd ever need.

They never made it to bed that night, had slept on the rug, wrapped in an afghan, Sam's big, muscular body so beautiful in that light.

It had been after they lost the baby, but before the other things, the things that had cemented that first, terrible loss and sealed their fate. Rachel frowned at the idea that their fate was truly sealed, that it had been years ago. What had all the intervening years been? Nothing but her and Sam playing out the hand fate dealt them? Was there no way to stop it? No way to change it?

And then there was no time for thinking at all. Because Zach was running for the ladder, and Sam was still three stories up. She managed to stop Zach from grabbing on to the ladder and knocking Sam down, but barely.

Emma took Grace into the house, and Sam climbed down. Zach was so excited, he was practically dancing at Sam's feet. He had all sorts of questions about the lights—how many were there, and how did they get them to stay up, and could he help. Sam answered all the boy's questions, and then Rachel gave Zach one of the smaller shopping bags and asked him to take it inside. He did, bouncing as he went, leaving her with Sam.

"The house looks good," she said tentatively.

Sam nodded, looking at it instead of at her. She thought about taking him by the collar of his coat and turning him to her, making him look, saying, *See me, Sam. Me. Think about leaving me now. Can you do it? Can you give up on us? After all these years? All we've been through?*

But she didn't. Not yet. She was still too afraid of what he'd say. Afraid he'd say, *Yes, I can go. Because I don't love you anymore, Rachel. Maybe I never did.*

"I spent a lot of money," she said instead. "I hope that's okay."

She went to the car and opened the door, showing him all the packages. He didn't say anything, just took what she handed him. And then the thought of money had her stomach clenching tightly. What was she going to do for money if Sam left? She made some money off her stained glass, but truly she'd always done it for the challenge and the sheer pleasure of it, not for the money. And what she'd made in the past wasn't enough to support herself, certainly not enough to keep up this house, which she honestly loved and would hate to leave. She hadn't even thought of it before, but what about the money?

Oh, she had people who wanted to hire her now. At least, they had after she'd finished the Parker mansion. Melissa Reynolds, whom she went to school with, had a gift shop in town and often talked to Rachel about selling small custom-made glass products, wind chimes, sun-catchers, small windows, mosaics, maybe even stained glass panels to fit in doors and windows. But Rachel had never talked to her seriously about prices or quantities of products or anything like that.

"Rachel?" Sam said. "It's fine, Rachel."

But it wasn't. She was an incredible anachronism in this thoroughly modern word. She'd never had a real job. Oh, she'd always been busy, and Sam had told her more than once, when she'd worried about what she was contributing to the family finances, that he never would have gotten the business off the ground without her. Truly, they'd worked side by side in the first few years. Every minute she hadn't spent taking care of her sick grandfather or her mother, she'd spent helping Sam.

But the business was his. She'd helped get it started, but it would never be hers. She would never claim a share of it. It wouldn't be fair. And she certainly would never expect Sam to go on supporting her once they were no longer man and wife.

She felt so ridiculous. She was a grown woman, thirty years old. How could she be so unprepared to take care of herself?

"Rachel, I don't care how much you spent on these kids, okay?"

She nodded, her gaze locked on his for a moment, that sense of panic rushing over her again. What was she going to do?

"Look," he said, still caught up in the kids and clothes, thinking that was all this was about, "I know what it's like to live in hand-me-downs. To have—"

He stopped abruptly, his face flushed in the cold, and she puzzled over what he'd been about to say. Sam had lived in hand-me-downs?

She remembered him in disreputable-looking jeans, the fabric worn almost white and so smooth, clinging to every muscle in his thighs, and some kind of shirt. Nothing that nice, but she hadn't seen Sam as the kind of boy who'd ever care that much about what he wore, and the snug, worn jeans fit with that bad-boy image of his. She'd never given his clothes a second thought. His grandfather was known as a tightwad around town, but she didn't think he was poor. She hadn't thought much about the way they lived at all, except that his grandfather was a grouch. She'd wanted to make it up to Sam for the lack of closeness between them, for what she suspected was a lack of love, by lavishing him with love of her own and pulling him into the midst of her big, loving family. She had wanted to be the one who made that all better for him.

Rachel frowned. What a joke that was. How long had it been since she'd lavished her husband with any kind of love?

"Are you okay?" he asked, finally looking at her.

"I will be," she claimed, an optimistic boast at best.

"Come inside. It's freezing out here."

And she followed him inside, trying to fight off that sense of melancholy, trying to live in the moment—the children, Christmas—instead of what was sure to follow.

It turned into a good day. They all finished decorating the house together, something usually accomplished with a good deal of order and precision, all of which was lost with two children helping them. Zach wanted to pull everything out and examine it, and he had his own ideas about where things should go. He was also determined to climb the biggest ladder they had. Sam pulled him off of it three times, only to find him right back up there a second later. Finally, Sam put Zach on his shoulders with the white lights they put on the fir tree in the front yard. They went round and round, circling the tree with lights, Zach cackling with delight as they went.

Emma and Rachel twisted red ribbons onto the branches once the lights were up, Grace hanging quite contentedly from a backpacklike thing on Rachel's back. She seemed enthralled by all the colors and made cooing sounds and sucked on her fingers through her gloves, which perplexed her greatly. She found Rachel's ear and tugged on that, on Rachel's hair, wouldn't leave a cap on Rachel's head.

They laughed more in that day than Rachel could remember in months. Even Emma, somber, serious Emma, had laughed. Sam was still hiding behind the gruff exterior, still seeming a bit uncomfortable, but even he had cracked a smile or two when he and Zach had gotten into a scuffle in the drifting snow.

Finally satisfied and freezing, they'd all stood on the sidewalk in front of the house, staring up at it and deciding all their hard work had been worth it.

"It's just like in the book," Zach said. He finally believed he was living in the Christmas house. Maybe he still believed in magic, just a little bit.

"Come on," Rachel said. "We've got to get inside."

"I'm not cold," Zach said.

"I am," Rachel insisted.

They went to the back door, she and Sam brushing the snow off the kids as best they could before they all traipsed inside and made a mess of the laundry room, with wet boots and coats and hats and gloves everywhere.

Rachel insisted that Zach have a hot bath, and Emma volunteered to give him one. Rachel sent them up with hot chocolate, and a moment later, her middle sister, Gail, dropped by with hot homemade soup and fresh bread. Gail who had four children of her own, the youngest of whom just started school this year, and a husband, Alex, whose work as a pharmaceutical salesman kept him on the road a good bit. She'd been a bit lost herself lately, and Rachel found herself wondering how her sister had coped.

"Thanks," Rachel said.

"It was nothing. I was just so excited for you, and I had to see the kids. Besides, it's tradition. You always bring me food when I have a baby."

It was true. She cooked for both her sisters when they had new babies. Still, "I didn't have a baby."

"You have one right there," she said, pointing to Grace, who was sleeping happily in Rachel's arms.

"But I can't keep her. She has a mother somewhere, and Miriam's going to find her."

"Couldn't I just hope this works out for you? Finally?"

"It would be easier for me if you didn't, because I'm trying to be very careful not to."

"Well, maybe you shouldn't," Gail insisted. "I don't like it that you always expect the worst."

Rachel thought about telling her sister that life had always brought her the worst, but it wasn't true. She'd had bad times—maybe more than her share—but there'd been good, too. Seeing these children made her realize that. It had her thinking of the value of hope. Did that include letting herself be hopeful about these children, that . . .

"No," Rachel said. "I can't forget that they'll go

someday. I can't . . ." Sam and the children were both going.

"Are you okay? There's nothing else going on? Ellen said you seemed strange at the store."

No surprise there, either that Ellen had told her or that Gail had rushed right over here to see what she could find out, and, granted, to help if she could. "Look, just forget it. It's been an odd day, but I'll be fine. And thanks for the meal."

"Of course."

Because there was nothing Rachel could say to dampen her sister's optimism, she finally gave up trying and accepted the hugs, the good wishes, and the prayers, and then Gail went home to feed her own family.

Chapter 6

On the third day of Christmas, Rachel's father showed up to watch the Christmas parade with them and to stay for dinner, something he did at least once a week.

"Hi, Daddy," she said, kissing him on the cheek.

"How's my baby girl?" he said in his big booming voice. He was sixty, a retired insurance agent who was almost always happy, if a bit lost since her mother died, and he still called her his baby girl. Her whole life, he'd lavished her with love.

"I'm fine," she said.

"That's not what I hear."

"Oh?" she asked, not surprised. "Ellen?"

"I may have talked to your sister. And I wanted to see this one," he said, coming closer until he could see Grace's face, which was pressed against Rachel's shoulder. "Now there's a beauty for you. Almost as beautiful as you were when you were a little thing."

"Do you want to hold her?"

"Well, I guess I could do that. Your arms are probably tired by now."

Actually, they were. She wasn't used to having a baby in her arms for any length of time. She passed Grace off to her father, who made himself at home in the rocking chair in the corner and settled in to fussing over the sleeping baby.

A minute later, Zach came bursting down the stairs at full speed, practically skidding down the last three but somehow not landing in a heap on the floor. Rachel held her breath and managed not to yell. He'd scared her half to death. He walked right over to her father and said, "Hi, I'm Zach."

"Hi," her father said, "I'm Frank. I'm Rachel's father."

"Whatcha doin'?"

"Getting acquainted with your sister."

Zach wrinkled up his nose and said, "She's not much fun to play with. She can't do much of anything yet. She can't even walk."

"Oh?" her father said, the sides of his mouth crinkling into a smile.

"I can do lotsa stuff," Zach bragged.

"I'll bet you can."

"I'm gonna watch the Christmas parade later. San'a's comin'. Right here!"

"Zach, he's coming past the house. He's not stopping or coming inside, remember?"

Zach frowned. "But I gotta talk to him."

"We will. Just not tonight, okay?"

"Okay." He turned back to her father, obviously disappointed. "Wanna see my cars?"

Her father agreed, handing over the baby and letting Zach take him by the hand and lead him from the room. They seemed to be the best of buddies when she glanced into the room twenty minutes later on her way to the kitchen to set the table for dinner.

A few minutes later, her father came into the kitchen. "That's some boy."

"Isn't he?"

"They seem to be taking this well. When I heard what they'd been through . . . Well, I wondered what you were getting yourself into, little girl."

"They're good kids," she said.

"I can see that for myself, and I'm proud of you for taking them this way."

"Oh, Daddy." Rachel stopped in the middle of setting the table. He just didn't know how bad things had been, how badly she'd handled it all. If Miriam hadn't barged in with the children two days ago and shamed Rachel into taking them, she'd still be sitting here lost in her own misery. He didn't even know about Sam yet. He was going to be so worried about her and so disappointed.

"It's a good thing you're doing," he said.

"No, I'm not," she told him. "Everyone's said that, too, how kind we're being, how generous, but the truth is, they're helping me much more than I'm helping them, because they've finally made me see what I've been doing with my life. I've been so wrong, Daddy, about so many things."

She fought with everything she had not to cry. It had to stop sometime, and she'd cried too much already.

"You're doing a very good thing, Rachel, and I'm proud of you. And I can't think of anything you've done that's been so wrong."

"I've been selfish, and . . ."

"No. Your sister told me you were spouting off some crazy talk like that, and I'm not going to listen to it."

"I have. I haven't been thinking of anyone but myself for so long."

"You've been grieving," he said. "And maybe it's

gone on for a long time, but it's hard to lose people, baby girl. I know that. And you've lost so much. I wish I could have spared you that, but don't let anyone tell you that you've been selfish or that any of this has been your fault."

"I just been feeling sorry for myself, and it's gone on too long."

"Rachel, I don't recall anyone telling me I'd spent too much time grieving for your mother. Nobody tried to rush me into getting over her, and don't you let anyone push you, either."

"No one's pushing me," she said. Except maybe for Miriam, but she thought Miriam was justified in what she'd done. Rachel should probably thank her. "I just need to get on with my life. I need to figure out what I'm going to do with myself. I started thinking the other day that I really need to find a job."

Her father eyed her sharply at that. "What kind of nonsense is that. You have a job."

"Taking care of the kids, for now. But once that's over . . ."

"Rachel, I'm not talking about the kids. I'm talking about everybody. You take care of everybody. You always have. It was kittens and baby birds that fell out of that nest in the big tree in the backyard when you were growing up, and now it's everyone around you."

"It's not a job." It was just what she'd always done.

"Of course it is, and it's an important one, too. Maybe it's not the kind of job where people see you heading off to work every morning and where they give you a paycheck once a week. But it's much more than that. When your grandfather got sick, I didn't know what we were going to do. Your mother had spent a lot of years taking care of this whole family, but she wasn't as young as she used to be and maybe she was already sick herself and we just didn't know it at the time. But I worried that she'd wear herself out taking care of your grandfather and I didn't want her to do that. I didn't want you to have to do it, either, but you stepped in and did, and I have to tell you, it was a relief to me and your mother. You and your grandfather had always been so close, and you and Sam were here, and . . . Well, after the baby, I thought you needed something to keep you busy, someone to take care of, too."

"I did." It had been hard, but it had given her a reason to get out of bed every morning, and she'd needed one back then.

"He needed you, and you were there. You were there for your mother, too. Did you know that your sister Ann almost dropped out of college? Thinking that someone had to be here to take care of your mother, and she didn't think it should be you after all you'd gone through with your grandfather?"

"No. She never said anything about that." Everybody had helped in that time, but Rachel had been the one who was there day after day. She'd felt like she had to be, that there was nowhere else she could have been while her mother was so sick.

"And that's just what you've done for the immediate family," her father said. "That doesn't begin to cover what you've done for the whole town, from Meals on Wheels to the art classes at the community center to the work you and Sam have done with the Chamber of Commerce to put this town on the map. I'm very proud of you. I always have been, and don't you dare let anyone say you haven't spent your life doing a lot of very important work."

Rachel had never thought about it that way. In truth, she'd always been busy, had always tried to help out in any way she could. But still . . .

"It's a gift, Rachel. The way you try to make things easier and better for everyone around you. I don't want to think about the kind of place this world would be without people like you. You know, you," he added, "are your mother all over again. You know all that she did. You know how much she added to your life and to everyone's lives around her."

"She did," Rachel agreed. Everyone loved her mother. Everyone depended upon her.

"She'd be proud of you, too. In fact, if she were here, she'd be able to say this a lot better than me. But I did my best."

"Oh, Daddy," she said. He was the best. "I love you."

"I love you, too, baby girl."

She turned weepy on him for a moment and just let him hold her, and then got herself together and called everyone to dinner.

Sam slipped in the back door just in time for dinner, finding his father-in-law still here. Sam had seen his car in the driveway and wondered if Frank was staying for dinner. It looked like he was. He was deep in conversation with Zach, Zach eating up every word, when Sam came in and took his seat at the crowded table in the kitchen.

It was an unusual meal for them all, the room echoing with conversation and laughter. The kids had all new clothes on, and Emma thanked him rather shyly for everything they'd gotten the day before. She had on a soft, pink sweater and a matching skirt, and it looked like Rachel had braided her hair, because the style looked like one his wife sometimes wore. She was a pretty girl, he realized, thinking that she seemed impossibly young and somehow very hopeful, reminding him long, long ago of his wife the first time he'd seen her coming out of church one Sunday with her family.

He'd been standing in the park across the street—anything to get out of his grandfather's house—and he heard her laughing and turned around to see who'd made that sound. She looked like a girl who'd been pampered her whole life, which was true he found out later. But instead of turning up her nose and looking away or staring at him as if he were some foreign creature caught under a microscope, she smiled at him, just as shyly as Emma was now.

Sam had to look away for a moment, too caught up in the past to say or do anything. He hadn't believed then that Rachel could truly be his, and before too long, she wouldn't be.

They finished their dinner and all of them helped the kids pile into coats, hats, mittens, and boots to go outside and watch the Christmas parade. It came right past the house.

Sam hadn't intended to go, but Frank was here and he suspected Frank would think it was odd if Sam didn't go. So they all traipsed out into the cold, and Sam stood there on the fringes of the scene, Rachel holding the baby, rubbing her nose against Grace's tiny one, and Grace laughing at that. It took Emma and Frank to keep Zach out of the street and out of the way of the parade, he was so full of energy.

The whole scene was so perfect. He had the oddest sensation of standing on the edge of what his life with

Rachel might have been. That he'd found a wrinkle in time, and slipped through. That somewhere, this was his life, completely different and as full and wonderful as anything he could have ever imagined. One step to the right, he thought. Or to the left. And this is what he could have had?

Instead, he was about to end up with nothing.

"Sam?"

He heard Rachel calling his name and realized he'd turned and started walking away. He couldn't let himself get any closer, couldn't stay.

"I have to go inside," he said and fled.

Fifteen minutes later, Frank caught him and said, "I think you and I have some things to talk about."

Sam hesitated a moment, then looked his father-in-law in the eye. Instantly, he felt every bit as guilty as he had the night he and Rachel had gone to tell her parents that she was pregnant and that they intended to get married. Frank had never forgiven Sam for daring to touch his precious little girl.

"What can I do for you?" Sam asked.

Frank's gaze narrowed in on Sam's, his big bad father expression coming across his face. "Anything you want to tell me, son?"

Sam took a breath and squared his shoulders. "About what?"

"You and my little girl. Because she hasn't looked too happy lately, and I've been hearing some things, things I don't like."

Damn. It was starting to come out.

Sam hadn't remembered until after he'd agreed to take the room above Rick's garage that Frank used to play poker with the guy who was currently renting that room from Rick. And his buddy Rick never shut up. He could just see Rick saying something to the man who was moving out of that room about the fact that Sam was moving in and the news getting back to Frank.

He wondered if it was too late already but tried to brazen it out. "I don't have anything to say, Frank."

There'd come a day when he'd have to explain himself to his father-in-law. This wasn't it. Not when he hadn't even told Rachel yet.

"You promised me," Frank said, scowling at him and suddenly full of fatherly outrage. "You promised you'd do anything in the world for her."

"I would," Sam said, but there were some things that were simply out of his reach.

Frank swore softly. "One thing about you—I've never known you to turn around and run when things got tough, and I know, things between you and her have never been easy. But you never ran out on her. You better think about what you're doing, son. You better think long and hard."

Sam had thought about it. He'd thought of nothing else, it seemed.

"You told me you'd always be there for her," Frank said. "That you were going to take such good care of her."

"Well, we all know how good a job I've done at that," Sam said, leaving unspoken their memories of what until now had been the worst day of his and Rachel's lives.

He still remembered the look on Frank's face when Frank had rushed into the emergency room after learning about the car accident so many years ago. They were quite civilized in front of Rachel's mother, who was scared to death, but the minute she was out of sight Frank backed Sam up against the wall. With sheer terror and a burning anger on his face, he demanded, "This is how you take care of my little girl? And my granddaughter?"

Sam still felt sick thinking of it, of how he'd failed them and how everything his father-in-law had worried about when he'd surrendered his daughter to the likes of Sam had come true that day. Their baby was gone. They'd almost lost Rachel, as well. And now, years later, there were no children. Rachel had been flirting with depression, and they were headed for even more heartache than before.

Sam had done a hell of a job of taking care of Frank's little girl. He couldn't blame the man for hating him. He looked up at his father-in-law now and knew he hadn't seen Frank looking so devastated or so angry since Rachel's mother had died, and he was sorry. But Frank adored Rachel, and Sam honestly thought he might be relieved to know she was finally done with Sam.

He thought about trying to tell Frank he'd done his best, that he just couldn't do it anymore, and asking him to take good care of Rachel when Sam was gone, but Sam didn't have to ask. Frank would do that.

Finally in frustration, he said, "What? Do you want to hit me? Go ahead. Get it over with."

"No, I want you to get your head on straight, boy. For some reason, my little girl loves you. She's always loved you. And I may not have approved of her choice at first, and I certainly worry about her being happy, but dammit, at least you've always been there for her. I never worried about that."

* * *

Rachel came inside with the children and found her father and Sam in the middle of a shouting match.

"What in the world is going on?" she asked.

They clammed up the minute they heard her, both looking guilty.

"Nothing," her father said, glaring at Sam for another long moment, then turning to her and the startled children. "Why don't you let Sam put them to bed, Rachel. And you can walk me to the front door."

"I can do it," Emma volunteered.

"I'll help," Sam said, taking Zach by the hand and heading for the stairs.

Rachel walked her father to the front door. "What was that with you and Sam?"

Her father took her chin in his hand. "I asked him if he was taking good care of my girl."

"Oh, Daddy," Rachel said, her heart sinking.

"I'm your father. I have a right to make sure my girls are being looked after properly, and you . . . You're worrying me right now, little girl."

"I'm not a little girl anymore, Daddy. And Sam . . ." She fought back tears. What had he said to Sam? "This isn't his fault. None of it."

"You're sure about that?"

"Yes." Oh, she was upset because he was leaving, but she couldn't blame him for that. She blamed herself. "He's a good man."

"I know that, baby girl."

"And he's my husband." Rachel felt the need to point that out even now. Sam and her father had never gotten along the way she would have liked.

"I know that, too. But I've also got eyes of my own, and I know when my little girl's unhappy. I'm wondering what he's going to do about that."

Rachel knew. He was going to leave. She could just imagine what her father would have to say about that, and again, she felt the need to defend Sam.

"Did you ever really accept him, Daddy? I know we disappointed you years ago when I got pregnant and we got married, but it wasn't just Sam. It was me, too. I loved him. I always have. Right from the start."

"You were just a girl."

"And he was only two years older than I was. He was just a boy. And it wasn't like anybody took advantage of anybody else. If anything, it was my fault. I went after him, and I wasn't fair to him. He tried to stay away from me, because he knew how you all felt about him. How the whole town did. And it just wasn't fair. Don't you see that now? No one was ever fair to him."

"Well, life isn't fair to us, is it? You know that. And I wish you didn't."

"And I wish you could really accept my husband. He's been so good to me, and he's worked so hard."

"I know that, Rachel."

"Did you ever tell him that? Did you ever apologize to him and try to make him feel like he really was a part of this family?"

"Maybe I do owe him an apology for that," her father admitted. "But I think you owe me an explanation. At least, one of you does."

"What are you talking about?"

"I think you do know, Rachel. I didn't want to bring it up earlier with you, especially not with you already being upset. Besides, I thought this was for me and Sam to settle, but I think something's going on here. Something between you and him —"

Oh, no, Rachel thought. Her father knew. Somehow,

he just knew. Maybe he was just guessing and maybe he wasn't. It was a very small town, and it was hard for anything to happen without everyone knowing sooner or later. "That would be between Sam and me," she said.

"Rachel, I'm worried about you. I have a right to worry. I'm your daddy."

"Then you can worry," she agreed, then insisted, "but that's it. And I want you to be nice to my husband."

"All right, baby girl. I will. But I want you to promise me something. If you need anything, you come to me. And bring that little boy to see me. The girls, too. My house is too quiet these days. I need all the grandchildren I can get to liven the place up."

"They're not your grandchildren, Daddy."

"Not yet," he said. "But you can bring them by anyway. You could come see me yourself sometime. You still know where I live?"

It was the same house she'd lived in her whole life until she'd moved in here with Sam. She knew.

"I think I can find it," she said as he finally walked out the door and into the night.

So, it seemed he knew and there was no telling who else did. She wouldn't be able to hide from it for much longer. She had to figure out what she was going to say to Sam, what she was going to do.

Rachel stood there for a long time, heard Sam's footsteps on the stairs and then the back door open and shut. So, he'd gone out. She wasn't surprised. He was always going somewhere these days.

She had just about given up on seeing him again that night. She was just making a final check of all the locks and turning out the lights when he came back inside. He had snow in his hair, and she remembered days before when they'd come in like this, and she'd brushed it away for him. When she'd taken his hands in hers to warm them and drawn him to the front of the fireplace, and how often on those nights they curled up here in front of the fire.

Here he was on a cold night with snow in his hair, a fire in the fireplace.

Oh, Sam, she thought, finally knowing what she was going to do.

She reached up and brushed the snow away now, and he froze, just staring down at her, and then she let her hand linger there, in his damp hair, against his cool cheeks, his chin.

Gathering her courage, she raised up on her toes and planted her hands against his chest and pressed her mouth to his. His lips were cold, and she felt his quickly indrawn breath, felt him brace himself, as if he had to before she touched him. He hardly seemed to do much more than breathe after that, and his breath, like his lips, was cold, too. She wondered if she left him cold, wondered again if there might be someone else, some woman he did want.

Rachel pulled back instantly, shaking and hurting and staring up at him. Could it be that? Another woman? She felt so stupid for how long it had taken her to think of it in the first place, how little weight she'd given the possibility. She'd never have believed Sam would cheat on her, but why did men leave their wives? Wasn't there always someone else?

He stared down at her, obviously puzzled, maybe a bit embarrassed, seeming as unsure of what to say or do next as she was. *How incredibly awkward we've become,* she thought bleakly.

"I . . ." What could she say? She knew she'd made this mess, that it was mostly her doing. Didn't that mean it was up to her to fix it, if it could still be fixed. And then told him again, "I do miss you, Sam."

Just in case he hadn't believed her the night before. Just in case he wondered if she missed touching him, holding him, making love to him.

He seemed to draw himself up even more painfully erect, more distant, more closed off than before.

"I do," she rushed on, worried that it didn't mean a thing to him, that it was too little, too late. "And I'm sorry."

"For what, Rachel?"

"Everything," she blurted out, meaning everything she'd done wrong. It seemed now that over the years she'd done everything wrong.

And it was only later, once he'd recoiled as if she'd slapped him and then turned and walked away from her, that she realized he might think she meant absolutely *everything*.

Marrying him.

Having a baby with him.

Loving him.

Every moment of their lives.

Chapter 7

On the fourth day of Christmas, Sam woke on the sofa in the family room feeling raw, all his emotions exposed in the harsh light of day.

His wife was driving him crazy. She'd touched him. He couldn't remember the last time she'd touched him. And then, when she'd kissed him . . .

He swore softly, and when he looked up there she was standing in the doorway wearing a familiar terry-cloth robe in a soft pink color, her hair caught in a careless knot on her head. Her face was totally bare, her toes, too. He could see them sticking out from under her robe, her nails painted a soft pink, too.

He took the sight of her, all rumpled and soft and so touchable, like a kick in the gut. Once more, he feared he was a split second away from grabbing her and locking his arms around her and kissing her as if he'd never, ever let her go. He'd barely gotten a sweet, familiar taste of her the night before, when she'd pulled away, looking every bit as surprised and uneasy as he'd been.

She didn't look so uneasy this morning, just surprised and a bit self-conscious as she held the robe together with a hand between her breasts. Now that he looked closer, he could see the damp tendrils of hair that escaped to unfurl against her neck, that flushed look to her skin, and that faint smell of lavender that told him she'd just gotten out of the bathtub. Looking closer still, he thought she must not have a thing on under that robe.

"Hi," she said.

He nodded, unable to get a word past his too-tight throat. God, he wanted to touch her so badly.

Crazy as it sounded, he'd actually decided it was better that they'd hardly touched at all in weeks. He thought he might wean himself off of her little by little, but still here so he could see her, sometimes smell her delicate lavender scent, still hear her voice. He was backing away one step at a time, doing all he could manage.

And now he wanted to grab her so bad he clenched his hands into fists, then didn't dare move a muscle.

"I . . . That last load of laundry wasn't quite dry when I went to bed, and my favorite pair of jeans are in there. I wanted to wear them today, but—"

"What?" he asked. What did laundry have to do with anything?

"Nothing. I just came down to get my clothes, and . . . Well, I'm surprised to find you still here."

Surprised he wasn't still avoiding her, she meant.

It was late for him to be getting up. He hadn't slept well at all. He'd been thinking of her, her soft, sweet mouth on his, her curled up under the quilt on their bed, her body all warm and soft and ready for him. And he thought it was a good thing to wean himself of her slowly? It was hell. Especially after last night.

"I'll just grab my clothes," she said, backing out of the room and disappearing through the laundry-room door.

Sam just stood there. He couldn't seem to do anything else.

She was back a moment later with her jeans in her hand and one of her favorite sweaters, a fuzzy blue thing that cupped her breasts in a way that used to make him ache to touch her, as well.

Every time he looked at her now, he thought about kissing her or touching her or even more than that. *Loving her.* There was a time when the best thing in his entire world had been loving her.

She disappeared upstairs as if someone were chasing her and she had to get away. Sam stood there for a full two minutes. He watched the time go by on the clock on the kitchen wall, and then he headed for the stairs. Their bedroom was the last door on the right. He walked in like a man who had every right to be there, caught her in the middle of tugging on her jeans, giving him a gut-clenching view of her bottom encased in a little pair of pink panties and long, smooth thighs that had him nearly groaning out loud.

She glanced over her shoulder at him, her cheeks even more flushed, and tugged on her jeans, her bra, her sweater, and even when that was done, she didn't turn to face him.

"What is it, Sam?" she asked, sounding as weary as he felt.

"You kissed me last night," he said, and it came out sounding like an accusation.

"Yes."

"Why?"

"Because I wanted to," she said carefully.

"You haven't wanted me near you in weeks. Probably longer than that."

"I know. I'm sorry."

Which meant what? That it had finally registered in her head that he hadn't touched her in the longest time and that maybe something was wrong. That maybe she should do something about that.

"Is it so wrong for me to kiss you?" she whispered. "Because I still want to, Sam."

He glared at her. The ache in his chest just got bigger. It was growing like a balloon that might pop any moment.

"Is that so hard to believe?" she asked. "That I might miss you?"

"Yes," he said raggedly, reaching hard for every breath. She was going to kill him, right here and now.

Instead, she came to him, tentatively put her hands on his arms and stroked up and down. He thought her hands were trembling and knew he was, just from having her hands on him and feeling as if she wanted him.

She had the tiniest, most delicate hands. They'd almost not found a wedding band small enough to fit without it having to be sent off to be sized, and they hadn't had time for that. They'd run away to get married, because her family was still so upset with them and the baby was coming. Rachel didn't think they could wait for everyone to calm down, and she didn't want a lot of upset, unhappy people at their wedding. And Sam . . . well, he'd just wanted it done. He'd wanted his ring on her finger, her life seemingly irrevocably tied to his.

Right now, his ring was still on her finger, and her hands were on his body, and he had no idea what it meant. Because the ties had certainly unraveled over the years. They were frayed and worn and ready to snap in two at any moment.

Still, he wanted her. He was trying very hard to ignore the fact that they were in their bedroom and she'd come straight from the bath. He loved the taste of her skin, the smell of her, straight from the bath. Especially when he caught her just as she climbed out, her skin still warm and glowing and a bit wet. He loved backing her against the vanity, then lifting her onto it and sliding between her thighs and taking her, right there. So fast it made his head spin and hers.

She eased herself into his arms now, and his head went spinning just the same. His arms came around her, crushing her to him. He felt the contact down to his toes, and the next thing he knew, he was kissing her like the dying, starving man that he was. He pressed his mouth to hers and she opened to him. He let himself inside of her in that one small way. She tasted faintly of coffee and sugar, and herself, so familiar he shuddered and ached and pulled her harder against him.

"Rachel," he groaned, his hand at the small of her back, arching her to him, to fit into the cradle of his thighs and nestle against his hardening body.

She wound her arms around his neck, and he felt her hands in his hair, holding him to her. She was so soft, so touchable. It had been so long since she'd come to him so eagerly. He'd almost convinced himself she didn't want him at all anymore.

He kissed her again and again and again, was just backing her toward the bed when the baby started to cry. He didn't even realize what it was at first, and when she went to draw away from him, he simply couldn't let her go at first. His thoughts were so jumbled, all that registered was that this little bit of heaven was ending and that they might never get it back.

It seemed he wasn't as ready to give her up as he thought.

The baby cried again, the sound echoing around the room.

Rachel mouthed, "I'm sorry," as she slipped out of his arms and down the hallway.

Sam stood there, breathing hard, his head still filled with the scent of her, and he was getting angry. Because he'd made up his mind, made his peace with this. They were simply disaster together, him and Rachel. For half his life, he'd wanted her and tried to make her happy, and never been able to do it. Trying anymore seemed as futile as banging his head against a brick wall and nearly as painful, and yet he still wanted her.

Rachel was back a moment later, the baby he simply couldn't look at in her arms. She sat on the bed, her legs crossed, a pillow in her lap, the baby lying across it. He could hear her sucking contentedly on her bottle, and it was so odd, hearing a baby in this house, seeing her.

It felt different from all the times her sisters' and brother's kids had visited, because it was just him and Rachel and the other two children. It felt like their little family, in moments when Sam's control slipped and he let himself think dangerous thoughts like that. And it hurt. Even now, it still hurt.

He'd never held their baby. The doctor had tried to talk him into it, to hold her and build some memories of her and then let her go. He hadn't seen how anything could have helped him let her go, particularly holding her in his arms. But he was sorry now that he hadn't. He was so sorry for everything, still felt so guilty. How could a marriage possibly survive under a burden like that?

"Sam?" Rachel asked tentatively.

He turned his head away. "I've got to go, Rachel."

He headed down the stairs, ignoring her calling to him. He did it by remembering how it had ended last night, that broken look on her face when she'd apologized and he'd asked what she was apologizing for.

Everything, she'd said with heartbreaking sadness. *Everything.*

That one word had carried so many regrets, so much pain. There was nothing left between them. He deeply regretted it, but he couldn't fix it.

Sam would have rushed out the door and not come back all day, but when he walked into the kitchen, Emma was there sipping a glass of milk. Emma with her sad eyes that saw too much and an expression on her face that said she still thought he was something akin to the big bad wolf who snarled at little boys and girls over the breakfast table.

"Hi," she said, just as tentatively as Rachel had only moments ago.

Was he really such a bear? So scary and snarly? Was this what he'd become? A grumpy old man at thirty-two.

Sam stifled the impulse to swear once again and went to the counter to pour himself a cup of coffee, thinking he might still escape somewhere to lick his wounds and shore up his defenses against his wife, maybe keep his distance from these kids.

"Good morning," he said, once his back was to Emma.

"I heard the baby. I got up to get her, but Rachel was already there."

"Rachel's enjoying herself with the baby," he said. "With all three of you. Why don't you relax a little and let her take care of all of you."

Emma said nothing. He turned around and judging by her expression, she didn't like what she'd heard from him. He couldn't seem to do anything right this morning. He felt so totally inept when it came to dealing with these children. He was searching for something to do, something to say to her, when the phone rang, saving him. He grabbed it, hearing Miriam's voice on the other end.

"How is everything with the children?" she said.

"Peachy," he replied, growling at yet another woman this morning.

"This is getting old, Sam."

"Yes, it is." He knew it. He'd griped at Miriam the day before and griped at the world in general lately. He had to stop. Leveling his tone, he asked, "What can we do for you, Miriam?"

"I just wanted to check in on you all. Make sure everyone's all right."

"Everyone here is fine," he reassured her.

"Good. I also need for Rachel to do something for me. I need for the two oldest children to be at Dr. Wilson's office sometime this morning. He's doing me a favor. He agreed to draw some blood today for testing, even if it is Sunday. I'm glad his office is at his house."

"Why do you need blood drawn?"

"We sent out bulletins about the children, all over the country, and there's a couple in Virginia whose two children were kidnapped by their nanny almost four years ago, a newborn boy and a girl of seven, and they have never been found. They think the photos of Emma resemble an age-progression photo of their daughter, and the ages are similar, the eye color, and the hair color. We have to check it out."

Sam didn't know what to say to that. He looked at Emma, imagining her at seven, snatched away from the only home she'd ever known, something he knew a whole lot about.

Oh, Emma, he thought. *What has the world done to you?*

Sam turned his back to her once again, because the girl seemed to know something was going on. Which made Sam think about Grace.

"What about the baby?" he said.

"I don't know. If the older two belong to that couple, it's no telling where Grace came from. Maybe snatched from another couple. First things first. Let's get the blood test and go from there."

"How long?" he said. "Before we know?"

"They'll do blood typing, because that's quickest and not as expensive, and we should have that on record anyway. If the blood types match, they'll move onto DNA testing. The couple hired an independent lab to do the test. No waiting for backed-up state agencies. We may know tomorrow."

Sam thanked her and hung up the phone.

"Is my mom back?" Emma asked.

He turned and studied her face, so hopeful, so trusting, as if she had all the faith in the world in the woman who'd deserted her. How could that be?

"Is that woman your mother, Emma? The one who left you?"

"Of course."

"She's always been your mother?" he asked.

"Yes. Why?"

Sam shook his head back and forth. "I just can't see her leaving you like that, if she was your mother."

"She didn't want to," Emma insisted. "She just had to see somebody."

"Who?"

"Somebody who could help us."

"Help you? How?"

"She was sick."

As in . . . mentally ill? That was Sam's first thought. It was easier to think the woman had mental problems than to think she'd simply abandoned them.

"What was wrong with her?" he asked.

"I don't know. She didn't want to talk about it because it scared me. She was all we had left, and if anything happened to her, I didn't know what would happen to us. I was afraid I couldn't take care of us, and I—"

"Okay," Sam said, carefully touching his hand to hers, wanting to soothe her if he could. "I don't do this to upset you, Emma. I want to help. I swear to God, I do. And if your mother's out there somewhere, we need to find her."

"Do you think something happened to her? Something bad?"

"I don't know."

"Because she loves us. She wouldn't just leave us there like that—"

"Emma, she did."

"She wouldn't," the girl sobbed.

"Tell me her name, Emma."

"I can't."

"Of course you can."

"She made us promise not to tell."

Sam did swear then. "Why?"

"She said it was dangerous for us to tell and that no one could know where we come from or we might have to go back there, and I don't want to go. I just want to be with her."

Ahh, damn. Had they been snatched away from their parents by a mad woman? "You love her?" he asked, having to know.

"Yes."

"And she takes good care of you?"

"Yes. When she can. When she's not sick."

"She gets sick a lot?"

"Yes."

"Emma, if she's sick now and can't come back for you, she may need help. If you tell us her name and where to look, we can find her. We'll help her. I promise."

"They'll send us back," Emma said.

"Back to whom?"

"I can't tell. I promised not to tell that, either. But she loves us."

"I never said she didn't."

"But you think it. You all think she's a terrible person because she left us there, and she's not. She's a wonderful person, and she's coming back for us. You'll see. She's coming back."

"Okay," Sam said. "I'm sorry."

Emma looked even sadder. "She's going to be so worried when we're not there waiting for her."

"She'll find you. The man at the motel knows where you are. The police know—"

"She doesn't like the police. She wouldn't go to them. We're not supposed to go to them, either. Not ever."

"Oh, Emma," he said. Everything she'd told him fit.

No police. Being scared of having to go back to a place Emma was obviously afraid of. What could this woman have told Emma about her real parents to make her fear them? If she even remembered them now.

"She'll be worried," Emma said. "I was supposed to take care of Zach and the baby, and I couldn't. But if I had, we'd still be there when she came back and everything would be fine. And it's all my fault that it isn't."

"No, Emma. No," he said. "None of this is your fault. It was wrong of her to expect you to take care of your little brother and sister for days at a time all by yourself. And you couldn't help it that the motel manager found you all there and brought in social services."

"I always take care of them."

"I'm sure you do. But it's not right. Taking care of a baby and a five-year-old is a job for grown-ups, Emma."

"I can do it."

"But you shouldn't have to."

Sam stood there and waited until she calmed down a bit, and then he sat down in the kitchen chair, so they were eye-to-eye. She looked so sad, so lost. If she belonged to that couple in Virginia, she would have been seven when she'd been taken away.

Seven.

It hit way too close to home to Sam, thinking of what it must have been like for her. She would have been terrified and lost and so very sad, and . . . He pushed the thoughts right out of his head, as he always did.

Except this time, they wouldn't stay buried. This time, though he resolved to simply think of something else, he kept looking up and into her teary eyes and thinking not of himself, but her, and he thought maybe he did have something to give this child. Maybe he could help her after all. Maybe he was the only one who could, because he truly understood.

"Emma, when I was a little older than Zach, one of the neighbors came to pick me up from school and said my parents couldn't come get me that day, that I couldn't go home, either. And they were upset. Everybody was upset, and nobody wanted to tell me anything. I think maybe I was afraid to ask because I already knew something terrible had happened.

"The next day, they took me to my house, and my parents still weren't there. My great aunt and her husband were. I didn't know them that well. They lived fifty miles away. And they told me my mother and father weren't ever coming back. That they'd gone to live with God, and that I had to live with my great aunt and her husband. And I did. I never saw my parents again."

"My mother's coming back," Emma insisted.

Sam waited, thinking she might see some parallels between his story and hers, fighting off his own memories of that time. He'd been six and terrified. Everything familiar in his world, he'd lost. From that point on, no place he'd ever been had felt like home. He'd thought for a while he'd find that with Rachel. Not that it mattered now. This was about Emma.

"You've never been through anything like that?" he asked carefully. "You don't ever remember living with anyone else?"

"No." Emma eyed him suspiciously. "She's always been my mom."

But Emma was hiding something. He could tell. As sad as she was, she was also very nervous. She'd also cried her eyes out. Yesterday, he'd done this to Zach, and today he'd done it to Emma. Would the baby be crying because of him tomorrow? Was he going to terrorize all three of them?

"All right." He sighed, letting it go, and got to his feet. "I'm sorry I upset you. I'm just . . . I do want to help you. Rachel and I both do. And I know how scary it is, to have to go live in a new place where everything is different. I've done it so many times, Emma. That's why I know this is a good place for you. Rachel is a wonderful person, and she'll take good care of you and your brother and the baby."

"Okay," she said miserably.

"Try not to worry so much, okay?" he said, feeling about a hundred years old at the moment.

"Okay."

And then he heard the baby going, "Muh, Muh," which Rachel thought was Grace's attempt at saying Emma. When he turned around, there was Rachel, the baby in her arms.

The baby grinned at Emma, but Rachel was staring at Sam, what might have been shock and surprise, probably even hurt in her eyes.

He turned away, not able to even look at her then, thinking, *What had he said?* But he remembered. He'd told Emma about losing his parents, about all the other places he'd been. And that was something he'd never told his wife, something he never told anyone.

He couldn't explain anything in front of the children, just said that they had to rush to get to the doctor's office, Miriam's orders. They fed the children and left for Dr. Wilson's.

Zach was uneasy. Emma tried to comfort him. Sam

pulled Rachel aside and told her quickly about the couple in Virginia and what Emma had said. Rachel hugged the baby closer and asked, "What about Grace?"

"They don't know. Miriam said it may well be nothing, that people who've had children snatched away from them look at a lot of photographs of children and always want to believe they've found theirs."

"It's so awful." Rachel rubbed her cheek against the baby's head.

"Miriam said not to borrow trouble. To just wait for the test results."

Rachel nodded and she looked so sad. Sam found himself wanting to reach out to her in a way he hadn't in a long time. She was still his wife, he reminded himself. He still had the right. So he did. His hand cupped her cheek, and it was every bit as smooth as he remembered, every bit as soft to touch. He came a step closer, ran his thumb along her cheek, and fought the urge to take her mouth beneath his, to comfort her. There'd been a time when she'd found comfort in his arms, in his kisses.

"We'll get them through this, Rachel. We can do that for them."

"I know," she said. "Sam?"

"Yes?"

"What you said earlier? To Emma. You moved around a lot, to lots of different homes after your parents died?"

"Yes," he admitted.

"But . . . I thought . . . it was just your grandfather. I thought your parents died and then you came here to be with him."

"Not exactly," he said, not liking at all the look in her eyes.

He'd expected pity, and he knew what that looked like. No matter where he'd lived before, people always found out. The grown-ups, when he was smaller, fussed over him and did that fake, cloying kindness bit he found so humiliating. Kids were mostly curious and asked all sorts of questions he didn't want to answer. Later, when he was older and—granted—much angrier, they'd been wary of him and sure he was trouble. The worst had been coming here at fifteen to live with his grandfather, who had to have been one of the most miserable human beings on earth. Everyone had hated his grandfather. God knew, his grandfather had hated him and his mother, too.

"But, Sam . . ."

His hand dropped to his side. He didn't want to touch her anymore, and he certainly didn't want to talk about this.

"Not now, Rachel," he said. "Not here."

Chapter 8

Rachel held Zach on her lap trying to comfort him after the prick of the needle scared him and maybe hurt him, too. Surprisingly, Emma cried a bit, too. Grace, watching the two of them, dissolved into tears herself, and Rachel wished she could join them, but she was the grown-up here. She was supposed to cope.

Still . . . she was a bit dazed by it all. By what might have happened to the kids and by what she'd overheard Sam say.

They drove home in a tense, miserable silence broken up only by Zach's sniffling and Emma's soothing words to him. Rachel made sandwiches for lunch, and they ate in somber near silence, even Zach having nothing to say.

Sam disappeared before anyone else was even done eating claiming he had work to do. Rachel held Grace close and rocked her until she was asleep. Zach lay on the rug in front of the fire, supposedly watching a video but looking as if he might drop off at any moment, and Emma hovered close beside him. Rachel left them there like that, Emma promising to listen for the baby and to keep an eye on Zach, and went to find Sam.

He was in his office with his back to her standing by the narrow window, simply staring at the snow, and he didn't turn around when she called his name. He was closing her out yet again. So often of late, that was his answer, to close her out. To be fair, she'd done the same thing to him.

What did one more secret really matter when he was leaving her anyway? she asked herself. But it did. It felt like such a betrayal. He'd been her husband for twelve years, and she thought she knew him, as someone can only know a person after years together. How could he not tell her something that obviously hurt him so much?

"Is it true?" she asked. "What you told Emma?"

"What did you hear?"

"That your parents died when you were in kindergarten. That you lived with an aunt for a while and a lot of other places over the next ten years before coming here to your grandfather."

"That's true," he said bleakly.

"Sam! I thought it happened right before you came here. That you had your parents until you were fifteen." That until then, he'd had a good life, a good loving home.

"I never told you that, Rachel. I didn't lie to you."

She paused, considering exactly how she'd come to her mistaken conclusions. He hadn't ever wanted to talk to her about it. Oh, he'd told her about his parents. It was obviously painful to him, and she'd taken his reluctance to talk as that—memories that were too painful. But if he'd only been five or six, how much did he even remember? How much more had he lost than he'd ever explained to her? How much was he holding deep inside?

"Maybe you didn't lie," she said. "I suppose I heard stories around town, and you let me go on believing them. But you certainly didn't tell me the truth."

His life must have been so much more chaotic than she'd ever imagined, so much worse. And he'd never let her inside even enough to tell her.

"I suppose I didn't," he admitted. Then, "Does it matter?"

"Of course it matters," she cried, thinking of every bad thing they'd ever gone through together. "I always thought you were so strong, and I always admired that. God knows, I needed it, too. But there were times, Sam, when I wondered, too, if you just didn't care that much. I'd look at you, and it seemed like you were never upset, never hurt, never scared, and I'd think, maybe it just doesn't matter to him. Maybe nothing does."

"It's not that, Rachel," he whispered, looking every bit as stern and untouchable as she'd ever seen him. "It was never that."

She supposed it wasn't, now that she knew his big secret. How could she have hoped to understand him without knowing that?

In her family, if someone was upset everyone knew about it. Sorrow and joy were shared with equal abandon. There were many tears and much laughter, and there had never been any doubt that anyone had to go through anything alone. Help was there, given as freely as the love. She'd never doubted that she was loved, that they'd always be here for her. She'd always believed Sam would be, too, but at the same time, so often she'd doubted his love, never quite able to tell if it was her own insecurities talking or simply his lack of feelings for her. Or both. Maybe it was both.

Finally she understood at least a part of it. This distance he kept, the way he could close himself up so tight and not let anything get to him. Because he'd been hurt too much over the years. He didn't have to tell her that part of it for her to know without any doubts. Her big, strong, so-capable husband hid a world of hurt inside.

And for the first time in a long time, she wondered if maybe he did love her. Maybe she'd read him all wrong. Maybe it was just the way he was, what he'd been taught, shuffled from place to place over the years.

"I thought I knew you," she said, despite the fact that she was talking to the wall again. Sam was so good at the wall. "But I can't imagine what you must have gone through—"

"Don't," he said. "Don't do that."

She backed up a step, bruised by the harsh tone, even knowing it was simply him trying to protect himself and why he did it now. Even now, he wasn't going to open himself up to her.

She sat there simmering with anger and so much hurt, ready to scream at him to pull some kind of reaction from him, when his phone rang.

"Don't," she said. "Please."

But he picked it up, and she could tell from the part of the conversation she could hear that it was a work problem. She intended to sit there, to not let him out of this room until they talked about this. But the next thing she knew, Zach showed up in the door to Sam's office, a big smile on his face for Sam and a slight frown when he saw Rachel sitting there.

"Hi," he said tentatively.

"Hi, Zach," she said. "Does Emma know where you are?"

He shook his head back and forth, caught but clearly not regretting it too much. He seemed inexplicably drawn to Sam and kept sneaking out here to find him, disappearing from the house and worrying her and Emma both.

"What did we talk about earlier, Zach?"

"I'm not s'posed ta come out here without telling you first?"

"Right." She looked from the boy to Sam, only now realizing the powerful connection between the two. They'd both lost their mothers, lost everything familiar to them, around the same age.

Sam, she thought, looking at Zach, imagining her husband nearly as little as Zach and just as lost. She wondered if Sam had ever ended up in foster care, wondered what might have happened to him there. When they'd discussed foster parenting and possibly adopting through the program, he'd said, "How could we ever know what had happened to a child there? What kind of damage that might have been done?"

What in the world had they done to her husband?

She let go of the anger that he hadn't been able to tell her then his true fear, that he was afraid of looking down into a little boy's eyes, hearing what the boy had been through, and being reminded of all he'd been through himself. He'd been worried about seeing someone exactly like Zach. It was almost too painful for Rachel to bear, because she loved Sam so much.

He probably wouldn't believe her if she told him,

and she didn't think she'd said the words to him in a long time, something that made her sad all over again. But she loved him. She'd loved him her whole life.

"Miss Rachel?" Zach asked.

Turning back to him and forcing a smile across her face, she said, "Yes."

"I'm sorry," he said sincerely.

"What?" And then she remembered. He'd come out here without asking. "It's all right, Zach. I'm not mad at you. But I bet Emma's worried, if she's figured out you're gone."

She glanced back at Sam, still talking on the phone. This wasn't the time for the discussion they needed to have. They didn't need an audience, and she needed to calm down.

She turned back to Zach. "I think you'd better come back to the house with me. Sam's busy. Okay?"

He nodded, waved shyly at Sam, and then slipped his small, cold hand into Rachel's.

"Forgot your gloves?" she said as they walked back to the house.

"I guess. Can we play in the snow later?"

"Maybe. If we have time. My aunt Jo called. She said we can have the sleigh tomorrow night. You want to go with us to get the tree, don't you?"

"Yes." He grinned at her, the best grin she'd ever gotten out of him. "Sam said we can cut it down. With an ax!"

"You think you're big enough?"

"Uh huh. I'm strong."

He was excited, too. They stomped the snow off their boots and went inside. Rachel tugged off his boots and unbuttoned his coat. That's when she found the book tucked inside.

"What's this?"

"My Chris'mas book," he said.

"Can I see?"

He nodded. She took it, turned it over, and found an edition of *The Night Before Christmas* illustrated with her grandfather's work. Not her first edition, but an inexpensive one, with the same story and the same illustrations.

"It's magic," he whispered.

Delighted, Rachel asked, "Really?"

Zach nodded and pointed to the cover. "It's the Chris'mas house! We're in it now!"

"That's right. And you already had this? Before you came here?"

He nodded mischievously. "I di'n't reco'nize it at first. 'Cause the lights 'n' stuff weren't on it. But it's a sign. Emma said so."

"Oh?"

"Ever'thing's gonna be all right. Nothin' bad can happen in this house."

Rachel wished nothing bad had ever happened here, and she didn't know what to say to that statement. She had a little boy who desperately needed reassurance. She settled for telling him, "I used to come here when I was a little girl, as little as you. It was always a happy house."

"Magic," he insisted, satisfied and happy at the thought.

Rachel thought of letting herself believe just for a moment. It was seductive, the idea of Christmas magic, of any kind of magic at all. But once, she'd believed that there'd been magic in this house and in the season. Love and light and all that goodwill, all swirling together to make Christmas magic.

She took it inside of her, just for a moment.

Magic.

What would that be like?

Maybe like someone bringing her children after she'd wished and hoped and prayed for so long. Long after she'd despaired of it ever happening?

What if this was meant to be? That seductive thought crept into her head, swirling around like fake snow inside one of her grandfather's snow balls. Part of her wanted to believe these children were meant to be here. That someone or something had brought them to her because they all needed one another so desperately.

There'd been a time when she'd believed in so much goodness in the world and in God's guiding hand in it all. But she'd stopped asking God for anything years ago and had never felt the distance between her and whoever might be running the universe more than when she and Sam lost their baby, more recently when they'd lost Will. It had been the last blow. The one to end all blows. She'd given up then. No wonder she was such a mess.

"Miss Rachel?" Zach whispered again.

"Yes."

"Are you sad?"

"Sometimes," she admitted.

At the moment she felt utterly lost, found herself questioning all the anger she'd directed toward a God she thought had let her down and betrayed her in the worst way. Questioned the way she'd always found someone to blame for the bad things that happened to her. It was so much easier than blaming herself or accepting the terrifying notion that bad things simply happened in this world. Very bad things. That at times there seemed no rhyme or reason for it.

How could someone ever accept that? It was terrifying.

Zach tugged on her hand until she bent down, and then he wrapped his skinny arms around her and gave her a big squeeze. Rachel thought he might have ripped her heart in two at that moment. She slipped to her knees, kneeling in front of him, and found her arms full of little boy.

"Mmmmmm," he hummed, squeezing tighter. Finally, he stepped back and asked, "All better?"

There was an adorable grin on his face, a wealth of warmth in his deep brown eyes and that childish belief in magic, including the magic of hugs. She blinked back tears and smiled a genuine smile.

"My mommy says hugs make everythin' better," he confided.

"She does?"

He nodded vigorously.

"She's a good mommy?"

"The best."

He seemed to genuinely believe that, and Rachel wanted to believe it for his sake. All morning she'd been imagining what the couple in Virginia had gone through, all these years never knowing if their children were alive and where they were and how they were being treated.

It made her think of her baby. At first, she'd tried not to imagine exactly where her daughter might be, except maybe in nothingness. Not lonely. Not cold. Not hurting at all. Simply suspended in nothingness. Her grandfather, even as angry as he'd been, had never questioned the notion that her daughter was in heaven, even as she'd all but threatened God that if her daughter was there, he'd certainly better be taking good care of her.

When her grandfather had passed away soon after that, Rachel had been by his side in the end. He'd whispered with his last breath that he saw her baby. That she was beautiful, and that he planned to spend his days rocking her in heaven, and that was an image she found comforting, if fleeting. She wasn't at all sure what she believed. She'd come to a sort of armed truce with God after that, even if he did have her baby and her grandfather and her mother in all that nothingness. And as hard as Rachel had tried to get there herself—to a feeling of nothingness herself—she hadn't been able to. She'd been tugged back to life.

Maybe for a purpose? For this purpose? She had Zach, who was so terribly funny and so happy, and Emma and Grace. She wondered if someone up there was trying to fill up her empty arms, finally, wondered again if this was somehow meant to be.

It was a dangerous thought. She'd promised herself she wouldn't do this, and yet here she was. The little boy smiling brightly at her most certainly was a rare and precious gift, one that just might save her.

"I love you, Zach," she whispered as it welled up inside of her, warming her through and through.

He just grinned, as if people told him that every day and he was quite used to being loved. Which is exactly what she wanted for him.

"Come on," she said, rising to fight another day. "Let's see if Grace is awake yet. And tomorrow, we'll get our tree."

*   *   *

It snowed again on the fifth day of Christmas. Rachel didn't remember the last winter they had this much snow. And it was altogether lovely snow. The kind that floated gently from the sky in big, fluffy balls.

They arrived at her aunt's farm as it was getting dark, a sliver of a moon hanging low in the sky. Zach danced in the snow beneath it.

Aunt Jo, Rachel's mother's youngest sister and the kindest, the most fun one, was waiting for them. She fussed over the children, especially the baby, and then took Rachel aside and slipped an arm around her.

"They're wonderful," Aunt Jo said.

"Yes, they are."

"It's going to work. I know it is. This time, it's going to work."

"Oh, Jo," Rachel insisted.

"I know it in my heart, Rachel. This was meant to be. And I'm so happy for you. I know it's been a long road, filled with a lot of pain, but you have to believe in something again someday. Until then, I'll just believe for you."

"I'm trying," Rachel said. "Miriam told me not to even think this way, but—"

"Miriam has seen too many bad things happen to people and too few miracles," Jo insisted, then pointed toward Zach, practically beaming up at the sleigh and the horse pulling it. "It's almost Christmas. It's a beautiful night and you're going off into the snow in a sleigh to find a Christmas tree. Anything can happen tonight, Rachel."

And Rachel supposed it could.

She thanked her aunt and approached the sleigh.

The horse was pitch black and regal looking. His mane and tail had been braided with red ribbons and bells, which he seemed to bear with great dignity, and there were ribbons and bells on the reins, as well. The sleigh was at least seventy-five years old and painted red. It might have come straight out of a 1940s movie.

Even Emma seemed enchanted with it. She ran a hand tentatively along the side and looked almost blissful.

"Do you still believe in magic, Emma?"

The girl frowned at first, then sighed. "I don't know."

"Zach showed me his Christmas book yesterday."

"He did?"

"Actually, he went to show it to Sam, but found me there. When I took him back inside, he showed it to me. It's really something that he had a book with a picture of this house on it, and now the three of you are living here."

"I guess," she admitted. "I've read him that book lots of times. It's one of his favorites."

"So you knew?" And Emma hadn't said anything about it?

"Yes. It's silly, but I used to think that nothing bad could happen in that house. I used to think nothing bad could happen to me, if I could find a way to live there," she confided. "It looked . . . magical. It's silly, I know, but—"

Rachel pulled the girl close. She wasn't one to lecture anyone about hope, but she thought it was what Emma needed to hear, and maybe Rachel did, too. It was leap-of-faith time. They were down to nothing but that. Did Rachel have any faith left?

"I don't think it's silly at all," she said. "And we all need reasons to hope."

"I want to. I want to believe," Emma confided.

"Then just do it, Emma. I'm not very good at it, either, but maybe if we both help each other we can manage. Let's believe something good is going to happen, rather than something bad. We'll make a pact. Okay?"

Sad eyes slowly came up to hers. "You get scared, too?"

"Of course." Emma leaned in closer. Rachel held on tight. "Did you think it was just you? That you were the only one who got scared?"

Emma nodded.

"Oh, baby." Rachel fought back tears. "You're so brave. I've been watching how you are with Zach and the baby through this whole thing, and you're so strong, Emma. You've inspired me and made me ashamed of myself. I've wished I were as strong and as brave as you."

"But you're a grown-up," Emma said.

"Supposed to be, anyway," Rachel said. "You know what? Why don't you let me work on being the strong one, the brave one. I need the practice. You let me do your worrying for you."

"I could try," she said.

"Good. Why don't you start by telling me what's been bothering you all day?"

Emma shrugged and looked over to Zach, who hovered in obvious fascination around the horse.

"Sam will stay close," Rachel said, knowing what the girl was thinking. "He'll make sure Zach doesn't get hurt. I know it can seem like Sam's kind of . . . mad at times. But it's not that. He's been through a lot. He's been hurt, too. He tries not to show it, and sometimes when he's hiding it . . ."

"You think he's mad?"

"Yes. It can look like he's mad. Or that he doesn't care. But he does. I think he cares a lot about you and Zach and the baby."

"He doesn't like holding her," Emma said.

"It's just hard. It reminds him of bad things that happened before. But it's not about Grace. Not at all."

"Okay," Emma said.

"You were upset when I walked into the kitchen yesterday morning. When you were talking to Sam. And at the doctor's. Can you tell me why?"

Emma's face fell. "What was the blood for?"

"It's a test." Rachel didn't suppose she could do anything but level with the little girl. "A test to see where you and Zach belong."

"We know where we belong," she insisted.

"And you won't tell us. So we're trying to find out. Emma, you can't expect us not to try to find out where you belong."

"But the blood? It's for that stuff, isn't it? That stuff in blood . . . With the letters?"

"DNA," Rachel said. "It can tell you who your parents are by matching your blood to theirs."

"I know who my parents are."

"Both of them?"

"Yes," Emma said.

"You could tell us where your father is?"

"No. But I know who he is."

"Then give us his name, Emma. We'll find him."

"No. We can't go there."

"Why not?"

"We just can't. And I can't talk about it. I'm not supposed to."

"Did your mother take you away from him? Is that why she's afraid of the police?"

"I can't talk about it. Rachel, please . . ."

"Grandparents?" she tried. "Aunts? Uncles?"

"I can't say."

"Okay." Rachel put her arm around the girl.

"You said we could stay here. You said it was all right."

"It is. I'm not trying to make you tell us about your parents to get rid of you, Emma. I'm just thinking that if I were your mother and I didn't know where you were, I'd be so worried. I'd want you back as soon as possible. And I know you and Zach and Grace would feel so much better to know where your mother is."

Which was something Rachel didn't understand about this at all. All the children had to do was give them a name and a town, and someone would go find her. And yet the children wouldn't. They claimed that the same woman who abandoned them at that motel made them promise not to tell anyone who they were or where they belonged, and they'd kept that promise they made to her, even though they had to be terrified. It didn't make sense—this faith they had in the woman who'd deserted them.

"Emma," she said. "Listen to me. I would do anything for you and Zach and Grace. Anything at all. And I'm going to be here for you, as long as you need me. Do you understand that?"

"You said it was just until Christmas."

"I know that's what we said at first." But Rachel couldn't turn her back on them now, and there was no reason to. As Miriam pointed out, she had the time, the energy. She had the love, too.

She'd probably had all of that from the first moment she'd seen Emma and Zach on her porch in their pitifully inadequate clothing, from the moment Miriam showed up like something out of Rachel's dream and put the baby in her arms. Certainly from the time Zach had wrapped his arms around her and asked solemnly if his hug made everything all better. She was in it for the long haul. She would not desert them now.

Emma stared up at her, so troubled, so hesitant, so much need and longing in her eyes.

"I'm not going to kick you out after Christmas," she said, trying to lighten the mood and keep herself from saying something so heartfelt she'd burst into tears right there. "You can stay as long as you need to. I promise."

And it wasn't until she looked up into her husband's grim features—he heard everything she'd said to Emma—that she realized she'd done it again. She'd made a monumental decision without ever considering his feelings in the matter, without ever talking to him about it.

Was she simply going to sit back and let him go without trying to salvage something of the last twelve years? Did she think to use these kids as a way to fill up her life when Sam was gone? She looked at them, Zach and Emma piling into the sleigh, down at the baby in her arms, and felt again that connection between herself and them. It was real, Rachel thought. It was powerful and filled her inside in all those empty places she'd lived with for so long.

But it was no substitute for what she felt for Sam. She still ached at the thought, was still panicked.

Then she thought of one more thing. Could she keep the children without Sam? They'd been approved as foster parents as a couple. She didn't even have a job. Maybe she had made rash promises she wouldn't be able to keep. She'd have to check with Miriam right away, hopefully without going into all the specifics of what was going on between her and Sam.

She looked up, finding he was closer than she realized, that closed-off look to his face replacing the anger and shock she'd seen moments ago when she'd made her promise to Emma. Did he really want the children to go? Or was he thinking like a man who was leaving his wife, a man who knew the promises she'd just made, she might not be able to keep because he was leaving.

"Rachel?" he asked.

"Yes?" She was suddenly scared of what he was going to say. She still wasn't ready to talk about him leaving. God, she didn't think she ever would be.

"Get in," he said.

She looked at him once more, lost in her thoughts, only then realizing they were all waiting for her, staring at her.

"Sorry," she said, putting the baby in his arms.

He looked startled and uneasy at that, and his eyes seemed to accuse her of things she didn't quite understand. He might come off as gruff as a bear at times with the children, but she could swear it was pure defense mechanisms. He didn't want to get attached to them, didn't want to get hurt when they left. He was still trying to protect her from that, too. Didn't that mean something? That even as he was leaving her, he still cared enough to want to protect her.

For so long, they'd lived their lives trying not to get hurt, curling up inside themselves and being wary of where the next blow was coming from, but it had to stop. It was time to reach for something better, something wonderful, and she wanted to reach out to Sam, the man she used to know. The one she'd fallen in love with. Laughed with, cried with, and lived with for a dozen years.

Rachel held out her hands for the baby, and Sam climbed in, having no choice but to sit beside her, his body pressed close to hers. He pulled a big, green blanket around all five of them and picked up the reins and off they went.

Emma sat with Zach on her lap. He talked the whole time, so excited he couldn't even sit still. There was the big yellow moon and all the stars, the snow, the horse, the sleigh, all the trees. He couldn't imagine Christmas trees growing in a field and kept saying theirs had always come from a box and had to be put together, kind of like his Tinkertoys.

He squirmed and grinned and seemed totally happy, and Emma was glad for that. Grace, too, seemed perfectly content here with Sam and Rachel. But Emma was getting more worried every moment.

It had been eight days since she'd seen her mother, and she simply couldn't imagine what could have kept her away for so long. She knew her mother loved them. She knew it. But she was gone. She'd been gone for so long.

Emma was afraid something awful had happened to her.

She remembered the place where they used to live, remembered how it had been there. All the yelling and how afraid she'd been. She and Zach and the baby couldn't go back there. Not ever. And yet if their mother was gone . . .

Emma looked over at Rachel, who said they could stay as long as they needed to. She wasn't going to make them leave after Christmas.

Emma wanted to believe Rachel about that.

Of course, she'd believed her mother, too, when her mother said she'd only be gone for a day and now it had been eight.

Chapter 9

Sam held the reins as the horse made his way along the path through the woods to one of the back pastures. There were rows and rows of trees for the public at the front of the farm, but the family got the privilege of taking the sleigh and finding a tree in one of the back fields.

It was beautiful back there, the light of the moon shining off the snow, the utter silence. There had been times in the past that it seemed he and Rachel were the only two people in the world.

They'd made love in the snow one night when they set off to find their tree, and had nearly frozen to death. It had started as a snowball fight, back in those years when they still laughed together, and the next thing he knew, he had her pinned to the ground beneath him, tugging at her clothes, crazy to touch her and have her touch him. It had been urgent and frenzied. Cold hands and cold skin, her warm mouth and welcoming arms. Now he had trouble remembering the last time she'd welcomed him into her arms, had opened herself up to him and truly wanted him, needed him.

A part of him wanted her so badly he could hardly stand it. Rachel, the woman he'd loved for so long. Sometimes he thought she had truly loved him, that she was the only one who ever had. And sometimes, he thought she'd willingly give him up now in favor of what was truly important to her. Children. They'd always seemed more important to her than he was.

And here he was, hurting and acting like a child himself, foolishly wanting to measure her feelings for them against her feelings for him, sometimes even resenting the fact that they made her happy when he never had. It made him feel as if he were six again, or eight, or nine or twelve or fifteen. How many places had there been? How many relatives and strangers who'd found a way to let him go?

Shit! Sam wasn't going to spend his life whining about how difficult his childhood had been. He didn't want to examine it in minute detail and make excuses for everything in his life. These kids just reminded him too much of himself, and damned if there wasn't a part of him who wanted to save them from all he'd endured.

He and Rachel could give them what they wanted—a place all their own, a place to belong and feel safe and be loved. He went to sleep and it was the last thing he thought of. Woke up, and it was the first thought that rushed through his head. If they had no place else to go, he and Rachel could keep them. She would be happy, and if she was happy, he could be happy, too.

Of course, there were only about a dozen little variables capable of ruining that whole plan, like the fact that he was supposed to be leaving her in eight days.

He'd been so sure nothing could save their marriage, and now he wondered if he was about to give up the best thing he ever had. The only woman he'd ever loved and the closest thing to a home he'd ever known.

These children had done that to him. They were

really good kids, and they'd made him hope again. He wasn't that comfortable around them or that sure he could be a good father to them, but he understood them. He had something to give them.

It had been that way with Will. He'd seen so much of himself, of his past and the chaotic life he'd led, in Will. One of the hardest things about letting Will go was knowing what Will was going back to. But he wasn't going to think about Will today. He couldn't.

Sam thought about what he had in this sleigh, his wife and a worried almost teenage girl, a funny, adorable, lost boy, and a beautiful baby girl born near Christmas, like a gift. He saw them all as a gift, as elusive as all those things he'd always wanted and never gotten as a boy.

Or was this his gift to treasure? Would the world finally send him something as precious as everything he had in this moment in this sleigh?

"That's it!" he heard Zach shout, realizing they'd come to one of the clearings, deep in the woods. Zach stood and pointed to a huge fir tree.

"That's two stories high," Sam said.

"Is that bad?"

Sam couldn't help but smile. He smiled a lot around this kid. "We couldn't get it in the front door, Zach."

"How 'bout that one?" He pointed to one that was maybe fourteen feet.

"We could probably get it in, but we'd have to cut a hole in the ceiling if we wanted it to stand up."

"We could do that?" Zach asked earnestly.

"No, but keep looking. You'll find one that's just right."

They drove on. Somewhere along the way, Rachel

relaxed against him, the baby held snug in her arms, looking truly like an angel.

He'd almost gotten to the point where he could look at her and not think of their daughter, and not hurt, and he'd almost managed to stop thinking about having to send such a truly innocent, helpless child off into the world with someone who might abandon her again someday. He could almost look at her and simply smile back at her and appreciate how soft her skin was, how sweet she was when she cooed and patted his cheeks with her tiny hands. He could almost hold her in his arms and be happy, just to have her close.

If he believed in miracles, he'd have said this was all meant to be. That he and Rachel were meant to come to exactly this point in their lives so they could be here for these children, just when the children needed them and when he and Rachel had to have the children to save themselves and their marriage.

But Sam had stopped believing in miracles a long time ago.

Hadn't he?

Just then, Rachel slipped her hand into his, leaned her head against his shoulder. He didn't pull away, didn't try to harden himself against the feel of her so close to him. He just savored it and the moment and all the possibilities of what their lives might be.

It took an hour to find a tree everyone agreed upon, even longer with Zach helping to cut it down, tie it to the sleigh, and load up again.

They were all so cold by the time they got back home, but so happy, too. Even though it was late, they built up the fire in the fireplace. Rachel made hot chocolate while he and Zach carried in the tree. They'd decorate it tomorrow, but they didn't want to leave it outside tonight. So they put it in its place in the front room, in front of one of the biggest windows, where it could be seen from the street. And sometime later, once the kids were in bed, Sam found himself sitting there staring into the fire, with Rachel, who sat down on the floor beside his chair, her head resting against his knee.

"It was a good day," she said.

"Yes," he agreed.

"Zach adores you."

"Zach's obviously in desperate need of a man in his life."

"He adores you," Rachel insisted.

"He's a great kid."

"They all are," she said. "And I want to keep them. I promised Emma they could stay as long as they needed to."

"I know. I heard."

"I'm sorry, Sam. I shouldn't have said that without talking to you first. I . . . I don't know what happened. She was so worried, so sad, and I hadn't really thought it through. I didn't mean to say it. But it's what she needed to hear, and as I said the words, I knew they were true. I couldn't turn them away."

"I couldn't, either," he conceded. That was probably inevitable, right from the start. It still had him angry and uneasy that she'd decided all on her own without talking to him first, but he let it go. He'd known she wouldn't be able to stop herself from loving them, which had him warning, "I'm afraid you're going to get hurt again, Rachel."

"It's a risk, I know. But I can't tell them to go just to

save me from the possibility of getting hurt again. Did you really think I was that selfish, Sam?"

"I don't think you're selfish at all."

"I do," she claimed. "I think I've spent too many years thinking about what I wanted, what I thought I deserved, and too little time thinking about you and what you want, what you deserve."

"What are you talking about?"

"Me. Being unfair to you."

"You haven't been unfair to me."

"I have. I've put my own wants and needs ahead of yours for years, for all the time we've been together."

"Rachel, all I've ever wanted was you," he admitted. "For you to be happy."

"What about you? When do you get to be happy?"

"Is this about the baby? About you getting pregnant? Rachel, you didn't do that alone. You had help. I'm every bit as much to blame for that as you."

"Blame?" Her face fell.

"I didn't mean it like that," he said. "We talked about this the other day. The timing was awful. We both know that."

"But I was happy about it. I'm sorry. I know the timing was awful. I know what it cost you. But as scared as I was, I was happy, too, because I knew you'd marry me. I knew my parents would have a fit and worried that they'd dislike you even more and I knew you probably wouldn't get to go to school the way you wanted. But I knew we'd be together and I was happy. How selfish is that?"

Sam stared at her, wondering why they kept coming back to this point and why it was so important to her. Could she possibly not know how he felt about her? How he'd always felt?

"Did you think you had to get pregnant for me to marry you?"

"Yes," she admitted.

"Rachel—"

"There's more," she said. "I . . . I wasn't sure I'd ever find the courage to tell you this. I should have, I know, but I was so ashamed. . . . Sam, I wanted to marry you. I was afraid you'd never ask me, because of my parents and because of everything else. And . . . remember the night we were out by the lake, and we didn't have a condom, and we wanted to make love, and I told you it was safe?"

"Yes."

"It wasn't. At least, I didn't think it was, and I didn't plan that, Sam. I didn't. It was one of those things, those split-second decisions. It was wrong. I know it, and I'm sorry. I didn't think it was safe at that time, and I lied to you and told you it was. I thought we'd leave it up to fate that night. That if we were meant to be together, it would happen. But I wanted to get pregnant, because I wanted your baby and I wanted you to marry me."

Sam didn't say anything at first. He was too surprised.

"That must have been when it happened," she said. "And I'm sorry."

"Sorry about what?" he asked carefully.

"That I misled you. That I was selfish and unfair to you and took that decision out of your hands by getting pregnant. I'm sorry for everything that happened after that."

"Sorry that you married me?" he found the courage to ask, something he should have done years ago.

"Sorry that I forced you—"

"Rachel, you didn't force me to do anything. I knew we were taking a risk that night. I knew we shouldn't have. We did it anyway. Both of us. Because we wanted to." Once he'd finally given in and let himself have her, he'd hardly been able to keep his hands off her. "And nobody forced me to marry you."

"You couldn't have walked away. Not with me pregnant with your child."

"Men do it all the time."

"Not you. You're not like that. I knew exactly what you'd do."

"I did exactly what I wanted to do," he said. "I wanted to marry you. I was grateful for the excuse."

"Sam?"

"Didn't you have any idea how much I wanted you? How much I needed you and loved you? All these years, Rachel, how could you doubt that?"

"I made you give up so much—"

"Did you hear what I said a minute ago? You were the only thing in this world I ever loved back then. The only thing left now. I loved our baby, and I loved Will and you. That's it."

She was crying then, and he pulled her up onto his lap and into his arms.

"I thought it was all my fault," she sobbed. "Our baby . . . I thought I deserved to lose her, because I'd tricked you. Because I'd been selfish. I thought that was my punishment."

"Oh, Rachel." He tightened his arms around her, pushed her hair back from her face, and kissed her forehead. She was shaking so hard, he thought he might be the only thing holding her together at the moment, and it scared him. He'd never realized, never imagined. "You've been feeling guilty about this all these years?"

"Yes. I didn't have the courage to tell you."

"Rachel, we made our daughter together. Both of us. And we would have loved her, if she'd lived. But it wasn't your fault. Innocent children don't die because their parents . . ."

"What?" she asked. "Because their parents made a mistake? Is that what you were going to say? It was more than a mistake."

"It's no reason for a child to die. There's no damned reason for that," he argued. "God knows we've tried to make sense of it long enough. We both know there's no sense to make of it."

"It was wrong," she said. "I was wrong to do that."

"Maybe. But it's not like you're the only person in this world who's ever made a mistake. Do you think they all deserve to lose their children?"

"No."

"God," he muttered.

He'd always thought it was him. That he was the only one who'd felt so guilty when their baby died. Who still felt guilty to this day. But she did, too, and it seemed that's where all the distance between them had started. A fissure in the rock of their marriage that lengthened and widened with time, until she was on one side of it and he was on the other, so that he could hardly reach her anymore.

"This has been eating away at you? All these years?"

She nodded.

"Oh, Rachel."

He knew how terrible that was, knew all about locking the pain inside. They had done so many things wrong, he saw now, both been hurt in so many ways. When she'd said that all along she'd wanted him, just him, some terrible knot that had been in his stomach almost since the first time he'd seen her had eased. He'd always wanted her. Hadn't he shown her that? Hadn't he loved her enough? So that she felt secure in that love? Believed in it?

He didn't think he'd ever felt secure in hers, but . . . "All that time, all I had to do was ask, and you would have married me? Without the baby?"

"Of course," she said.

He took a minute to absorb that, to draw the knowledge inside, to let it spread throughout his entire body and warm him right down to his soul. It didn't solve everything that had gone wrong over the years, but she had wanted him, despite everything.

"I would have asked, Rachel," he told her, "if I'd ever thought I had anything to offer you."

She raised her head from that spot where she'd buried it against his shoulder and looked him right in the eye. "You would have?"

"Yes."

He both saw and heard the little catch in her breath, the flicker of need in her eyes, the way she just melted against him, boneless and tired and spent.

"I didn't care about those other things." She curled up against his chest, clinging to him. "I just wanted you. If you'd asked, I would have said yes."

Rachel stayed there for a long time, just holding him, not wanting to let him go. The guiltiest secret she'd ever had was out now, and he'd forgiven her. She'd sat there in the sleigh and thought about how much she wanted to know about him, how much he'd kept from her, and realized that she was being a hypocrite for being so angry at him when she'd kept things from him, as well. And maybe it was a tiny inkling of maturity inside of her that instead of asking him about his childhood secrets, she'd bared a secret of her own.

And now she had his forgiveness, a gift she'd never expected. His absolution for the worst of it—that irrational yet nagging sense of guilt that she'd made one split-second judgment, one mistake, kept one secret, but that wasn't anything that should cause anyone to lose a child.

She was letting herself dream Christmas dreams where everything just worked out when she drifted off to sleep. It was much, much later, once it was pitch-black outside and the fire had burned down to nothing but embers that she came awake, startled by something.

"Shh," Sam said. "It's late. I'm just taking you to bed."

"What?"

"Go back to sleep, Rachel."

She wanted to sleep in his arms. She wanted him to make love to her, the way he once had, when he'd wanted her so desperately, before all the sadness had crept in.

He carried her up the stairs and laid her gently beneath the cold sheets. He tucked her in, kissed her forehead, and when he would have left, she grabbed on to his hand and wouldn't let him go.

"It's cold in here," she said. The bed was always so cold without him.

He hesitated. She closed her eyes and wished so hard. *Stay with me, Sam. Just stay.* Still he turned to go.

She set aside every bit of pride she had. What did it matter in the face of this? Of losing her husband.

"Couldn't you just sleep beside me?" she asked. "Please?"

"There are things we haven't talked about, things I haven't told you."

"I know," she said, thinking, *Not now. Don't tell me now when we're so close to fixing things.*

"I . . . I don't even know how to tell you."

"Just sleep beside me, Sam. Sleep in our bed and hold me. Let that be enough for now."

And so it was.

He slipped out of his clothes and shoes in the dark, leaving on nothing but his briefs, and slid between the sheets, lying on his back, his arm stretched out above his head. Which Rachel took as an invitation. She settled herself against his chest, one of her legs entwined with his, her breathing a little easier once his arm came around her.

She was starting to think there were miracles left in this world after all.

Chapter 10

On the sixth day of Christmas, Rachel woke slowly, having slept better than she had in ages after drifting off in front of the fire in her husband's arms and sleeping that same way in this very bed.

She rolled over onto his side of the bed and caught the faint scent of him there on the sheets and a hint of the warmth of his body. He had been here.

And Sam McRae loved her at one time. If he had once, maybe he still did, or maybe he could again.

She wished he were still here. That she'd woken up with him beside her, the way he used to be. She wished she'd come awake to him kissing her, his big, warm body on top of hers, his body already hard with need, him slipping inside of her when she was still warm and boneless with sleep. Mornings had been like that once. That dreamlike quality. The ease of long-time lovers. The need that could come so quickly and be so strong, they'd both be in a frenzy in moments, her body shuddering and her crying out and him lying heavily on top of her fighting for air. Sometimes the whole thing seemed like a dream.

She realized she hadn't needed him like that in a long time—in a strongly sexual way. It was like her body had been in a deep, deep sleep, her emotions frozen over, out of pure self-preservation, and now she was coming back to life.

He'd brought her back. Him and these children.

She felt everything now. She smiled. She laughed. She looked forward to each new day, even though the closer they came to Christmas the closer she came to the day Sam was supposed to leave.

She had hope for the first time in ages. What a wondrous gift. Hope.

It was going to get her through the day and maybe all the ones that came after. Hope that she could still fix this with Sam, and that maybe these children could stay.

They decorated the tree without Sam, popping popcorn, which Zach ate and Rachel and Emma strung onto thread to make a garland to hang on the tree. It went on first, then the lights, and then the little red balls.

"Do you have any more ornaments?" Emma said, standing back and surveying it critically. "It looks a little empty, like it needs more."

"We do, but they don't go up until Christmas Day," Rachel explained. It was a tradition in her family, one she would share with them if they were still here at Christmas. And then she thought about something else. "How are we going to keep Grace from pulling it all off and trying to eat it?"

Emma frowned. "I don't know."

"How did you keep Zach from pulling the whole tree over on himself?"

"We didn't," Emma said. "He did that once."

"Did not," Zach said.

"Yes, you did. Don't you remember?"

"No," Zach said.

"You were little, Zach."

He frowned up at the tree, his little brow wrinkling in concentration. Rachel could picture him lying on the floor, a decorated Christmas tree on top of him, and she started to laugh. Emma did, too, and finally Zach joined in.

Sam came in in the middle of that and hovered in the doorway watching them, the way he often did, and Rachel wondered what it would take to draw him inside, to keep him from lingering there on the edge. She wanted him with them, always.

"What's going on?" he asked finally.

"I didn't pull the tree over," Zach insisted.

"Well, that's good to know," Sam said.

"Emma says he did that when he was little, and we're wondering how to keep Grace out away from this one," Rachel said.

The baby was napping at the moment, but she crawled all over the downstairs, fast as she could go, and she hated the playpen Rachel's neighbor, Mrs. Doyle, had brought over for them to use. So far, they'd mostly been chasing her all over the house.

"We could confine her to the family room, with a few more baby gates, like the one on the steps," Sam said.

"She'll hate that," Emma said.

"Probably," Rachel agreed. Already, she hated the one on the steps. She crawled up to it, pulled herself up so that she was standing, grabbed the gate, and shook it and fussed. "We can't let her eat the tree and all the stuff on it."

And then Rachel laughed again. She feared she had a Christmas-tree-eating toddler on the loose in her house, and they needed to cage her to keep her from pulling the tree over on herself, like Zach had one year.

When she looked up, everyone was smiling and her house rang with laughter, just the way it had when she was a girl.

Rachel caught a glint of light out of the corner of her eye and when she looked up, sunshine was streaming in through the diamond window. The bevels in the glass turned the light this way and that, and as the sun set the light did seem to dance across her living-room floor.

Magic, she thought. There was magic streaming into her house on this day.

Sam didn't sleep in her bed that night, not that she was surprised by that. Apparently it took begging on her part to get him there, and she hadn't sunk to that level that night.

Still, she woke on the seventh day of Christmas feeling just fine. Her youngest sister, Ann, called that morning right after Rachel got downstairs and started the coffee. Ann was the only one of Rachel's siblings who'd had the audacity to move away from Baxter, Ohio, something seen as an absolute sin in Rachel's family. Ann lived an entire two hours away. She and her husband were expecting their first child in the spring.

They talked for a few minutes, Ann mentioning something about her back hurting and being tired all the time, and then said abruptly, "Can we talk about these things, Rach? I wasn't sure. . . . I don't want to make it any harder for you."

Rachel closed her eyes and said, "I want you to be

happy. I want you to have a healthy, happy baby, and I want to hear all about it."

"Still, on Daddy's birthday, when we told everyone . . ."

"I'm sorry," Rachel said. "I didn't want you to see that. I would never want to bring you down at a time like this. It's special, Annie. You've waited a long time."

Their father had despaired of his third daughter ever settling down and having children. He'd hounded Ann and her husband mercilessly. This had been a long time coming.

"Enjoy it," Rachel said. "Every bit of it."

"Thank you. And I want you to enjoy the three that you have. I wish I could see them."

"Well, if they're still here at Christmas, you will."

"Good." Annie hesitated. "Is everything else okay?"

"Uh hmm," she claimed. "Why?"

"Oh, I just talked to Daddy the other day, and . . . You know how he is. He worries. About all of us," she rushed on.

And right now, he was worried about Rachel and Sam. And he was taking it to the family. *Damn.*

"You have enough to worry about," Rachel said. "Baby names and baby furniture. What color to paint the baby's room. How you're going to rearrange your whole life. All that stuff."

"I know. Still, if you need to talk . . ."

"I'm fine," she claimed. "And right now, I have to go. Dave Sharp has his photography equipment set up at the town square, and he's taking family photos today. I want to get a photo of the children."

"Okay. Call me," her sister said.

Rachel hung up thinking of calling her father and

telling him everything, begging him not to say anything to anyone else about her and Sam, but it was
probably already too late. She was afraid everyone
knew by now or if they didn't, they soon would.

And that wasn't her real problem. Her problem was
that she had to stop hiding from it, stop pretending she
didn't know, and figure out how to deal with it. But not
today.

Today she was going to have the kids' picture taken.

Zach fussed as she and Emma dressed him up, and
Emma smiled shyly as she put on her best dress, a new
green velvet one, and Rachel fixed her long hair and
put a Christmas-plaid ribbon in it.

Grace was already in her Christmas outfit, a red
plaid dress made along the same lines as Emma's, and
they were almost out the door when Zach decided to
give her a drink of grape juice from his cup. Rachel
and Emma both grabbed for the cup, but none of them
faster than Grace. She grabbed on to anything that
came within six inches of her and the next thing they
knew, she was dripping with juice and looking quite
happy about it.

Zach apologized three times, and Rachel assured
him everything would be fine. They stripped Grace
and washed her off and then thought about what to do.
They could go buy a new dress or try to get this one
clean. But they were ready to go. Like Grace, Zach
never stayed clean for long. They'd be pushing their
luck, either way.

"I know something we can try," Rachel said.

She headed upstairs, Emma following her with
Grace, once they'd given Zach a very stern warning to
stay put and not get dirty. Rachel walked into the bedroom Emma was using. She lifted the lid of the old

cedar chest in the corner, the scent alone bringing back so many memories her throat nearly closed up completely.

"What's this?" Emma got to her knees beside Rachel. Grace stood in front of her, hanging on to the sides, patting her hands against the top.

"My grandmother's cedar chest," Rachel said.

"It smells funny," Emma said. "But good."

"That's the cedar. The wood the chest is made from."

"You have baby things," Emma said, picking up a tiny pair of booties.

"Yes." Rachel dug through the chest that hadn't been opened in years.

"Whose baby things? Yours?"

"A few of them," Rachel said. Her mother had saved some of the things Rachel had as a baby for Rachel's own children.

She came up with an old white box, fished out of the depths of the chest, and laid it on the bed. Opening it, she pulled back layers of tissue paper and found a very old, slightly yellowed, once-white gown and held it up to Grace. It was musty, and Grace wrinkled up her little nose and sneezed once, then again, then laughed. Her smile could just about light up the world.

"She's so beautiful," Rachel said. "Let's try this on her. It's going to be long and maybe too tight through the chest. It's made for younger babies. But it just might work."

"What is it?" Emma said.

"A christening gown. One that's been in my family for a long time."

They put Grace on the bed, and she immediately reached for the box, wanting to chew on it. Emma took it away, and then Grace got her hands on the tissue paper, obviously fascinated with the noise it made when she grabbed it. They took that away, too, and then Grace grabbed for the gown.

"Maybe we should wait until we get there to put it on her," Emma suggested.

"I think you're right," Rachel agreed, holding the gown up to her and deciding it would do, just for the picture.

Grace rolled over and got up on her hands and knees, grinning like a wild thing set free, and lunged for the tissue paper again. Emma laughed and took it away from her again, then set her on the carpeted floor and gave her a rattle from inside the chest, which held her interest at the moment.

"It's okay?" Emma said.

Rachel nodded, still holding the gown, still feeling as if she might choke at any moment.

"Why do you have all the baby things in the chest?" Emma asked.

"Sam and I had a baby once. A little girl."

"Oh. What happened to her?"

"We were in an accident before she was born, and she died."

"Oh." Emma didn't say anything for the longest time, and then she slipped her hand inside of Rachel's and gave it a squeeze. "That's why you and Sam are so sad?"

"Part of it," Rachel said. "Probably the biggest part."

"I'm sorry." She slipped an arm around Rachel's back and leaned against her. "I didn't know little babies died."

"Not very often, thank God. But sometimes."

"Do you want to tell me about her?"

"I think I do," Rachel realized. "Her name was Hope. It was a family name, after one of my favorite great aunts. We'd already decided on the name, even though she wasn't due for another eight weeks. It was March, and we'd had sleet and snow. The roads were a mess, but I had a doctor's appointment. Sam and I were on our way there when we had a car accident."

Rachel remembered the slow, sickening slide. The light changed, and they hadn't been going that fast. There was a firm layer of snow on the roads. Snow wasn't that hard to drive on. As long as they took it slow, they were fine. But the ice . . . Ice was a different story, and apparently they'd had ice overnight, a layer of it under the snow. In spots the snow had melted away, leaving just the ice. Ice was nearly impossible to manage.

"We hit a patch of ice," Rachel said. "Just one of those things. There it was all of a sudden, right in front of a traffic light that had just turned to caution, then as we slid into the intersection, to red. Someone coming from the other direction had probably done the same thing—hit ice—and we slid into each other. We weren't going that fast, but the car we were in was tiny, and the other one was huge."

She omitted a lot after that. Being trapped in the car. Bleeding. Knowing she was losing the baby. Sam's ashen face in front of hers, him trying to calm her, trying frantically to get her out, making all sorts of rash promises if only she and the baby would live.

It had taken a long time for the emergency crews to cut her out of the car, and she hadn't known then but it was already too late for the baby. The force of the crash had torn the placenta loose, cutting off the baby's oxygen supply. When they finally got her to the hospital and got the baby out, the damage had been done. After that, they'd simply waited, waited for the baby to die, and wondered if Rachel might die, too. Her mother had told her all of it later, as her mother sat by Rachel's bedside and wept.

The baby had been without oxygen for too long, and there was nothing to do but let her go. They could have kept her on the machines, but there was no point. Her brain . . . There was no point.

Rachel had lost too much blood. The doctors couldn't get it to stop. She'd been outside in the cold for so long and in shock and they'd had to do something quickly, or she would have died, too. As a last-ditch effort at saving her, they'd removed her uterus, which had stopped the bleeding. It also meant she'd never have children.

"They couldn't save the baby," Rachel said simply. "And I had some trouble afterward, and I couldn't have any more children. It was just one of those things. We hit a patch of ice on the road. That was it."

Emma stayed there close by Rachel's side, and they watched Grace, shaking the rattle and smiling and trying to get it into her mouth.

"I'm sorry," Emma said again.

Rachel pulled the girl to her and gave her a big hug. Or maybe Emma gave her one. Grace sat in the corner with the rattle that should have been Rachel's daughter's, and in a little while, she'd wear the gown that should have been her daughter's, as well.

Life went on, it seemed. She'd opened the chest she'd planned to fill with keepsakes from all the special moments in her life, as her mother and her grandmother had done before her, and she hadn't fallen apart.

She remembered so clearly her grandmother's cedar chests. On slow winter days, when it was too cold to go outside and they'd exhausted every possibility for playing indoors, her grandmother would take them upstairs to one of her chests. They'd open them up and one by one pull things out, and her grandmother would tell them stories about each thing and the person it belonged to. Rachel always thought it an incredible sign of riches—all the memories, all the little stories. There were old dresses of her mother's and aunts'. Drawings. Report cards. Postcards. Letters. Photographs. Toys. Baby blankets. Tiny shoes.

Rachel had long ago stopped putting mementos in her cedar chest. She didn't open it up and remember. Not until now. She supposed that was progress.

"Do you ever wonder why God lets bad things happen?" Emma asked.

It took Rachel's breath away. "Yes."

"Me, too."

"Bad things have happened to you?" she asked carefully. "Before your mother went away?"

The girl looked so sad. "Yes."

"What happened, Emma?"

"We . . . we had to leave. . . . My father," she said haltingly, fighting to get out each word.

Barely breathing now that Emma was finally giving up some of her secrets, Rachel whispered, "Why?"

"He was bad," she said simply, as if that were all she could bare to say.

"Bad . . . how?"

"He yelled a lot." Emma looked up with frightened eyes.

"What else?" Rachel coaxed the words out of her.

"He scared me, and . . . and he hurt my mom."

Oh, no. "He hit her?"

Emma nodded, tears in her eyes now.

"And you and your mother and Zach and the baby ran away from him?"

"We had to," Emma said in a rush, now that she'd gotten that much out. "Mom said he would have hurt us one day if we hadn't."

"And you believed her?" Rachel said. "That he would have hurt you?"

"I guess. . . . Maybe. He scared me."

"Then you had to get away," Rachel reassured her. "If that's the way it happened, you did the right thing."

"You think?"

"Yes. I'm sure."

"I still miss him," Emma confessed. "Even after everything, I miss him."

"That's why your mother's afraid of the police? Afraid they'll make you all go back to your father?"

Emma nodded. "Zach doesn't know. Just me and Mom."

"Oh," Rachel said.

"She told me in case anything ever happened to her. In case I was the only one to take care of Zach and the baby. She didn't want us to go back." Emma started crying then. "You won't make us go back, will you?"

"Oh, Emma."

"I'm not supposed to let anyone take us back there, and I'm scared. I'm scared my mom won't come back and that we'll have to go back there and that he's really mad at us now."

"Emma, I don't know what's going to happen. I don't know where your mother is or when she's coming back, and I don't know anything about your father. I don't know a lot about the law in cases like this, but

I meant what I said earlier. You and your brother and the baby can stay here as long as you need to. I promise. And if . . ."

She was going to say she'd protect her from her own father, but honestly, how could Rachel do that? She'd already seen how the system worked, and a biological parent's rights were so hard to break. They'd learned that with Will. Will had gone back to his biological mother, despite everything Sam and Rachel had done and everything his mother had done. What if someone decreed that these children had to go back to their biological father?

"Emma," she began. "I . . . I—"

And then Sam appeared in front of her, taking Emma by the arms and gently turning her to face him. "Emma?"

"Yes," she whispered.

"Don't tell us who your father is," he said.

"What?" she and Rachel said at the same time.

"If no one knows who your father is or where he is, no one can take you back to him. Don't tell us, Emma."

Rachel gaped at him, hardly able to believe what he was saying. Sam, who'd been so diligently trying to get the kids to talk. Now he was telling Emma not to.

"Do you understand what I'm saying, Emma?" he asked.

Emma nodded.

"You don't have to tell anyone anything. I know I tried to get you to, but I didn't know why you couldn't, and now that you've told us, I understand. It's okay. Just don't tell. Don't tell me or Rachel. Don't tell anyone else."

"Okay."

Emma gazed up at Sam with what could only be awe, Sam who looked fierce enough to break someone in two at the moment. But obviously, Emma didn't see that in him. Or maybe she did. Maybe she saw it for what it was. He was furious on her behalf and on behalf of Zach and Grace, and he was ready to take their so-called father apart with his bare hands. Sam could be so hard when he was pushed too far. Rachel had seen it in him as a teenager, when life had been so cruel to him. And she'd seen steel in him over the years. When she'd leaned on him in bad times, and he'd held himself together and her, too.

He was the kind of man a woman could depend upon when times got tough, a solid, unshakably strong, brave man, and at one time, he'd loved her very much. He'd loved their baby, too, and it seemed he loved Emma, Zach, and Grace, maybe just as much. And this was just what the man she'd always loved would do. He'd keep these children safe.

Rachel was scared now that they knew the kind of battle they were facing, but they had Sam. He'd decided for all of them. They simply wouldn't tell. If Miriam asked if the children had told them anything, Rachel wasn't sure what she would say. But she wasn't going to worry about that now.

She went to Emma and put one of her arms around the girl, the other around Sam. They were in this together now.

Sam stayed there until Emma lifted her head and dried her wet eyes. She looked embarrassed when it was all over and a bit self-conscious, and Sam found himself rashly promising her that everything would be okay.

Then he asked her to take Grace downstairs and wait with Zach so Sam could talk to Rachel. Rachel, who'd opened the cedar chest and gotten out the christening gown and the rattle that was supposed to belong to their baby. The one she'd felt guilty for years for losing.

Life was so strange, he realized. All those things they'd never said that had eaten away at the foundation of their marriage all these years. Things that had festered and grown and ached and threatened to rot it at its core. He hadn't quite been able to take it all in the night before. It had literally made him dizzy, just thinking of how she must have felt, how much it had to hurt, all this time. He knew, because he'd felt the exact same way, and there had been days when he'd thought it might well kill him, days when he wished it would. Guilt was a powerful thing, an irrational, powerful thing.

"I always thought it was my fault," he said.

"What?" She looked up from her spot on the floor, where she'd sat down to play with Grace for a moment.

"Our baby. I thought it was my fault we lost her."

Rachel looked genuinely puzzled. "Why?"

"Because I was driving. Because the car needed brakes and the tires were bald. Because it crumpled like the tin can it was when we hit the car, and I should have been able to afford a safe car to put you and the baby in."

"Sam—"

"Your father said as much to me that day at the hospital, and I thought he was right. I thought the same thing myself."

"Oh, Sam. He was angry. He was hurt. It was a terrible day."

"I know."

"You can't still think it's your fault," she began.

"You do," he said. "You blame yourself because you wanted to get pregnant and you made love to me that night knowing it was possible. And that's not why we lost our baby, Rachel."

"I did." And then she began to understand. Her eyes filled with tears. "You felt that way, too? All these years? That it was your fault?"

He nodded. "And afterward, when I was trying my best to help you, and you pushed me away—"

"Because I felt so guilty," she said.

"I thought it was because you blamed me, too."

"Sam, I never did. Never."

"And I never blamed you. As much as I wanted someone to blame, it was never you."

He didn't know what to say then, what to do. He ended up walking over to the chest, which was still open, and pulling out the pair of booties. So tiny, so delicate. He forgot sometimes how truly tiny she would have been, even if she'd been born at the right time, and he really didn't want to cry right now. He despised tears; he'd been taught to at a very young age and he didn't care about any of this new-age man shit that said it was perfectly fine for a man to fall apart. He didn't think it was.

But the booties were tiny. What in the world would her feet have looked like? Suddenly, he wished he'd looked, wished he'd held her, as the doctors had told him to do. He wished he'd had just that little bit of time with her and that maybe the memories he had left were even stronger, the way she smelled and the feel of her in his arms.

He wished he and Rachel had done this a long, long time ago. Had talked this out, had gotten the poisonous grief and guilt out of their systems before it had taken such a toll of them.

He felt her hand on his arm, and then her cheek pressed against his shoulder.

"We have to stop this," he said, more gruffly than he intended because he was trying to keep his voice from breaking. "We have to stop hating ourselves. We have to let it go."

"I know. I've just held on to it for so long, I don't know how to let it go."

He got himself under control, at least enough to face her, and for the first time, he thought about the future, about all the possibilities. Him and Rachel and children. And then he had an idea.

He took her face in his hands and tilted it up to his. His gaze locked on hers, and in a moment, he saw everything there. The young girl he'd first known. The one he'd fallen in love with. The one he'd held so tightly while they'd buried their baby, and the one he'd ached for, for so many endless nights. She was still his, despite all they'd gone through and all the things that had threatened to tear them apart.

"Do you trust me?" he asked.

"Yes," she cried.

"Then listen to me. I forgive you, Rachel. I know what happened. I know what you did. I know why you did it. I know how much you've suffered over the years, and I don't blame you at all for what happened to our baby. I don't think it was your fault. I never thought it was."

She closed her eyes, dipped her head until it was nestled against his chest, and she was trembling. He held her even tighter.

"I forgive you, too," she cried. "Can you let me do that for you? Can we do it for each other and put it all behind us? Finally?"

"We can try," he said.

"I want to, Sam. I want that more than anything."

By the eighth day of Christmas, Sam still felt shell-shocked, like someone who'd been purged of a poison or had woken up after a long, long sleep.

He knew enough about guilt to realize that it took more than a few words to absolve a person of emotions he'd hung on to for more than a decade. But things definitely looked better.

He was actually looking forward to Christmas, and since he couldn't get any work done, he might as well get ready for it. Rachel and the children were baking today. She always made baskets of goodies she delivered to the neighbors, and she had a whole crew of women baking for the elderly people served by the Meals on Wheels program she helped start. He was no help when it came to baking, and Rachel had given him a pointed look when he'd claimed he had nothing to do that day, reminding him that Christmas was next week and then looking over at the children.

He suddenly found himself with a large number of people on his Christmas list this year. He was in the bike department at the town's only toy store when he ran into Miriam.

"Bikes?" she asked.

Sam ignored that. He felt foolish enough, looking at bikes while there was snow on the ground. Bikes implied that the person riding them would still be around in the spring when the snow thawed.

"Did you hear back on the blood tests?" he asked instead.

Miriam nodded. "That's why I came over to talk to you. They were negative. The children don't belong to the couple in Virginia."

Sam nodded. He'd known that after what Emma told them yesterday.

"Still," Miriam went on, "from what Emma said, about being afraid of the police and running away, someone's probably looking for them. Someone other than their mother."

Oh, hell. Sam forgot about mentioning that. "I thought you sent out all sorts of bulletins about them."

"We did, but bulletins about a mother who abandoned them. If we focus on the father, children taken by their mothers from their fathers . . . Those cases aren't as clear-cut. Lots of times, law enforcement isn't exactly jumping up and down to get involved. It's a custody issue, for the courts to handle."

Sam nodded, feeling sick inside, thinking what he'd told Miriam before he'd understood what the children were facing might help send them back to an abusive father. And then, he had to ask one more question. "What happens if you don't find anyone for them?"

"We look for a long-term placement. If we're very, very lucky, an adoption, if it goes that far. Most people don't truly abandon their children, Sam. They might dump them somewhere for a while, but things get better. People sober up. Or feel guilty. Or panic and come back. Or we find out where they're from and that leads us to someone who can take them. A grandmother, an aunt, someone."

"Anyone?" he asked, offended by the thought.

"What are their options? They're three children. Do you have any idea how few people are willing to take on three children at once? If we split them up, I could place Grace in a second. People would fight to get her. And I might be able to place Zach. He's still young enough. But Emma . . ."

"You can't split them up," he said.

"I may not have a choice. I'd be out begging, just like I was when I showed up at your and Rachel's door," she said. "Oh, I have a few possibilities. People call me from time to time who are looking to adopt, and there might be someone on my list I could talk into taking them all. In fact, now that I think about it there's a woman I know in her mid-forties, someone who's spent the last twenty years building up a business she just sold. She's regretting never having a child, and she certainly has the financial resources to raise three children. She's looking for one child, but she might be convinced to take them."

"A single parent? You let single people adopt?"

"Yes. We'd prefer two-parent families. They tend to get priority, especially with infants. But it's not always possible to find two-parent homes for all the children up for adoption. If it's a choice between long-term foster care and a single-parent adoption, we'll go for the adoption."

"So if . . ." God, he was going to say that even if he and Rachel split up, Rachel could still keep the children.

She didn't need him as much as he thought she did.

"Sam?" Miriam asked. "Are you okay?"

He nodded. All these years, children had been the one thing he and Rachel hadn't had, one thing he hadn't been able to give her. Now he found out she didn't need him at all for that. Not to keep these children.

"What's going on?" Miriam asked.

"Nothing," he insisted.

"Do you and Rachel want them if they become available for adoption?" she asked. "I have to warn you, I don't know how long we might be living in limbo here—how long we'll look for their parents, whether we'll ever find them, whether the children will ever be free for adoption. There are no guarantees here, and I thought after what happened with Will . . ."

"I don't know," he said. "I have to talk to Rachel."

And then he thought of what his wife had already done, the promises she'd already made on their behalf, and took a leap of faith himself.

"But you don't have to look for someone else to take them after Christmas. They can stay at our house. Rachel already promised them that. It's not a problem, is it? We've still got all our paperwork in order?"

"Yes. You and Rachel can have them for as long as you want them, provided we don't find where they belong."

"Okay." He frowned. "You have single-parent foster homes, too?"

"Of course."

"It's not a problem? Being a single parent?"

"We're not exactly overwhelmed with people dying to take foster kids into their homes, Sam. We have plenty of kids to go around." She frowned at him. "What's going on?"

"Just curious," he said, shaking his head back and forth.

A few days ago he felt trapped because of the kids. He couldn't have walked out on Rachel and the kids. Now he worried that they didn't need him at all. Oh, he could probably take the coward's way out, stay for the sake of the children, and maybe Rachel would keep him around for the same reason.

But it was about the saddest reason he could think of for him and Rachel to stay together, and he didn't think it was enough for him anymore. And he didn't know what to do.

Chapter 11

On the ninth day of Christmas, Rachel got out of bed very early, dressed quickly, gave Grace a bottle and put her back down, then went downstairs to find Sam still asleep on the sofa in the den.

Good. She'd made it down here before he crept out the back door. She'd waited up for him the night before and the one before that, but he hadn't come in until very late. He was doing it again, sometimes disappearing before she woke up, sometimes coming home long after she'd gone to sleep at night.

Not today, she vowed.

She went to work in the kitchen, intending to have him wake to a house filled with the smell of homemade biscuits baking and bacon sizzling in a skillet. It was going to smell so good, he wouldn't be able to leave without eating, and she intended to make him do it sitting across the table from her. He couldn't ignore her sitting across the table from her. She wouldn't let him.

It was time they got on with this. He didn't blame her for anything that happened in their past, had generously offered his forgiveness for it all, if that wasn't enough. He'd said he would have married her anyway, even without the baby, and she was trying to make herself believe it.

He'd decided not to ask the children anything else about their mother and didn't intend to let them tell him or Rachel anything about their father. Rachel had never been prouder of him than she was in that moment. That was the man she knew, the one she'd loved for so long. A man three lost children could count on to stand by them, to help them. A man she could count on, as well. When he wasn't hell-bent on avoiding her.

That seemed the way it had always been for her and Sam. Two steps forward, one step back. They had just been coming out of the fog of losing the baby when Rachel's grandfather had died. Two years later, her mother had died. The next year, they'd gotten involved in an adoption gone wrong. A birth mother who had changed her mind at the last minute. They'd actually seen the baby at the hospital. Rachel had held him in her arms, but they'd never been able to take him home. And then there'd been the adoption that was nothing more than a scam. A woman who'd been pregnant and promising her baby to a half-dozen couples throughout the Midwest and in the process managing to scam them out of thousands of dollars. And then there'd been Will.

It was like they'd hardly been able to breathe between one tragedy and the next, and considering it all together, Rachel supposed it was a miracle they'd made it this far, her husband's post-Christmas plans notwithstanding.

But they were still together. They were talking about things they'd never been able to discuss before. There was a long way to go and no guarantees of any kind regarding these children. But they had reason to hope.

Rachel was just putting the biscuits in the oven when she thought she heard a car out front. Glancing at the clock, she couldn't imagine anyone showing up at her door this early unless . . .

She hurried to the front door, afraid of finding her father or one of her sisters there, but it was Miriam climbing the porch steps.

"Good morning," Miriam said.

It scared her, seeing her aunt here so early, so unexpectedly. "What did you find out?" she asked.

"About the children?"

"Of course, about the children."

"Nothing. Just what I told Sam yesterday. That the DNA tests showed they couldn't possibly belong to the couple in Virginia."

"Oh."

Miriam frowned at her. "Can I come in, Rachel? It's freezing out here."

"Oh. Of course." Rachel stepped back and held open the door. "Sorry."

She took Miriam's coat and led her to the kitchen, where she offered her fresh coffee, conscious of the fact that Sam was still asleep on the sofa in the family room. Which Miriam would know instantly if she took three steps down the back hallway. That was all she needed—Miriam to see that, if she hadn't heard from someone else about all that was wrong at the McRae house.

"Sam said you'll keep the children after Christmas if I still haven't found out where they belong."

"He told you that?"

"Yes. I assume you'd both agreed . . ."

"We had," Rachel claimed. It wasn't exactly a lie. "I just didn't know he'd told you. That's all."

Miriam was giving her that all-knowing mother look, the one Rachel's own mother used so often. She'd claimed mothers just knew things, that one day they were going to find a gene for it on the X chromosome. The all-knowing-mother gene. Rachel had hardly ever been able to put anything over on her mother or Miriam.

"Sam and I talked about a lot of things. Oddly enough, he was interested in the fact that single people could be foster parents or adoptive parents."

"What?" What did single people have to do with anything?

"Singles. Foster parenting. Adopting. For instance, if you were single and wanted to continue foster parenting these children or to be considered as an adoptive parent, we could probably make that work just fine."

"Oh." Rachel was suddenly feeling awful.

"Why would your husband ever be interested in something like that?"

Miriam headed down the back hallway before Rachel could stop her. She stood in the doorway leading to the family room, Sam just waking up and staring at the both of them as if he weren't quite sure where he was. But Miriam knew exactly where she'd find him this early in the morning, and it wasn't in his wife's bed where he should have been. Miriam gave Rachel another one of those mother looks. That I-knew-it and why-didn't-you-tell-me look, all at once.

"Dammit," Rachel muttered under her breath. She did not need this. She didn't intend to explain her marriage to anyone, especially not her entire family.

Rachel grabbed her aunt by the arm and tugged her back into the kitchen. "This is none of your business," she said.

"Rachel, I'm not trying to be nosy. I'm worried about you. I was worried before I brought these children here, and now I'm worried even more. You and your husband aren't sleeping together?"

"I don't think it's any of your business where we sleep," she said.

"If you're going to try to adopt these children someday, it is."

"We can't adopt them now, can we? They're not free for anyone to adopt."

"No. Not now."

"Then until we can, it's none of your business."

"Rachel," she said, the hurt obvious in her voice. "I care about you very much, and I promised your mother before she died that I would look out for you, as if you were my very own daughter. And obviously, you've needed a mother now for a while, and I haven't been here. Not the way I should have been. I love you. Don't you know that?"

"I know it," she said wearily, then pulled her aunt close for a quick hug. "I do. I'm sorry. I . . . I didn't want to talk about it. Not to anybody."

Not even her husband. Obviously that had been a mistake. Maybe keeping it from Miriam was, as well.

"Okay. We can talk." She glanced nervously toward the stairs, could hear Sam climbing up—leaving her to deal with Miriam alone, which she actually thought was better. Maybe she could calm Miriam down and convince her not to talk.

But a moment later, she heard one of the children coming down the stairs. Her household was coming to life. This wasn't the time for this conversation. She needed to tell her aunt about Sam. About him losing his parents at five, not fifteen, and what in the world had likely happened to him in the meantime and what it might still be doing to him today. "But not now. I'll call you, okay?"

"All right. How are the children?"

"They're fine. We had pictures made in front of the town tree, and we baked like crazy yesterday."

"Good. I may be able to use one of the pictures on some new bulletins. Lost kids in their Christmas best. That ought to get people's attention."

Rachel nodded, thinking that was the last thing they needed.

"They still haven't said anything that might help us find them?"

"No," she claimed, not liking the lie at all. But she and Sam had chosen their path. They'd made a promise to Emma. As Rachel saw it, little rights or wrongs didn't matter nearly so much as the promise they'd made to keep these children safe.

"I told Sam before, and I want to tell you today that we'll find someone who knows them," Miriam said. "People abandoning their children, unfortunately, is not that rare, but their consciences will finally kick in and they'll come back. Remember that, Rachel. I really don't want to see either you or Sam hurt again. I thought long and hard before bringing them here. I worried about what I'd be doing to you."

"It was the right thing," Rachel reassured her. "The best thing you could have done. We needed them, and they needed us."

"Good. Just be careful. Remember what I said about liking them a lot—"

"Too late," Rachel said with a wary smile. It was probably too late right from the start. "I couldn't stop myself from loving them."

Miriam looked even more worried at that.

"I couldn't," she said. "But I'm stronger than I used to be. And more determined this time."

She was going to do her best to save her marriage and to help these children, no matter what. It felt like the most grown-up decision she'd made in years. Maybe in her whole life. And there was nothing Miriam could say to change her mind.

Rachel put breakfast on the table twenty minutes later, and a sleepy but hungry Zach dug in. Even Emma ate more than usual. Grace was after the jam more than anything else. She kept grabbing at the bits of a jam biscuit Rachel was trying to feed her until she got her hands on the whole thing. Quite pleased with herself, she tried to shove all of it in her mouth at once and ended up with jam everywhere, all over her hands and her mouth and her bib, even in her hair.

It was strawberry, and she looked like she'd decorated herself for Christmas. Everyone laughed at her, and she laughed, too, then started sucking the jam off her tiny fingers. Sam stayed to eat with them and to help clean up. He and Emma loaded the dishwasher while Rachel got the things for Grace's bath, and they put her in the sink again.

Emma went off to help Zach get dressed, and Sam stayed in the kitchen with Rachel. She probably could have bathed the baby herself, but maybe Grace wanted Sam closer, too, because she squirmed for all she was worth and generally gave Rachel a hard time until Sam stepped in and held her slippery, soapy body while

Rachel did her best to wash her. All the while Grace gazed up at Sam adoringly and batted her wet lashes at him, temptress that she was. Rachel laughed at her, wondering if some females were just born with that gene.

"She's flirting with you," Rachel said.

"She's a baby."

"Look at her. She's flirting. You haven't been out of circulation so long that you don't recognize flirting, do you?" Rachel said, and then had a terrible thought.

He *was* planning to leave her. She forgot that at times, and she thought she knew the reason—that it was simply too painful to stay. But there were other possibilities. Scared, she looked up at him, so tall and so strong. So solid. Her rock. She spoke before she even thought about it.

"Tell me no one else is flirting with you, Sam."

She saw his gaze narrow in on hers, saw the questions in his eyes. "What are you talking about?"

"I—"And then it was gone. All that courage, that reckless impulsiveness, gone. She couldn't ask. She wasn't ready for what he'd say when she did, was hoping the last few days together had changed everything.

"What?" he asked again.

"Nothing. I was being silly. That's all."

"You think I've been seeing someone else?" he asked.

"I . . . I don't know what I think." She knew she'd reached out to him, that she'd kissed him and talked him into sleeping in their bed, but he hadn't stayed for long and he hadn't made love to her. And he was planning to leave. "Except that I wish things were different between us."

"It's not another woman, Rachel," he said softly,

taking her chin in one hand and turning her to face him. Looking right into her eyes, he said, "It's never been that."

"Okay."

He frowned. "You don't believe me?"

"I have to." She couldn't let herself believe anything else.

"I would never do that to you," he said. "I'd never hurt you like that."

"I didn't really think you would. But . . ."

"Things still aren't right," he finished for her.

"No, things still aren't right," she said, curling her body against his, her forehead against his shoulder.

Grace sat quietly in the shallow water for a moment, gazing up at them, as if to say, *What's wrong? What could possibly be wrong?* Sam had one of his big, strong hands at her back, ready to catch her should she topple over, and Rachel touched a fingertip to the baby's delicate, upturned nose, and then her chin, winning a broad smile from her and a cooing sound.

"It's helped having her here," Sam said, his arm slipping around Rachel's waist. "And maybe it even helped to talk about our baby. I . . . I've always wanted to tell you how sorry I am for that," he said raggedly. "It feels so stupid, to ever think words could matter in something like this, but I've still felt the need to say them. More than anything, I wanted to hear you say you forgive me, but I didn't see how you possibly could, so I just never said the words. I didn't think I could, not without . . ."

She looked up and saw tears in his eyes.

"Shit," he muttered. "Not without this."

"I don't blame you. I never did. Can you believe me about that?"

"I'm trying. I'm trying to take it all in. It's hard to let go of things when you've held on to them so tightly for so long."

"I know. So many times, you seemed so distant. I thought it just didn't matter that much to you—"

"Oh, Rachel. It mattered."

"I could feel you pulling away from me then. I thought you were impatient with the fact that I was still consumed by it at times. I thought you were shutting me out because of that."

"No," he said. "It wasn't that."

"And I thought you never really wanted children. Not the way I did. Especially when we started talking about foster parenting . . . You seemed . . ." Cold, she'd thought. Unfeeling. And now she knew. He felt too much. "We have to talk about it, Sam. You were one of those children, weren't you?"

He nodded.

"And it was bad?"

"Sometimes."

"I just didn't understand." Maybe she hadn't paid attention the way she should have. Maybe she'd simply focused so sharply on herself and her own feelings, she'd missed so many of his. "I guess we still have some things to work through."

He nodded grimly, and she wondered, Would he stay to do that? Or had he had enough? She would promise him anything for another chance. She couldn't imagine her life without Sam.

But he was talking to Miriam about single-parent foster homes and adoptive homes. The only reason she could imagine him doing that was because he was wondering if she could still keep the children herself if he left.

She slid her arm around him and held on tight, thinking what an odd triangle they made. Sam holding on to her, her holding on to him, and both of them holding on to the baby.

A real baby this time, not the memories of the baby they'd lost. They'd both been warned in those early, crazy days after the accident that most couples didn't survive the loss of a child. It was simply too stressful. Rachel vaguely remembered warnings about feelings of guilt—however misplaced they might be—and grief that tore couples apart. She hadn't wanted to deal with it, and neither had Sam, and it seemed they'd nearly lost themselves by refusing to talk to each other.

Rachel was scared, so scared of what the coming days would bring. She could end up with everything. Or nothing.

At other times in her life, the changes had come so quickly, so unexpectedly, she hadn't had time to think. But this . . . She could see it all staring her in the face, and she didn't think she'd ever had so much at stake.

Her and Sam.

Her and the children.

For so long she'd just wanted children, and now when she might finally have them, she might be losing Sam. She felt so foolish now for taking her marriage for granted, for thinking he would always be there.

Rachel held on to him more tightly, soaking up that heat and the solid feel of his chest, his heart beating beneath her right ear. She was afraid to let go, afraid of what would happen once she did.

"Will you tell me about what happened after your parents died?" she asked, because it was still between them, and they had to deal with it. He tensed immediately, would have pulled away if she hadn't been holding him so tightly. "Please, Sam."

"I never wanted you to know. I never wanted anyone to know."

"Why?"

"Because I didn't want your pity, Rachel. I still don't."

"I think I need to know. To understand you. It's part of who you are."

"Not anymore."

"Sam, it is. If losing the baby taught us anything, surely it's taught us that we can't run from the past or our feelings. We can't afford to keep hiding things from each other. Look at what it's already cost us," she said. "I'm not going to judge you. I just want to understand. I want to help you. Will you let me help?"

"I don't think anything helps with this," he said.

"Please, Sam." She waited. He didn't say anything, and he was tenser than she'd ever seen him. His entire body was as unyielding as a stone, as straight and tall as a statue. "Sam—"

And then Zach burst into the room with the speed of a small tornado, chattering the whole way. He saw them standing there all together and came up to Sam and wrapped his arms around Sam's legs and grinned up at Rachel.

"Hi," he said.

Rachel took a breath and said, "Hi, Zach."

He really was an absolute joy, and he adored Sam.

Rachel stepped away from Sam and Zach beamed up at him. Sam ruffled the boy's hair and asked, "What are we going to do today?"

"Build a snowman," he said.

Sam nodded. "Let's get to it."

And Rachel let them both go, comforting herself with the fact that she still had three days until Christmas. Even if he left, he wasn't planning to go until after Christmas.

Her whole life had been turned upside-down in the last nine days. She figured anything could happen in the next three.

Miriam came by after lunch. Grace was napping. Emma was in her room, and Zach and Sam had gone to town on a mysterious mission that Rachel suspected had to do with Christmas presents.

Rachel made tea, and she and Miriam sat in the family room in front of the fire, sipping slowly. Finally Rachel asked, "What does it do to a child to be passed around from home to home, never staying anywhere for long?"

"You mean like in foster care? Kids there want the same thing all kids want. Adults they can trust to care for them. Security. Love. They're always trying to find it. Forming attachments, hoping, worrying. Break those bonds too many times, and it makes it that much harder for them to form those kinds of bonds again."

"Into adulthood?"

"Yes. Think about it. If you'd seen every bit of security you'd ever had yanked away from you time and time again, what would you want most of all?"

"All those things," she said. Hadn't she loved Sam enough? How could he not see how much she'd loved him?

"And what would you do, if you'd grown up that way and you wanted to protect yourself from ever being hurt again?"

"I'd put up a wall between me and everyone else.

And I'd try to never let anyone that close to me. I'd pull inside myself and try not to get hurt again." That was it. Rachel knew. She'd thought so many times he just didn't care when he'd been desperately trying to protect himself.

Oh, Sam.

"Want to tell me what's going on?" Miriam asked.

"Sam's parents didn't die right before he came here. They died about ten years before, and I guess he got passed from house to house after that. Relatives. Foster homes. I'm not sure exactly."

She looked up to find an expression on her aunt's face that she'd seldom seen. The one she'd worn the day she came to tell them Will had to go back to his mother. In her job, Miriam knew too much, saw too much. There must have been more days than her aunt cared to remember when she'd been the one taking a child from one home to another, one more time. When she'd taken children out of horrendous situations and likely been unable to forget them, unable to sleep at night for wondering what was going to become of them. Miriam knew what Sam's life had been like. She knew kids who'd been Sam.

"What do I do?" Rachel asked, afraid of what her answer might be.

"He never told you?"

"No. He told Emma."

"Oh, Rachel. All these years . . ."

"I know." She'd been married to him, and she hadn't truly known him. She couldn't help but believe she'd failed him completely, and she wanted to make it up to him, if she could. "What do I do?"

"Get him to talk about it. If not to you, to someone.

I have the name of a great psychologist in the next county."

"I can't see Sam ever talking to a stranger about this."

"He has to talk to someone. If he's kept it a secret from you all these years, I doubt he's ever talked to anyone about it, and you know what holding things inside of you that way can do to a person."

"Yes." They were so good at that, her and Sam. "I don't know how I can get him to talk about it. And I was wondering if you could find out about what happened to Sam? It would be in the social services records, wouldn't it?"

"Rachel, those are private."

"I know. But he's my husband."

"And those records are private," her aunt said firmly.

"Okay. I'm sorry. I just thought . . ." She was married to the man. She thought she had a right to know.

"I think you and I should start with what's going on now. Like why he's sleeping on the sofa?"

"I guess things just got too hard for us—all the bad stuff—until we were drowning in it. It was all I could do just to try to keep going. I didn't even see what it was doing to him. I don't even know if he wants to be here anymore."

"But he is still here," Miriam pointed out.

"I'm afraid he won't be for long. I don't know how to get him to stay."

"You start by telling him how you feel."

"We've been doing better. But there's so much. How can you be married to a man for twelve years and have left so much unsaid?"

"Say it now. If he's still here, he's still interested in hearing it."

"I want to tell him. I want to make him happy." And then she got to the scariest part of all. "I'm afraid he's never been happy with me."

"You haven't had a lot of time to be happy, but you've stuck together just the same. That says a lot, Rachel."

Rachel hoped it did. She hoped there was something left the two of them could build upon.

Something like love.

Chapter 12

"Emma said we get to stay here after Christmas," Zach said.

Sam paused with his hands deep inside a box of dusty odds and ends at an estate sale in the next county. He was always on the lookout for period things that could be used in his restoration business, and this sale looked like a good one. There were several old doors and light fixtures, mantelpieces, maybe some furniture. Zach found it all fascinating, and he'd proven to be good company.

"That's right," Sam said. "You can stay as long as you need to."

"Till Mommy comes back?" he asked quite seriously.

"As long as you need to."

Sam was starting to wonder if their mother was ever coming back, starting to think it was up to him to make sure these kids were taken care of. Miriam wasn't making any progress, and it seemed so odd that no one was looking for them. If they had the kind, caring mother Emma claimed, surely she would have come back by now, if she was able. Emma was convinced her father was a monster, and Sam wondered if the man had already gotten his hands on their mother.

After all, she seemed to have disappeared off the face of the earth.

"Zach?" he asked very gently. "Did your mother get sick a lot?"

Emma said that, and he'd thought the woman might be a drunk. Being sick was a euphemism drunks hid behind. Sam certainly knew that. Drunks blacked out, too. Lost days. But it had been almost two weeks.

"Yeah," Zach said. "She got sick."

"Sick how?"

"I dunno. Just sick," Zach said.

"Fever? Cough? Cold? Throwing up? Sleeping a lot?"

"Uh-huh," he said.

They weren't going to get anywhere with that line of questioning. "Did you all live around here?" he tried instead. "I mean, you were at the motel. You'd been in the car, right?"

"Uh huh."

"How long?"

"Forever," Zach said, giving a long-suffering sigh.

"You mean a few hours? A few days?"

"Days and days," he said dramatically.

"Where were you going?"

"I dunno."

"Do you remember your dad, Zach?"

He shook his head back and forth.

"You haven't seen him in a long time?"

"Uh-uh."

"You mean not for months? Or years?"

"Years," Zach agreed.

"Was he there . . . say on your last birthday?"

"Uh-uh."

"The one before that?"

"Uh uh."

Okay, so they hadn't been running away just now. Which meant they had to be trying to get to someone or someplace. But who? And why?

"When you got in the car, did your mother say why you were doing that? Were you trying to get to someone?"

"Someone who'd help us, because Mommy was sick and having trouble taking care of us."

So there was someone out there somewhere. "Do you know that person's name?"

"No," Zach said. "But we don't need 'em, right? 'Cause we can stay with you and Miss Rachel?"

"Yes. You can. I just . . . I know you want your mother back. I'm trying to figure out where she might be so we can get her back for you."

No matter what his mother was like, Zach probably still wanted her back. To most kids, any mother was better than no mother at all. Sam knew that.

"Where's your mommy?" Zach asked.

"She died," Sam said gently.

"And she didn't come back?"

"No," Sam said. "When people die, they don't come back."

"Do you think my mommy died?"

"No. I don't have any reason to think that," Sam said quickly.

"But she promised she'd come back." His lower lip started trembling.

"I know."

"I do remember somethin'," Zach offered. "I heard Mommy and Emma talking when they thought I was asleep. They said the name of the town, and my mommy got all upset."

"What was the name?"

"I can't remember." He frowned. "But it had a funny name. Like a dog. I remember that part."

"A name like a dog? That's it?"

Zach nodded.

A dog? Nothing came to mind.

"Hey, are we gonna buy somethin'?" Zach asked, his attention caught on an old bicycle in the corner of the barn.

"If we find what we're looking for," Sam said.

"What are we lookin' for?"

"Something for Rachel. Something very special, and I think I see it over there. Can you keep a secret?"

Zach nodded vigorously.

"Okay. Come on. I'll show you."

And he took the little boy by the hand, struck by the trust he offered so freely and by how much the boy needed. He could do this, Sam told himself. He could help this child through whatever lay ahead. He could make sure Zach never felt the way Sam had when he was a little boy, and he hoped to God he could make sure he never went back to a father who abused his mother.

On the tenth day of Christmas, they all went to see Santa Claus. It was a clear, merely cool December night with a full harvest moon hanging brightly in the sky, and the town was lit up from end to end in Christmas finery, like something out of Zach's book. Greenery and bright lights draped from anything that didn't move. People were out in force shopping and eating and happily thinking about the days to come. There were carolers strolling the streets in downtown, hot cider for sale in the town square, and Santa presiding over the festivities.

There was a line of kids waiting to see Santa, but Zach started playing with the little boy in line in front of them. Grace was enchanted by all the lights, and Emma seemed to be covertly eyeing a boy about her age who'd been given the task of taking his little sister up to see Santa, but she was too shy to even say a word to him.

"I used to look at you just like that," Rachel said to Sam, but she didn't seem sad about that. She seemed to be merely caught up in the past, a time when their lives seemed filled with infinite possibilities.

Sam edged closer, slipping his arm around her. Grace gurgled up at him and cooed. He brushed a hand down her back, and she smiled at him, making his chest feel full to bursting.

"Hold it. Right there," someone said, and the flash of a camera went off in their faces.

When the flash faded, he looked up to see their neighbor, Mrs. Watson, smiling back at them.

"You all make such a lovely picture," she said. "I couldn't resist."

Rachel chatted with the woman for a few moments, and it was typical of the conversations they'd had with so many people that night.

"How are these fine-looking children doing?"

"They're fine," Rachel assured her.

"Still no news?" she whispered, although neither Zach nor Emma was paying any attention.

"Not yet," Rachel said.

"Well, maybe this time. I just know that one day, everything's going to work out for the two of you, because you're such nice people. I've been praying for you all along."

"Thank you," Rachel said.

Everybody in town knew they'd always wanted children, and there would have been a time when Sam would have resented that. But standing there in the town square at Christmas hearing about their good wishes and their prayers for the two of them, he saw, too, that everybody in town seemed to want them to have children.

It was all a part of that small-town mentality he'd resented so much as an angry, sometimes reckless teenager; they'd all talked about him then, too. But it was different tonight. Everyone was pulling for them now. He felt it, suddenly felt very much a part of this community. It was a nice town, and they were mostly good people. He couldn't imagine living anyplace else.

"Now, let's get all five of you together," Mrs. Watson insisted. Rachel drew the children in close. They all crowded together and the flash went off again. "Got it. Your first Christmas together. First Christmases are so special. You'll remember this your whole life."

Sam looked down and saw Zach standing grinning next to Emma, who was tucked against Rachel's side, the baby in her arms.

Their first Christmas . . .

He didn't want it to be their last.

"I'll send you a copy of the picture," Mrs. Watson promised. "Oh, and thank you for the basket of goodies, Rachel. Not that we needed them, but we sure will enjoy them, and it is Christmas, after all. The calories shouldn't even count this time of year."

Rachel laughed at that, and Mrs. Watson moved along. It wasn't long after that when it was their turn with Santa. Grace refused to get anywhere near him. She curled up her nose and made a face and cried, clinging to Rachel for all she was worth, while Sam deposited a suddenly shy Zach on Santa's lap.

Dave Nelson, one of the town's firemen, was stuffed into the Santa suit. He gave a credible version of "Ho, ho, ho! What have we here? A little boy? What's your name, little boy?"

"Zach," he whispered.

"And have you been a good boy, Zach?"

Zach hesitated, looked a bit worried. Sam put a hand on Zach's shoulder and reassured Santa that Zach had indeed been very, very good this year.

"And what do you want for Christmas, little boy?"

Zach leaned over and whispered in Santa's ear. Santa gave another hearty "Ho, ho, ho!" and when Zach turned his head to look back at Sam and Rachel, Santa mouthed, "Bike."

Sam nodded. The more practical side of him—and maybe the one who still feared his good fortune might not last—had been leaning toward a sled, a good one, but a bike was doable. Hell, he could do a bike and a sled.

"Anything else?" Santa said in his booming voice.

"I get another one?" Zach asked.

"Of course. Anything you want!" Santa said, winking at Rachel. Apparently Santa had them pegged, and his aunt and uncle ran the town's only toy store. But so far no one had objected to that little conflict of interest.

Zach hesitated once again. "Anything?"

Santa gave a hearty "Ho, ho, ho," and nodded.

Zach, very solemnly, very hopefully asked, "Could you bring my mommy back?"

* * *

Rachel held Grace close, singing to her and swaying back and forth on her feet. She was standing by the window, and everyone in the neighborhood had their Christmas lights on. Grace was wide awake, still staring at the lights, trying to reach out and touch them.

"You want her back, too? Don't you?" Rachel asked softly. "You want your mommy?"

Rachel had done it again, she realized. She'd been thinking of herself and her marriage, what she wanted and thought she needed, maybe what she thought she deserved. She hadn't been thinking of Zach or Emma or the baby, except to tell herself she could be so much better a mother to them than this woman who'd abandoned them and never came back.

But the children still loved that other woman. She was still their mother, and they wanted her back. Rachel had forgotten all about that, and she was so ashamed.

She kissed the baby's soft cheek, smoothed down her wispy hair and put her down, then went in and kissed a sleepy Zach and a troubled Emma.

Suddenly she just couldn't be here, couldn't stand even her own thoughts. Everything was swirling around inside her head—all the questions, all the doubts, and none of the answers. She didn't know what to do, hadn't felt this lost since her mother died.

She ran downstairs, headed for the back door.

"Rachel?" Sam was there, coming toward her.

"I—I forgot something," she stammered. "Something I have to do . . . I have to go out."

"Now?" he asked.

"Yes."

"What's wrong?"

"I . . . I just have to go," she insisted.

She grabbed her coat and her gloves, shoved her feet into her boots before he could catch her, and she ran out the back door. Literally ran.

"Rachel?" he called after her. "Wait!"

She hadn't grabbed her purse, she realized. She didn't have her keys. And she just had to go. There were tears streaming down her cheeks and the sidewalk was slick. She knew Sam was worried, but she had to get away.

She walked for blocks and blocks, and finally the sound of singing brought her out of her daze. She looked up and realized she was only a half a block from the church. Standing outside, she could hear the words to a familiar Christmas song drifting out, a song about having a merry, little Christmas, if the fates allowed. Rachel winced at the idea of her holiday or anything else in life being left up to fate. Fate had not been kind to her.

Still, she was cold, and the church seemed to beckon to her. She slipped in the back door, finding herself in the middle of practice for the Christmas service. The choir was down front singing, the organist playing, the children arranged in a scene from the first Christmas, complete with the three wise men and a little boy she knew from down the street costumed as a glittering cardboard star.

Rachel sank into a seat in the last pew at the very back of the church and hung her head and cried. Father Tim, the man who'd presided over her grandfather's funeral, her daughter's, her mother's, found her there. He sat down beside her and didn't say a word at first, just handed her a cup of what turned out to be hot cider. She took it between her cold hands and sipped slowly, her tears still falling.

"It can't be that bad," he said finally. "It's Christmas."

Rachel tried to smile and failed. He was one of the most cheerful people she'd ever known.

"Want to tell me what's wrong?"

"Do you have all night?" she asked.

"I know it's not that bad," he claimed. "Tell me the worst of it. The absolute worst."

"I've done it all wrong," she said. "Everything."

"Absolutely everything in your whole life, Rachel?"

She did smile a bit then. He always knew how to make people smile, too. "Is that so hard to believe?"

"Yes. I know you. I would never believe you've done absolutely everything wrong. A few things. But not everything."

"I haven't been fair to Sam," she said. "Or to Emma and Zach and Grace. You know about them, don't you?"

"The children left at the Drifter? Of course. You and Sam took them in. Surely that wasn't wrong. Surely that's one little point in your favor."

"I didn't do it out of the goodness of my heart. Miriam bullied me into it. She had to, because all I was thinking about was myself. I was thinking that I was scared, and I didn't want to get hurt again. I wasn't thinking about them at all."

"But you took them into your home, and I saw the five of you tonight in town. They looked quite happy. I'd say you've done them some good."

"They've done more for me and Sam than we could ever do for them."

Father Tim gave her a stern look. "Rachel, I'd say you've done a whole lot if you managed to soothe their fears at a time like this. They must have been terrified, being left there like that. So you helped each other. Nothing wrong with that. Nothing selfish about it, either."

"I want to keep them," she confessed. "I thought if they could stay, we could all be a family, and that Sam . . . Sam would stay, too. And everything would be okay."

"Sam?" He gave her a gentle smile. "I heard something about that. You can tell me, if you want."

"He's leaving me," she said miserably. "Right after Christmas. At least, he was, before the children came."

"You've agreed to separate?"

"No. He's decided to go. He hasn't told me yet. I just . . . I heard him on the phone with Rick Brown. You know? He lives over on Elm Street. He has a little apartment above his shop, and Stuart Ames is living there now, but he's moving out. And Sam's moving in. Right after Christmas. I hadn't told anybody that." She hadn't been able to say it out loud. "Not until just now."

"So you and Sam have been having problems. He was going to leave, but now he might not. Because of these three children? And you think you're selfish for wanting to give them that home. And keep your marriage together."

"I was just thinking of me. I'm always thinking of me and what I want. I saw that tonight. All they really want is their mother," she said. "How could I want them so badly? How could I be wishing so hard and praying that they could stay with me and Sam, when all they really want is their mother?"

"You want to take care of them," he said. "That's not a bad thing."

"But I wasn't putting their needs ahead of mine. Or

Sam's. Maybe Sam needs to leave me. Maybe it's unfair of me to even try to stop him."

"Do you love him?" Father Tim asked.

"Yes."

"Does he love you?"

"I don't know," she whispered. She certainly hadn't
found the courage to ask that. Still, "How could he still
love me, if he's going to leave me?"

"He's the only one who can tell you that, Rachel."

"I've been too scared to talk to him about it, and I
guess I hoped we'd never have that conversation. I
hoped the children would stay and Sam would stay because of them, and I'd get what I wanted. *Me.*"

"Could you be a good mother to those children?" he
asked.

"I hope so."

"I think so. After all, you're doing it right now,
Rachel. You're asking what would be best for them,
not you. That's what mothers do."

"But I—"

"We all think of ourselves. It's only natural. And it's
not such a bad thing. Figuring out what you want in
life, what's important to you, and how to get it, is usually what makes people happy in this world. Provided
we've got our priorities straight and are after the right
things. What do you really want? Deep down in your
heart?"

"I want Sam to be happy, and I want the children to
be safe and happy and loved," she said.

"And you'd really like it if Sam and the children
could be happy with you?" he suggested.

"Yes."

"If they could only be happy without you, you'd let
them go?"

"Yes," she cried.

"So you're not putting your welfare above their own. You just love them and want to take care of them. You want them in your life."

"Yes."

"I don't suppose you climbed onto Santa's lap and told him all that?"

"No." She laughed.

Father Tim nodded toward the altar, lined with greenery and candles and all sorts of finery, and Rachel's gaze caught on the stained-glass window behind the altar, a depiction of Jesus awash with light, ascending into heaven. The whole image seemed to glow tonight. There was such power there. It seemed to radiate warmth and reassurance and something else that just made her heart feel so heavy it might overflow in a moment. She wanted so much right now. She needed so much.

"Want to sit here and tell the big guy?" Father Tim asked.

"The big guy?" Rachel laughed again. "We haven't exactly been on speaking terms lately."

"Not since you lost your baby," Father Tim said. "I won't pretend to think I know how that felt, because I don't. But I asked you one question back then, and you weren't ready to hear it. I think maybe you are now."

"What's that?"

"There are some things you can only take on faith, times when that's all we have to fall back on. I want you to look in your heart. Deep inside. You've been a part of this church your whole life, and I think that still means something to you. But I know, too, that real faith comes in times like this. When we're tested. It's not until we ask ourselves the really hard questions that we know whether or not we truly believe," he said. "So I want you to think about this. Where do you think she is, Rachel?"

"My baby?"

"Yes. In your heart, don't you know? Don't you know she's with God, and she's fine? That He's taking good care of her? Don't you believe you'll see her again someday? Because that's what true faith is. It's knowing. I think in your heart, if you dig down deep, you'll see that you know. She's just fine where she is. I know it's terrible that you had so little time with her here, but you don't have to worry about her. She'll be yours again one day. Do you believe that?"

It was a question Rachel usually avoided at all costs. Where was her baby? Had she simply ceased to exist? Or was she out there somewhere? Sometimes she had nightmares that her baby did exist somewhere, that she was crying and she needed Rachel and Rachel simply couldn't get to her.

So usually, she tried not to think about it at all.

But she'd been raised in the church, had sat here at Sunday school and grown up on the stories in the Bible.

Stories? Or something real? Something she believed in and could rely upon? Was this all there was to this earth? Only what she could see and touch? She didn't believe that. She couldn't.

Was someone watching over her and everyone else? Some order to what sometimes seemed chaos? Some master plan?

"There are so many things I don't understand. Things that made me so angry."

"I know. Me, too."

"You?"

"I'm as human as you are," he said.

"But—"

"Now we're talking mysteries of the universe, Rachel. I don't have those answers. I struggle with them myself. Are there things in this world I'll never understand? Yes. Do they trouble me? Yes. Do I get angry at times and even ask God what in the world He thinks He's doing? Yes. Even I do that. But I still believe. I believe in Him and His innate goodness and His guiding hand in my life and in yours. I think you believe in all that, too."

Rachel looked back up at the stained-glass window, at beautiful golden light streaming out of heaven and Jesus' open arms, waiting, just waiting.

"Think He's going to wink at you or something?" Father Tim asked.

Rachel smiled through her tears. "Does He wink at you?"

"No. I stopped asking Him to. I stopped asking for proof or for any kind of a sign. That's the faith part, Rachel. The hard part. Sometimes you have to take it all on faith, because that's all you've got. Not just faith in God. Faith in yourself, too. Faith in the people around you, the people who love you. Sometimes you have to make that leap. Reach out to the people you love, the people who need you. Believe that things are all going to work out somehow."

"I don't know if I remember how to do that," she said.

"Of course you do. You took the children into your home and you've taken them into your heart."

"That was an act of pure selfishness."

"It was an act of faith. At worst, something you did because you needed them and had faith that they could help you. At best—which I choose to believe—something you did because they needed you, too, and you believed you could help them. And it looks like it worked out just fine."

He gave her a handkerchief, and Rachel dried her tears.

"Think about it. And if you need to talk some more, I'll be here." Father Tim nodded toward the image of God and put his hand on her shoulder, smiling at her. "So will He."

"Thank you," she said.

"My pleasure. I've been waiting for you."

"All this time?"

He nodded. "I knew you'd come back sooner or later."

"Faith?" she suggested.

"Of course. I always knew it was somewhere inside of you."

Chapter 13

S am was about to go out of his mind.

Rachel had been gone for an hour and a half. It was below freezing outside now, and he had a houseful of kids. He couldn't go look for her.

And he was scared. Scared in an illogical way of what she might do. Scared he might lose her forever. It was the kind of fear that grabbed him by the throat, making it almost impossible to talk, grabbed him in a tight band around his chest and made it hard to breathe.

He couldn't imagine his life without Rachel.

He could start calling her family and tell them she was gone, but they'd want an explanation, more of one than he'd given her father a few nights ago. He could call the sheriff. Not because he thought someone had grabbed her or hurt her, but because the deputies would keep an eye out for her. They were certain to spot her before long. But again, there'd be explanations to give, and he didn't know what he'd say.

He was afraid Rachel was upset because of what Zach said. They'd both stood there, frozen with guilt for wanting these children so badly while Zach told Santa that all he really wanted for Christmas was to have his mother back.

Maybe that's what Sam needed to give the boy, too.

Frowning, Sam looked at the clock once more and then his gaze caught on the road map on the table in the corner. He'd been sitting here staring at the map, looking for a clue, when Rachel had run out of the house.

And now there it was. Right in front of him.

It was as if the name leaped out at him.

Shepherdsville.

Zach said the town had a funny name. Like a dog. That must have been the one he was talking about. Shepherdsville was just across the border in Indiana, about forty-five miles from here. Emma said when her mother left, she promised to be back that day. She should have been able to make the trip there and back in a day with no problem. Except she hadn't come back.

Sam had found it easy to blame her for that at first, to think she must be scum to leave her children that way. But these were good children. Well behaved, well mannered, self-assured. Obviously someone had taken good care of them, at least at some point as they were growing up.

So, if she was a good mother, running away from an abusive husband, but she had to go back there for some reason. . . . Could she have left them, thinking they were safer here in a motel with Emma than in Shepherdsville with a man who beat her?

Sam stared down at the map and frowned.

He'd never been particularly good at taking care of the people he loved, and he had to do something.

He'd had enough experience with the social services system not to trust it to take care of the kids. Maybe that wasn't fair, because he knew Miriam, knew she worked hard and that she cared as much as she could about everyone she tried to help, as much as she could without going nuts doing the job. And he knew it was a hard job. He hadn't been fair to her over Will. It wasn't her fault. He was sure she'd done all she could. But he didn't trust the system.

Shepherdsville was only forty-five minutes away, and it wasn't a very big town. It was up to him, he thought. It wouldn't be that hard to spend the day there and see what he could find out. He didn't have to tell anyone what he was doing. If it was a dead end, it was a dead end. If he found the kids' mother and she had a good explanation for what she'd done, maybe he'd tell her where she could find her children. If their father was there and he'd done the things Emma believed, Sam didn't know what he'd do to the man. Likely get himself arrested.

No, he thought. He wouldn't. Because that would lead the man right to his children, and Sam wasn't going to be the one who did that.

He'd made up his mind—he was going to that town to see what he could find out—when he heard the back door closing softly and hurried to it, expecting to find Rachel there. She wasn't. And there was no way anyone had slipped past him and gone upstairs.

Which meant . . . Someone had gone outside. At this hour?

Sam pulled open the door and saw someone disappearing around the side of the house and it didn't look like his wife.

"Emma?" he called out.

She turned for a moment, a lost little girl wrapped up in her new coat and with her new boots on her feet, something he couldn't make out clutched in her hand. What in the world?

Sam waited, thinking she'd come back. But he'd made that mistake once already tonight. He grabbed his coat off the peg on the laundry room wall and took off after her.

"Emma!" he said again as he came to the front of the house and found her standing on the sidewalk on the opposite side of the street. She just looked at him, all sad eyes and what he suspected were big tears. Was every female he knew crying tonight?

Sam was afraid she'd make him chase her, but she didn't. She stopped right there, staring up at their house. So he took his time walking across the street to her, wishing he knew this child better, wishing he would somehow just know what to say to ease her mind.

"Out for a stroll?" he said, as casually as he could manage and noting that she was in her nightgown. It was long and the edges were hanging down below her coat, brushing the top of the snow. She was going to freeze.

"No," she said. "Just to here."

"What are you doing, Emma?" She finally looked up at him and he frowned. Those were definitely tears. Emma, who'd been so brave, was now reduced to tears.

"I had to see the house," she said.

"Why?"

"It's a secret."

"I think you're going to have to share it with me, Em."

She frowned up at him, tearing up again. "My mom called me that."

"Does that mean I shouldn't?" Sam asked gently.

Her bottom lip trembling, she said, "I don't know."

He slipped an arm around her thin shoulders and pulled her to his side, something he'd wanted to do for a long time. She bent her head against his chest and rested there for a moment.

"You want her back, too. I know that."

She nodded. "Do you believe in magic?"

"You mean like rabbits coming out of hats and stuff like that?"

"No. I know that's not real."

"Then what?"

"Signs?" she tried. "Do you believe in signs."

"I don't know. Do you?"

"I want to."

"What kind of sign, Emma?"

"This."

She finally showed him what she'd been holding so closely to her, hidden in the folds of her coat. It was a snow globe. He took it in his hands. A cheap, plastic copy of Rachel's grandfather's work, the kind they mass-produced here at the factory in town.

"It's this house, isn't it?"

"Yes," he said.

"It's one of my most favorite things. Zach's and the baby's, too."

"Where did you get it?"

"I don't know. For Christmas, maybe. A couple of years ago. I've had it for a long time, and I love looking at it. It's so beautiful, and I thought it was a sign. That I had this, and I always thought nothing bad could ever happen in a place like this. And now I'm here. I'm living in this house . . ."

"So you thought everything was going to be okay?"

"I was sure of it. I came outside and checked the first night we were here, and even before the Christmas decorations were up, I could tell it really is the same house. That's why I knew it was okay that we were here."

"You checked? The first night you were here?"

She nodded.

Sam decided to let that one go. They had bigger things to worry about tonight. "So you thought everything was going to work out? But now it's almost Christmas and your mother's still not back. Now you're not sure."

Emma nodded.

Sam turned her fully into his arms, drawing her close and wrapping her up inside his coat with him. She acted so much like a grown-up at times, he often forgot how little she was. She felt so fragile now, seemed so young.

He thought about all the platitudes he could offer her, about things just magically working out and signs and hope, and he just didn't have it in him to say any of those things. Not now.

He had no idea if she'd ever see her mother again, and he'd love to promise her that he and Rachel were going to make it and that Emma and her brother and sister could stay. That they'd love them and keep them safe forever. But Sam knew there were damned few promises he could make with any certainty, damned few certainties at all. So he thought of what he could do.

"Sometimes, you just don't know what's going to happen, Emma. Sometimes you're going along and things are fine and someone comes along and yanks the rug out from under you. I know that's scary. But I'm afraid it's just the way things are sometimes. But it helps to have people around you that you can count on. I know it's been a lot easier for Zach and Grace because they've got you, and you're so good with them. It's been easier for me and Rachel because you're here, too."

"I'm glad we're here," she said. "If we can't be with Mom, I'm glad we're here."

"I'm glad, too," he said. "And you can count on us. Will you do that, Emma? Will you let us do what we can to help you? And when you're worried or scared, you should come to us, okay?"

She nodded. "I will."

"Good. I don't know where your mother is. I don't know what happened to her, but I was thinking that I could go look for her."

She brightened at that. "You would?"

"Yes. And I don't want you to be scared of that. I don't have to tell anybody why I'm looking for her or where you and Zach and Grace are. I'll just go see if I can find her."

"My dad . . ." she began. "He gets really mad sometimes."

"I'm not going to let him find you."

"But, he might . . . hurt you."

Sam would like to see him try. "I think I can take care of myself, Emma. It's different when a man's trying something like that with another man. It's not as easy to push a man around as it is a child or a woman. "

"Okay."

"So tomorrow, I'll go see what I can find out about your mother."

"Do you want me to tell you her name? It's not the same as my dad's. Not anymore," she said. "We changed it. We changed 'em all. So if anybody asked, you still wouldn't know my dad's name. You still couldn't tell. Nobody could send us back to him."

Sam hesitated. They were splitting hairs here. He didn't want to know her father's name before because he didn't intend to ever say anything about her father to anyone. But if that's where Emma's mother went and something happened to her . . . The situation had changed. He wasn't sure he could explain that to Emma without scaring her. Shepherdsville was a fairly small town. He didn't think it would be that hard to find out about her mother.

"You don't have to tell me her name," he said. "But she was going to Shepherdsville, in Indiana, wasn't she?"

"You know?" she asked breathlessly.

"I just figured it out. But I haven't told anyone."

"Okay."

"Okay. Let me see what I can find out. If I need her name, I'll call from there. We'll let this be our secret, okay? I don't think we should tell anyone about it until we know something, okay?"

"I can keep a secret," she said.

"I know. I'm going to do my best to bring her back to you, Emma."

"She's going to be in trouble, isn't she? For leaving us like that. I heard that lady—Miriam—talking about it. Mothers get in trouble for things like this."

"They can. It depends on why she left you, why she didn't come back."

"Something must have happened to her," Emma cried. "She's a good mother. Something must have happened."

"I'll find out," he promised. "Do you trust me to do that, Emma?"

"Yes," she cried.

"Okay."

He looked down at the snow globe, still clutched in her hand like a talisman to ward off evil, and thought about the chances of Emma having this with her when she ended up here. He thought about signs and faith and hope and what little he had left that he truly believed in, that he'd ever believed in in his entire life.

Of course, Emma was here, and she was safe. She and her brother and sister had arrived here just in time to save his wife from what he feared now would have been a serious depression and they'd gotten him and Rachel to talk about things they hadn't dared mention in years. What were the chances of that? Of anything saving them at this late date?

"You don't believe, do you?" Emma asked solemnly, holding her prize possession out to him.

Sam took it and gave it a little shake. The snow started tumbling down on the little house, and it did indeed look like something out of a fairy tale. He'd thought that the first Christmas after he and Rachel had finished restoring the house and then spent money they didn't have to deck it out for Christmas. It had looked like a fairy-tale place.

Of course, they'd already lost their baby by then and Rachel's grandfather had been sinking fast. Her mother was soon to follow. A pretty place didn't make a pretty life for the people inside of it.

"Rachel said she used to believe this was a magical house," Emma said.

He wondered if that was before or after they'd come to live here and thought it must have been before. And there was no sense thinking of things like that. They couldn't go back, and he wasn't sure if they could go forward. He wasn't sure of anything anymore except that he was going to do all he could to help these lost, scared kids.

"I don't know what I believe in anymore, Emma. But I'll go tomorrow to look for your mother," he said gently. "Can we go inside now?"

"I guess so."

He left his arm around her shoulders and kept her close. "You have to promise me something else."

"What?"

"You will never sneak out of this house again."

"Okay. I'm sorry."

"It's all right. I just worry about you. I don't want anything to happen to you."

"Okay."

He walked inside and up the stairs with her, waited out in the hall while she changed into a dry nightgown, and then tucked her into bed and kissed her cheek.

"Sam?" she whispered when he was nearly out the bedroom door.

He turned back around. "Yes."

"You're really a nice man. I wasn't sure when we first came here. I was—"

"Scared of me, Emma?" he suggested.

"A little."

"I'm sorry. Rachel and I were going through some rough times."

"Because of the baby?"

"That was part of it. That's always been part of it. But other things, too. We haven't had a lot of reasons to be happy lately. But it's better now. Having you and Zach and Grace here has helped a lot."

"You're going to be sad again if we go?"

"I don't know what's going to happen here if you go," he told her quite honestly.

"We could come back and visit," Emma suggested.

Sam nodded, touched. "That might help."

"I'd miss you both if we left."

"We'd miss you, too," he said. So much so that they wouldn't survive it? Sam just didn't know. He turned out the light and said, "Go to sleep, Emma. Try not to worry so much."

And then he walked downstairs, feeling about a thousand years old and every bit as lost as he'd ever been in his life.

He walked into the front room and found his wife there, her arms wrapped around her midsection as she stared down into the fire. Sam was so shocked he nearly stumbled over a toy Zach had left on the floor. He swore, barely managed to catch himself. Rachel jumped and whirled around herself.

He checked his first impulse, which was to grab her and demand to know where she'd been and what she had been thinking worrying him so. But there was something in the way she stood there, the way she held her body. He was suddenly afraid of what she might tell him and what had sent her rushing off into the night away from him.

It had torn him up to see her walking away from him. He wanted her so badly he ached, wanted her in every way a man could want a woman.

There wasn't as much standing between them as there used to be. It didn't seem as insurmountable as before. But he was going to Shepherdsville tomorrow. He might well find the children's mother, and then where would he and Rachel be?

"Hi," she whispered.

"Where have you been?" he practically growled, as he had at the kids that first night. When he was worried or scared, he sounded way too much like his grandfather.

"I just had to get away for a few minutes."

"Rachel, it's been nearly two hours."

"Oh." She looked surprised. "I'm sorry. You were worried?"

He wanted to throttle her. "Yes, I was worried."

"I'm sorry."

She looked a bit dazed, and she'd definitely been crying. "Where did you go?"

"Walking."

"In this? It's twenty-eight degrees out there." He knew because he'd checked. It was probably colder than that by now.

"I ended up at church. The kids are practicing for the Christmas program, and Father Tim was there. We talked. About a lot of things."

Sam waited, wondering what took her there. Rachel hadn't had much use for church in years. She'd dragged him there with her when they'd been younger, and he'd gone to please her. And maybe he'd found some comfort there, too, before. Before they'd both gotten so angry at the world and felt so betrayed by everything, so lost.

"We talked about the baby," she said.

Always the baby, he thought. They couldn't seem to get past the loss.

"It helped," she said. "And talking to you helped. Or maybe I'm just ready, finally, to deal with it. We never really dealt with it, Sam, and it's been like a poison to us."

He knew that. He'd just never known how to change that.

"Do you ever think about where she is now?"

"No." He wouldn't let himself.

"I used to try not to. I used to have nightmares where I'd hear her crying and I couldn't find her, but I thought about it tonight. Father Tim made me, and she's okay, Sam. I know she's okay."

"How do you know?" How could anyone?

"I just do. I believe it. And I'm not worried about her anymore. I may always be sad that we had so little time with her, but even that doesn't seem to have the sting it used to. I think she's out there waiting for us somewhere. I think we'll have her again someday."

Sam would like to believe that. As skeptical as he'd always been about anything to do with heaven and anyone's ideas of what it would be like, he would love to believe that their daughter was somewhere safe and happy and waiting for them, that they'd see her again someday. He'd never seen Rachel so calm when she talked about their daughter.

He frowned at her, looking at her more closely now. Yes, there was evidence of tears in her eyes and on her cheeks, but she was different, too.

"I'm going to put this behind me," she said. "For the first time, I believe I can. When I was on my way back here, I ended up walking past the Parker mansion. I don't think I ever saw it at night, not once all the work was done. And I stood there staring up at the windows I did, and they're beautiful, Sam."

"They are," he said.

"And I thought, I did that. They were such a mess when they came down one by one. There were all those little bits of glass, some of them dirty, some of them broken and chipped, some of them worn down over time, the colors all fading away. I remember how overwhelming the whole project seemed at first. I didn't think I'd ever manage it or why they would have put such faith in me. But you told me how to do it, and before you, my grandfather had. You said to take it one step at a time, one piece, that it was like a puzzle and if I stood there just staring at how big it was and how much had to be done, I'd never finish it. I'd likely never start it. I'd give up without really trying.

"It took the better part of a year, and there were lots of times when I thought I'd never be able to put all the pieces back together in the right way, never make anything of it. But looking at it tonight, I can see that I did. There was a place for everything. I put it all back together and it's beautiful now," she said. "Do you know what I'm getting at?"

"I'm not sure."

"This is my place. It's a mess right now, and I've been standing back staring at it and thinking it was just too much, too overwhelming, that I'd never get it all back together. I think that paralyzed me for a while, but I'm done letting it. I'm ready to go to work now, no matter what it takes, no matter how much time, and you and I both know how to do that, Sam. We both put things back together. I'm going to stop being so sad and so angry all the time. I'm going to believe that you married me because you loved me—"

"I did," he said, feeling hopeful for the first time that he'd actually made her believe that.

"And I know I married you for the same reason. I will never understand or be able to explain all the things that happened to us later, but I think things can get better, Sam. I think we can put all the pieces back together. I have so much faith in you—"

"In me?"

"Yes. And in us."

Oh, damn. Look what she was giving him. So much faith. He never dreamed . . . And he owed her. He owed her the truth about himself. "Rachel, you don't really know me. There are things I never told you."

"About when your parents died?"

He nodded. "Things I never wanted you or anyone else to know."

"Sam, it doesn't matter. It doesn't change who you are now. It all happened before we ever met. All those things are just what made you the man I've always known, the one I've always loved."

He thought about that. Really thought about it. By the time she'd met him, all of those things had already happened. She'd never known him the way he'd been before, had never known the little boy nobody wanted, who got passed from house to house seemingly at a whim. He'd never wanted her to know. He hated that boy, hated the weakness in him, the neediness, the sorrow.

All that had ever come out was the rage. By the time someone found Sam's paternal grandfather and convinced the man to take him in, Sam was capable of being every bit as nasty as his grandfather. He had been consumed with anger and stubborn pride and shame, illogical as that was.

"I can't imagine what you ever saw in me," he said.

"I saw you, Sam, and all those things you tried so hard to hide."

And in her, he had seen everything he'd ever wanted. She was the most beloved daughter of one of the oldest families in town, with two parents who obviously loved her, three sisters and a brother, all of whom indulged her terribly, plus a host of aunts, uncles, and cousins. Her roots were as deeply imbedded in this town as the massive hundred-year-old oak tree in the town square. Her place in the world had been absolutely assured. It was here, in that old house of her grandparents', surrounded by people who loved her.

"You should have hated me on sight," he said.

"Never. I could never hate you."

Somehow, she'd been practically the only one in town to see through that sullen look that was so often on his face. The one he hid that pitiful little boy he used to be behind. That and the I-don't-give-a-damn attitude.

"I would have thought you'd run from me as fast as you could," he said. Instead, she'd followed him around the way Zach did now, giving him those same shy smiles and that insane amount of trust Zach did. Why would either of them have ever trusted him? Or wanted to be with him?

"Sam, think about it. I've spent my whole life running after you."

And she had. She'd been as gentle and happy and hopeful as he was sad and angry and gruff. She'd always been so sure she could draw him into her life, into her family and make a place for him there, just as strong a place as she had. She just kept coming back, kept after him with a stubborn kindness and teenage admiration he hadn't been able to resist.

"I tried, Rachel," he confessed. "I tried so hard to resist you."

"I know," she said.

He'd never quite believed he was good enough for

her. Her family saw that, even if she did not. But there was only so much a man could do when faced with a woman who represented everything he'd ever wanted, everything he'd never had. She'd accepted him just as he was, and saw him as he'd always wanted to be, believed in him somehow. And one day, he'd given himself just one oh-so-innocent taste of her, and she'd gone straight to his head.

There'd really been no going back then. Not for either of them.

He still wanted her every bit as much. Wanted all that kindness and happiness and sunshine. He wondered if there was any sunshine left inside of her, and thought maybe he was seeing it tonight for the first time in ages.

"I guess I'm still chasing you, Sam," she said. "I've missed you."

Like he had in the old days, he took a step back, thought about saying something to try to make light of the situation. To dismiss everything that had always been between them.

But this was Rachel, and it was gut-level honesty time.

They'd hurt each other so much over the years, and he'd decided, right before the children came, that he simply couldn't do it anymore. He was sick and tired of feeling like he'd failed her in every way possible and he'd given up hope that they'd ever be happy together. Too many bad things stood between them for that.

So now, here they were, about to get their hearts broken again if he was any judge of the situation. And he still wanted her every bit as much as he always had, probably more. Still needed her. Still wished for something he could give her, and still worried that someday she'd see the real him and not the man she'd always believed he could be.

"I can't do this halfway, Rachel. Not anymore."

She put her hands against his chest, fingers splayed wide, palms warm enough that he felt it through the fabric of his shirt. It seemed like it had been decades since she touched him.

"What do you mean, halfway?"

"It means I don't want to live the way we have been. I can't."

"I don't want to, either, Sam. I want so much more. I want to give you so much more. I think we can make a new start. Right now."

"With these children," he said.

"Maybe."

"We don't know what's going to happen—"

"We never really know. Maybe for a while we thought we did, but we were wrong. Whatever happens tomorrow or the next day or the next, I want to spend those days with you."

He closed his eyes, letting the words sink into him, letting her touch him, running her hands lightly up and down his chest, soothing him and heating him through and through and making him want to grab her and take her upstairs and kiss every inch of her. That used to make things better. At least for a while. While he could hold her close and feel as if he were truly a part of her and lie to himself that he'd never lose her.

"You don't really know me," he said.

"I don't know the little boy who lost his mother when he was so young. But I know the man. He's my husband. He has been for twelve years."

He waited, not saying anything, not able to.

"Sam, whatever it was, whatever happened, it's not going to change the way I feel about you."

"I never wanted you to see me that way," he said. "To look at me that way."

"What way?"

"The way you look at Zach. The way I do," he choked out.

"How do I look at him? Like I pity him?"

Sam nodded. "I never wanted your pity, Rachel."

"I don't recall ever offering it. Not to you or to him. I love Zach," she said. "I hate what's happened to him, and I wish I could take him in my arms and make everything all better for him. I think about those things when I see him. But mostly, I just think about how precious he is to me and how much I love him. I couldn't help myself any more with him than I could with you."

And still, he stood there.

"I've never been any good at hanging on to the people I love," he said.

"I am," she said, wrapping her arms around him. "I'm never going to walk away from you. I'm never going to leave you, and I'll never ask you to go."

And maybe she wouldn't. After all, she never had. Despite all they'd been through. That should have told him something about her and about the two of them. She wasn't going to give up on him, and there was a new strength and determination to her these days. There were times when she seemed determined to have him back, the way things had been before.

She was right here, too, and he was trying so hard to keep his hands off her. He'd been counting on it getting easier with each passing day, but the last few days, it had been anything but easy.

"Rachel." He stepped back, trying not to look at the hurt on her face.

He'd almost given up hope of her ever really wanting him again. But everything could change in a heartbeat. He could find the children's mother tomorrow, and then where would he and Rachel be? He couldn't go back to what they'd had before.

So when she came toward him again, he blurted out the only thing he could think of to keep her away, the worst thing. "I had a brother once."

"What?" she said.

"A brother. Four years younger than I am. You asked me to tell you the worst of it. I had a brother. I told you I have a hard time hanging on to the people I love . . ."

"What happened to him, Sam?"

"I lost him," he said.

"*Lost?* How?"

"At one of the places we went to live. I think, the third place we went, after some time at our great aunt's and our other grandmother's. It was a couple having problems having a baby. They decided to take a chance on me and Robbie. He was only about a year old when our parents died, so he would have been about two and a half when we went to live in that house. I think right from the start, they wanted him. He was so much littler. He didn't have any memory of our parents. I think they liked that. I think they believed they could erase any memories he had of any other home but theirs, and I was the only thing standing in their way. I was . . . angry. I was so angry, Rachel. And Robbie . . . he was mine. I was supposed to take care of him. I was all he had left."

"And he was all you had left," she said.

Sam nodded. His heart hurt. It hurt so bad.

"Anyway, they wanted him, and they didn't want me. And in the end, they got him. I got into trouble at school one too many times, and before long I was seeing a counselor and labeled a troublemaker. They told everyone all kinds of stuff about me, and I was so mad by then. I knew what they were after. They adopted Robbie, and they gave me to social services. To a foster home. I didn't care about anything then. Not after they took my brother from me."

"You never saw him again?"

"Not until right after you and I lost our baby."

"You found him?"

"I had to know what happened to him. Losing the baby . . . I just had to know."

"And he was okay?"

"Sure. Had a great life. Had no idea who I was."

"Oh, Sam," she gasped.

He shrugged his nothing-can-hurt-me shrug. What a crock.

"You left it at that?" Rachel asked. "With him not knowing?"

"He didn't even recognize me. He introduced himself to me using their last name and asked if he was supposed to know me." Sam winced at the way that hurt, even now. "What was there to say to him? I told him I thought I knew him, asked him about his family. He was happy, Rachel. They'd never even told him about me or our parents. He was only about four when they got rid of me. I guess it's not that surprising he wouldn't remember."

"And you just let it go? You let him go?"

"Think about it. He missed all the crap. Losing his parents and getting passed around from place to place.

I wouldn't give that back to him for anything in this world. As far as he knew, he just had two parents who'd always loved him and wanted him. The truth was that his so-called parents had been lying to him his whole life and had neatly disposed of me. Do you think he would have thanked me for telling him that? It would have destroyed his whole life, and I know what that feels like. I wouldn't do it to him."

"Oh, Sam," she said. It seemed that was all she could say.

He finally looked at her, not wanting to think about what he'd see in her eyes but unable to stop himself from looking. Pity? He couldn't say. Horror? That part he was sure of. Shock? No surprise there. Anger? He loved her for that, for her outrage on his behalf.

"He'd be an adult now," she said.

"Who would still be seeing his whole world fall apart if I told him the truth."

"Oh, Sam. I love you," she said, looking as fiercely protective of him as anyone had ever been. "And I want you. I want you here with me."

Sam actually smiled then. He took her chin in his hand and filled his lungs with the sweet scent of her, rubbed his cheek against the side of her face.

"I've missed you, Rachel. I don't want you to be hurt anymore."

And he was afraid he was going to hurt her. Maybe if he didn't find the kids' mother. Maybe if no one ever found her. . . . What a terrible thought. Sam was ashamed of himself for how badly he wanted that to happen, so the kids could stay here with him and his wife and maybe they would all be okay.

But until he knew, there was nothing to say at the moment.

"It's late," he said, pulling away from her. "You should go to bed."

She wavered back and forth on her feet for a moment, as if she'd taken a blow. And he felt like a heel once again. He thought she might argue with him once again. Or even worse, that he might touch her and simply not be able to let her go this time. But she didn't. Her gaze dropped to the floor, and without letting him see the look on her face again, she turned and headed for the stairs.

He stayed down there, trying to close his mind to everything and everyone. Trying to block out everything but what he had to do.

Tomorrow was Christmas Eve. He'd go to Shepherdsville, and he'd try to find out something about the kids' mother. And then . . .

He had no idea what was going to happen then.

Chapter 14

On the eleventh day of Christmas, Rachel could have wept when she woke up and found Sam gone with nothing but a hastily scribbled note saying he'd driven to the next county. After all he'd told her last night, he'd turned around and left before she could say another word this morning.

Two steps forward, one step back. Or maybe she'd gotten the ratios wrong. One step forward, two steps back. They couldn't make it that way.

Rachel was standing there in the kitchen still holding his note when Emma came downstairs, Emma who looked as sad as Rachel felt. They stood there staring solemnly at each other, and finally Rachel held out her arms and said, "Come here."

Emma dipped her head and stumbled forward, her arms outstretched, and soon they were standing there holding each other in the cool of the early morning in the kitchen.

"What's wrong?" Rachel asked.

"Nothing," Emma said, apparently having learned a thing or two from Rachel. "Where's Sam?"

"Gone," Rachel said. "Work."

"Work?" Emma frowned.

"I assumed it was work. What did you think he was going to do today?"

The girl looked surprised and then she looked guilty. What in the world? "Emma, do you know something about where Sam is?"

"Yes. But I can't tell. It's a secret. I promised him."

Rachel frowned. She would love to believe it was something other than work that had sent Sam out of the house so early this morning.

She was running out of time. It was Christmas Eve. What had he said that day on the phone about leaving? Tuesday after Christmas? Just her luck, Christmas came on a Monday this year. Two days, and he was supposed to go.

Merry Christmas, Rachel, and by the way, I'm leaving you.

"Are you okay?" Emma asked.

Rachel didn't know what to say, and then she remembered Father Tim and what he'd said. This was the hard part. The faith part.

So it was going to be harder than she thought. She couldn't shy away from it for that reason.

"Okay," she said, pulling herself together and looking at the worry on Emma's face. "It's Christmas Eve. We have things to do."

"What things?" Emma asked skeptically.

"Things." There must be something. And then she remembered, "Presents? Do we have enough presents? Besides the ones Santa's going to bring, I mean?"

"I know Santa doesn't bring presents," Emma said. "But Zach doesn't. Neither does Grace. So I pretend."

"Oh." Of course. Emma was almost twelve. She'd know.

"You didn't get enough to do Santa?" she whispered, seeming truly worried now.

"No. It's not that. I was just thinking about Sam."

"You didn't get Sam anything?" Emma asked.

"I did."

She'd gotten him some very practical things. He was a practical man, after all, but some occasions called for more than the practical. Surely this Christmas was one of those times. Months ago, when Will had still been here, he'd been interested in her stained glass. They'd started a project together to give to Sam for his birthday. But Will left before the birthday, before the project was ever finished. It was still probably right there in her workshop in the basement where she'd left it.

Looking at her watch, Rachel frowned and wondered what kind of shape it was in and how much she could get done today with the children here.

"Will you help me with something?" she asked Emma.

"Yes."

"Okay. We just might make it." And it would keep them busy, keep them from wondering where Sam had gone and how the children would manage tomorrow if their mother didn't show up.

Sam drove into Shepherdsville around seven-thirty, spotting a diner a block off main that had a cluster of cars around it. He took a seat at the crowded counter and ordered coffee, thinking he'd make his way to the newspaper office, hoping it was open on a Sunday. On his second cup of coffee, he struck up a conversation with an older man sitting next to him about what a nice little town this seemed to be. The man had lived there his whole life and was more than happy to talk about it.

Sam tossed out a casual, anything-interesting-happening-here remark, and the man told him a woman was found nearly beaten to death in a ditch on the outskirts of town almost two weeks ago. She was in a hospital on the outskirts of Indianapolis, and so far no one had figured out who she was or who had hurt her so badly. Last the man heard, she hadn't regained consciousness.

Sam felt sick inside. Literally sick.

He went across the street to the newspaper office and bought a copy of last week's paper from the rack outside, and there was the story, right on the front page. An unidentified woman, believed to be in her forties, average height, average build, no distinguishing marks on her. Nearly beaten to death on the outskirts of town. The sheriff speculated that she must be a transient and hoped the person who hurt her was, too. He'd even suggested someone might have gotten off the highway, dumped her body here, and taken off.

Sam didn't think so. He was afraid her husband had done it and wondered how he could find out without leading anyone to the kids. He didn't have a great amount of trust in the law enforcement profession, and he couldn't tell Miriam. She'd be obligated to follow certain procedures here.

He ended up driving to the hospital, forty minutes away, and saying he thought he knew the woman. The nurse in ICU eyed him suspiciously when he asked more questions than he answered about how he might know her. But she'd remained unconscious for two weeks and they let Sam see her.

"I don't know what you're going to be able to tell us

from looking at her right now. Her face is still a mess, and she's got tubes coming out of just about everywhere," the nurse said. "But at this point, anything would help."

Sam nodded as he stood outside the cubicle. He didn't know what he expected to see. Something of Emma maybe. What he saw nearly made him sick. She was so pale, except for the bruising still evident and the reddish abrasions. Her face was still swollen, and he couldn't imagine what she'd been through. He also couldn't imagine bringing Emma here to try to identify her.

The woman was so still, save for the motion caused by air being forced into her lungs by the machines, that if he hadn't been looking at the monitors that proved her heart was indeed beating, he wouldn't have believed she was alive.

Why in the world had she come here knowing there was a man in town capable of doing this to her? Sam had to find out. Fast.

"Do you know her?" the nurse asked.

"I'm not sure," he said. "Is she going to make it?"

The nurse frowned and offered a noncommittal, "She's been unconscious for a long time."

Sam nodded, thinking of Emma and Zach, imagining the look on their faces if he had to tell them they'd lost their mother for good.

"What's the name of the deputy in charge of her case?" he asked.

She gave it to him, and Sam headed back toward Shepherdsville. He had to do something. He had to protect the children; he'd promised Emma he would, but he couldn't do this alone.

He needed someone who understood the legal aspects involved, because Sam certainly didn't. And he needed someone to deal with the sheriff in Shepherdsville, who wouldn't know Sam from Adam. He supposed the logical choice would be an attorney or another person in law enforcement. Sam had an attorney who handled the few business matters that required legal expertise, but he didn't think his attorney did much in the way of criminal law.

He knew a lot of the deputies in Baxter, some of them from all the way back when he was a two-bit hood who got hassled by the law regularly and often without even having done anything. Of course, he'd known some of them for years now as an adult, as a businessman, and as Rachel's husband. They were all civil to him now and a few even friendly on occasion.

Sam frowned. He didn't like it, but he had to trust someone. Deputy Joe Mitchell came to mind. They'd built a playground together at the community center last year with about a dozen other volunteers, and despite the fact that Joe had picked Sam up for questioning more than once when Sam was a teenager, he liked Joe and thought he was a fair man.

Sam called Joe, asking to meet him at the café in Shepherdsville, and spent the rest of the drive there worrying about whether he'd done the right thing. When they sat down at the café, Sam decided the best thing to do would be to put the whole thing to Joe as a hypothetical situation.

"You know about the kids found abandoned at the Drifter last week?"

"Of course. I hope everything works out there, Sam. I know you and Rachel have wanted kids for a long time."

"Let's say, just for the sake of conversation, that I

thought I knew what happened to their mother and that maybe I knew where their father was, too."

"If I knew that, I'd have an obligation to do something about it, Sam."

"I know. But, just for the sake of more conversation, let's say those kids are scared to death of their father. That he hit their mother and they're afraid if they tell who their father is, they'll get sent back to him."

"Without any proof of abuse, they probably would," Joe said. "I'm sorry. That's the law. He's their father. If he has legal custody, they go back to him."

"I don't know who has legal custody."

"The mother took them away from him? She ran away?"

"Let's say she did."

"Sam—"

"There's more. Let's say that I think their mother went back to the town where they all lived. But she was scared of what he might do and didn't want to risk him seeing the kids, so she left them forty-five minutes away in a motel room, thinking they'd be safer there than anywhere near their so-called father."

"Okay. The oldest girl's eleven?"

Sam nodded.

"Someone might be able to argue that's not abandonment. A judge might believe it."

"It's not the real issue, I'm afraid. Let's say she found her husband or he found her and beat her half to death. I can't be sure, but that's what I'm afraid happened. There's a woman who was found in a ditch on the side of a road here the day after the kids' mother left them in the motel. A woman beaten so badly, it's hard to even know what she looked like before. One with no ID who hasn't regained consciousness. No one knows who she is."

"Damn," Joe said.

Sam nodded. "What do I do? If I start asking questions, it's going to come out that I've got those kids. If there's nothing to link what happened to that woman to her husband, the kids might go back to him, and I'm not going to let that happen."

"That's a problem. If the woman can't tell us anything . . ."

"She may never be able to. They don't know if she's ever going to wake up."

"You don't think the daughter could identify her?"

"I'd hate to ask her to, given the shape the woman's in."

"You know where the husband is these days?" Joe asked.

"I don't even know his name. I made Emma, the oldest girl, promise not to tell me. I figured if I didn't know, I couldn't tell anybody. But now . . . I have to do something."

"Well, if the mother had trouble with the husband in the past—if the sheriff had been called to the house or the woman treated at the hospital before and someone had suspected abuse . . . That ought to be enough to point the finger in the direction of the husband, but—"

"Not good enough," Sam said. "I promised those kids they'd be safe. I'm not turning them back over to a father who abused their mother."

"I know the sheriff over here. We've worked together on a couple of cases over the years that straddled boundary lines. I guess I could have a hypothetical discussion with him, a lot like the one you just had with me."

"I don't know, Joe."

"He's a good guy. He's got kids the same age as mine. He's not looking to let anybody else's kids get hurt. But I guess I don't have to tell him anything about the kids, although if I show up asking questions, from a town where three abandoned children turned up around the same time this woman was found, he's going to put it together. But, as I said, he's a good guy. I don't know what else to do, Sam. We're going to have to trust somebody."

Sam nodded. Trust had never come easily to him.

"I promised these kids," he said again. "You'll be hunting me down one day if you ever try to send them back to a man who frightens them."

"Hey, if that's the way it is, I'll give you a good head start," Joe promised. "Give me a few minutes. I'll see what I can find out."

The wait seemed interminable, although in truth it was less than a half hour. Joe came back with a man who introduced himself as Sheriff Whit Simmons, and the three men sat down at a booth in the back of the room.

"Whit thinks we're on to something," Joe said.

"We had a couple named George and Annie Greene with two kids, a girl about eight named Emily Ann and a little boy who was about two. I don't remember his name. We never got called to the house, but Annie ended up in the emergency room a few times. Never would say what happened. Not the truth, anyway, but I think we all knew. One of my brothers went to school with George, and he always was a nasty little shit. Didn't lose his temper that much, but when he did, somebody got hurt," the sheriff said. "I wish I could have helped that woman, but without her testifying, there really wasn't anything I could do. She took the kids and left him a couple of years ago, I heard. George made some noise about his wife stealing his kids, and wanting me to do something about it. I told him I hadn't done enough while she was here. I sure wasn't going to help him find her now. He didn't like it much, and he could have made something of it. Lucky for us, he let it go. He's taken up with somebody else these days, and I think he probably beats her, too. But she's as scared of him as Annie was."

"So you don't have any proof he was abusing his wife?"

"We could probably get the hospital records from before. Show broken bones, reports of injuries. But when you come into a hospital, they ask how you got hurt. They'll likely have records of Annie herself telling them she fell down again," the sheriff said, shaking his head. "I never would have put this woman we found together with Annie. We were guessing she was about ten years older, but I guess life's aged her some. Other than that, she fits the general description of Annie Greene. I would have thought I'd know her, if I saw her again, but this Jane Doe's too much of a mess for that now."

The sheriff looked troubled. "I know where you two are from, and . . . Well, I get the bulletins that go out to all the sheriffs in the state. I think I can put together what happened here, and I understand your not wanting to say too much. I don't want to do anything to put those kids in danger."

"So what can we do?" Sam asked.

"The way I see it, this Jane Doe is my problem. I

need to know who she is. Now that you've given me a lead, I think I'll ask somebody from the hospital to pull the records from the time Annie Greene was there in the past. We'll check the blood types, maybe see that Annie had broken the same bones in the same places in the past as my Jane Doe. If they match, I'd say I have cause to go see what George's been up to in the past couple of weeks. Maybe I can scare him into talking. That woman dies, I'm looking for a murder suspect. I want that man in jail every bit as much as you do," the sheriff explained. "The way I see it, the safety of my town's my first priority. I don't see any need to go looking for Annie's kids right now. Besides, she had two kids. Not three. And her oldest girl had a different name. I don't see the connection. At least not now."

"Thanks, Whit," Joe said. "We appreciate it."

The man nodded and got to his feet. "I'll be in touch."

Sam waited until the sheriff was gone and then looked across the table to Joe, who'd been with the sheriff's office since Sam first came to Baxter. Sam laughed, thinking about the irony of what just happened.

"What?" Joe asked.

"I never expected to have a couple of cops helping me with anything."

Joe smiled, too. "Hey, it's been a long time."

"Yeah, it has."

"I never expected you to stick around or to make something of yourself," he admitted. "I think I owe you an apology, too. I think we hauled you in for questioning a few times at least when you really hadn't done anything."

"Don't worry about it," Sam said. "I think I did a few things you and your boss never found out about."

Joe laughed with him then. "It's funny how things turn out."

"Yeah, it is."

"Which reminds me. Sally and I've been meaning to call you. She's got her eye on the Wallace place, has for years. I know the damned house has to be a hundred years old. Can't imagine what she's thinking, but she wants it and that woman's almost always found a way to get anything she wants from me. She thinks we might be able to make something of the place. Or that you could."

Sam grinned. "You have a small fortune hidden away somewhere?"

"I'm a small-town cop. What do you think?"

"We could take it slow," Sam offered. "You could probably do some of the work yourself. Isn't one of Sally's brothers a plumber?"

"Yeah."

"That ought to be worth something to you right now."

Joe rolled his eyes and swore. "Just what I need. A money-guzzling shack."

"Give me a call. I think I'm going to owe you a favor."

"Oh, hell, Sam. I'd have been mad if you hadn't called for something like this. You're a part of this town now. We stick together, look out for each other."

Sam nodded. He knew the people of Baxter did. He just hadn't realized he was considered one of them.

"I need to get back," Joe said. "I'll call you as soon as I hear anything."

Sam thanked him again and headed home himself,

just remembering as he came into town that it was Christmas Eve. He didn't know whether to hope this woman in the hospital was Annie Greene or not. She was so sick she might never wake up, and he didn't want Emma or Zach to lose her. Grace was so young, she wouldn't remember her, but Emma and Zach would. He didn't want to have to tell them their mother was gone, and at the same time, he didn't want Rachel to have to let these children go. He didn't want to do that himself.

And he had no idea how to work out any of this so that no one ended up with a broken heart.

When Sam got home, Rachel was getting Zach ready and Grace was asleep, but Emma was waiting for him. From the worried look on her face, he knew he had to tell her something and he didn't want to do it here.

"I need some help," he told Emma, before she could ask him a thing. "I'm not quite done with my shopping . . ."

Rachel laughed. God, he loved hearing Rachel laugh again. "He always waits until the very last minute," she told Emma.

"Will you come with me?" he asked. "And help me?"

"Okay," Emma said.

Rachel looked surprised and he knew she wanted to ask what was going on, but he cut her off.

"We'll hurry," he promised.

"We have to be at church at six," she reminded him.

"Church?" Zach frowned.

"Yes, church," Rachel said. "There's more to Christmas than Santa."

Sam promised he and Emma would be back in time. Emma followed him to his truck and said, "We're going shopping?"

"Yes," he said. "Rachel needs a present."

"Oh."

She let it go at that and Sam tried to figure out what to say to her about her mother. He really didn't know anything for sure.

He glanced over at her finally, after driving for a few minutes, sitting silently beside him looking at all the windows of the shops. She looked so sad. He didn't want her to be sad.

"Rachel really should have something from you and Zack," Sam said, hoping to distract her and give himself some time to think. "Will you pick something out?"

"I don't have any money," Emma said.

"That's okay. You pick and I'll pay. It'll come from all of us. Do you know of anything she needs?"

"No."

"Well, maybe we'll find something." He parked in front of one of the two women's clothing stores in town and they walked in. There was Christmas music coming through the speakers in the store and a festive, if slightly desperate air about the place. It was Christmas Eve after all.

The clerk, Jamie Cousins, whose husband worked with Sam, greeted him by name and gave them a warm smile. "Waiting til the last minute again, Sam?"

Emma laughed a bit at that and Sam admitted that he was. They wandered around the store, Sam following Emma, who paused in front of a display of thick terry-cloth bathrobes.

"Rachel's has a hole in it," she told him.

"It does?"

Emma nodded. "And Zack spilled grape juice on it the other day. Grape juice is hard to clean up."

Sam frowned, thinking a bathrobe was as good a present as any. He'd gotten Rachel something else already, something he hoped she'd like, and this would be fine coming from the kids. He fingered the thick material in a pale, pale pink. It was soft, and he supposed it would be warm.

"You don't like it?" Emma asked.

"No. It's fine," he claimed, picking it up.

And then his gaze caught on a flash of blue in the corner. He liked Rachel in blue, and this was the color of her eyes. Sam walked over to the silk robe and pulled it off a dainty, thickly padded hanger that was more suited to one of those lingerie stores at the mall than downtown Baxter.

Jamie walked over to him and took the terry cloth robe from him. "Going to be practical, Sam? Or not?"

He flushed a bit, caught fingering the silky robe and thinking about what his wife would look like in it.

"That's pretty, too," Emma said, oh so innocently.

"Practical is nice, but it only goes so far," Jamie claimed. "Especially at Christmas."

Sam wasn't thinking of being practical at all. He was thinking of what his chances were of seeing Rachel in the midnight silk robe. Maybe he had some hope left in him after all.

"We'll take both," he told Jamie.

Jamie smiled knowingly.

"Both?" the ever-practical Emma asked.

"Yes," he said, refusing to be embarrassed. "You and Zach can give her the pink one, and I'll give her the other one. Or maybe I'll save it for another day.

Her birthday's not long after Christmas. Maybe I won't wait for the last minute for that."

Emma still frowned, probably at what she saw as the extravagance of buying two robes at a time, Emma who'd likely spent her whole life in hand-me-downs, too rapidly outgrowing everything she had when there was little money to buy more.

He paid for the robes and waited while they were wrapped. He and Emma were back in the truck, almost home, when he couldn't wait any longer to bring up the subject of her mother.

"I guess we need to talk about something else, too, before we get back to the house."

Emma just looked at him, with so much hope it nearly broke his heart.

"I'm sorry, Em," he said quickly.

"You didn't find my mom?" she choked out.

"Not yet."

"But you tried? That's where you were all day?"

"Yes. I tried." He felt as if he'd failed her and hated the idea. He wanted to make everything all better for Emma, too.

Her face fell. Her bottom lip quivered but she stubbornly fought back tears.

"Hey, this was just the first day," Sam said. "Just because I didn't find her the first day . . ."

"You won't give up?"

"No," he promised. "I'll never give up."

Chapter 15

Rachel had never faced a Christmas Eve with as much anticipation or dread. It seemed her whole life had come down to what happened in the next twenty-four hours. They'd have this one day, and then her husband would make his decision. He would either stay or go. Her whole life was about to change, and she had to keep reminding herself—one good Christmas. That was what she'd vowed to give them all, and it was upon them. She wouldn't let herself ruin it by worrying about what would come later.

Sam and Emma came home, and they had to rush to get to the six o'clock service at church. The bells atop the old stone church were ringing when they arrived, the front steps adorned with poinsettias and greenery strung along the rails. Inside, the lights had been dimmed and there were candles burning on the altar, the whole place seeming to glow.

The organist was already playing Christmas music softly and people spoke in hushed tones, feeling the reverence of the evening.

Rachel remembered the feeling of peace she'd found here the night before, the sense of hope, and it was all here tonight. She still felt it as they settled into a pew near the back and on the right.

"Is it almost time?" Zach asked, still looking for Santa.

"Not quite," Rachel said. "What did we say? Church. Dinner. A story. Bedtime. Then Santa."

He gave a long-suffering-child sigh.

Someone else crowded into the already packed pew, and Rachel found herself pressed tightly against her husband's side. Grace started babbling, trying to get Sam to talk to her. Sam put his arm around Rachel's shoulders and touched a fingertip to Grace's chin. She giggled at him and cooed and batted her eyelashes.

"She is going to be a knockout someday," he said. "She'll give her father fits for sure."

"I know," Rachel said, wondering if he wanted to be her father. If he'd stay if the children did.

He'd said no more half measures between them, and she supposed staying for the children would definitely be that. What would it take for him to want to stay?

He looked so handsome tonight and smelled faintly of Old Spice; she'd bought him his first bottle of it their first Christmas together, and he'd never worn anything else. His hair was still damp from his quick shower, and it was jet-black and curling a bit at the ends. He hadn't shaved, and it was late enough in the evening that she knew just how his slightly roughened cheek would feel against her skin. She knew how soft his mouth was, how strong his arms were, how safe she'd always felt there.

Seeing him now with Grace . . . She loved seeing him like this, seeing all the gentleness and kindness and love inside of him that she always knew was there. He might hide it from the rest of the world most of the time, but she'd always known. These children did, too, despite the rocky start they had with Sam.

He bent over to tickle Grace's chin again, and she cackled in delight, then held her arms out to him. Sam took her, one-handed, with Rachel's help. She was standing on his lap, his arm around her middle, and she put her chubby little hands against his cheeks and patted them, then either tried to kiss his nose or take a bite out of it. Grace laughed at that, and she made Sam laugh, too.

Rachel felt a twinge in the region of her heart and said, "You would have made a wonderful father."

Sam looked at her, unsettled and too serious in a moment's time.

"It's okay," she said. "I'm not going to cry or run away from it anymore. We had a child once, and you would have been a wonderful father to her. You still could be."

Sam still didn't say anything. Grace looked a bit puzzled and stared from one of them to the next. "It's all right," Sam whispered to her.

"I'm better now, Sam," Rachel said. "I've changed. I think you've changed, too, and that I've finally grown up. I'm not that silly, spoiled girl anymore."

"I liked that girl," he said. "I didn't think she was silly at all. I thought she was sunshine and laughter and everything good in this world. And I always wanted to spoil her myself. I wanted to give her everything."

"She just wanted you," Rachel said. "All along. Just you."

He was going to say something else. She could see it in his eyes, but Grace started making a racket and the service was starting. They concentrated instead on quieting her and keeping her entertained, and then it seemed they'd lost the moment to talk.

Rachel sat there with Sam's arm around her and let

herself rest against him, let the music and the beauty of the place settle over her once more, calming her, giving her strength.

It wasn't over yet, this battle she faced to keep her husband and maybe these children. She was ready to fight, and she wasn't afraid anymore. She wasn't afraid of anything.

Emma used to go to church with her mother but she hadn't been in a long, long time. This one was especially nice. It was big and crowded tonight, but she liked the way it felt in here—warm and hopeful. She liked the Christmas music, the candles, and the fancy windows, like the ones in Sam and Rachel's house. They seemed to glow tonight. She liked Sam and Rachel, too, felt safe with them and trusted them. Honestly, she did.

It was just that the world was such a mixed-up place right now. At least, hers was. When Sam said he'd go look for her mother, she'd been so sure this would be the day she'd have her mother back. But he hadn't found her.

Emma was scared now.

She'd trusted Sam to find her, but she was afraid he was keeping something from her, something bad.

And tomorrow was Christmas.

She sat there as still as possible in the crowded church, wishing and praying as hard as she could and feeling more lonely and more miserable with each passing moment, and still her mother was nowhere to be found.

They went back to Sam and Rachel's house. Emma picked at her dinner, not caring a thing for anything like food. She got out of her church clothes, the prettiest dress she'd ever owned. She wished her mother were here to see her in it. Then she put on her pajamas and went back downstairs.

Sam read *The Night Before Christmas*, the one with his and Rachel's house on the cover, and Emma thought about that some more, about being in the Christmas house at Christmas.

Where was the magic? she wondered. Where was her mother?

Grace was asleep by the time Sam finished the story. Emma gave her a kiss and then Rachel took her upstairs. Sam took Zach, telling her that she should go on up to bed, too, because they'd all be up early in the morning.

Emma slowly climbed the stairs and sat down on her bed in the unfamiliar room missing her mother so bad it hurt to breathe. Rachel came in a moment later and sat down beside her. She didn't say anything at first, just pulled Emma against her side and held on to her.

"What's wrong, Emma?"

"It's almost Christmas. I was sure that if I could just hang on until Christmas, my mom would be back."

"And now you don't think she's coming?"

"I don't know. I don't know anything anymore."

"You know she loves you," Rachel reminded her.

"Yes." She was sure of that. She could hold on to that.

"And Zach and Grace love you," Rachel said. "I love you, too."

She gave her a big squeeze and Emma thought about that. About having Rachel love her. Rachel was a good person. She was kind and nice and she'd taken such good care of all of them. Sam, too. She thought

Sam might love them a little bit, too. And this was a good place to be. She didn't want them to think she was ungrateful.

"I like you and Sam a lot," she said. "I do. It's just . . ."

"You still miss your mother. I understand that. And how much you want her back. I know it's hard, but sometimes we just have to hope, Emma. Sometimes that's all we have to hold on to. Hope. Do you think you can hold out just a little longer? Can you find just a little bit of hope and a smidgen of faith? And believe that everything's going to be okay?"

Emma nodded, too upset to even say a single word. She just leaned into Rachel and let Rachel hold her, which was almost as good as having her mom's arms around her.

She thought she had just enough hope and faith left to hang on until Christmas, but that was it.

Tomorrow . . . She didn't know what she'd do tomorrow if her mother wasn't back.

Rachel went back downstairs to sit in front of the fire, brushing away a few stray tears. She didn't want Sam to see them, had promised herself she wouldn't cry at all. But Emma was so sad, and Rachel knew what her Christmas wishes were all about, Zach's too.

Not tonight, she told herself firmly. Not tomorrow, either. They would take the day and all it had to offer, worry later about what came after.

She looked up and saw Sam standing in the doorway looking so handsome in the gentle light of the fire. She forgot sometimes; she'd been looking at him for so long, but he was a truly handsome man. There was still a hint of that bad boy she'd fallen in love with so long ago, the slightly dangerous one. But there was so much more, too. So much more she loved about him.

Which made her think about what *she* wanted for Christmas. She wanted him to stay.

"What in the world are you thinking?" he asked.

"About what I want for Christmas," she said, way too seriously, then, determined to lighten the mood, imagined what he'd do if she walked over to him, tied a red ribbon around him, and said she'd picked out her own present, thank you very much. She'd take *him*.

He arched a brow at that and looked puzzled. She remembered Christmas mornings they'd spent snuggling in bed, hiding from the cold in what was once this drafty, old house. Christmases spent laughing and playing in the snow. Christmases spent missing all the people they'd lost. So many Christmases. So many years with Sam.

"I can't imagine my life without you," she said, remembering courage, faith, hope, a vow she'd made to do her best to salvage this marriage.

"Why would you be thinking of your life without me, Rachel?"

She gathered up all her courage and knew it was time. It was long past time. "I think you know why, Sam."

He shook his head back and forth, but she saw the tension coming into his entire body. She hadn't meant to do this on Christmas Eve, but she was all out of time. In a day and a half, he was supposed to go, and the hardest thing of all to admit was that she would let him go, if that's what he had to do.

"I told you I want you, and I'll never ask you to leave, but, Sam, if *you* want to go . . . If you don't think you can be happy here with me. If I haven't loved you enough or made you feel like you belong here with me. If it takes leaving me for you to be happy, then go, Sam. Because I want you to be happy."

She did it without a single tear falling, did it looking him straight in the eye, and thought he looked as miserable as she'd ever seen him.

"You know?" he whispered.

"I heard you talking to Rick on the phone the day the children came."

He looked away for a moment, looked as if the breath simply left his body. "Oh, God, Rachel," he said. "I'm sorry."

And then her tears wouldn't stay away. They rolled down her cheeks.

"Don't be sorry," she insisted, her head held high. "I know how unhappy you must have been for you to think you had to go, and I can't blame you for that, Sam. I know what it's been like between us for a long time. I know what *I've* been like."

"You've been so sad," he said.

She nodded.

"I never wanted to hurt you," he said, then took her face, her wet cheeks, between his hands, bent down, and touched his forehead to hers. "It seems like we've been sad forever."

"I know. I never wanted to make you miserable, Sam. I wanted you to be happy. I still do. Whatever it takes," she said. "Even if it's leaving me."

She let the words sit there between them, not liking at all the way it sounded, as if she were offering her permission for him to go, but not knowing how else to say it. She was going to think about what he needed now, what it would take for him to be happy.

She was setting him free and yet . . .

"Hey, it's not a hint," she said as lightly as she could. "I meant what I said yesterday. If it were up to me, you'd always be here. But I'm not going to try to hold you here if you believe you have to go."

"I don't know what I want." He shook his head back and forth and said, "I thought I did, but . . . Leaving you would be the hardest thing I've ever done. Harder than losing my parents, my brother, our baby. It would be the worst thing."

Rachel stood there, afraid to even breathe, wanting to plead her case and not sure if she had the right. Was that setting him free? Did that cross the line?

"I think things can be different," she said tentatively. "I think I've done so many things wrong for so long, and I'm sorry."

"It's not your fault," he insisted.

"A lot of it is. I couldn't control all the things that happened to us, but I had a say in how I dealt with them. Or didn't deal with them."

"It's been hard," he said. "All of it."

"And it shouldn't all have been hard. We still had each other. We have a whole lot of family left, more than most people ever have to start with, and we have this house. I know it's not what you wanted . . ."

"I've gotten attached to this old house," he said.

"But it's not what you wanted. I was happy to stay here, because I have so many happy memories here. I know it's always going to be my grandfather's house in a lot of ways, but it's ours, too, Sam. Do you remember how it looked when we first moved in? How much it's changed? We did that together, you and me. I can look in any corner of this house and remember you and me here. We made it what it is today, and that makes it special to me."

"The house is not the problem, Rachel."

"I know. It's just that . . . If you want something else, that's fine with me. If you want to go back to school, it's not too late, Sam. You could take classes at night at the community college right here in town. There are programs now where you take classes just on the weekends, classes over the computer and on TV. If you still want an architecture degree, it's not too late."

"Rachel, that was something I wanted a long time ago. When I wanted out of this town—"

"And we can go. If you want to go. If you want me with you."

He stood there, looking surprised and confused and at a loss. "I haven't thought about leaving this town in years. It's different now. It's where we live, Rachel."

"I thought I'd taken so many things away from you, and I wanted you to know that I'm ready to put you first and what you want. And I know that's something I haven't done before, and I'm sorry. I'm sorry, Sam."

"Rachel, you didn't do this to us. Life just worked out this way. And maybe it's been more about what you wanted than what I thought I wanted, but mostly it's been what life did to us. I'm not sorry about ending up in this town, or in this house, or with the business. I like it. Maybe more than I ever would have liked being an architect. I don't know. All of those were things a teenage boy wanted a long time ago."

"And he wanted me," she said. "That boy wanted me."

"He still wants you." Sam reached out to take a strand of her hair between his fingertips. "He's always wanted you."

"But you were going to leave me. Why did you think you had to go, Sam?"

"I . . . It was Will, Rachel. I think it must have been losing Will. I . . . I know we didn't have him for long, but I loved him. I hadn't let myself love anyone but you in so long, and I thought things were finally going to be okay for us and that we'd have Will. And then when his mother came back and they took him away from us . . . It was like everyone I'd ever lost in my life, like losing them all, all over again. It was like life was showing me one more time that I always lost everything and everyone I'd ever dared to love, and I couldn't run anymore from the idea that no matter what I did, one day I'd lose you, too."

"You're not going to lose me," she promised.

"I thought I would. I was sure of it. We were both miserable, and I thought if I was going to lose you anyway, it was better to go ahead and go."

"You're not going to lose me," she said again. "Although I think maybe I deserve to lose you. All this time, I've been thinking about all the things I didn't have, instead of what was right here in front of me. I feel like I've been blind, like I've been so careless and so ungrateful—"

"No," he said. "You've just always known exactly what you wanted and where you belonged. It's one of the first things I loved about you. You had this place in the world that was absolutely yours, and you were always sure you could make my own place right beside you. I loved all of your dreams for us. I loved your vision of our life together."

"But, the children . . . Sam, I know—"

"I've always wanted to have children with you. Always. I wasn't sure what kind of father I was going to be, and I was for damned sure scared of having anything to call my own because I was so afraid of losing

it. Think about it, Rachel. Until I met you, everything
I'd ever loved I'd lost. Except for you, I've still lost
everyone else."

She started to cry again. She'd never thought about
it quite that way. "Is there any little bit of hope left inside of you where we're concerned? Any little part of
you that thinks this could still work out?"

He looked as if she'd slugged him, as if he might
double over in pain at any moment, but he didn't. He
just stood there and looked as if she'd knocked the
breath out of him, too.

"I think about that," he said, "and I come back to the
children. What's going to happen to you and me if we
lose them, too?"

"You think I'd fall apart if we lost them?" Rachel
straightened her back, lifted her chin. "That I'd just
shut down again and push you away? Like I did when
we lost Will."

"I don't know," he said.

"I'm not going to do that, Sam," she said, although
she couldn't blame him in the least for thinking it. "I'd
be sad and I'd worry about them, but I'm through sitting here feeling sorry for myself. I've actually learned
some things in the past few days. I don't know how to
prove that to you. I know you've spent a lot of years
taking care of me and trying to hold things together
here. I'll understand if you can't do it anymore. I really
do want you to be happy now."

"I can't imagine being happy without you," he said.
"I can't imagine being without you at all."

Which gave her hope, but still, "It's up to you. This
time, it's your choice."

"I don't know what's going to happen, Rachel."

"We never do. Never."

"The kids' mother could show up tomorrow."

"I know. It's what they want. What about you, Sam? Right now? In this moment? What are you waiting for? What do you want?"

Sam stood there, not moving a muscle. There'd been times in his life when he felt as if he wanted so much and had absolutely nothing to call his own. And there were times when he thought he was asking for so little, surely he ought to be able to have it.

Right now his whole world seemed so full, here in this house with three children he'd come to love sleeping upstairs and his wife practically in his arms. And it was all balanced so precariously, he felt as if it could slip through his fingertips in an instant. One wrong move, and it would simply disappear.

His first instinct was to hold on as tightly as he could to her and everything they'd ever shared. There had been joy mingled with all the sorrows, love unlike any he'd ever known.

He did love her, and he believed more than ever that she actually loved him. He didn't even want to tell her how hard it was for him to believe it—that someone could love him, that it could last. But he supposed she already knew because he'd told her what his life had been like.

And it seemed they were at a crossroads. Tomorrow was Christmas. He was supposed to go away in a day and a half. He had a feeling if he didn't go then, he never would. And as she'd said, there were no guarantees. Not ever.

Which meant this was a question of faith, of what was left of their feelings for each other and whether they could muster up any hope that the future could truly be better, different, that what they'd found now could last.

How much did he love his wife? How strong did he think she was? How strong was their commitment to each other?

He wanted to let go of all doubts and bask in the love she seemed now to offer so earnestly, so generously. He wanted all those dreams for the two of them he'd once seen shining so brightly in her eyes.

Still, the smartest thing to do right now would be to wait until tomorrow. This whole thing with the children might be over by then. They'd know, and they could decide what to do from there.

Nevertheless, he eased an inch closer to her, because he'd been without her and missing her for so long.

What if this was all he ever got? All they had left? It seemed selfish to reach for her feeling like that, but there it was. He still wanted her, wanted anything he could have with her right now.

Sam went to say something to her; he wasn't even sure what. But his throat felt too tight and the words never made it past that point. He felt as if he could easily choke on the emotions running through him, felt as if he were about to go toppling over the precipice, and didn't really care at the moment where he was when the dust finally settled. Because he was doing it to get to her, for however long he could have her.

Looking for a way to lighten the mood, to maybe get through this without letting her see what it cost him, he glanced around the room and remembered . . . Christmas. It was Christmas Eve. She'd gotten out the wrapping paper, the ribbons and bows, while he was upstairs, and then he remembered . . .

"You never told me what you wanted for Christmas."

She looked puzzled for a moment, then hopeful, then very tentative as she reached for something on the table at his side and came up with a big, red bow. She peeled the paper off the adhesive on the bottom of it and stuck the bow on his shirt, squarely over his heart, and then left her hands there on him. He absolutely loved having her hands on him.

Giving him a shy, tentative smile, she said, "I was hoping I'd find you under the tree. All wrapped up with my name on you."

He closed his eyes and let himself enjoy the feel of her hands running over him. He bent his head until his cheek was nestled against hers, and he could smell her, the Rachel smell, mingling with that of the tree and the fire.

Rachel at Christmas, he thought.

Rachel in the light of the fire and the tiny, blinking, white bulbs reflected off her smooth skin.

He'd seen her like that once, late one Christmas night. A Christmas when there hadn't been a lot of money for any kind of gifts, and she'd given him herself, right there by the tree.

Sam's entire body started shaking with need. He reached behind him and flicked off the light, heard a little catch in her breath as his arms came around her and he settled her against him.

There was a tape of Christmas songs playing softly in the background, a happy, triumphant song. "Joy to the World." She was humming quietly to it even now.

She'd loved Christmas once, he remembered. Loved everything about it. Enjoyed it more than anyone he'd ever known. There had been joy inside of her once, and maybe life hadn't beaten it all out of her.

He slid his hands across her back, thinking about how small she was, how vulnerable she felt against him. He always forgot that about her until he had her this close, and he thought about how easy it would be to hurt her, how much hurt he'd seen in her face over the years.

She pressed her nose to the side of his neck, inhaling deeply of him, and he thought of doing the same thing in her hair. He loved the softness of her hair, the feel of it against his skin.

He let his hand slide into it, his palm cupping her cheek and his fingertips buried in the silky strands. She was wearing it down tonight, which he loved, and it was longer than it had been in a while.

He remembered one time lying flat on his back and her leaning over him, kissing him all over, him discovering how much he liked the feel of her hair on him. Remembered how she'd laughed and teased him with it.

He missed that woman, he realized with a stark longing that he thought might send him to his knees.

"I've missed you," he whispered. "Everything about you. It's been pure hell staying away."

"I've missed you, too," she whispered, kissing his neck, his jaw, his cheeks and finally his mouth.

She was very tentative about it; she'd seldom taken the lead when it came to lovemaking, even in all the years they'd been together, although she'd always been eager to please. Just shy. He'd take her hands and guide them to where he wanted them to be, show her, teach her. But he didn't do that tonight. He let her do what she wanted, let her set the pace for this sweet awakening, let all the memories come pouring back with such clarity, such poignancy.

Rachel.

She was like a song inside of him, a half-forgotten, sad, sweet, so sexy song. His blood was on fire, and yet he couldn't find it in him to rush this. He wanted to savor every moment, every touch.

She pressed her mouth to his, her lips soft and questioning. He let out a ragged breath, his heart settling into a strong, heavy thud, and the whole world seemed to slow down around them.

The lights were blinking on and off on the tree, and the fire crackled and hissed every now and then, the light from there flickering over them, as well. She teased at his mouth with her tongue, and he opened up to her, to that first heady taste of her.

He wanted to stay locked in the power of that kiss for days, wanted to take and take and take until she was limp in his arms. His hands started to move, running up and down her arms, across her back, tugging at the buttons on her blouse and then undoing her bra and slipping inside to the soft, soft skin of her breasts. He found smooth, heated skin and pearly nipples. She cried out when he touched them, when he bent her backward in his arms and laved them with his tongue.

She tasted so good, so soft, and the sounds she made and the fine trembling in her body drove him on. He could not get enough of her, kissed and suckled and outright devoured her until he sensed that she was very close to a climax and so was he.

It had been entirely too long, after all.

Sam backed up a bit, tugged off his shirt and threw it into the corner, unfastened his pants and pushed them and everything else off. Then he went to work on her clothes. Her shirt came off completely, her bra. He pushed her back onto the rug in front of the fire and went after the fastening of her skirt, tugging it down, pulling off her panties, until she was gloriously bare before him.

There was a scar on her belly, a not-too-neat one that for a time had been long and raised and hard, a constant reminder of the fact that he'd nearly lost her, too, and of all they'd gone through.

But it had faded over time. Quite often, he forgot it was there. She had always hated it, always tried not to even look at it, and didn't like for him to see it at all. But there it was. She wasn't trying to hide tonight, and he had the urge to press his mouth along every inch of that now faint, slightly pinkish line.

"Are you cold?" he asked as he eased down onto the floor beside her.

"A little," she said.

He pulled the afghan off the back of the sofa and covered her to her waist, and then he ran his hands along that scar, and then buried his face against her belly, right there along the thin line.

"I nearly lost you, too," he said. "All these years, not talking about the rest of it, I don't think I ever told you how scared I was that night. I was sure I was going to lose you, too, and that my whole life might as well be over."

"But you didn't lose me," she said. "I'm here. I'll always be here. And we're not done."

But he had nearly lost her again, he thought. In just the last few months, he'd nearly lost her. He still might.

Faith, Sam, he reminded himself. *Just a little faith.*

He could find a little. He had her in his arms, after all.

He sat up, leaning over her, his hand running up and down, watching the way she shivered beneath his touch, watching how responsive her body was. Seeming to reach for him and then shrink back when the sensations grew so intense it was almost too much to bear, but then she reached for him again.

He studied the contrast between his big, sun-browned hand on her delicate skin, the sight of which was always his undoing. There'd been a time when he thought he'd never touch her this way, that she'd never allow it and if she did, she'd come to her senses soon and be done with him. Or that her father would find out and kill him. But here she was, years later. *His.*

There'd been a time, too, early on when he'd been lost himself and so desperate for a connection with anyone. A time when he'd spotted her and found her fascinating and so confusing and she'd made him want things he knew he shouldn't. A time when she'd made him believe in things he never imagined for himself, a time when her dreams had become his.

She'd given him hope when there was none in his life, taught him all about dreaming. How could he ever imagine giving that up? She'd given him back his dreams once.

"Sam?" she said, her voice low and husky.

"Yes?" he asked.

"I want to touch you. I want to hold you. I want you inside of me. I want you to fill up all the empty spaces again."

And so he did. He teased her for as long as he could stand it, wanting her weak and nearly spent before he slid inside her, because he knew what it was like for her when he could hold out that long. He wrapped his arms around her like he'd never let her go and settled his body over hers and then kissed her some more, rubbing his body against hers. She started moving, unable to help it, moving in a slow rolling thrust of her hips against his. Her legs were restless, captured by his, and he could feel the little ripples of arousal running through her, could feel how close she was.

"It feels like it's been forever," he whispered. "A lifetime." A long, lonely one.

"I know," she said.

Sam knew just what she'd feel like when he slipped inside of her, just how smooth and slick and tight she'd be. He knew the way her body gripped his and held on, how hers needed time to adjust to his. He knew the sounds she made in the back of her throat and the way her hands clutched at him and how tight her entire body grew just before she came. And he knew what it was like to pour himself into her and all of her heat, and the way they both had to work so hard for air afterward.

Knew the way she liked him to roll sideways and take her with him, until she was lying on top of him, and her hair was everywhere, and she pressed little kisses along his chest. It would be damp with sweat, and his heart would be pounding, and he'd want to sleep just like that, all night long. With her on top of him, utterly spent in his arms.

He knew all of that, and she was all he remembered and more. When he couldn't wait any longer, he nudged her thighs apart and pushed his way inside of her, barely, pausing right there on the edge while he tried to get himself together so that maybe he could make this last. Just maybe.

He felt all the heat of her, all the need. Her hands were pulling him closer, and she was whispering, "Please, Sam. Please."

And then he slid home.

There was no other word for it.

It had been just this way, just this powerful, just this certain, the first time he'd ever done it.

He felt as if he'd finally come home.

Chapter 16

He lost all track of time. It was that powerful, that shattering, being with her again, holding her close as she lay bonelessly on top of him. The side of her face was pressed against his chest, and it took a moment to register, but when he realized what was happening, he froze, the hand lazily stroking through her hair tightening into a fist.

She had her tears running down her cheeks, and he felt as if someone had knocked the breath out of his body in one killing blow.

She raised herself up on one arm and took his face with her other hand. "No," she said. "It's not that. Not at all. It's just been so long, and it makes me feel so much. Sometimes I think you can rip my soul right out of my body, it's so good. And I need that, Sam. I need to feel that close to you when we're like this, because sometimes, that's the only time I do. It's the only time I feel like I can really touch you."

"Me, too, Rachel. For me, too." He pushed her head back down to his chest and locked his arms around her. "Stay here. Stay a while longer."

He didn't think he could give up the feel of all her silky skin, her delicate hands, her warm, eager mouth, her shy touches. He'd always been greedy for all he could get of her, had always been reluctant to let her go afterward, though in truth she'd never given any indication of wanting to leave his arms, not even in the worst days.

Trust, he told himself. It wasn't that he had no trust in her. It was himself. He had trouble trusting that anyone would want to have him stay.

But she always had. Always.

They dozed for a bit in front of the fire, and luckily woke around midnight and remembered all that they still had to do.

Rachel went to get dressed again, but Sam stopped her. He went to the closet and dug into the back and pulled out the box wrapped in town that afternoon, and handed it to her.

"Now?" she asked

He nodded.

She slowly pulled off the paper, starting with the corners first and then the bottom, unfolding it delicately, with no haste at all, enjoying every moment. She'd always taken such pleasure in anything he'd ever given her. He'd worried that he'd never have enough to give, whether material or emotional, and watching her now, he remembered. She'd always seemed so excited by anything he had to give her.

Finally, she pulled the top off the box and pulled out the robe. It shined in the light of the fire and slipped through her fingers like water, the midnight-blue color setting off her eyes perfectly, just as he'd known it would.

"Emma told me you needed a new robe," he said.

"I doubt this is what *she* had in mind."

"She picked out what she thought you needed, and

I picked out what I wanted you to have." And then he'd hidden it away, not sure if he'd give it to her, but he did.

Rachel leaned over and kissed him on the cheek. He caught her by her hair, tugging gently to bring her back to him when she would have pulled away.

"You can wear hers tomorrow," he said, pushing the afghan off her shoulders and leaving her bare once again. "And tonight, you can wear mine."

He put it on her himself, wrapping it around her, pulling her hair out from beneath the collar, smoothing the lapels together, tying the belt at her waist, and then sat back and admired her in it. He'd been right. It was the exact color of her eyes, and he liked the way the silk felt on his skin, loved imagining the way it would feel encasing her naked body, and thought of how easy it would be to get it off of her when he wanted her again. Which he did. Already.

He reached for her, and she smiled. God, she was beautiful when she smiled like that.

"We have so much to do," she protested. "And I've always wanted to do this. To sit down here by the fire and the tree and listen to Christmas music and dig out all the presents we've hidden around the house and wrap them."

He took the ribbon from the chair behind him, a bright red velvet one, and wrapped it around her.

"Sam!" she protested.

"Don't worry. I'll unwrap you."

And she laughed. Rachel, he told himself, laughing, wrapped up in silk and tied with a ribbon into a slightly mussed, thoroughly beautiful package. His once again, at least for the moment. He sat back and admired what

he'd done to her, admired the smile and savored the
laughter.

"Now all we have to do is put you under the tree,"
he said.

On Christmas morning, Rachel woke with an arm
wrapped firmly around her waist and anchoring her to
the big, warm, blessedly familiar body of her husband
pressed against her from head to toe. She was lying on
her side, as he was, her head pillowed on one of his
arms, his other arm hanging on to her.

She was still wearing her robe—kind of. He liked
having it wrapped around her, liked the fact that it
was easy to push it away and get inside of it. The fabric was cool and slick, still cinched around her waist,
but most of her legs were bare, as were her shoulders
and her breasts.

She knew she wore the look of a thoroughly disheveled woman and a very happy one. When she felt
Sam's prickly cheek moving slightly against hers, she
shivered. The things he could do with his mouth . . .

"Cold?" he whispered.

"No."

"It's still early. We don't have to get up yet, do we?"

"No." She slid around in his arms until she could
face him, give him a slow, steamy, good-morning kiss.
"I don't think I said thank you for my present."

"You didn't?"

"Not the robe," she whispered. "For you."

She looked at him and saw dark, smoky eyes, sleep-
glazed and lazy with satisfaction, but the heat was still
there. She saw the blackness of his hair, the breadth of
his shoulders, and she wanted her hands all over him
again.

Sex really was an amazing thing, a powerful thing, a healing thing, a thing to bind them together, to strip away the pretense and the images they all carried with them to get down to the elemental nature of a relationship. She felt bound to Sam, felt as if no one and nothing could come between them this morning. If they could hang on to that feeling, remember it, savor it, surely they'd be okay.

She slid closer, feeling the little hairs on his legs tickling at hers, feeling hard muscles in his thighs and his chest and his arms, the first stirrings of arousal in his body and hers. How could she have ever given this up? Forgotten how much she needed him? Wanted him? Wanted this?

"Merry Christmas," she whispered, rolling onto her back and pulling him along with her.

It didn't take much that morning for either of them. They'd been in a state of semi-arousal all night, and her body was already alive with the memories of what they'd done, already soft and empty-feeling and wanting him.

He was hard in an instant, kissing her deeply and breathing raggedly, inside her a moment later, and she was right back there. To sheer bliss. She closed her eyes and tried to simply hang on to him and let him do with her what he would, and in her head she was thinking, *Stay with me, Sam. Stay.*

They woke abruptly the next time, woke to find Zach sitting on their bed tugging at Sam's arm. Rachel blinked twice, not quite sure she was awake and this was real. But there they were, in their bed, thankfully mostly covered. Sam jerked the quilt up around them both and looked at Zach, who was chattering a mile a minute, and frowned.

"What?" he said, breaking into the stream of excited chatter.

"It's Christmas!" Zach said, pure glee on his face. "Isn't it? Isn't it morning yet?"

Sam frowned once again and looked at the clock. "It's six-fifteen, Zach."

"Isn't that morning?"

"Technically, I suppose so."

"And Santa came?"

Sam rubbed his hands over his face and turned to Rachel for help. "It is morning?"

"Morning comes extra early on Christmas Day. I think it's a rule," she said. "A Christmas rule."

"Can we go downstairs!" Zach asked. "Can we go see!"

"In just a minute," Rachel said. "It's cold down there. Give us a minute to build up the fire and check and make sure that Santa's already gone. He doesn't like for anyone to see him, you know. If you catch him, and he gets mad . . . Well, we wouldn't want him to get mad at us."

"Uh-uh," Zach said quite seriously.

"Why don't you go see if Emma's ready to get up," she suggested.

"Okay!" He bounced off the bed and took off at a dead run, yelling Emma's name as he went.

"Well, if she's not up yet, she will be," Sam said.

Rachel just grinned. It was the best Christmas ever. She gave Sam a quick kiss on his mouth and got out of bed herself, gasping as her feet hit the cold floor. She opened a drawer and pulled out a pair of her warmest pajamas and fled into the bathroom to throw them on.

"I want to turn on the lights on the tree and in the windows and grab the camera before they get down there," she said, coming out of the bathroom.

Sam snagged her with an arm around her waist and pulled her to the side of the bed. He still hadn't put on anything. "You need clothes," she said.

He gave her a dazzling, disheveled Sam-in-the-morning smile. "I think you're almost as excited as they are."

"Maybe I am," she admitted. "I want them to have a great day. I want you to have one, too."

"I will." He studied her for a moment, not letting her go, then put his mouth next to her ear and whispered, "I still love you, Rachel."

She let out a shaky breath and felt tears flood her eyes. "I'll always love you."

"Hey, I got Emma!" Zach called out from the doorway. "Are you two comin'? Should we get Grace? I think I hear her, too!"

"Go on." Sam nodded toward the stairs, his gaze steady on hers, and for a moment, he looked so much like that beautiful, bad boy from days of old, the one she'd fallen in love with in what seemed like a lifetime ago. Her heart just melted. "I'll contain them somehow and buy you a few minutes down there."

Rachel turned and rushed to the doorway and sent Emma and Zach to get Grace, who she could hear babbling in her room. She allowed herself one quick glance at her husband, sitting there in her bed watching her with an expression on his face that warmed her entire body, before she ran downstairs to check on what kind of job Santa had done.

The day was a blur from there on, of presents and too much food and utter chaos. The kids were beside themselves with excitement. Zach was ripping into packages and practically dancing. Even Emma seemed especially pleased with the clothes Rachel had picked out and the CDs that came at the suggestion of two of Rachel's nieces. Grace mostly played with the empty boxes, patting their sides, climbing in them, crawling under them, hiding inside, and trying to eat the wrapping paper.

"She's like a puppy," Sam said, sitting on the floor in the corner of the room and laughing at her antics. He grabbed her every now and then to take away wrapping paper when it became necessary, putting her inside the biggest boxes himself, and getting her out when she was tired of one and ready for another.

By midmorning, the floor was covered with boxes, paper, toys, and clothes. Sam had cleared a path in one corner where he and Zach were working on putting together Zach's new bike, and Rachel warmed up muffins she'd made the night before and put the turkey in.

She was planning to sneak upstairs to have a shower and get dressed before the family descended upon them but Sam stopped her.

"I still haven't given you your present," he said.

She blushed, thinking of the robe and the way they'd spent the evening. "I thought I got my present last night."

He actually blushed a bit himself. "I have something else."

"I have something else for you, too. Wait just a minute."

She went downstairs instead, to the basement. When he renovated the carriage house and moved back there, she'd taken over the space to work on her stained glass. And yesterday, despite having the children underfoot, she'd managed to finish a present for Sam.

He'd had a logo made for the business six months ago using an image of their own house with the business name, and Rachel had decided he needed a sign to go with it. She'd been working painstakingly on re-creating the logo on a sign made of stained and beveled glass. It was a foot and a half square, held within a wooden frame, and she planned to hang it from the mailbox, and when sunlight went streaming through the glass, it would be wonderful. Her favorite part was the names, *McRae Construction,* and underneath that in smaller script, *Props. Sam and Rachel McRae.*

Zach and Emma had helped her wrap it the day before, and Grace had been persuaded to stick on a big red bow. Rachel carried it upstairs and put it at Sam's feet. The children gathered around, and he let them rip off the paper for him. They giggled as they worked and then beamed up at him when he got his first sight of it.

Rachel worried that perhaps she'd overstepped, giving him a sign for his business that listed both their names as a couple on it and one that showed his business being located here, at this house. She was nervous about that—overstepping—but Sam seemed genuinely touched by her gift. He stood there staring at it for the longest time and had to clear his throat twice before his gaze met hers and he thanked her for it.

"It's beautiful."

He touched it reverently, tracing the image of the house, and she thought, *Oh, Sam. Please stay.*

* * *

Sam was touched. He loved the sign. When Sam managed to drag his attention away from it, he remembered what he'd found for her at the auction he'd taken Zach to. He brought it to her then, and she let Zach open it.

"Careful," Sam warned.

Zach frowned as he uncovered the dusty, even rusty piece. "It's that old thing."

"Very old," Rachel said, getting down on her knees and inspecting it more closely.

Zach shook his head. He hadn't seen the appeal when they'd bought it and now maybe even thought Sam was insulting his wife. "It's broken, too," he complained.

"Chipped," Rachel said, reaching for one of those places. "Still, it's in remarkably good shape given how old it is."

"What is it?" Emma asked.

"A rose window." She said it almost reverently. "They used to put them in churches. In the grand cathedrals in the Middle Ages. They'd be down front, behind the altar."

Beautiful circles of stained glass.

"I've always wanted one," Rachel said. Turning around, she pointed to the landing where the stairs made a right-hand turn. "For there, right above the stairs. There used to be a rose window there. The oldest photos we have of this house show it, but it must have gotten broken a long time ago and someone just took it out, rather than try to get it repaired."

"Can you fix this one?" Sam asked.

"I don't know if I can match the glass exactly. I don't even know if anyone makes it anymore. But it'll be fun trying to find out, trying to see how close we can come to restoring it to its original shape."

And Rachel would do that. She liked putting things together, fixing them. She was good at it. Look what she'd done with Sam so long ago.

"I can fix it," she said, then looked up at him. "It's the one we saw in that old house in the next county, isn't it? The one that was sold before we got there?"

"Yes."

"How did you find it?"

"The dealer who bought it had an estate sale three days ago. I took a chance he might sell it there."

"It matches the colors on the house," Emma said. "It has the same blues and lavenders in your stained glass and the same gray that's on the outside of the house."

"Yes, that's another reason I wanted it," she said. Then she stood up and wrapped her arms around Sam and gave him a kiss, a not-too-fast one on his mouth. "Thank you. I love it."

"You're welcome," he said.

"I love you, too."

The kids giggled, probably because of the kiss. Emma looked shyly fascinated, and Zach was making faces. Grace clapped and beamed up at him. Rachel wiped a tear away and said, "We have so much to do."

"More?" Zach asked.

"Lots more," she said. "I have to have a shower, and we all have to get dressed, and before long, lots and lots more people are coming."

"Who?" Zach asked.

"My family. My entire family. My father . . . Remember him?" Zach nodded. "And my sisters."

"You have sisters?" he asked.

"Yes. You know that. You met them. Or you met two

of them. But I have three and a brother. And Aunt Miriam and Aunt Jo—the one with the sleigh."

"Will she bring it? Can we go for a ride?"

"No, she won't bring it today. She'll come in her car. With her husband and her kids and grandchildren."

"Oh." Zach was disappointed now.

"But she'll probably bring more presents," Sam said. "Everybody will bring more presents." The house would be overflowing. Christmas with Rachel's family was like nothing he'd ever imagined before he married her.

"And little boys," Rachel told Zach. "My sisters and my brother together with Miriam's and Jo's children have eighteen kids, ten of whom are boys."

"Wow!" Zach said. "I like boys."

"I know. We'll have so much fun. But for now, we have to get ready because everyone will be here soon."

They managed to talk the kids upstairs. Not easily, but they did it, and rushed through the morning routine. Sam made it downstairs with Zach first, and soon Emma was back with Grace and finally Rachel.

Sam watched her come down and the smile on her face took his breath away this morning. She'd lost that pinched look to her face, those little lines of tension in her brow, all that sadness she'd worn for so long. It was gone, and she was beautiful this morning.

Her hair was shining and her eyes. There was a hint of color in her cheeks, and that smile. There'd been a time when he couldn't take his eyes off her, that she'd absolutely dazzled him and he'd been so proud, so happy to know that she was his. He'd forgotten all about that.

She came to his side, and he eased his arm around

her waist and kissed her softly. "You look beautiful this morning."

She caught her breath and said, "You're going to make me cry."

"No," he said. "Not anymore."

"I can cry if I'm happy, can't I?"

"No, Rachel. Not even happy tears. I want to see you smiling like this again."

She sniffled and worked hard to put a smile across her face, and he just wanted to grab her and hold on to her, hold on to this day, this newfound happiness.

The doorbell rang a few minutes later, and the house started filling up. Rachel's father arrived with Gail and her husband, Alex, and their four kids. Gail kissed him, and Alex slapped him on the back. Their two oldest sons walked in with a football and big grins.

"I brought the ball," Alex Jr. said. He was as tall as Sam now and might even outweigh him.

"You're nuts," Sam said.

"Hey, it's tradition. Snowball."

Sam frowned. They'd nearly ended up with frostbite some years playing tackle football in the snow, a viciously brutal game played not so much for touchdowns as the opportunity to shove someone down in the snow and pile on top of them. He'd had snowballs shoved down his shirt, down his pants, had eaten mouthfuls of snow, in last year's game.

Alex Sr. gave his son a playful shove and said, "It was more fun when they weren't so big. When we could push them around."

"I know." Alex Jr. grinned and shoved right back. "It's revenge time."

Sam was saved from agreeing to anything when Rachel's sister Ellen and her husband, Bill, and their four came in. Davy, Rachel's brother, a miniature version of her father, and his wife, Jane, a petite, perky blonde, and their three arrived next.

Davy held up his watch to show Sam the time. "Three hours and counting. I'm counting on you to move this along. Get this meal served so we can sneak upstairs by kickoff time."

"Hey, I don't have anything to do with this meal. Talk to your sisters and your aunts."

"It's your house, Sam. Be a man. Put your foot down."

Jane got her coat off and slipped in beside him, hearing the tail end of the conversation. "You mean, like you do at home, honey?"

Davy frowned. Sam laughed.

"He can live without football for a day," Jane said, dragging him into the midst of the crowd.

The next time the doorbell rang, it was Miriam, her daughters and grandchildren. Rachel's Aunt Jo and her husband came next, followed by their children and grandchildren. Rachel's sister Ann and her husband, Greg, came last.

Everyone came with a stack of presents, which they piled under the tree.

Zach gaped at them and tugged on Sam's pants leg. "Are all those for us?"

"For everybody here," Sam said.

"Wow! Can we open 'em now?"

"In a minute," Rachel said. "We have to do something first."

"What?"

"The ornaments," she said.

He pointed to the tree. "It's got orn'ments."

"Special ones," Sam said.

"Those look special."

"Extra special," Sam said, nodding toward Gail and Ellen, who'd come into the room with three boxes. "You'll see."

Miriam and Jo took their places beside the tree, because this was Rachel's mother's family tradition, and damned if it didn't get to him every time they did it. Gail and Ellen put the boxes down beside the two women, who looked very much alike at the moment and reminded him of Rachel's mother. Frank tapped a spoon against a glass to get everyone's attention and welcomed them all, telling them he was happy they were all here to see another Christmas together, and then he turned things over to Miriam and Jo. They opened the first box and from among the tissue paper pulled out one delicate glass ornament each.

"It looks like a snowflake," Zach said. "Or a star."

And they did. They were some of the first projects Rachel's grandfather made when he started working with glass, long before he hit on his success with snow globes.

One year, he had some diamond-shaped pieces of beveled glass, and he put them together into three-dimensional ornaments. He trimmed them in a gold tone and engraved each one with his three daughters' names and the date of their birth.

They loved them, and the next year, all the relatives had their own ornaments that went up on the tree Christmas Day as they all gathered together, and one of their most sacred traditions was born. It was a way of remembering everyone they'd loved and lost, of remembering all the blessings they had and the strength that comes from family.

This was the house where the tradition first began.

Sam and Rachel were the caretakers now of both the house and the ornaments. Jo still made them, just like her father had taught her. One day when she was gone, Rachel would make them.

Miriam and Jo put their ornaments on the tree, then ones for their own mother and father. Frank put up his and his wife's next, and they went on like that, one by one.

Finally, it was Rachel's turn. She took Sam by the hand and pulled him to the tree with her. Jo handed him his ornament. It read *Sam, 1988,* the year he and Rachel were married.

He remembered that year so well, how bewildered he'd been to find himself in the middle of a Christmas celebration like this. It had awed him, thinking Rachel had come from this, something this strong and this enduring. All of this love.

She put her ornament on the tree, and he hung his next to hers. *Sam and Rachel.* And when he would have stepped back so the others could hang theirs, she held him there and took another ornament from Jo.

It said *Hope, 1989.*

"You do it," she said, giving it carefully to him.

"You're sure?" he asked.

"Yes," she whispered.

They'd never hung this ornament before. He knew it existed at one time. Her grandfather had it ready for them the first Christmas after they lost her, and it had caused a horrible scene. Rachel had refused to put it on the tree, had run out of the room in tears. Sam had never seen the ornament again, but Rachel's grandfather must have saved it. Maybe he'd been trying to tell them even then that they had to deal with the loss, they had to remember her. Maybe he knew what it would cost them if they didn't.

Sam reached out and found a branch, a sturdy one, right below where his and Rachel's ornaments were hanging, and with a hand that positively shook, placed their baby's glittering star carefully on the tree.

He and Rachel stood there together, looking at the three ornaments rotating slowly and glittering in the light. Sam took a breath, a slow, deep one, and Rachel slipped an arm around his waist.

"No more tears," she said. "You made me promise. She'll always be a part of us, but no more tears."

Sam nodded. It was all he could do.

They went to step back once more and Jo said, "Wait. We have new people in the family. We can't forget them."

And then she held the box out to them, three ornaments left.

"Oh, Jo," Rachel said, taking the box, turning the ornaments over one by one so she could read the names. *Emma, 2000. Zach, 2000. Grace, 2000.*

"I believe," Jo whispered.

"What's that?" Emma said tentatively, crowding in beside them and looking over the sides of the box to what was inside.

Rachel held it out to her.

"For me?" Her voice was filled with awe. Sam knew just how she felt. He remembered being awed himself the first time he'd taken part in this.

"Yes," Rachel said, and it looked as if all they'd said about tears was going down the drain right now.

"And me?" Zach asked, bouncing over to them.

"Careful," he and Rachel said together as Zach reached for his.

"Wow!" He held it up and let it spin on its string, and then he laughed. "It says Zach! Right there!" And it did, etched into one of the pieces and painted in gold.

"Let's get it on the tree, while it's still in one piece," Jo said, stepping in when he and Rachel seemed hardly able to move. She guided Zach and Emma to safe places on the tree, to sturdy branches, and then said, "One more."

Rachel's sister Gail had Grace, who came quite happily into Sam's arms. She was grinning at him and pressing her tiny hands against his cheeks, was about to start sucking on his nose when he sidetracked her and kissed her instead. She gave him a dazzling smile, and then her gaze caught on the ornament Rachel held up in front of her.

"See," Rachel said, "it says *Grace*."

Grace reached for it, batted it just enough to send it spinning, too, and then she started babbling a mile a minute.

Rachel kissed her, too, and said, "I know. It's so special, isn't it? And it's just for you."

"I think she likes it," Emma said.

"Uh-huh," Zach said.

Rachel handed the ornament to Emma and said, "Why don't you put it on the tree."

She reached for one of the lower branches, near the right side, but Jo guided her to another spot, so that all of theirs ended up together. Sam, Rachel, Emma, Zach, Grace, and Hope.

There was absolute silence in the room when Emma was done. Sam didn't remember the house ever being quiet at Christmas.

Emma came to stand on Rachel's side, Sam on the other holding the baby, Zach in front of them, and for a moment all five of them just stood there, staring at the tree and all their names, sparkling and shining and so full of promise.

"There," Jo said finally. "It's done. Merry Christmas, everybody."

Chapter 17

So, the tree was done. He and Rachel turned to each other, and he pulled her close, as close as he could with Grace between them.

"Merry Christmas," he whispered, kissing her softly.

"Merry Christmas," she said.

They both kissed Grace, too, at the same time. She was sandwiched between them, looking surprised and then very pleased.

"What's goin' on?" Zach asked.

"Tradition," Rachel whispered, grabbing him and lifting him into her arms.

"Trahh . . . Huh?"

"Something we always do," she said. "Now you're supposed to hug me and wish me Merry Christmas."

He did and then said, "Now what?"

"Now you hug everybody in this room. You can kiss them, too, if you want. And wish them Merry Christmas. And let them do the same to you."

"Ever'body?" He looked skeptical.

"Everybody," Jo insisted, grabbing him away from Rachel for her hug. Rachel's brother grabbed her, and Sam lost her for a moment in a flurry of hugs and kisses that he still found a bit awkward and disarming, too.

When that was done, Rachel's father settled into his place by the tree and started handing out presents, one by one and very slowly, telling stories about each of the recipients as he went. The rules said nobody got to open a thing until all the presents were passed out, which had the kids groaning and trying to make their grandfather speed up. He never did.

Emma was standing beside Sam, and he could see the surprise on her face when Frank called her over to him and treated her as he did all the other grand-children. Zach wasn't surprised at all. He seemed to expect it, but Emma still didn't, even with her orna-ment on the tree.

She came back to stand by Sam's side, inching closer and closer. He put his hand on her shoulder and said, "What did you get?"

"I don't know."

"No guesses?"

She shook her head.

"Anything wrong?"

She shrugged and looked around the crowded room. There were about sixteen conversations going on at once, not a spare inch of floor space in the room. All those happy faces, all the laughter.

"Is it always like this?" Emma asked.

"At Christmas. Easter. Memorial Day. Fourth of July. Labor Day. Thanksgiving. Christmas again. Rachel's family loves to celebrate."

"They're all so nice," she said.

"Yes, they are."

"They . . . they all act like they know me. Like they like me."

"It's the way they are," he said. Maybe not with him, but they would be with Emma and Zach and

Grace. And even that probably wasn't fair, Sam realized. Rachel's father hadn't really accepted him, but
the rest of the family had. They'd drawn him in, at
least as much as he'd let them. He was a part of them
now.

They were ready to draw Emma and her brother and
sister into their midst, just as generously and eagerly as
they'd welcomed Sam. He'd never loved them more
than he did right now for the generosity they'd shown
toward the children. He was awed by it, all choked up
by it. He'd never thought to belong to anything like
this family, to anything this strong, this enduring.

"They're good people, Em," he said.

She nodded. "I like the snowflake ornaments."

"Me, too."

"I like it here."

"I'm glad."

"And . . . I like you, too."

Sam nodded, thinking about grabbing her and just
holding on to her, too, but she looked so shy at the moment, so ready to bolt and run. Emma would be slow
to accept things like that, and he didn't want to spook
her. So he just gave her as much of a smile as he could
manage and said, "I like you, too. Merry Christmas."

She slipped away from him, as if the conversation
had become too much for her. Oh, Emma, he thought.
They had a lot in common.

He was still sitting there a few minutes later when
Rachel came to him. She sat on the floor, settling in
with her side pressed against his leg, her head against
his knee.

"Your family really is amazing," he said, his hand
teasing at the ends of her hair.

"Our family, Sam. They're yours, too."

He nodded.

She went to turn to face him and bumped into the sign she'd made for him, which he'd stashed in the relative safety of the corner. "Careful."

"Oh. I didn't know that was there." She reached for the sign again, tracing his name and then hers. "You know, it didn't turn out quite the way I expected."

"Rachel, I love it. It's perfect."

"That's not what I was saying. I love the way it turned out. It's just not what I thought it would be. I always start with an image in my mind of what it's going to be, but it's like projects take on a life of their own. Like there's something else they were just meant to be, and it used to drive me crazy. I'd work so hard to force my vision onto the work. It seemed like I ought to be able to do that. After all, I could hold all the pieces in my hand, the design and all the different kinds and colors of glass. I'd cut them and grind them and shape them into the pattern in my head, and no matter how careful I was and how determined, it never came out exactly the way I expected.

"My grandfather used to try to explain it to me—that I hadn't failed just because in the end, I had something that was different than I envisioned. That part of creating art is letting it just be what it wants to be, accepting what comes, rejoicing in it, even," she said, laying her head on his knee again. "And he was talking about life, too, I think. All those things I thought I had to have, all that time I spent trying to make all the pieces fit together the way I imagined they should."

"What are you saying, Rachel?" he asked quietly.

"I'm saying, look around this room, at all that's here. This place and these people are all the pieces of our lives. We can make something so beautiful of this, Sam. It is beautiful. It's beautiful right now."

And it was.

She was still waiting for what he might have said a moment later when Zach brought a present to Sam and one to Rachel. They'd missed her father calling their names. And a moment later, Frank said, "Let 'er rip!"

Everyone tore into presents all at once in a race to get them opened, and general chaos ensued once again. Sam and Rachel got separated as he supervised a marginal cleaning of the living room. At least enough that they could walk through the room, and she went to the kitchen. The meal had to go on the table soon because all of her siblings' spouses had family in the area, too, and they spent the evening with them.

Late afternoon and evening, by tradition, was drop-in time for neighbors and various other relatives who didn't make it to Christmas dinner. Soon after they finished the meal, the house was overflowing even more with people, and it seemed a general Christmas truce had been lifted—the subject of the truce, Rachel's troubled marriage. She could just imagine them all getting together and deciding they couldn't ruin Christmas with all this talk. But the presents had been opened, the ornaments were on the tree, dinner eaten, and soon her siblings would be leaving. They couldn't leave without saying anything.

Her first clue was her brother, who came up to her and hugged her and said, "I don't know what's going on. That little scene with the ornaments?" He placed a hand theatrically over his heart. "Got me right here. And I don't know if that was staged—"

"We didn't stage anything," Rachel said.

"Okay, I just wondered. I wondered too if maybe you wanted me to beat him up?"

"Sam?" Rachel asked.

"Yes, Sam."

"Why?"

"I don't know. What's he done?"

"He hasn't done anything," Rachel said. "And your wife's looking for you. I think she managed to corral your entire crew and wants to escape before they get loose. You have to go to her parents', right?"

"Yes."

"Go," she said, shooing him away and retreating to the kitchen.

Her friend Mary Ann, from the shoe shop, caught her there and rambled aimlessly for ten minutes about nothing, which was a relief. But then Mary Ann's face fell and she whispered, "I just can't imagine you without Sam."

"Neither can I," Rachel said, smiling and playing dumb about it all.

She stuck her head in the refrigerator and when she emerged from there, her neighbor, Mrs. Potter, was giving her a kindly smile and patting Rachel's hand.

"You can never give up, my dear. Never," Mrs. Potter said.

"I'm not," Rachel promised.

Her sister Ann confessed, "I was about to strangle Greg if he didn't get his mother to leave me alone about the fact that we hadn't had children yet. You think Daddy was bad? Greg's mother was relentless. I couldn't have a conversation with her without her asking me about it and making me feel like a bad wife because we hadn't reproduced yet."

"Oh?" Rachel said.

"Yes. She's never liked me, and I can accept that. But I don't think it's any more her business than Daddy's when Greg and I chose to have children, and don't get me wrong, I'm glad it's happening. But we just weren't ready before. We wanted a little time to ourselves. I think we deserve that."

"Of course," Rachel agreed.

"But his mother just kept pushing, and Greg kept telling me to just ignore her. I guess that's how he's dealt with her all these years, but I don't have to do that. She's not my mother. All I wanted was for him to stand up to her for me, and for the longest time, he wouldn't. We used to fight all the time about it."

"You did?" Rachel had no idea.

"Now she's driving me crazy *about* the baby. You'd think she was the only woman on earth to ever raise a child successfully. She thinks she knows everything, and I can already see it's going to be trouble. Greg doesn't always do what I think he should to get her to just butt out of our marriage, and as much as that irritates me, I still love him," Ann said.

"Of course." Rachel had never doubted that part.

"Sometimes it just gets so hard," her sister Gail added quite sincerely, then stood there waiting expectantly.

"Oh," Rachel said, beginning to see where the conversation was going. She had honestly thought for a moment it was going to turn into a gripe session about men, and she hadn't understood what brought that on.

"Alex wanted to take a job in Phoenix the year Mom got sick," Gail said finally, when it was clear Rachel wouldn't say anything more. "Can you imagine? I mean, it was a good opportunity for him, but we were doing fine here, and there was no way I could have left with Mom so sick. I couldn't believe he'd even suggest it. We had terrible fights about it, and one night I told him if he had to take that job, to just go ahead and go. The kids and I would stay right here, where we belonged."

"Really?" How had Rachel missed that?

"We all have problems," Gail said.

"I know," Rachel agreed, but really, she hadn't known any of this.

"I wish Mom were here. She'd know what to say," Gail said, sighing and looking around. "It's almost like old times, you know? Like when we were kids. Being here in this house at Christmas, with the family all around. Ever since Mom was gone, we've all been together here. It's the Christmas house and the Thanksgiving house and the Fourth of July. All of those things. I can't imagine us all not being here, and . . ."

Her sister broke off, almost in tears.

"I'm sorry. Here I am thinking of me and my holidays, when—"

"It is a holiday. Today. Let's think of that," Rachel suggested.

"But—"

"Let's," she said. "Or even better, how in the world did you keep all these problems from me and from Dad and everyone?" That part absolutely fascinated Rachel.

"That's not the point," Ann said.

"Maybe not for you," Rachel said, but right now everybody in the world was sticking their collective noses into her marriage.

"The point is that marriage is hard. You don't just give up," Gail said.

"I'm not giving up," Rachel insisted. "And right now, I'm going to find my husband."

She thought she should probably try to rescue him from the same treatment she was getting. She saw him being cornered as often as she was, and she could tell from the knowing look in his eyes that they were hearing the same things. Right now, her father had him at the foot of the stairs.

She made her way, as fast as she could, to Sam's side, just in time to hear her father say, "I think I said a lot of things over the years that you didn't deserve. That day at the hospital, especially."

"What?" she asked, surprising them both. "What did you say to him?"

"Rachel, don't," Sam said.

"No, I want to know. Daddy, what did you say to him?"

"Something along the lines of him not doing his job, not doing what he promised me he would—which was to take good care of you and that baby."

"Oh, Daddy," Rachel said, then looked to Sam, who stood there staring back at her father.

"I'm sorry," her father said.

"It wasn't his fault," Rachel said.

"No," her father said. "That was a father talking, a father who was scared he was going to lose his little girl and thinking he'd failed her somehow. I thought I hadn't done enough to keep you safe and happy, little girl. It's hard for a man to let his daughter grow up. To give her into the safekeeping of another man. I don't think any father thinks the man who wins his little girl's heart is good enough for her, but I should have gotten over that a long time ago. It's been obvious to anyone who wasn't blind that you love Sam and that Sam's loved you for a long time."

He turned to Sam and stuck out his hand.

"You've worked hard, made something of yourself, and I know you've been good to my little girl. After twelve years, I guess it's a little late to welcome you to the family. But I'm proud of you, Sam. Proud of what you've done here to this old house and to this town. And I don't think you're the only one who needs to hear that."

Rachel didn't know what he planned to do, but before she knew it, he'd dragged her and Sam a third of the way up the stairs, where they could see everyone in the front part of the house and everyone could see them.

Her father had a glass of spiced cider in his hand. He called for everyone to be quiet, then raised his glass and announced that he had a toast to make. He talked about how happy he was to be there, to have all his friends and family around him, how blessed he felt. And then he turned to Sam and Rachel.

"To my little girl, whom I love dearly." He raised his glass. "I'm so proud of her, for all that she does for our family and for this community. I can't imagine where any of us would be without her. Especially her husband and my new best friend Zach, and his two sisters."

He leaned down close and kissed Rachel's cheek. "This is what you were meant to do, little girl."

And it was. She realized that there wasn't anything she'd ever done in her life that gave her the kind of satisfaction that came from taking care of the people she loved. For so long, she'd honestly thought she was just drifting along, following where life led her, but in truth, she'd done exactly what she should have been doing. She'd been taking care of everyone. It was the only thing she could have done.

And these children . . . Zach was standing there grinning at the bottom of the stairs, and Emma was standing by the fireplace watching with an eagle eye as Rachel's fourteen-year-old niece held Grace. Her father was right. This was what she was meant to do. This felt better and more important than anything she'd ever done.

"I love you, Daddy," she said.

He winked at her as he addressed the crowd again. "And to my little girl's husband of twelve years. I was just thinking of how nice it is to be in this house on this day. The place where my wife and her sisters grew up, a place that holds so many memories. I don't think the house ever looked as good back then as it does now. Sam and Rachel made it glow.

"I was thinking about my own father-in-law and all the joy he's brought so many people with his work. He loved this town, too, and I realized that my son-in-law's brought the town back to us with all the work he's done to restore so many of our grand old buildings. He's made the place look as good as it did fifty years ago or better, and now we have all these nice people from all over the place coming here to see it and enjoy it over the holidays.

"I know we had some hard times in this town and that there are lots of downtowns dying all over these days, but this town's alive and prospering. It glows with all the magic of Christmas, and I just wanted to take a moment to tell him how much that means to us. And that I'm proud of him and my little girl."

There were cheers and raised glasses and well

wishes all around. Rachel gave her father a big hug and a teary smile.

"You were right," he said. "I hadn't been fair to him, and if I've made your marriage any harder because of it, I'm sorry. I thought I owed him a very public apology."

"You did good," she said, looking over at her clearly stunned husband. And then she had an idea. They'd show them this marriage wasn't done, no matter what they'd heard. She wrapped her arms around him and said, "Kiss me, Sam. Right here. In front of them all."

And Sam did. He caught her close and gave her a long, leisurely kiss that had their entire audience cheering before they were done.

She eased back in his arms, remembering the look in his eyes, the husky roughness in his voice that morning in their bed when he'd told her he still loved her. What more could a woman want from Christmas than all that she had in this moment?

She was in the kitchen cleaning up later that afternoon when someone's cell phone rang. When she turned and saw the look on Miriam's face, Rachel knew right away who this call was about.

The children.

A moment later, Sam was at her side, his arm firmly around her waist. When Miriam finished the call, Rachel said, "You found their mother, didn't you?"

"Yes. About two hours from here by car. In a hospital near Indianapolis. She's been there unconscious since the day after she left them in that motel."

Rachel drew herself up a bit straighter. Sam was right beside her, hanging close, maybe waiting for her to fall apart. Well, she wasn't going to. She'd known this day was likely coming, and this was what the children wanted.

"Is she all right?" Rachel asked.

"I don't know. But she's conscious now, and she wants to see the children, if that's possible. Today."

Rachel nodded, her heart withering just a bit. *Today.*

"It's the woman they found in Shepherdsville, right?" Sam asked.

"What woman?" Rachel asked.

"Someone found a woman dumped on the side of the road two weeks ago. She'd been beaten half to death and was unconscious, with no ID. Nobody had any idea who she was."

"And you knew about this?"

"Yesterday," he said. "I found out yesterday. Not that she was their mother, just that she might be. I didn't see any reason to say anything until we knew for sure."

"Oh."

"What about their father?" Sam asked.

"I don't know," Miriam said.

"You're going to find out. He used to beat her up, and I'm betting he's the one who put her in the hospital."

"You've talked to the sheriff about all this?"

"Yesterday," Sam said. "He was working on identifying her, but I guess if she's awake, we don't have to worry about that. We do have to worry about him. If he's the one who did this to her, those kids aren't going anywhere near her until he's behind bars."

"Sam, it's not for you to say," Miriam argued.

"Forget it, Miriam. I promised them they'd be safe from him, and I'm going to keep that promise. The man's going to be behind bars. That's it."

Sam didn't give an inch. It was an hour and a half later before he heard from the sheriff. They had taken Annie Greene's statement from her hospital bed and used that evidence to arrest her husband, who was behind bars on a charge of attempted murder.

"Okay. It's getting late," Miriam said to the two of them, then checked her watch. It was almost five. The hospital in Indianapolis was almost two hours away. "Maybe we should wait until tomorrow."

"No. It's Christmas. We have to take them today," Rachel said. "It's all they really wanted for Christmas. To see their mother."

"Are you okay?" Sam asked.

"Yes," Rachel said, feeling more calm than she would have expected. "This is what they want, and I want them to be happy. Just like I want you to be happy. Whatever it takes."

Chapter 18

They told the children together. Zach jumped up and down, he was so happy. His whole face lit up, and he was practically running for the door, leaving Rachel to chase him.

Emma looked up at Sam with a mixture of hope and love and fear on her face that left him practically paralyzed, finally whispering, "You found her?"

Sam nodded.

She flew into his arms and held on tight, her whole body shaking. "Oh, Sam. Thank you."

"You're welcome, Em." He waited until she'd calmed down a bit, wishing he didn't have to tell her the rest, wishing he could really be her hero, the one who made everything all better for her. "There's something else."

"What?"

"She's in the hospital."

Emma's expression froze. "Is she okay?"

Sam dodged that one. He didn't know the answer himself. "She's been unconscious. You know, when you're asleep and can't wake up?"

Emma nodded.

"She's been like that the whole time. That's why she didn't come back to get you. And now she's awake."

"Is she still going to be in trouble?"

"I don't know. All I know right now is that we found her, and she wants to see you. Rachel and Miriam and I will take you to her."

"And then she'll take us home?"

"I don't think she's well enough to come home yet. But you can stay with Rachel and me awhile longer. You don't have to worry about that part."

"Okay."

She was still trembling, still worried. He could tell. Finally, she looked up at him and said, "Was it my dad? Did he find her? Did he hurt her?"

Sam nodded. "But you don't have to worry about him, either. He's in jail, and even if he wasn't, he doesn't know where you are and nobody's going to tell him. You're safe here, Em."

"Okay," she said breathlessly.

"Come on," Sam said, his hand firmly on her shoulder. "Let's go see your mom."

It was a quiet, somber drive to the hospital. Rachel sat beside him, her hand clasped tightly in his for most of the journey. Zach and Grace dozed off on the way, and they had to wake them when they arrived. Miriam went into the room first, and came back looking pale and worried. Sam knew why. He'd seen Annie Greene the day before.

"They're going to turn down the lights. I think that might help a little to hide the bruises. But she looks awful," Miriam whispered.

Sam took Emma and Zach aside and told them, "Your mom looks bad."

"Bad?" Zach said. "She's been bad?"

"No. Not that. She just . . . She has some bruises on her face, and it's kind of puffy, too. She has some machines hooked up to her, some tubes and wires and things, but don't worry about those. They're all helping her."

"Tubes?" Zach said.

"She's sick, Zach," Emma explained.

"Yes, she's sick. You need to be careful about jumping on her. Even about hugging her. I know you want to, but you don't want to hurt her."

Zach looked perplexed. "She can't hug me?"

"I bet she can. You'll just have to be careful. Let her hug you, okay? Don't run in there and grab her. You might grab on to a part of her that's sore."

"Okay." Zach was ready. "Can we go now?"

Miriam took him by the hand and said, "Come on. I'll take you."

Emma waited, looking up at Sam, getting ready to cry.

"I know you want to see her," he said. "Everybody here is working to make her better, but I bet seeing you and Zach will do more to make her feel better than anything anyone else could do."

"I'm scared, Sam."

"I know." She started to cry. Sam dried her eyes as best he could. "She needs to see you. She needs to know you're okay."

"Okay."

"Rachel and I will be right here waiting for you."

Emma disappeared into the room. Sam felt sick to his stomach, wishing he could spare her this, hating the powerlessness he felt in this moment. There should be a way for a man to protect the people he loved, and he loved these kids. There should be a way he could take the hurt himself and spare them.

And then there was Rachel, standing by the wall

holding the baby, looking more angellike than ever as she slept with her face tucked sideways against Rachel's shoulder. Grace's cheeks were pink and full, her nose like a button, her lavish eyelashes lying against those silky cheeks, one hand clenched in a fist that was half in her mouth. She was sucking and smacking her lips against it in her sleep.

Sam smoothed down the flyaway baby hair and kissed the baby's forehead, then wrapped his arm around her and Rachel. Rachel was trembling, too, and she leaned her head on Sam's shoulder, and he could feel the misery coursing through her.

For a second, he thought of last night and this morning. Thought of how close they'd been, how hopeful he'd been. It was selfish, he knew, and he didn't wish any more misery on Annie Greene and certainly not upon her children. But he and Rachel had been so close, so close to having everything.

He pulled her closer, wishing he could stop her from hurting, too. Wishing he could give her strength and somehow make this bearable for her. But he didn't have any words, couldn't think of anything to do except hold her.

They were still standing there a moment later when the door to Annie Greene's room opened again. Zach and Emma came out in a rush, Zach looking scared, Emma almost as pale as her mother had been the day before. They came to him and Rachel. Sam picked up Zach, and he and Rachel pulled Emma into their embrace, the five of them locked there together in their shared misery.

"Mommy's really sick," Zach said.

"I know," Sam told him.

"Is she gonna get better?"

"I hope so, Zach."

Emma's head came up at that. She was studying Sam's face, looking for reassurance, and he couldn't bring himself to lie to her. *I hope so* was the best he could do with any degree of honesty at all.

Her lower lip started to tremble, and then her eyes and her mouth took on that pinched look a moment before she bent her head until it rested on Rachel's shoulder, and she started to weep. He would have done anything, he thought, anything at all to spare her this.

Miriam ended up taking the baby from Rachel and disappeared into Annie Greene's room once again. Sam took Zach down the hall to a vending machine and bought him a drink, because seeing Emma so upset was worrying Zach, too. It also bought Emma some time alone with Rachel. It was a while after that before they got everyone settled down in a small waiting room down the hall. Miriam came back with Grace and asked Emma to take her for a moment while she pulled Sam and Rachel into the hall and told them Annie Greene was asking to see them.

"I think she just wants to know who has her children for now," Miriam said. "Will you talk to her?"

Rachel agreed, and then Sam led her down the hallway. He'd hardly let go of her since the phone call, hadn't wanted to. She was obviously upset and shaken, but she hadn't fallen apart, not like she had when Will had been taken away from them, and it hadn't been that long ago. Sam was proud of her. She was obviously intent on trying to make this as easy as possible for the children, no matter what it cost her.

He stopped her at the door to the room, trying to prepare her. She still gasped at the figure on the bed, who seemed so desperately frail, her face a bruised, swollen mess.

Sam guided Rachel into the room and down into a chair at Annie Greene's bedside. Annie held out her hand to Rachel, and Rachel took it. Sam stood behind his wife, his hands on her shoulders.

"I just wanted to see the two of you," she whispered weakly, haltingly. "And to thank you. Emma and Zach said . . . you've been very kind."

"You have wonderful children," Rachel said, her voice trembling.

"I'm afraid I'm going to be here for a while," she said. "Your aunt said you're willing to keep them . . . for as long as it takes?"

"As long as it takes," Sam said.

"Thank you. It . . . I was so scared when I realized how long I'd been here. I imagined all sorts of terrible things happening to them . . ."

Sam stifled the urge to ask why she'd taken such a risk by coming here. Why she'd ever married a man who beat her and stayed with him all those years or how she came to be in a situation where there was no one but two strangers and the child welfare system to take care of her children. He was angry, but he could contain it for now. It wasn't the time to demand explanations of anyone.

"We'll take good care of them," he vowed.

"Thank you," she said, and a moment later had drifted off, either asleep or unconscious again, they couldn't tell.

"Come on." Sam tightened his hands on Rachel's shoulders. "Let's go."

They were just outside the door, in the hall, when Rachel turned blindly into his arms and started to cry.

He held her for a long moment, feeling helpless once again and hating it all the more.

"She looks so bad," Rachel said, her face against his shoulder. "I can't imagine what she's been through, can't imagine a man who's supposed to love me, one who's the father of my children doing something like that to me. And the children . . . No wonder they were so scared."

"I know."

Sam heard footsteps and looked up to see a woman in a white coat coming down the hall, a tag that identified her as a doctor. She paused in front of them and said, "You're friends of Mrs. Greene's?"

Rachel hastily dried her tears and together they faced the doctor. "We're taking care of her children," Sam said. "They want to know how she is."

"She doesn't seem to have any neurological damage from the head injury, which had us worried because she hadn't regained consciousness before today." There was an odd look on the doctor's face. "But . . . it's going to be a long road. I would say as little as possible at this moment to her children."

Sam frowned, wondering what was being left unsaid. Finally he settled for asking, "She's going to be here for a while? Days? Weeks?"

"Weeks, at least," the doctor said, excusing herself and walking back into Annie's room.

Sam stood there for a moment, facing his wife, holding her by her arms, hating this look on her face. It brought back too many memories of too many bad times. "It's late," he said finally. "The kids have to be exhausted. Let's take them home."

Rachel nodded, slipped her arm around his waist, and together they walked back down the hallway to the waiting room and tried not to look so grim once they got there. They had children to take care of.

They'd talked briefly with Miriam before she left the house. She said as far as they were concerned, nothing had changed. The children were still wards of the state, and Sam and Rachel were still their foster parents. It was hard to say what would happen next. There might be relatives of Annie's or even her husband's who might come forward and want to take care of them. Relatives who could provide a stable home were normally favored over strangers.

If there was no one but Sam and Rachel to care for them, Miriam didn't know what might happen when Annie Greene was released from the hospital, how a judge might view her leaving them alone in that motel, even if it was only supposed to be for the day. They'd all have to wait and see.

They got back to the house and put the kids to bed, and then together they faced a house filled with the ghosts of the Christmas just past. Someone had left the lights on the tree and the ones on the outside of the house on. They blinked with annoying regularity, seeming to mock the events of the day. There were presents all over the place. Everything seemed as disorganized and scattered as the house was, and the day that was supposed to be so special, so magical, was ending in such disarray.

Sam didn't even know what to hope for anymore. He wanted the children to be happy and safe. He wondered if they ever would be with their mother. He had a knot in his stomach just thinking about giving them back to her. He wanted to be their safe harbor, the one place they could always turn to.

And then there was Rachel. He was supposed to leave in the morning, but he wasn't going anywhere for now. And he owed it to his friend to tell him something about the apartment. If it had been just twenty-four hours ago, Sam would have said he was staying, that he and Rachel could make this work.

But this was his and Rachel's worst nightmare come true.

Sam looked up the staircase and dreaded going up there, had a sinking feeling about what he would find. She hadn't come down since she went to check on Emma, and that had been thirty minutes ago.

Just a month ago, Sam would never have thought of going up there to see if she was okay. He'd have known she wasn't and been out of ideas about how he might help. He'd have hidden in his office and hoped she was asleep by the time he came inside. Because he would have exhausted every bit of energy he had trying to make her feel better and been dying to escape the misery in this house. He didn't feel that way now, but he was simply afraid of going back to living the way they had for so long.

Slowly, dread dogging his every step, he climbed to the second floor and went from bedroom to bedroom. Zach and the baby were asleep. So was Emma. His and Rachel's bedroom was empty, but the bathroom door was closed.

How many times had he found her weeping in the bathtub? How many times had he walked away. This time he stood by the door and said, "Rachel?"

"Yes?" she called out.

He heard the sound of water lapping against the sides of the tub and sagged against the door. "I just wanted to know where you were."

"I'll be right out," she claimed.

He sat on the bed and waited, looking out the window at the lights still on in the neighborhood. He'd actually looked forward to Christmas this year, and now he was so tired. He didn't even know what to wish for, what to pray for.

Rachel had talked about taking things on faith. He'd only known one kind—the kind that told him no matter what, nothing was going to work out, that it never had.

And yet, some things had.

He looked around at the house and realized it was their place, the keeper of their memories, the stage of their lives. He couldn't imagine being anywhere else, couldn't imagine doing anything else with his life but taking old things and making them new and strong and whole again. It wasn't what he'd always wanted, but now that he had it, he realized how much he enjoyed it, how satisfying it was to him. To make something tangible and enduring. He could drive through town and look at building after building and think, *I did that. I helped make it what it is today.*

Life here hadn't been without its satisfactions.

Sam heard the bathroom door open with a slight creak and Rachel was standing there in a mix of heat and enticing smells. The lavender she put in her bathwater or rubbed on her skin, now mixed with the heat and the condensation in the bathroom, unfurled like a cloud into their bedroom, billowing out and surrounding him. He loved this smell, the Rachel-straight-from-the-bath smell.

She had her hair piled haphazardly on top of her head, little bits of it escaping in damp curls at her nape, and her skin had that rosy glow. He knew how dewy soft it would be right now, how warm, how good it would taste.

She had on the robe he'd given her and, he thought, nothing else. It was paper thin, enticing more than covering, and clinging to every inch of her slightly damp skin. Her eyes showed evidence of recent tears, but again, she didn't look like a woman on the verge of falling apart. She looked sad and oddly tentative, but determined, as well.

"The children are asleep," she said. "Miriam's gone?"

Sam nodded.

"She didn't say anything else to you about what's going to happen?"

"No."

"You're not keeping anything else from me? About them?"

"I'm not keeping anything at all from you."

"Okay. I didn't mean . . . I understand why you didn't tell me about Annie—"

"I didn't know, Rachel. Nothing for sure. I didn't even have my suspicions about it until I talked to Emma a few days ago."

"I understand." She stood there, not coming any closer, not seeming any surer than he was about what to do next. Finally, she said, "You told Annie we'd keep the children, and I wondered . . . I assumed . . ."

"I'm not going anywhere, Rachel. I'll call Rick tomorrow and tell him."

"You mean, you're not going while they're here?"

"That's right."

"And after that . . ."

"I'm not sure," he admitted, taking a deep, slow breath. He felt as if he were on the edge of a cliff all of a sudden, like one misstep and he'd lose everything.

"This changes everything between us?" she asked tentatively.

"I don't know. Does it?"

"I . . . I don't know." She stood there a moment longer. Finally, sighing, she said, "And I'm tired. I think I'll go to bed."

She flicked off the bathroom light and then the light on the bedside table, the room suddenly bathed in shadows and the glow from the front window that faced the well-lit street. She was close enough that he could smell her now, as he had in that moment all the fragrance wafted out of the bathroom in her wake. He wanted to touch her. He wanted so much. But he was worried, too.

"I know you wanted to keep them," he began.

"I did."

"And I know it hurts—"

"This is what they wanted, Sam. She's their mother. I know how powerful that bond is. I still miss my own mother, and I was more than twice Emma's age when I lost her. I wouldn't wish that kind of sorrow on anyone."

"Still . . ."

"I'm sad for us. Of course I am. But I'm not sorry we took them into our home. They needed us, and we helped them through this. I'm glad we could do that. And they've been good for us," she said. "I don't know why this happened, why these children came here now. I don't know why anything ever happens, but I don't regret this. Not one bit."

She had tears in her eyes by the time she was done, but then he did, too, and he couldn't hide them from her.

"You are so good with them," she said, reaching out

and taking his hand. "I've never seen you open up to anyone like you did with them. They needed things that only you could give them, and you did it. It made me love you more than ever."

"Rachel—"

"It's all right." She stopped him. "I'd like to get in bed now."

"Okay."

He stood up, pulled back the sheet, and let her climb in. He pulled the covers up around her and put his hand to her cheek.

"You can sleep here, if you want," she offered.

And he wanted. He wasn't sure if it was smart, but he wanted.

"I didn't lock up before I came upstairs," he said.

"Okay."

"I'll be up in a minute."

Rachel watched him go, feeling utterly drained and empty. She had no idea if he would come back, and she wanted so badly to have his arms around her, have the familiar bulk and warmth of his body next to hers in the bed.

She wasn't going to beg him to stay. She didn't have the right; after all, she'd promised him if they could just have the children here until after Christmas she wouldn't ask him for anything more. And Christmas had come and gone.

She lay perfectly still in the bed, conscious of every sound in the house, waiting for that faint creak of foot-steps on the stairs, thinking, *Come back to me, Sam. Just one more time. Come back.*

And he did. She heard him coming up the stairs. He

went into the bathroom, and she waited some more. If he walked away now . . .

The bathroom door opened. She heard him shedding his clothes, draping them over a chair in the corner. He had drawn back the covers and was slipping inside when she realized she was shaking badly. Delayed reaction to the events of the day and the depths of her fear about what was going to happen tonight with her and Sam and tomorrow with the children.

He lay on his back, not touching her at first, and then he extended his arm off to the right, between the top of her head and the headboard. That was the invitation she'd been waiting for. She rolled onto her side and then settled herself against him, her head on his shoulder, her hand on his chest, their legs intertwined.

Rachel let out a shaky breath, her heart racing.

"You're trembling," he said, angling his body toward hers, pushing her face down to his chest.

She was also fighting to keep her breath slow and even, to hold back her tears, because he hated it when she cried. Or maybe she'd simply spent too much time crying in the last few months. It had truly been an awful time.

"I'm going to miss them, too, Rachel," he said, as if they were already gone.

"I know."

"But I am glad we had them, too. You're right. It was the right thing for us to do."

He stroked a hand back and forth along her back, rubbing at the tension in her shoulders, at the base of her spine. Slowly, she was relaxing, the shivering lessening. He had wonderful hands—strong and warm and a bit rough from his calluses—and it was good to have his hands on her, to have him here in her bed. She turned her head and dropped a kiss onto his chest, then tilted her head back, turned his face to hers, brushed his lips with hers. The kiss was hesitant at first, questioning, and then deeper and needier.

He pulled away and put his hand on the side of her face, staring down at her through the darkness. He was shaking, too, she realized, not sure why, not sure why he was holding back now.

"Is it so bad to want me? To want to be with me?" she asked. "I'm still your wife."

"No. I just . . . I wonder how long this is going to last, Rachel. Any of this. I told you I can't go back to the way things were before."

"Neither can I."

"I'm afraid of what's going to happen to us when the kids go."

"So am I," she said. "But we never had any guarantees to start with about how things were going to turn out, Sam. We just thought we did. And now we've both seen what it would be like to lose each other. I don't want to lose you."

"And I don't want to give you up," he said.

"I'll never ask you to," she said. "Never."

And then finally, his mouth came down to hers, and he kissed her deeply, needily. She felt every bit of the frustration in him, frustration over the events of the day, the uncertainties that plagued them both in the night.

She felt as if she were in the middle of a storm, a roaring, swirling storm. It felt dangerous and like it had the potential to blow them both away. But they clung to each other, were bound together and determined to ride this out.

He stripped her efficiently and quickly, and then he

was devouring her body, fighting against what was inside of him and everything that was between them. She knew all his frustrations and fears, and she wanted him desperately.

It was a greedy, breath-robbing journey, and her hands, her mouth, were every bit as busy as his. They couldn't get close enough quickly enough. He couldn't get deep enough inside of her, and she couldn't draw in air quickly enough or in sufficient quantities to stop her head from spinning.

Her back arched and her legs parted, and she rocked against him, trying to draw him in even deeper. He moved with such strength, such need, ruthlessly pushing her up and over the edge. She dug her nails into his back and cried out his name, dizzy from the heights to which he'd taken her, all the while conscious of the fact that having taken her so high, she now had to come back down to earth.

If they'd both been trying to outrun this thing, the sorrow, the anger, they'd succeeded but only temporarily. It was right there waiting for them in the end.

Sam buried his face in the side of her neck, and lay heavily on top of her, laboring for each breath, and she was trembling once again, every bit as hard as before. She still had a grip on him. She was afraid she would leave marks on him, and even knowing that, had a hard time loosening her hands.

He kissed her cheek, nuzzled the tip of his nose against her, and then kissed her mouth, still needing something she wished she could provide. She knew what he wanted, what he needed. Oblivion and a place to hide from the pain, and she would give it to him, if she could. She would offer whatever comfort he could find in her arms.

"Did I hurt you?" he said warily.

"No."

"I was rough with you," he said grimly, and he never, ever was. He was considerate and patient and always conscious of her needs, her pleasure.

"I was rough with you, too," she said. "Did I hurt you?"

"No, Rachel."

"Don't worry about it. We needed each other. That's all."

"It scares me sometimes how much I need you."

"I need you every bit as much, Sam. I have the whole time. I was just afraid to let you close enough for me to see that, because I think I didn't want to love anyone else for a while, not even you. I was so sure I was going to get hurt again."

He bent his head and kissed her once more, slowly, softly. Still breathing heavily, he rolled off of her, and she followed him, until they ended up on their sides facing each other. She touched him lightly on the cheek and found it damp, his eyelashes, too. The corners of his eyes.

"Loving them wasn't a mistake," she insisted.

"I know." He touched his forehead to hers, stared down at her. "But I didn't want you to be hurt anymore."

"How do you ever ensure that? By not caring for anyone anymore? I tried that. We both know it didn't work. It failed miserably, and I'm not going to do that anymore. I'm still afraid, but I'm not going to let that fear rule my life. I love these kids. I love you. I'll accept whatever risks come with that because I can't stop myself from loving any of you."

"It's going to hurt both of us in the end," he said.

"And we've been hurt before. We're still here. It hasn't destroyed us. This won't, either."

His doubts might. The memories of what they'd become, what he feared they'd become again. But there was nothing left to say to convince him to take one more chance on her, one more leap of faith. It was up to him and the whims of the world now. She'd done all she could. She would survive, no matter what happened. Older and wiser and stronger, she would survive. Please, God, she thought, don't let her have to do it without him.

Chapter 19

They were sitting down to lunch the first day after Christmas when Miriam called and said Annie Greene wanted to speak to Sam and Rachel again. She came over and stayed with the kids, and they made the two-hour drive in a strained silence.

Sam held on to Rachel's hand as they walked into the ICU to find Annie asleep. Rachel sat in a chair beside the bed and Sam stood behind her, his hands on her shoulders, rubbing slightly at the tension there. She leaned back against him thinking that everything she had was on the line now.

Annie stirred in her bed and moaned. Her eyes opened slowly and seemed to have trouble focusing at first, and then she gave Rachel a weary smile. "You came."

"Of course," Rachel said. "What can we do for you?"

"A favor . . . An enormous favor," she said slowly, as if each word cost her a tremendous effort that was nearly beyond her at the moment. "I wanted to try to explain. I want you to know . . . I love my children . . ."

"Of course," Rachel said. She believed it.

"I never meant for it to end this way . . . I . . ." Her breathing grew more labored. There was a monitor measuring her heartbeat, and it was speeding up, even as she spoke. "I should have done more . . . Protected them . . . Taken better care of them . . ."

"They're fine," Rachel said. "Honestly, they are. They're wonderful, and they have absolute faith in you. They knew you'd never willingly leave them all by themselves. They've been telling us all along that you'd be back."

"I . . ." She gasped.

The beeping of the monitor was starting to really scare Rachel. Sam was reaching for the call button to summon a nurse when one walked in, going straight to the monitor and then to Annie.

"I was afraid this would happen. Annie, you can't do this to yourself."

"Tell them," Annie said, catching the nurse's hand. "Tell them for me."

"Of course." The nurse smiled back at them. "You're the ones taking care of her children?"

"Yes," Sam said. "What's going on?"

"I've been with her most of the day, and we've talked a good bit in bits and spurts. It's all she can manage right now. She's been waiting for you, and there's a lot she wants to say, but I'm afraid it would take too much out of her."

"Tell us, please," Sam said.

The nurse gave them a kind smile and kept hold of Annie's hand, looking from her to Sam and Rachel. "She wants you to know their father wasn't always like this, that he was a good man once."

Rachel felt Sam tense. They didn't want to hear about the so-called good man who'd done this to Annie Greene.

"She said he got sick—really sick. Not because he

was drinking. This was before all that. He missed a lot of work, lost his job. They lost almost everything. She said it was like they'd fallen into a string of bad luck and couldn't get out. About that time, she got pregnant with Zach. That's when things got really bad and when her husband started drinking. She never thought he'd hurt her, but of course, he did. She kept telling herself it would get better. It didn't. She didn't think he'd ever hurt the children, but one day her oldest daughter got between her and him, trying to save her . . . And that's when Annie knew they had to go."

"So ashamed . . . of myself," Annie whispered, tears in her eyes. "Should have known."

"It's all right," the nurse told her, and picked back up with the story. "She didn't really have anyone to turn to. Her husband's family . . . they all drank, too. And her family had been against her marrying him all along. They weren't interested in helping her out of the mess she'd made, and they were scared to have him coming around. So one day Annie packed their things and left. It wasn't until later that she realized she was pregnant again with Grace."

"Sweetest thing," Annie said. "Sweetest, happiest baby."

"She is," Rachel assured a crying Annie Greene.

"Don't want her to know . . . What she came from . . . How it was . . . Doesn't have anything to do with her."

"I understand," Rachel said. She was sure there weren't a lot of tender feelings left between husband and wife by then, but she doubted that would have stopped Annie's husband from taking what he wanted from her.

"She did the best she could, but it wasn't enough.

She'd hate for people to judge them based on what their father was like or what she's done."

"We would never do that," Sam said.

"Thank you," Annie whispered.

"She would never have come back here, but she was sick herself," the nurse said. "A problem with her kidneys from the beatings. They'd damaged her kidneys, and she hardly ever got proper medical care. Battered women seldom do. The damage was done, and getting pregnant again . . . Well, pregnancy takes its toll on a woman's entire body. It's especially difficult for someone with kidney problems. Honestly, I don't see how she made it through the pregnancy, and afterward, Annie was getting weaker all the time. She knew she wouldn't be able to go on taking care of the children on her own.

"She risked calling her mother, who refused to help. But Annie was desperate. They were losing their apartment in Georgia. She hadn't been able to work. There wasn't any money. She thought maybe if she told her mother the whole story in person, her mother would listen. But she was afraid to take the children anywhere near her husband, afraid of what he might do.

"She knew all about Baxter, Ohio. She'd read about the Christmas festival there. It seemed like a nice town, and she thought if anything did happen to her, someone there would take care of her children. So she left them, thinking it would just be for a few hours. She was so scared when she finally regained consciousness and realized how much time had passed. I didn't think we'd ever get her to calm down enough to even tell us what was wrong. And when she found out they'd spent three days there all by themselves . . ."

"Monster," Annie whispered. "You must have thought . . ."

"It's all right," Rachel claimed. "They're fine now. Emma took good care of them. You would have been so proud of her. This whole time . . . She's so good with them, so strong."

Annie nodded gratefully.

"She didn't get very far with her own mother," the nurse said. "Her mother's already raising two of her other grandchildren, and she didn't think she could handle any more. And someone Annie knew must have seen her in town and called her husband, because the next thing she knew, he took her and left her for dead on the side of the road."

"I messed it all up," Annie said. "Everything."

"You don't have to worry about the children right now," Sam said. "Whatever time you need to get back on your feet . . . And Rachel's family knows almost everybody in Baxter. I'm sure we know someone who could help you get a job, a place to stay. Whatever you need."

Annie smiled at him, truly smiled. "I forget sometimes. . . . There are good people left in this world. . . . But . . ."

"It's more than that," the nurse said. "She's had me asking about the two of you. She knows how much you've always wanted children, that it's just never worked out. Your aunt said the nicest things about both of you, that she's sure you'd make wonderful parents. So did your minister. And even the mayor."

"I don't understand," Sam said. "What does she want from us?"

"Dying," she said. "I'm dying."

"No," Rachel said.

"It's not the beating," the nurse said. "It's her kidneys. Really, her whole body now. That's why she was so desperate, why she came back here. She's dying, and she needs someone to raise her children for her."

"You," Annie whispered. "Both of you."

Rachel didn't say a word. Neither did Sam. They were too stunned.

"She wants you to be sure. To take some time to think it through. She doesn't have long, but she wants you to be sure."

"What's wrong with her?" Rachel asked.

"She developed kidney disease, from the damage done years ago from the beatings, which worsened with the added strain of the pregnancy, and now with the added stress of the beating, her kidneys have shut down."

"But she could get a transplant, couldn't she?" Sam asked.

The nurse shook her head. "Maybe if she'd tried to get help sooner. But she let it go on for so long. The damage adds up, and at times, if the kidneys shut down, the whole body starts to shut down. I'm afraid she's also developed congestive heart failure and with that, no one would even put her on a waiting list for a transplant."

"Not now, you mean?"

"You don't understand. She's not going to get better."

"You're just going to let her die?" Sam asked.

"She probably wouldn't live through the surgery, even if she could get on the list and last long enough to get a transplant. I'm sorry. I know that seems harsh. But there are never enough organs to go around. We set strict criteria for patients who get them. The idea is that if only so many people are ever going to get a transplant, we want it to be people with a good chance of surviving," the nurse said. "Annie's accepted that. The only thing she's worried about now is her children."

"What about her husband?" Sam asked.

"The sheriff's been here. They videotaped her testimony, and he promised her husband's going to prison for what he's done to her. Her mother doesn't want the children. Annie's afraid no one will," the nurse said. "Your aunt told her if she picked someone to take them that the courts would likely give a great deal of weight to her request. Your aunt didn't think you'd have any trouble getting approval to adopt them, if that's what you want."

Again, Rachel just sat there, overwhelmed. This woman was dying. She was going to have to leave this earth and leave three young, helpless children behind. It was staggering to think about.

It was only three days ago that Rachel had really come to terms with the loss of her baby and truly known in her heart that her baby was fine, in a place where no one would ever hurt her. But Annie Greene was leaving her children to the mercy of an often cruel world, faced with no one to trust but people who were all but strangers to her. Rachel couldn't imagine how difficult that must be.

And Emma and Zach and the baby were going to lose their mother . . .

"You're sure?" Rachel asked. "There's nothing anyone can do for you?"

"Sure," Annie said.

It seemed she wasn't even going to fight anymore.

Rachel started to cry. She couldn't help it. The tears just rolled down her cheeks as she sat there hardly making a sound and struggling to breathe. Sam's hands tightened on her shoulders, and she leaned back against him, hardly able to look at the woman on the bed anymore. It was so sad. Emma and Zach were going to be devastated.

"She wants you to be sure," the nurse said. "If you can't love them, the way they deserve to be loved . . ."

"We can love them. It's not that. Not at all. But we need to talk," Sam said. He put a hand on Annie Greene's shoulder, told her, "We'll be back."

Rachel wasn't sure how they got outside, but there they were. Out in the cold, the automatic doors of the hospital swishing closed behind them, snow flurries rushing at them on the cold breeze.

There were Christmas lights strung up around the entrance of the hospital, the lights blinking on and off in a way that seemed to mock everything to do with Christmas.

Annie Greene was dying, and she wanted Sam and Rachel to take her children. Rachel, it seemed, was going to get what she'd always wanted.

"Not this way," she said, conscious of the fact that Sam had steered her to the side of the main walkway, out of the line of people rushing in and out. He held her by the arms, held her hard, maybe to keep her from falling down in the snow, maybe to get her attention. "Oh, God. Not like this."

"Rachel, we did not do this," he said. "We didn't wish that woman dead. She isn't dying because of anything we did."

"But I wanted them. I wanted those children, and they're hers. The only way we're going to get them is if she's gone."

"Wishing doesn't make things happen. You and I

both know that. If it did, our entire lives would have been different. Things just happen. This is just one of those shitty things that happens."

"Emma . . ." she said. "Oh, God, Sam. Emma! And Zach! Grace won't even remember her, but the other two . . ."

"I know," he said, pulling her close. "I know."

And he did. They both knew. Him better than her.

"It's so awful. How in the world are we going to tell them?"

"We're not. It's not up to us. It's up to Annie. They're still hers."

Rachel nodded. Still, it would be up to her and Sam to pick up the pieces. So much sadness . . . She could see it all coming. How odd to be able to sit here and see it all coming.

They stood there for a long time. Finally, her tears subsided and she stopped shaking so badly, and Sam let her go. Then he stood there staring at her with the saddest look on his face, as if he felt every bit as weary as she did.

It occurred to her that she'd stood outside a number of hospitals just like this. Feeling as if someone had shoved a booted foot into her midsection. And every one of those times, Sam had been right here beside her.

She was awed by his strength, by the sheer determination with which he'd stayed by her side through the years. She reached for him, taking his face in her hands, finding his cheeks damp and his mouth trembling.

He frowned down at her and asked, "What are you thinking?"

"That you've been with me through the worst days

of my life. That I've depended on you and leaned on you and taken and taken and taken without—"

"It wasn't like that, Rachel."

"Wasn't it?"

"No. It was a marriage. Two people together through good and bad. Doing our best to take care of each other. To love each other and to stay together."

"There's more inside of me to give, Sam. Not just to these children. To you. And . . . I don't even know how to ask you what's going to happen now. Because I know you love these children, and I can't imagine you leaving when they need us so much. And that's not fair to you at all. I don't want you to have to stay because of the kids."

"Single people adopt all the time. It wouldn't be a problem. And I can't imagine Annie would object, not if you told her how much you love those kids. You don't need me to have these kids."

"Of course I do."

"No, you don't. I talked to Miriam. There wouldn't be any rules standing in your way."

"I know. I talked to her, too. She told me you'd asked her about that. But I thought you were going to stay. I thought . . . after Christmas Eve. All the things we said to each other. All the things we figured out about each other, I thought you'd stay."

"I didn't say I was going anywhere. I just said that if you're thinking the only way you'll be able to have these children is by having a husband—having me—that's not true."

"You think I want them more than I want you?"

"I think the way either of us feels at the moment isn't as important as how those kids feel and what they need."

"No, it is, Sam. You're important and how you feel is important. You think I could be happy with them, but without you?"

"You've never really been happy with just me, Rachel," he said.

"That's not true."

"Isn't it?" he asked, then held up his hands. "No. Forget it. Forget I ever said it."

"I can't do that. I won't. Sam . . . you're the only man I've ever loved in my whole life. The only one. I never wanted anyone else. I never will. And there has to be some way of making you believe that, short of giving up these children and having just you in my life. Because I know you. You would never ask that of me. We would never abandon them now."

"No. We won't, and I wouldn't ask that of you."

"Is it so hard for you to believe I love you?"

"Maybe it is," he said. "Maybe that's what the problem's always been."

"I'm not your mother or your father. I'm not all of those cold-hearted people who took you into their homes when you were little and sent you off to someone else without a backward glance. I'm your wife. I've always seen the real you, the man at the core, and I've always loved him." She put her hand over his heart. "Give me another chance. Give us a chance. And try to believe me when I say I love you. Is that really so hard for you to believe? Have you lost every bit of faith you had in me? In us?"

"Rachel—"

"I can't believe you have. And you know something else, you haven't given me a fair chance, either. You kept things from me, important things. You didn't let me into your life, Sam. Not really. You kept things bottled up inside, and now they're tearing you up. They're tearing us up. You want me to accept you as you are, to understand you and fulfill every need you have? You have to tell me. I can't help heal what I don't know is hurting you. Give me a chance to do that now that I finally know everything. I do know everything now, don't I?"

"You know the worst of it," he said. "I never wanted you to know. I never wanted you to see those parts of me."

"I want every part of you," she said. "The good, the bad, everything. I deserve it. Can you give me that?"

"I have, Rachel. I've given it all to you now."

"Then things should get easier from now on. At least between us. The kids . . . That's going to be hard. Do you think I can't handle it? Do you still think I'm going to fall apart on you?"

"I think together, we can do this. We can help them." He smiled at her then.

"What, Sam?"

"I'd forgotten what it was like to see you spitting fire, the way you used to do for me, back when you were defending me to the whole damned town. I guess I wasn't sure you had any of that left in you."

"You found it and dragged it out of me." She sighed, trembling again, because she thought it was going to be okay. She took hold of the side of his coat and pulled him closer, until they were almost nose to nose. "I meant what I said Christmas morning. I still love you, Sam."

He held her for a long moment. She felt each shuddering breath, felt the fine trembling in his body. Sam, her rock, trembling.

She looked up at him and kissed him quickly on the lips. "What are we going to do?"

He frowned and glanced back up at the hospital. "It's going to be a long night for Annie."

"Yes," Rachel said, hope unfurling madly inside of her.

"I don't see any reason for her to be up there worrying, do you?"

"You mean—"

"We might as well go back inside and tell her we've made our decision. That we'll take the kids."

She waited, waited for more, hoped for it, needed it. "You mean . . ."

But all he did was slide his arm around her waist, turn her back toward the building, and say, "Let's go back inside and tell her the kids can stay with us."

Epilogue

On the first day of the new year, Sam was sitting on the floor of the family room trying to explain to Zach the intricacies of pro football and watching a very determined Grace head for the fireplace one more time.

He caught her by the foot and dragged her back once again. She had on one of those warm, fuzzy, one-piece pajama things, like long underwear with feet in them, and the floor was a heavily varnished hardwood. She slid along quite easily, and it had become a game to her now.

He finished tugging her back, and she pivoted around on her belly to face him and giggled. Great. They could make a game of her trying to get close enough to the fire to singe her gorgeous eyelashes.

"She dudn't understand," Zach said, shaking his head.

"No, she doesn't." And he couldn't turn his back on her without finding her in some sort of trouble. It was definitely a whole new lifestyle.

"Is Emma comin' back soon?" Zach asked. "Sometimes she listens to Emma."

"Emma should be back anytime now." Sam glanced at his watch for the third time in ten minutes. Annie

had decided it was time to tell Emma what was going
to happen, and Sam had wanted to be there but their
baby-sitter—one of his nieces—had canceled at the
last minute, so Rachel took Emma and Sam was here
trying to keep Grace out of the fire. But he was anx-
ious to know how Emma was holding up.

"I think I hear 'em," Zach said, racing for the door.

"Don't go outside without your shoes, Zach!" he
called out, maybe already too late. Kids were impul-
sive. About everything, it seemed.

Meanwhile, Grace crawled over to him and pulled
herself up until she was standing beside him, hanging
on to determined fistfuls of his shirt and wobbling
back and forth. She was determined to walk and fell
down at least a hundred times a day.

"You're going to give me heart failure," he told her.

She patted his cheek. Hard. They hadn't convinced
her yet to be gentle. Sam made a growling sound and
went after her, his mouth landing against her soft,
fabric-covered belly. She howled with delight and
latched on to his hair. It was her favorite game of all.

When she finally let go and he looked up, Emma
was standing there staring at the two of them, looking
a bit lost and afraid as she had that first day.

So much had changed so quickly, he could hardly
believe it. He'd growled at Emma for real that first
day, scared her, resented her presence here, and been
scared to death by her, too.

This time he held out his arm to her and said,
"Come 'ere, Em."

Her face fell. She dropped to his side and buried her
head against his chest. Her shoulders were shaking.
She was crying, and he was fighting not to himself.

Grace didn't understand this, either. She thought it

was yet another game and soon she was hiding her face against his chest, too, and trying to get Emma's attention. Sam gently pulled her back, so she'd leave Emma alone.

"Give us a minute, Grace," he said.

She frowned—she was used to being the center of attention—and pointed to Emma and said, "Muh, Muh."

"I know. It's Emma. She'll play in a minute." He reached behind him for her ball. Zach was trying to train her to fetch. Sam thew the ball into the corner farthest from the fire and said, "Get the ball, Grace."

She didn't look happy about it, but she crawled off after it, her diaper-clad bottom swishing back and forth as she went.

Emma finally lifted her wet face from his shoulder and said, "She's not a puppy."

"Zach thinks she could be almost as good as a puppy. He wants to get her a leash and a collar, thinks we could keep her out of trouble easier that way. What do you think? We could stake her to the middle of the floor, give her some room to run, but still keep her out of the fire?"

Emma laughed a bit, and then bit her bottom lip and cried.

"We're going to take good care of her, Emma. You and Zach, too. We promised your mother."

"I know. She told me. She told me everything."

"We love you," he said.

"And I love you. But I'm scared. It's gonna be so hard . . ."

"I know, Em. But Rachel and I have been through a lot of bad times. We know how much it hurts sometimes, and I won't lie to you. Some things just always

hurt. But things can get better, too. You'll get to the
point where you can remember someone you lost,
someone you loved, without hurting so bad you want
to cry. Where you can be happy again. Where you
know there are still good things in life ahead of you."

"You think?" she asked.

"Listen to me." He turned her head up to his. "I
know it's true. All you need are people around you
who love you. You just hold on tight to them and you'll
get through it. You already know how to do that.
You've done it with Zach and Grace. Rachel and I
know how to do that, too. We'll hold on tight. Have a
little faith, okay?"

She nodded.

"Hey," he said, seeing something coming at him out
of the corner of his eye. "Look at that!"

Grace was up on her feet, in the middle of the room,
holding on to nothing at all. Just standing there grinning and wobbling back and forth.

"Careful." Emma held out a hand to her.

Sam did the same thing. Grace raced toward them,
three, four, five steps, more off balance with each one
she took. She *would* run instead of walk. Sam barely
managed to catch her before she hit the floor. It scared
her a bit. She fussed as he pulled her close and looked
bewildered and maybe a bit mad.

"So you're really mobile now?" he asked. "And
that's supposed to be a good thing?"

She blinked up at him and frowned.

Emma gave her a kiss on her soft cheek. Grace
threw her little arms around both him and Emma and
squeezed hard. Sam held on to them both and looked
up to find Rachel and Zach standing in the doorway.
Zach was grinning, and Rachel was about to cry. But

she was smiling, too. These days, she smiled through her tears.

They were going to be okay. Everything was going to be okay.

Sam and Rachel finished taking down the tree that night. By tradition, it didn't come down until New Year's Day.

Rachel worked so carefully, especially with the personalized ornaments. She wrapped them in specially made containers and stacked them in little boxes that would go on special shelves nearly at the ceiling in the basement, so they wouldn't get damaged from year to year.

Sam watched her, thinking about Christmas after Christmas in this old house. Rachel's grandparents had lived here. Her mother. Now Rachel and him and the children. Someday Emma would stand here carefully wrapping the same ornaments after taking them off her tree, he imagined, and felt once again that unending sense of family, of connections that were never truly broken.

A sense of place, of belonging.

He felt rich beyond anything he'd ever imagined. Rich in memories and in people around him who loved him, rich in the possibilities the future held, and he knew he'd done a great disservice to his wife, that it was time to put that to right. He thought he knew how.

There was some part of her that feared he'd remained here simply because of the three children asleep upstairs, and he didn't want there to be any doubts about that. Because he knew how painful those doubts could be. He didn't want her to live like that.

He put his hand in his pocket, pulled out a tiny box

wrapped in red. When her back was turned, he slid it amid the branches between the spot where his ornament and hers hung, then tried not to grin and ruin the surprise.

She turned back around and reached for another ornament, finding the box and just staring at it for a moment. He waited through three heartbeats before she reached for it. The tentativeness of her movements, the way she studied the package and her name scrawled across the front of it, told him how unsure of the two of them she still was.

"Find something?" he asked through an impossibly tight throat.

She nodded and held it out to him with a trembling hand.

"It has your name on it, Rachel. Open it."

She did, being careful with the wrapping paper, as she always was. It took forever, as it always did. She finally opened the lid of the box and then nearly dropped it.

Sam took it from her and pulled out the ring. He stuck it on the end of his index finger and held it out to her. She didn't say a word, just stared. He hadn't had the money to give her a diamond the first time around. It had been a plain gold band. A cheap one she'd treasured anyway.

"Do you ever watch those sappy diamond commercials on TV?" he asked.

"All women watch those, Sam."

"Really?"

She nodded.

"Diamonds are amazing. So strong. They last forever. And this one . . ." He held it up in front of her, showing the simple beauty of the ring. A solid band of diamonds, a never-ending circle. "It's forever, Rachel. I know so much more about that now—about the commitment it takes and what it means to me—than I did the first time around. It means so much more to me now. *You* do. I'm sorry I ever doubted that."

"Oh, Sam." She started to cry again. "I don't know what I'd do without you."

"And you're not ever going to find out," he promised, then remembered the ring and what he needed to tell her. "The sappy commercials?"

"Yes."

"The one I saw said this is what you give a woman to tell her you'd marry her all over again. I'd do it in a heartbeat."

And then he slipped the ring on her finger and dried her tears and carried her upstairs to their bed.

Turn the page for a preview

of Teresa Hill's next novel

of romance and family,

Unbreak My Heart

Coming from Onyx in 2001

Allie Bennett is back in her childhood home for the first time since she was nine years old. There's so much she doesn't remember; so much that she's not sure she wants to remember. And yet she knows, to move on with her life she needs to figure out what had happened to shatter her family all those years ago. Alone in a house with no electricity, overcome with emotion, Allie is seeking the truth. And then truth comes knocking on her door, in the form of the man next door. . . .

A bit of light flared between them—from a cigarette lighter, she realized—and Allie gaped up at the tall, dark stranger. He reached for her, and it wasn't until she'd likely made a fool of herself that she figured out he only meant to light the candle she held in her hand. She was trembling so badly he put his hand over hers to steady it, then took the candle from her. He slipped the lighter into the pocket of his raincoat and carefully shielded the candle flame from the wind as he held it up to her face. The man stared at her for a long moment. Then his eyes narrowed, recognition dawning. "Allie?"

"Yes." She gave him a tentative smile. "I'm afraid I don't remember you."

"I doubt you would. You were what? Six or seven years old? When you and your mother left town?"

"Nine," she corrected him. She'd just finished third grade and had so few specific memories of that time. Struggling with multiplication tables. Watching with curiosity and envy as a few of the older girls started filling out in all the right places and gossiping about boys.

She didn't remember this man.

Just then, the rain came thundering down, running off the sides of the porch and blowing toward them. The man came one step closer. Allie hesitated only a moment. She dreaded the idea of being alone in this house, and he had known her family.

"Would you like to come inside?" She would never have invited a stranger into her apartment in Connecticut, but this wasn't Connecticut, and he wasn't exactly a stranger.

"Yes, thank you."

As she closed the door she realized there was no other car in the driveway. He must have walked here before the rain started, and she wondered if he was a neighbor.

He set the candle on a small table at the bottom of the stairs, took off his obviously expensive and now very wet raincoat and hung it over the banister. He was wearing a beautifully tailored suit in a rich brown color, the jacket showing off the wide expanse of his shoulders. He ran a hand through his hair, which was short and dark and wet, then stared at her once again.

"Sorry," he said. "I can't get over how much you look like your sister, Megan."

Allie found herself absurdly pleased by the idea, and she liked knowing someone still remembered

Megan. Sometimes it seemed she was the only one. Her mother hadn't so much as mentioned Megan's name in years, and Allie had learned not to, either, as she'd learned not to ask about so many things over the years.

She let the man take his time looking at her, as she studied him. He was in his mid-thirties. Tall, trim, with the build of an athlete and an air of self-assurance and power. Money, too. It was evident in the cut and quality of the suit. He looked like a man used to having the best, to getting his way.

A second later, he turned his head a bit, and the light hit his face at just the right angle. Allie saw something there, something she recognized. The shape of his eyes, maybe the hint of gold in the dark-green irises or the shape of his lips when they stretched into the barest hint of a smile.

"You used to live next door," she said.

"Still do."

"Stephen Whittaker?"

He nodded. "I'm surprised you remember."

"I'm surprised now that I forgot," Allie said. "Megan talked about you nonstop from as far back as I can remember. She watched from the window of my bedroom when you went out on your first date. Then she cried for days."

He looked surprised, then a bit embarrassed. "Megan was a sweet kid."

Allie nodded. Stephen, if she remembered correctly, had been a few years older than Megan. Allie wondered if he'd always viewed her sister as nothing but a sweet kid, if there had ever been anything more between them.

Allie's memories of the time she'd spent here had

always been vague, but strangely, the closer she tried
to get to her memories of that summer Megan ran
away, the more difficult it was to recall anything at all.
Was it merely the fact that she'd been so young? Or
something else entirely that made it difficult to remember those last days with her sister?

Allie couldn't say. But Stephen would have been in
high school or college. He'd always lived next door to
her family. His mother did volunteer work at her parents' church, and his father was a judge. Surely she
could trust him.

Impulsively, Allie said, "Someone was kind enough
to leave me a casserole for dinner. I think it had enough
time to heat before the power went out. I also made a
pot of fresh coffee. Would you care to stay for dinner?"

"Coffee and a hot meal? In the middle of one of these
storms? That's an offer I couldn't possibly refuse."

By the time she served the casserole, Stephen was
sitting at the small table by the window in the kitchen,
the flames of a half dozen candles dancing around the
room. Outside, the thunder and the wind had subsided,
but the rain still fell heavily, the wetness glistening
against the windowpanes, the atmosphere suddenly in-
timate.

They ate hungrily. Stephen had her laughing as he
came up with news of people and places she remembered. The food was warm and settled her stomach.
She'd stopped shaking, was more relaxed than she'd
been in weeks.

"I don't remember the last time I enjoyed a meal
more," she said.

"Then the man in your life ought to be ashamed of
himself."

He grinned as he said it, and there was power in the

easy smile that rested so naturally on his lips, in the richness of his voice, the warmth in his tone, the mere hint of flirtation in his sparkling eyes. She couldn't help but admire the elegance infused within every move he made. Everything about the way he carried himself spoke of unfaltering self-confidence and an assurance of his place in the world and with women.

He had to know women found him charming. All women, she expected. Allie suspected he could get most anything he wanted simply by asking. She wondered exactly what was happening to her. If it was some trick of the soft, pretty light or her gratitude at having someone to keep her company tonight. Whatever it was, she was enchanted with him. And she found it was easy to sit here in the dark with him. She wasn't nervous or tongue-tied, as she often was around men like him, because she knew Stephen. It seemed she'd always known him, and that at the core, the man was not so different from the boy. He'd always been kind to her and Megan.

"So, who is this man who's treating you so shabbily?" Stephen asked.

"There is no man," she said quickly.

No one at all. The thought sobered her faster than anything could have. She was all alone, missing her mother, missing her sister and her father more than she had in years, and she still had to face the night alone in this house.

"So what brings you back?" Stephen asked. "The house?"

He'd poured her another cup of coffee when he'd gotten up to refill his own cup. Even lukewarm, it still tasted good. They'd pushed their plates to the side, and Stephen was leaning back in his chair now, watching her intently in a way she didn't think she'd ever feel comfortable with. And he would be gone soon. If she had questions she had to get to them.

"My mother died recently," she said.

"I'm sorry." His hand slid across the table to hers in a simple, eloquent offer of comfort.

"Thank you," she said, unable to remember the last time a man had held her hand. "I miss her. More than I had imagined I would." Particularly given the fact that she'd been angry at her mother for most of her life.

"It was just the two of you? Once you left here?"

"Yes."

"You must have been close. . . ."

"I wouldn't say that." Allie sighed. "We just never quite got it right, you know? The mother/daughter thing. I always thought one day we would, but we didn't and I let her rob me of all those years with my father."

The minute she said it, Allie felt the muscles in her stomach tighten, felt her throat go tight as well. Stephen just watched her. She could have sworn he knew just what she was thinking.

"I think this conversation's gotten too grim," he said finally, standing and walking across the room.

"I'm sorry."

"Don't be. I asked. And I'm willing to listen to anything you want to tell me, Allie." Leaning against the cabinets, his long legs stretched out in front of him, he again looked relaxed and perfectly at ease. "I just thought there must be something we could talk about that might make you smile."

She found herself unexpectedly touched. "Let's talk about you," she suggested.

After all, it would be no hardship to listen to that

low, soothing voice of his. Southern to the core, the sound of it was like an old familiar song, one she hadn't known she missed until she heard it again. She decided she'd been gone for too long when nothing but the sound of a man's voice could charm her so.

"What do you do?"

"I have a law degree I've never put to good use, much to my father's dismay," he said easily. "For the most part, I build things."

"You?" Allie doubted it. He certainly looked strong enough for manual labor, but that wasn't what he did. Not in a suit like that. Not with those hands. They were not the hands of a man who earned his living through hard labor.

"I rebuild things, actually. Old things. My company buys old buildings, restores them. Sometimes we keep them and manage them. Sometimes we sell them and buy more." Stephen took another sip of his coffee. "I find old buildings interesting. They have character, charm. I hate to see them torn down and replaced with modern ones that all look the same. I'd hate to see this town look like a cookie-cutter version of any other small town anywhere in America. Take this house, for instance. It's beautiful."

"I've missed it," she said, finding that she had and was happy to share this thing with him—a love of things old and solid and enduring. Did he see that in it, she wondered? That it had endured. That it had a history. That it no doubt held so many memories, so many secrets.

"What are you going to do with it?"

"I'm not sure." Allie sighed. "What would you do with it?"

"If I inherited this house? I'd keep it. Sink a small fortune into restoring it."

Allie didn't have the luxury of that kind of money or time. She was a classic example of someone house rich and pocket poor. She could not afford to keep the house. But she was intrigued enough by Stephen's idea to ask, "And then what? Once you'd restored it?"

"Live in it."

"All by yourself?" Or at least, she assumed he lived alone. He wore no ring, and he hadn't needed to tell anyone he wouldn't be home for dinner.

"Until I found someone to share it with me," he said.

She looked up to find him watching her again thoughtfully and tried to summon up a smile. He really had the most amazing smile. She wondered if he was consciously flirting with her or if he treated all women this way, if his natural inclination was to be polite and utterly disarming; wondered, too, if perhaps it wasn't a way of bringing people close to him but of keeping them away. A false kind of intimacy he used like a shield.

Did anyone ever truly get close to him? she wondered, and found herself wishing that she could. It was unsettling—to be so taken with him already, having spent so little time with him, to be so caught up in what she suspected was a flirtatious bit of nothing for him.

She was simply out of practice with the way things were between men and women. She'd been alone too long. The last few years had been busy, working her way through school, trying to take care of her mother. There hadn't been time for casual flirtations. Maybe that was why it felt so oddly sweet to be with him, why she was reluctant to let the moment end.

"So," Stephen said. "You never told me. What are you going to do with the house?"

"I haven't decided. It's one of the reasons I came back."

"What else brought you back?"

"I miss my father, I suppose. And my sister," she said, then admitted, "I don't even know why Megan ran away."

"What did your mother tell you?"

"It's so odd," she said, searching her memory, as she'd done a million times before. "I don't remember. Not exactly. I knew something was wrong that day we found her gone, but I didn't know what happened at first. My mother woke me up early and sent me to a neighbor's house. I think she must have worried about frightening me, because she was so frightened herself. She always tried to protect me.

"My sister was always quiet and a little shy." At least, that's what Allie recalled. She looked up at Stephen. "You must remember her so much better than I do. You were . . . what? Eighteen? The summer she disappeared?"

"Nineteen," he said, carefully setting his coffee mug on the counter. "You're right. Megan was quiet. Serious. A little shy. I'd watched her grow up, and it was hard for me to think of her as anything but a little girl, which is not something a sixteen-year-old girl wants to hear from a boy. I'm afraid I hurt her feelings that summer."

"So the two of you were never . . . involved?"

"No." He laughed a bit. "Nothing more than friends."

She couldn't help but ask, "Did you ever want to be more than friends?"

Stephen went to the window and looked out into the

rain once again. "I wish," he said carefully, "that I'd been a better friend to her."

"Why?"

"She ran away, Allie, and she never made it back. Whatever was going on with her that summer, it must have been bad for her to just take off like that. She must have felt so alone, like she didn't have anyone to turn to. I wish she'd come to me. Or to anyone who could have helped her."

"It was just a car accident, wasn't it?" Allie asked. "You never heard anything else, except that Megan was involved in a car accident?"

"No. Allie, what's going on?"

"I don't know. I— I've just always had all of these questions, and none of the answers."

And she wasn't leaving until she found them.

For only $3.99 each, they'll make your dreams come true.

LORDS OF MIDNIGHT

A special romance promotion from Signet Books—featuring six of our most popular, award-winning authors...

Lady in White by Denise Domning
❑ 0-451-40772-5

The Moon Lord by Terri Lynn Wilhelm
❑ 0-451-19896-4

Shades of the Past by Kathleen Kirkwood
❑ 0-451-40760-1

LORDS OF LOVE

Jack of Hearts by Marjorie Farrell
❑ 0-451-19953-7

The Duke's Double by Anita Mills
❑ 0-451-19954-5

A Perfect Scoundrel by Heather Cullman
❑ 0-451-19952-9